Sue

You are a

Treasure

Love and

Blessings

Elaine

2014

محمد

كارمس سوم م

أحمد يوسف عبد

على حسن هشام

اب المحدث انيم

علي المحمد الزائد

عبد ١٢

Georgia's Secret

by Elaine Jabenis

The deceiver's punishment is to be obliged to deceive again.
Countess Diane

Georgia's Secret
Copyright © 2014 by Elaine Jabenis

DISCLAIMER

This is a work of fiction. Names, characters, places, events, and incidents are created through the author's imagination. Any resemblance to actual persons, living or dead, is purely coincidental.

Published by

BOOKS INC.
www.collagebooks.com

Printed in the United States of America

ISBN: 978-0-938728-29-0

DEDICATION

To my beloved children and grandchildren.

Jon — Aliyah and Grant
M'Lee — Sarah and Jessica

ACKNOWLEDGMENTS

I don't know what positive force put us together, but I am deeply indebted to all these generous people.

LEANNA ENGLERT

A major blessing as editor, friend and morale booster. Her talent and endless heavy lifting brought me to a place I could not have reached without her. A friend forever.

MYRON HIRSCH

For his expertise and generosity. Bless you, Mike.

KATHY BYRNES

Kathy stepped up and helped get this effort to the finish line. She knows the true meaning of kindness.

MARALYN BURR & MANDY MAYNARD

For the beautiful cover picture.

JAN SAVOIE

Her eagle eye didn't allow me to get away with anything. How lucky I am that Jan shared her expertise with me.

KAREN SOKOLOF JAVITCH

Karen has other talents besides writing music and lyrics for her musicals. She's amazing at kindness, loyalty and friendship.

THE ANGELS

Lynne, Doris, Ruthie, Deana, Beth, Ann A, Ann P, Teresa, Kay Lynn, Ila Dean, Martha, Robyn, Mary Gay, Norma, Georgia, Carol and Suzy. I love you all.

JANET VAN DE WALLE & ROXY ORR

Generous with advice and guidance.

TECHNICAL AND SPECIALITY SUPPORT

Marilyn Hansen, founder of The Designers
Jamie Samuel
Jan Braun
Bob Ford
Mark Braun

PROLOGUE

1962

If there had been any neighbors living nearby, Georgia's screams for help would have been heard.

There were no neighbors. Her father had built this house outside of Lincoln in the center of three acres. Privacy was further guaranteed by an abundance of evergreen trees on one side and sprawling oaks on the other.

Before her attacker had ripped off her dress and thrown her to the floor, he grabbed her shoulders and shook her. "Everyone in Nebraska thinks you're white, but you're nothing but a nigger. Not nice to deceive people like that. I guess it's up to me to teach you a lesson you'll never forget."

The weight of his sweaty body rendered her motionless. Screaming was her only choice. He clamped a rough hand over Georgia's mouth and whispered into her ear. "Sweet fifteen and never been had? My, my."

Georgia bit his hand and he slapped her so hard she was sure he broke her jaw. The thought of being violated by someone she knew intensified the horror.

"If you don't want me to hurt you, you better do exactly as I say. Understand?"

CHAPTER 1

1969

Georgia Parker sped underground in to her reserved parking space, hurried out of her new Mercedes – a car of her father's choice, not hers. She dashed to the elevator that would take her to her top floor apartment – also her father's choice.

She punched the button repeatedly. No elevator.

Damn it, Dad, how meticulous did you build snazzy Regal Towers with an elevator that's always asleep.

Georgia paced. Finally," she sighed, darting through the shiny bronze elevator door. "Sorry to wake you," she said aloud, "but I have a gorgeous man waiting for me and I'm late. So, move."

Mr. Gorgeous, known since birth as Cliff Hudson, had arrived a week ago from New York. Georgia's joy had soared to a place it had never been before. Here was this remarkable newspaper journalist, who, after five years with the *New York Journal*, had a noted California newspaper beckoning. And on his way to LA he was spending ten vacation days with her. How could she have been so blessed?

Georgia caught a glimpse of herself in the elevator's mirrored panel. Was her skin as creamy white as her mother's . . . her lips too full . . . her eyes as black as her father's? Georgia smiled as she touched her long brown hair—straight, silky, smooth. Not at all like her father's—dark and nappy. No way did she resemble her black father.

Still, guilt followed her like a threatening shadow. She had avoided telling Cliff about her father too long. Today. She'd tell him today.

Georgia rushed from the elevator to her apartment door. She paused. A man as worldly as Cliff would understand. Hadn't he expounded often that only tolerance and love would bring peace?

Georgia opened the door. *Even if I don't find the right moment to tell Cliff today, there's still three more days.*

She stepped inside and shouted, "Cliff, I'm back."

No answer. All that greeted her was the hollow sound of her voice in this vast empty space. *He's too engrossed in his writing to hear me.*

She couldn't imagine these highly-polished oak floors, devoid of furnishings, translating into a place called home. Georgia groaned. *This looks like a damn dance hall. Almost a five or six-thousand square foot apartment for a twenty-two year old girl just out of college? Really, Dad.*

Cliff had called it obscene. Stepping onto the expansive shiny floor, he laughed. "Put in some bleachers and it would make a hell of a basketball court."

Georgia had gulped. If he thought she was tied to this life style, how could he ask her to move into an ordinary apartment?

"I'm here only . . . temporarily. My father's going to furnish it, to make it appealing . . . for sale." *I shouldn't have said that.*

Cliff?" She rushed to the kitchen where she expected him to be working at his portable Royal typewriter. Both were gone.

Georgia suppressed an anxious pang with logic. He finished writing his article and stepped out to buy a paper. He reviewed several major newspapers every day.

On the kitchen floor, inlaid with square black and white tiles, were several balls of rejected pages that had missed the wastebasket. His coffee cup was empty. The pecan rolls she had served him were gone.

With a weak voice she called out as she moved from room to room. *He's in the shower. That's it. He can't hear me.* Not only was his shower empty, but so were all the drawers and closets in the guest bedroom.

The phone rang. *There he is.* She grabbed the phone, got tangled in the cord and dropped the receiver. "Cliff? Sorry. I dropped the phone"

"What's going on there?"

"Dad?"

"Yes, dear. I just landed. I'm in a phone booth, waiting for my car. Furniture for your study should arrive tomorrow. You'll love it."

"Thank you, Dad, but slow down on furnishings for a while. Okay?" *I hope I won't be here long enough to need more furnishings.*

"You don't sound very chipper. Anything wrong?"

Understatement. "Cliff Hudson was here. Now he's gone."

"What happened?"

"Look, Dad, I don't want to tie up the line. As soon as I hear, I'll call you. I promise." Before he could protest she hung up.

I shouldn't have left here today.

Deeply shaken, she headed for her bedroom suite. She passed through her sitting room and opened the French doors to her balcony. Gripping the banister, she released imprisoned tears.

Just the night before, she and Cliff had stood here sharing an incredible sunset. *He told me he loved me. What went wrong?*

Georgia looked down. The new street, flanked with young linden trees and handsome light posts, was devoid of traffic. Empty land stretched in all directions. Her father's pledge that development was coming soon didn't help. The total quiet made her feel all the more deserted.

CHAPTER 2

Still on her balcony, Georgia had stopped pondering why Cliff had left. If she let go and examined what happened today, maybe, just maybe something might surface.

As usual, Cliff was up early working at her kitchen bar. Georgia walked in unnoticed and gasped with pleasure. He was bare-footed, dressed in jeans, and bare to the waist. His muscular, broad shoulders and shiny tanned skin beckoning to be touched.

She sneaked up behind him, put her arms around him, and laid her head on his back. His warm skin and fresh smell of soap almost brought tears of joy.

"Good morning," he mumbled and continued typing.

She kissed his shoulder and remained snuggled against his back.

"Please, Georgia, I'm on deadline."

Slowly, Georgia pulled her arms away. *I shouldn't be resentful. He told me when he arrived. He had to work.*

The phone rang. Her best buddy, Rudy, sounded almost pleading— he must see her. She couldn't leave Cliff. Absolutely not. Yet how could she ignore the need of a long-time, devoted friend?

After she dressed, she returned to the kitchen. "Cliff."

He continued typing. Nor did he look up when she served him coffee and warm pecan rolls. Not until she told him that she had to respond to an urgent call from Rudy Ascot. "Rudy sounded desperate. I need to go, only about an hour or so."

"Hope it's nothing serious," he said. "My, you look pretty. Is this a dressy emergency?"

"Just appropriate. I'm meeting him at Emeralds, where he works."

Still straddled on the bar stool, he drew her between his legs, and slipped his arms around her waist. "Don't go," he whispered.

"But you're busy working and . . ."

"Exactly. I work better when you're here. You're smile, your delicate fragrance and great coffee." His lips brushed her neck and she caved to the tantalizing sensation.

He needs me. I really should stay. What should I say to Rudy—that even though he's always been there for me, I can't be there for him?

"I'll hurry back." She put her arms around his neck and whispered, "Put a bookmark on this moment so we can pick up where we left off."

I'd better run before I weaken._

Georgia reached Emeralds Department Store in record time. She entered the new revolving door, but instead of going inside to meet Rudy, she continued to spin around until she was outside again.

Perhaps she should have explained to Cliff that she and Rudy had been buddies since grade school, and that Rudy saw her every day for months after her mother was killed. *I had to come.*

Outside Emeralds, the June noon sun was heating up Main Street's sidewalks. Georgia watched the lunchtime rush of chatty customers entering the store. Their energy pulled her inside.

How she had loved this store when she was a little girl. Her mother never minded the sixty miles from their home in Lincoln to Omaha, for shopping and lunch at Emeralds. Georgia always wore a pretty dress, patent-leather shoes and little white gloves. For years those mother-daughter trips to Emeralds became a treasured ritual. For Georgia's thirteenth birthday, her mother took all the girls in her class to Emeralds for lunch. A week later her mother died. Georgia never went back.

Omaha's popular downtown meeting place was still there. Its large white face with black numbers was surrounded by gold leaves and a generous array of precious and semiprecious jewels. Rudy wanted her to meet him here at twelve. She was prompt. He was late. As usual.

The jeweled clock was the only thing that seemed unchanged. The new 1969 look of Emeralds surprised her. Revolving doors had replaced the old push-pull ones with heavy brass handles. The huge pillars that stalked the main floor were no longer dull green but enriched by handsome wood paneling. Where lights once hung on long chains from the high ceiling, an updated lighting system now illuminated the store like daylight. Even the air smelled different. She remembered a dusty, musty odor. Today the store's air was as fragrant as fresh-cut flowers.

Georgia waited several minutes under the famous clock, until curiosity led her to a vibrant display, evidence of Rudy's skill as Emeralds display director. California beachwear was the theme. A pretty girl in a sundress offered samples of lemonade. Beside her was a cart of fresh citrus fruit—some painted with smiles and sunglasses, others with huge eyes and thick, black eyelashes. A definite Rudyism.

California. That's where she would live if she married Cliff. Suddenly, the oranges with smiling faces seemed to mock her.

Another look at the big clock indicated that Rudy was thirty minutes late.

"There you are, my love," came Rudy's exuberant greeting. He approached with arms open. "A fashion vision. How clever of you, Miss Georgia, to wear peach."

"You're half an hour late."

He glanced up at the clock, looking ridiculously innocent. "It's just twelve thirty. Lunch time."

It's amazing, Georgia thought, how Rudy can show a happy face to the world in the midst of adversity. He'd say, "It's not their problem, just mine." Even as a kid, she recalled, he was like that

Inside the new green and white Emeralds Tea Room, they were escorted to the reserved area that stretched across the back wall. It was separated from the rest of the room by a white wrought iron banister.

"This is charming," Georgia said, running her hand over the waist-high banister. "It reminds me of my father's front porch."

"That's where I got my inspiration," Rudy said, pulling out a chair for Georgia.

"You did this?"

"Yep."

"How wonderful. When did you become an architect?"

"Not an architect. Just a designer. However, management has assigned me to work with the architects on the departmental plans for the new store."

"I'm proud of you. I love this reserved area, especially how each seating space is enclosed with a vine-covered trellis. Feels private."

"Rudy nodded. "We have customers who discuss business during lunch. Everyone is welcome to sit here at no charge, but reservations are required."

Rudy ordered toasted BLT sandwiches and bottled Coca Colas, then fell silent.

He's not ready to talk. I won't rush him.

"The store looks great, Rudy."

He smiled his gratitude. "You mentioned your father's porch. How is the good doctor?"

"He attended a Chicago medical conference. He'll be home tonight. I'll get a date for the three of us to have our monthly dinner together. I'll let you know."

"How in the world does he manage to be a master builder and continue to achieve so much as Dr. Benjamin Parker in medical research at the same time?"

Georgia shrugged. "Medical research is his first love. Building is a new passion. He has all that money and property his white ancestors left him, so he does what he's always done—work day and night."

A streak of sunlight from a high window spotlighted Rudy's curly red hair. She saw no sign of stress in his boyish face, or in his alert hazel eyes. Nor did she find any clues in his voice or manner justifying his urgent phone call. *It's obviously not his work. He's come a long way from dressing plastic dummies and changing store windows.*

Rudy folded his arms. "Ready to talk?"

Thank goodness. "Ready to listen."

"Good. But first," he began, with an impish grin, "my best friend has been in Omaha for weeks, stomping around in her luxury apartment, and hasn't invited her adorable, handsome, lifetime buddy over to see it. What's more, the flowers I was bringing are wilted and the chocolates are gone."

She chuckled. "Rudy, I told you up front, there was nothing to see yet. Only the bedrooms and kitchen have been furnished. In fact, when more furniture arrives, I'm counting on you to arrange everything."

"I'd love that. So, tell me about Cliff."

He's dodging again. "Shouldn't we discuss Cliff after . . ."

"Now is better."

"Okay. He loves me, tells me so. We are planning a future together. You met him. Wouldn't you agree he's the poster boy for tall, dark and handsome?"

"He's certainly tall."

"Six foot six," Georgia exclaimed. "The perfect man for my five eleven."

"Imagine that. What else?"

"He writes for the *New York Journal* and slick magazines. Five years of training with the Journal and they say he has a great future."

"So he's going to leave the *Journal* for what?"

"The *LA World News*." Georgia's enthusiasm escalated. "Cliff has always wanted to live in LA and he likes the direction that paper is taking."

Rudy leaned back. "You don't have to tell me, but how attentive is this guy?"

"Very. But you're out of order."

"Sorry. We've always been so open with each other. Does your father like Cliff?"

"Rudy, back off."

Rudy jiggled the ice in his water glass. "Just answer the damn question."

Georgia bit her lip.

"You haven't told Cliff about your father, have you?"

"Okay, Ascot, enough. I came here to talk about you."

"Me?"

"I made a great sacrifice to come. You had such anxiety in your voice, I was afraid you were dying or something."

He gave her an enigmatic smile. "Well, I did break up with Stanley, but dying didn't come to mind."

"But you sounded so . . ."

"That wasn't an act. Well, maybe a little. I know how extremely kind you are to people who have extended even a small kindness to you."

"What's wrong with that?"

"Well, you can also be impulsive. I just wondered—have you met his family and friends?"

"There wasn't much opportunity while I was at school."

Rudy rubbed his ear. "What does he like?"

"Lots. He took me to the theatre, concerts, museums, great

restaurants. He showed me all of that when I came to New York on weekends."

"Anything else?"

Georgia leaned back. "I know what you're getting at, Ascot. Romance? For the first three months, I really didn't think this was to be romantic. He was like a friendly teacher showing a student New York's finest virtues. It wasn't until maybe, after four months that he even kissed me on the cheek."

"A teacher-student relationship?"

Georgia nodded. "He'd drop me at my hotel and go back to his apartment. I never saw his apartment."

"You're really serious about this guy?"

"Certainly. He says he's working hard for our future. When we're married I'll move to California with him."

"Has he mentioned marriage?"

A chubby, apple-cheeked waitress approached with their lunch. "I gave you extra potato chips, Rudy."

"Wilma, I love you."

"You're all talk," Wilma giggled, and left.

"Best BLTs in the world," Rudy said, rubbing his palms together. "Homemade bread, home grown tomatoes."

"It's huge. My father would like this. He thinks big. She took a bite of potato chip. "Okay, Ascot, I think it's time to talk about the reason I'm here."

"What do you think we've been doing?"

"Talking about me. I came here to try to help with what's worrying you."

His eyes widened. "Oh, my God. I didn't mean to sound like that. I felt urgent about you."

"Why?"

He averted her glare. "Are you going to eat that pickle?"

"No. You know, Ascot, I may have to kill you."

"Get in line. Look, kiddo, I was very happy that you had found someone special. However, after we three met for coffee the other day, I felt it was urgent that we talk."

"Are you nuts? I thought you liked him."

Rudy swallowed hard. "I do. I did."

"So?"

"When I asked him questions about his work, he was eloquent. He's smart as hell, very passionate about his work. I deeply felt . . . I mean, I always listen to my gut feeling, and it told me . . . he's too old for you."

"What? He's only twenty eight."

"He's almost thirty."

"You've dated guys older than you, Ascot."

"We're talking about you."

Georgia threw her napkin onto the table. "I came here for this? I'm leaving."

He reached across the table for her arm. "Please, Georgia. I know I've been dancing around the issue. It's been hard on me too. Just hear me out."

She folded her arms. "Make it short."

"Well, he's all the things you say he is. Brilliant, good looking, tall."

She glared.

"Cliff's been around the horn, and then some. You are a kid just out of college. You've never had a job, never traveled, or had a steady boy friend. I know you could have several times but they were either too short or too predictable. Predictable in what way?"

Georgia looked away. "You know . . . like all college guys."

Rudy nodded. "A bunch of raging bulls, hungry to collect the most notches on their belts."

"So what is your point?"

"Simple. You meet this older guy. He's respectful and patient. No pressure, just eager to show you the wonders of New York City. What's more, he's smart, good looking and has mucho inches—in height. So, he's it."

Georgia was gritting her teeth, trying not to explode or stomp out.

"Georgia, you graduated from Vassar at the top of your class. Give yourself a little time to find out who you are. This is 1969, women. Your sisters everywhere are finding opportunities. So can you."

Where is he going with this?

"If Cliff loves you, I'm sure he'd be willing to wait . . . a year or two."

"You've over-stepped the line, buster."

"I know. But, damn it, you're my family."

Georgia covered her face with both hands and fought tears. He had never used those words before. When they were growing up, Georgia envied how his parents and sisters showered him with love and praise. That is, until they discovered he had "given his soul to the devil" and shamed the family. Georgia knew, no matter how he had tried, Rudy hadn't seen or heard from them since.

When she managed to speak, the words came slow. "Of course we are your family."

How shall I say this? "I've never had a better friend, Rudy, but even a devoted big brother can be, well, a little over protective. Sometimes I don't know if you're a pal or parent."

She managed a half smile. "But looking back, I know I'm blessed—when sometimes you're both."

So there it was—a detailed review of the morning with Cliff, Rudy's urgent call, and lunch with Rudy. But not a clue about Cliff's leaving was found.

Georgia had been sitting on her balcony in the oversized lounge where she and Cliff snuggled every evening. Here she could revisit the heart-gripping memory of his strong arms folded around her. Forget such things? It was like asking her to stop breathing.

Quit avoiding the truth, girl. Cliff knows. He knows everything about the disingenuous life I've been living. He can't love the woman I really am.

She felt faint. Better go inside, lay down. As she touched the gold handles on the double doors to her bedroom, a wave of hope swept over her. *My God, this is the only room I didn't check.*

She envisioned Cliff's nude broad shoulders stretched across her bed. *Waiting for me, he fell asleep.*

He wasn't there but he had been here. A type-written page was propped up on her cluster of small pastel pillows.

Shame on me for doubting him. He didn't leave without explaining why.

She slowly approached the bed, picked it up, the page, and slipped into a chair,

I can't read this. With shaking hands, she held it in front of closed eyes. *I have to read it.*

The sound of his deep, authoritative voice painfully resonated with every word. What she had expected was anything but this.

"I thought I had found the girl I had always hoped to find—one that understood what I was trying to accomplish for my future. Maybe you're not the girl. You seem annoyed by my working and have priorities over and above me, even when my time with you is limited. Sorry—CH Thanks for the pecan rolls."

CHAPTER 3

Georgia's silent plea for sleep was denied. Viewing her large white bed, with a pale blue satin spread and a generous collection of pillows, she saw it only as a place where Cliff left his scathing note.

Stretched out on her chaise lounge, facing the bed, she pictured Cliff placing the one page, typewritten note on top of the pillows.

"Why in hell do you need so many pillows?" Cliff had once asked.

"The decorator chose them."

Why didn't I say what the decorator had said—the assorted pillows turn a dull bed into an artistic focal point.

She replaced the note to the pillows, after memorizing every word, comma and period. *These words don't sound like Cliff.*

Because the note was typed and unsigned, she fantasized that someone else had written it and dragged him away. *I'm getting delusional.*

By dawn, Georgia was out on her balcony again. The wind's bold fingers lifted her sheer nightgown away from her legs, the long legs she had hated since she was a teenager. They were responsible for making her so tall. But when Cliff came into her life, he said her legs were the most beautiful in the world.

Slipping into *their* lounge, she took a deep breath, hoping to recall the scent of his after-shave lotion. With eyes closed and only her own arms hugging herself, she fell asleep. Those weary eyes did not open until she heard the phone ring.

Please let me get there before it stops. "Hello? Hello?" No answer.

Not until she was completely dressed in khaki slacks and light blue shirt—Cliff's favorite color—did the phone ring again. She lifted the receiver but couldn't speak. *Please let it be Cliff.*

"Georgia?"

"Yes."

"Look, love. I want to apologize for yesterday." It was Rudy. "I guess my protective instinct interfered with good judgment. Georgia? You there?"

"Cliff's gone."

"Damn. I'll be right over."

"No. I don't want to see anybody."

"I'm not anybody. I'm Rudy. On my way."

The uncomfortable feeling of facing Rudy gave way to one of gratitude when her doorbell rang.

Before Rudy could step inside, she held up her hand. "You can come in under one condition. Don't ask for a tour of the apartment, and no comments. Just follow me to the kitchen."

Once inside he looked down at the white marble floor of the round foyer. "Wow. This is gorgeous. Oops. Sorry."

In the kitchen, he gasped. "You could put most of my apartment in this kitchen. And what's this? State-of-the-art cooking utensils and a rack of fancy knives? All for a girl who can't cook?"

"My father is an optimist."

Rudy made coffee and opened the paper bag he brought. "Cinnamon rolls or scones?" He paused. "Okay, if you're not going to talk, just point."

"Scones."

At the breakfast bar, they mounted the stools.

"No wonder Cliff liked to work here. Mighty comfy," Rudy said, patting the stools' white leather cushions.

"He sat where you're sitting."

"Want to tell me what happened?"

She handed him the note.

Rudy read slowly. "The bastard," he said half aloud. "Georgia," he began, obviously trying to keep his voice calm, "what was your reaction to this?"

"Confusion. Disbelief. Wished my mother was here."

Rudy nodded. "I wish she were too. She always made my favorite pie—Dutch apple. What about your father?"

"He wouldn't understand."

"I think he would. When those two guys beat me up, your father took me to the hospital and assured me he wouldn't contact my folks. He paid my hospital bill and paid my apartment rent until I was able to work again. I had asked for nothing. He just understood."

"I remember."

"Your wounds can't be patched up at a hospital. Besides cooking lessons, I need to hear what you need."

Georgia dismounted the bar stool and slumped down against a yet-unstained cabinet. "Bottom line? I need Cliff to come back. I love him."

Rudy slid down beside her. "I think better on the floor too. That's what we always did as kids—usually on the grass against a tree and talk about our dreams."

Georgia nodded. "Have any of yours come true?"

Rudy shrugged. "Not yet. A work in progress. So, can you tell me what transpired before you left to meet me?"

"Nothing special. He asked me not to go, that he worked better with me here. I kissed him goodbye and promised to hurry back."

Rudy shook his head. "Doesn't this note signal anything?"

"Of course. He found out I hid the truth from him about my father. I always made excuses that my father was out of town, had the flu, or some other creative lie."

Silence, the kind that screams to be ended, finally overtook Rudy. "Permission to speak freely?"

"Sure."

Rudy ran his fingers through his curly hair. "Well, first the good stuff. He's smart and he's tall."

Georgia managed a half smile "And the bad stuff?"

"He's a sadistic creep."

"I can always count on you to be sweet."

"I can get even sweeter. Cliffy boy is in love with Cliff. Just reread his note. It's loaded with 'I' and 'my' and his only reference to you is accusatory."

"I think you're reading something into that note that isn't there."

Rudy rolled his eyes. "Well, tell me this. What in hell could you have done that deserved such a brutal message?"

"I deceived him. How can he love someone he can't trust?" After a quiet moment, Georgia rested her head on his shoulder. "What are you thinking?"

"Nothing. Just another one of my paternal thoughts. Better stick to being a pal."

"Rudy, tell me."

"Now is not the time." He stood up, took her hand to help her up.

"What are you holding back?"

"I'll call you tomorrow, pigeon."

"Pigeon? You've never called me that before. You've called me dove but never pigeon."

Rudy looked bewildered. "Really?" His face reddened. "I guess it never came to mind before."

CHAPTER 4

Two weeks later, Georgia was reluctantly standing under the clock at Emeralds, waiting for Rudy. Too drained from Cliff's departure and no word from him since, she was without an excuse or energy to defy Rudy's urging. He had literally commanded her to come. "You need to get out, and I have a surprise. Wear something elegant."

His late arrival was tempered with exuberant approval. "White silk dress. Perfect." He led her to the elevator. "Please note, I was only fifteen minutes late."

"I hope this isn't another one of your—"

"Georgia dear," he interrupted as he punched an elevator button. "I have this brilliant idea, and I know you'll love it. Trust me."

"Trust you? I've known you since sixth grade, and I don't remember spending a single sane moment with you."

"Damn right. And be boring like all those rubber-stamp types cluttering up the universe?"

No arguing with that. Georgia admired the way he dressed. He usually followed the trends but sometimes created his own. Today he was very dapper in navy slacks, a pale blue dress shirt with white collar and cuffs, simple gold cuff links and solid navy tie. Great looking guy. How often had she heard girls moan, "What a waste."

"We're opening a store in Lincoln," he boasted, "and more are planned. You feel okay?"

"Fine."

"Have you heard from—?"

"No."

The elevator door opened and they stepped out.

"Here we are, my sweet. High fashion heaven."

"What's your brilliant idea? And what are we doing here?"

"I want you to meet Michelle."

"Who's Michelle?"

"She claims to be French, but I wouldn't bet on it. She's our Designer Salon buyer."

"And why would I want to meet her?"

"Well, actually," he gulped, "she wants to meet you, only she doesn't know it yet."

"I think Michelle and I are both in for a surprise." Georgia stopped just short of the Designer Salon. "I'm not moving another step until you tell me what's going on."

"Okay, okay. Michelle is having a Geoffrey Beene trunk show soon. Beene is particular about models. I heard Michelle say she doesn't have anyone suitable."

"So?"

"So . . . you're suitable."

"What? Forget it."

As she turned to leave, Rudy linked his arm in hers and spun her around. "Trust me, love. You'd make a great model. You're beautiful, tall, and move like a gazelle."

"No way, dear boy."

"Would you just try to—"

"No!" Georgia peaked behind Rudy.

Designer Salon was a spacious area set off from the rest of the floor by a majestic arch of carved dark walnut. Luxurious loveseats, satin chairs, and highly polished tables awaited the clientele. A stately woman about fifty, with perfectly coiffed auburn hair, emerged. Georgia recognized her suit as Chanel and her pearl necklace as top quality.

"Rudy, I'm getting nowhere with that idiot Jesse you call an assistant. Look at that dreadful mannequin. It belongs in Montgomery Ward."

"Sorry, dear heart, but first here's a model I want you to meet. Michelle, this is Georgia Parker." He caressed Georgia's name as though he had introduced Elizabeth Taylor.

Michelle's demeanor telegraphed that she'd require a Dun & Bradstreet report before condescending to say hello.

Georgia felt uneasy as Michelle scanned her with a critical glare, squinting as though the vision might damage her eyes.

Michelle folded her arms. "How tall are you?"

"Five-ten," Rudy said when Georgia hesitated.

"Five-eleven," Georgia corrected.

"You're experienced?"

"Uh, yes," Rudy said. "She's modeled at college and for the Junior League. Stuff like that."

Michelle turned a dark eye on Rudy. "Can't she speak for herself? Let me see you walk."

"What?"

"Walk," Michelle ordered.

Rudy nudged Georgia. "Walk, like you learned in modeling school."

"I never went to modeling school, you idiot," she whispered.

When Georgia walked back, she heard Rudy tell Michelle, "She's a Vassar girl, you know." He obviously knew how to push Michelle's snob button, because the woman's eyes brightened.

Michelle walked around to Georgia's back and Georgia felt a fist jabbed between her shoulder blades. "Pull yourself up to your full height. Stop denying that you're tall."

"I've had no training, and I was only in a couple of fashion shows in college."

Michelle almost smiled. "You have potential. You'll catch on. This is only June, but we preview fall with trunk shows. I could use you a week from Saturday. Are you available?"

"Sure she is," Rudy answered.

Michelle groaned. "You again?"

"If you'll give me some pointers," Georgia said, "I'll try."

"Good. Be here at nine. The show's from ten to three. The pay is fifty dollars for the day, plus forty percent discount on any Beene outfit you'd like to order."

With a strong finger, Michelle tapped Georgia's chin. "Don't lead with your chin, girl. Tuck it in." Michelle sighed. "Oh, well. You'll learn."

She walked away with not so much as a goodbye, and then turned to Rudy. "And, you, Ascot, get that ugly dummy out of here. It's destroying our image."

Destroying our image? For a harrowing moment, teenage Georgia was standing in her once favorite store, The Satin Bonnet, in

19

Landing, Mississippi. Without warning, the Bonnet's owner had shouted. "Leave. We don't serve the likes of you."

"We can leave now," Rudy said. "Georgia?" He touched her arm. "You okay?"

She shook her head. "Yes. Fine."

"You seemed far away. How about lunch?"

In Emeralds Tea Room, Georgia set the menu aside. "I'll just have coffee."

"Make that two," he told the waitress.

"Thanks for accepting the modeling job. To celebrate, I'm buying."

A page came over the intercom. "Number seven . . . seven."

Rudy stood up. "That's for me. I'll be right back." He leaned over to whisper. "Bring the coffee at your own risk."

Georgia noticed today, as she had before that not a single diner or employee was black. Even the busboys were white.

The waitress brought their coffee and a dish of cookies. "Home-made," she said, "no charge."

Rudy returned, his face flushed. "Jesse the jerk doesn't know one body part from another. We received a shipment of mannequins and he's overwhelmed. He's useless."

"Then fire him. You're the boss, aren't you?"

"Can't. He was a resident at Boys Town—sent there from Mississippi because of trouble with the law."

"That's why you can't fire him?"

"A priest at Boys Town asked our president to give him a job."

"So you're stuck with him."

"Yes. Truth is, he's talented, but he's a pain—an angry bigot. Mind if we stop by my office for a minute? It's on this floor, and then I'll walk you to your car."

Their trip to Rudy's office was interrupted when a blond young man stepped out of the door marked Display. His electric blue eyes glared when he saw Rudy approach.

I know those eyes.

"Where are you going?" Rudy asked. "You just paged me."

"That snooty French Michelle is driving me nuts. First she wants a new mannequin standing, then one sitting. Now she wants both. I can't put them together that fast. I'm going for a Coke." He disappeared down the hall.

Georgia shuddered. Something in his bold blue eyes and southern accent sent a disquieting twinge through her. The accent was a sound she loved when she arrived in Mississippi at age fourteen, but later, after she had been so brutally rejected, she found it frightening.

"That was Jesse," Rudy told her.

"I feel uncomfortable here," she said as they left the store. "Everything's gone wrong since I came here. I lose my job, I'm embarrassed by my over-the-top apartment, Cliff leaves and stabs me in the heart. Now I meet your man Jesse and I imagine that I've met him before under disturbing circumstances."

Rudy shrugged. "And don't forget our Tea Room's awful coffee."

"Thanks for your help."

Rudy opened her car door. "I thought you chose Omaha, instead of living in Lincoln with your father."

"I was supposed to have a job in Omaha, remember?" She closed her eyes. "In Lincoln I'd be afraid every day that Stratley would—"

Rudy touched her cheek. "Do you still have nightmares?"

"Yes, but not while Cliff was here." She bit her lower lip. "Cliff's leaving intensified how men hate me when they discover I'm not pure white."

"Would you consider calling Jon Roberts? You told me more than once, in high school that he was your first love. His heroism that awful day was incredible. He really cared about you, Georgia."

"Jon will always be my hero. After Stratley's attack—*why can't I call it what it was?*—Jon sent me daisies, even while he was in the hospital being treated for the beating he sustained. I tried and tried to reach him, but his parents kept us apart."

"Keep trying. You'll find him."

"It would be useless. Jon's family liked me, until they saw my father and his violent behavior that night."

"That's the Roberts' problem not your father's."

Georgia nodded and slipped into her car.

"And don't worry about Slimeball Stratley. He went to college back East and there's not a chance he'll come back here."

Georgia blinked. "How do you know?"
Rudy smiled. "Word gets around."

CHAPTER 5

Georgia thought modeling would be a piece of cake.

"Just move among the customers," Michelle told her. "Act as though you love everything you wear and smile." Georgia did love everything. In her first outfit she glided out gracefully, but she tripped on a rug, and almost landed in a client's lap.

"Pick up your feet," Michelle growled.

A nice flow of customers kept the department humming throughout the day. Judy, the pleasant uniformed maid, drew coffee from a silver urn into porcelain cups. While Georgia moved among customers seated on satin chairs or brocade loveseats, Judy moved about with pastry trays.

Georgia had changed into her next ensemble, but was having difficulty with the necklace. Outside of her dressing room she saw the maid refilling a pastry tray. "Judy, could you help me? I'm having trouble with this clasp."

"Of course," the gray-haired woman said. "Bend down a little. You certainly have style, Georgia. There. Turn around. Looks great. Best model yet, and I've seen a lot in the last twenty years."

"You've worked here for twenty years?"

"Yes, ma'am. And I've seen some of these customers at every show."

"Really?"

"Like it was the most important thing in their lives." Judy lowered her voice. "I've heard Michelle call them shallow and spoiled. I see them differently. Some have husbands too busy for them. Or have mistresses. Too many of these women have nothing to enjoy but a charge account. These poor dears are just plain lonely, you can see it in their eyes."

I wonder if Judy can see loneliness in my eyes?

At the outset, Georgia felt their rigidity was their expression of superiority. Later, she recognized forced smiles and heard laughter filled with pretense.

Georgia was changing when Michelle whispered, "Mrs. Farnsworth, my best customer, is here. Put on the blue suit. Hurry."

The moment Georgia emerged from the dressing room, Michelle gasped.

"What's wrong?"

"You're wearing the wrong skirt. Quick. Go change."

Too late. Mrs. Farnsworth saw Georgia and motioned her to come close.

"What a clever idea," the woman said. "A mix of patterns."

The Beene representative and Michelle tried to explain that a solid skirt was available.

"No," Mrs. Farnsworth said. "I like it this way. I'll take it."

At the end of the day, Michelle approached Georgia, her voice peppered with irritation. "Next time, ask the rep how he wants his clothes shown."

"There'll be a next time?"

"Maybe you'll learn from your mistakes. I suggest you cut your hair. You look like a school girl with it long. Be sure everything is hung up and shut the door when you leave."

Maybe you'll learn . . . hang up the clothes . . . shut the door. I don't need this stupid job. What she needed was to hear from Cliff. Three weeks and no word. If only he'd give her a chance to tell him the huge apartment means nothing to her. She'd tell him that Rudy had always been there for her, and that was the first time Rudy had urgently called her. And she'd explain why she hadn't told him about her father.

Maybe, if she called his newspaper they could tell her how to reach him.

The moment Georgia arrived home, she called Cliff's newspaper. He was out of the country, they said, but as soon as he checked in with their foreign bureau they'd pass on her message.

After a week and no word from Cliff, Rudy urged Georgia to let go. She knew he was right. Work would help.

The Bill Blass collection, proclaimed by the fashion press as superb, exemplified the way Georgia preferred to dress: chic, unique, comfortable. She had looked forward to this show, until she put on the first pair of shoes. Too small.

"Trunk show shoes rarely fit the models," Michelle said, "but it's only for a few minutes."

The few minutes added up to five hours.

"Just keep smiling." Michelle snapped her fingers for Georgia to hurry. "The Salon is packed. I'm calling for an extra clerk, more chairs, and another model. Mrs. Farnsworth and her entourage are here already. Hurry."

While dressing, Georgia heard a disturbance outside her dressing room. Voices expressing anger, mingled with words of reassurance and apologies, clashed back and forth. Georgia recognized only voices of Michelle and Mrs. Farnsworth. Georgia waited for the voices to disappear before stepping out into the Salon.

Seated on a loveseat was a stately, handsome woman about thirty in a bright orange dress and wide-brimmed matching hat. Her shoes had heels higher than Georgia had ever seen. Her unique handbag, covered with multi-colored beads, was held by a hand bearing a large diamond ring.

On the loveseat that could accommodate two more, she sat alone. She was black.

Michelle whispered to Georgia to bypass the woman in orange and go directly to Mrs. Farnsworth.

Georgia couldn't move.

Michelle was in her ear again. "Move." When Georgia didn't respond, Michelle took her arm and guided her to Mrs. Farnsworth. With a fabricated smile, Michelle asked her best customer, "Isn't this the dearest ensemble you've ever seen?"

"Rust? Not my color," Mrs. Farnsworth said.

"I will take it." All heads turned. It was the lady in orange.

One customer left, and two more followed.

While Georgia changed, Michelle told her she had asked Mrs. Farnsworth to go to lunch—on the store—and come back later for a private showing. "I've told the rep to get rid of that person."

Sometime later, Michelle came out of her office and passed the dressing room, now shared with another model. "Is that person gone?"

"Some time ago. Mrs. Farnsworth is back. Should we start over?"

"Yes."

Michelle and the rep fawned over the cherished customer. She bought three outfits and left pleased. Michelle was ecstatic. "This is the biggest day we have ever had for a trunk show." She turned to the rep. "How did you get rid of . . . that person?"

He looked at his shoes. "Well, actually, she left on her own."

"Really? Did she say anything?"

"She placed orders for six outfits, plus two in different colors. That made a sale of eight."

"You fool! She'll never pay for them and—"

"She paid cash," he whispered.

"—That's an order of thousands of dollars. She what?"

"Cash," he smiled, pulling out a wad from his pocket. "No one else would help her. That's why I'm here, Michelle. To sell."

As soon as Georgia reached home, she telephoned Rudy.

"I'm quitting." She told him about the lady in orange. "They treated her shamefully. I can't stay there. I can't believe this is happening here. Certainly Nebraska isn't like Mississippi."

"Of course not. Prejudice never crosses state lines."

"Don't play mind games with me, Ascot."

"I'm sorry. The treatment of that woman was rotten. I'll be in Lincoln for two days. When I get back we'll talk."

"There's nothing to talk about. I'm done with Emeralds."

CHAPTER 6

Georgia watched, appalled, as three delivery men carried in furnishings her father had ordered. A formal dining room in dark cherry, an ultra-modern living room—Rudy would love it—so bizarre she was moved to laugh or cry.

The designer for Mara-Lane Images had called to explain. "We felt someone as young as you would find it enchanting."

Enchanting, my ass.

"I'll drop by and review each piece for you."

I can hardly wait for that.

Only the study and the library were compatible with Georgia's idea of comfort. Off-white couch with large matching chairs in the study, and tall, copper-colored leather arm chairs in the library.

The phone rang. *Oh, please, let it be Cliff.* "Hello?"

"Georgia? Michelle. I only have a minute, but you're too tall for Halston samples. See you in two weeks for Anne Klein. Gotta run."

Damn. I didn't tell her I wasn't coming back. So, I'm too tall for Halston, my hair is immature—good riddance.

Georgia passed a mirror, then backed up. *Hmm. I'm not in college anymore.* She recalled how often people said her mother looked like Grace Kelly. *And didn't people say I looked like my mother?* She ran her fingers through her long, dark brown hair. She did look like a teenager, especially in a ponytail. What had she seen in fashion magazines? Sassoon's asymmetrical cut might work.

The following morning, Georgia made a trip to a beauty salon. She not only had her hair cut, but also changed the color. Surveying the result, she decided—good. Very good.

The evening Rudy returned from Lincoln, he arrived at her apartment with corned beef sandwiches. He gasped. "A blonde? Fabulous. Sassoon? Perfect."

In the kitchen he laid out the sandwiches, dill pickles and salad, seldom taking his eyes off of her. "You're stunning. Absolutely stunning. Why the big change?"

"Just a whim." She told him about Michelle's call.

"Did you tell her you quit?"

"No. Her call was such a surprise I was speechless."

"Good. Let me explain something. If Michelle had refused the lady service she would have been fired. That's why she wanted the visiting rep to get her to leave. You're not working for Michelle. You're working for Emeralds. Michelle just supervises the area in which you serve."

"Good try, but I'm not going back."

"Wherever you go, kiddo, you'll find people like Michelle. If you want to change things, be there. Walking away solves nothing. I've been shunned, laughed at, talked about, and beaten up. Where would I be if I walked away from every job where I felt disliked? On a bread line. You have two weeks before the next show. Think about it."

When Georgia walked into the Designer Salon for the Anne Klein trunk show, Michelle scrutinized her. "Well, I see you've respected my advice. Good cut. What was wrong with your natural color?"

Georgia flinched, said nothing.

During the show several customers raved about her new look. Georgia remembered customers' names, and learned about the designers' special merits. "The patterns are exclusive and the workmanship's impeccable," she'd say.

The representative asked if she would consider coming to New York. "Here's my card. Think about it."

"You're not ready for New York," Michelle said later. "I'll have plenty of work for you. Fall fashion shows start soon." Michelle dropped into a Salon chair. "I hate putting runway shows together. You've shown creativity in how you understand the designer's intent. I've not always agreed, but customers seemed pleased."

"Who will select the models?"

"If you know the merchandise, have to do the fittings, it would make sense, I suppose, to choose appropriate models. If you would do all that, I'll make it worth your while."

Georgia spotted Rudy standing outside the elegant archway. After Michelle dismissed her, she joined him.

"You were fabulous," he said. "I can tell the customers love you."

"Too bad styles like these aren't affordable for more women."

"Knockoffs are. If an Anne Klein is copied, the knock-off house blatantly boasts it's an Anne Klein look."

His page came over the intercom. "Gotta go. Probably Jesse with another problem."

Georgia winced. "Where in Mississippi is Jesse from?"

"Don't know. I'll find out."

"Rudy," she called after him, "Don't mention who asked."

CHAPTER 7

Georgia rushed into her apartment to grab the ringing phone. "Hello?"

"What time would you like dinner?"

Rudy. "Who is this?"

"Very funny. In the mood for Chinese?"

"Always. Pick up curry chicken for me, and come at six. Remember, six o'clock."

At six thirty, Rudy showed up with Chinese take-out.

"How do you always manage to be late?"

"It's a gift."

"Smells good. Let's eat."

"Wait a minute. I've been here twice and still haven't seen the whole house."

"Follow me." She showed him the two guest bedrooms. "Next, my bedroom suite."

"Good lord, this is an apartment in itself. Bedroom, sitting room, dressing room, home office. Do you ever get lost?"

"I try. You've seen the kitchen. Now, the dining room."

His eyes widened, as he ran his hand over the long table. "You'll never use this. You can't cook."

"I can always have you bring in Chinese. Follow me to the study."

"Great fireplace. White furniture. White rug." He inhaled. "I love the smell of newness. Why is this room called a study?"

"A place to study television, I guess. The small library is through here."

"Another fireplace? Love the leather chairs. Where are the books?"

"The two on the table."

"Romance novels? Any heroes resembling Cliff Hudson?"

Without responding, she led him to the living room.

"Holy Toledo. I love this modern stuff. And what's this?" He had walked to the tall windows, under which was a chaise lounge covered in black and white pony skin and splashed with red and purple pillows. He stretched out on it. "How glamorous."

"I'm sending all this back. Not my style."

"Don't. Please."

"Okay," she sighed, "I'll leave it to you in my will."

"I'll never get it. I'm going first." In the middle of the living room, he sat in one of four leather and chrome chairs. "Some graduation present. Your dad's gift of love."

"A gift of guilt," she corrected. "Since we left Landing, he's been leaning on his checkbook to appease me."

"Ah, come on, Georgia. If he could have foreseen how damaging Mississippi would be, he wouldn't have taken you there. Your father loves you."

"He had a strange way of showing it when I was growing up. Seldom around. His attention was lavish gifts for Christmas or birthdays."

"Harboring such feelings, why did you accept all this?"

"He insisted it was my mother's wish—a special home for me."

Rudy sighed. "Some day I'm going to make lots of money."

"My father says the only thing money does is allow you not to worry about money."

"I could handle that."

"Better to have goals and let the money follow. I'm quoting my father again."

"Some day, I'd like to go to design school in New York."

"That's a big leap—from display to fashion design."

"Not really, Georgio Armani did it. He went from window display designer for an Italian department store to fashion coordinator."

"Really? He gave up all that just to become a famous fashion designer?"

"The great Armani started out just like us." Rudy spun around, with arms outstretched. "Great floor plan—so open and bright. Lots of bare walls. We'll have to shop for décor. That wall—that's the place."

"For what?"

"Something spectacular. Like the jeweled clock at our store's entrance. It belongs in a place like this. Do you know the clock's history? The grandson of Emeralds' founder gave it to his bride. Know why?"

"Because he was rich and extravagant."

"It was a gift of love. He told his bride *time* was precious. So, he had it made with precious and semi-precious stones." Rudy paused. "Sad thing though, his bride died shortly after they were married from a ruptured appendix. Eighteen months later, two concerned friends of the still grieving Solomon Emeralds, urged him to join them on a trip abroad, Solomon Edwards and his friends chose to return home on the Titanic. He didn't survive."

"How sad. He and his bride were granted precious little time."

"Well put."

Georgia was silent, reflecting on the story. Rudy warmed up their curry chicken, and set two places at the kitchen bar.

"Rudy, why did they hang that clock in the store instead of a family home?"

"From what I've heard, they felt it would be a constant reminder of Sol's heartbreak. In the store, it served as a valuable reminder. Beneath the clock, they placed a large plaque with the words 'Time is Precious'. Customers found it an inspiring gift. I've heard customers brought friends and family in to read it. A few years ago the plaque was stolen. It's never been replaced."

Georgia nodded.

"Georgia, your father's monthly dinner is next week. Am I still the wing man at dinner?"

"You're still our cherished guest," she corrected.

"Has your father said anything about you two ever being seen in public alone?"

"He's hinted at it. I hope you're not tired of the Nebraska Steak Barn. He won't go anyplace else."

Located far outside the city, in a converted barn, the restaurant was rarely frequented by Omahans on week nights. Since her father chose Tuesday once a month, with Rudy along, they appeared to be a young white couple dining with an old black friend.

"Love that place. Best food in the state." Rudy picked up an almond cookie. "What I get tired of is the pretense."

"My father set boundaries when we left Mississippi. It was his choice never to visit me at school or attend my graduation."

Rudy's eyes flashed. "I thought it was your idea that he not attend."

"No. But I must confess . . . I was relieved." She placed their tea things and almond cookies on a tray. "If he had come, Vassar would have been Mississippi all over again. Dad knew it and I knew it."

The phone rang. She answered in the kitchen, and motioned to Rudy to take the tray into the study.

As soon as he left, she said, "Cliff?"

As soon as Georgia joined him, Rudy looked up from the chair near the fireplace. "I poured your tea, but it's cold by now. Must have been someone important."

She smiled. "Cliff." She sat on the white area rug, drew her knees up and held them tight. She stirred her tea.

"What did he say?"

"He was glad I called."

"You called him?"

"He sounded kind of formal at first, but became . . . enthusiastic when he was telling me about his work." She paused. "Mostly, I just listened."

"Did you ask him why he left that nasty note?"

She nodded. Raw feelings surfaced— feelings she hadn't been aware of before. "I asked him."

"You asked him," Rudy repeated, "and he said?"

"No."

"No? No what?"

"That's what he said. No. He wouldn't tell me. I felt he wanted to forget the whole thing and move on. Maybe he made a mistake, but so did I."

"What mistake?"

"I failed to tell him about my father's color and if he found out on his own, he felt deceived. But I couldn't explain on the phone. I felt, well, like I owed him something, so I apologized."

Rudy jumped up. "You apologized? For being beautiful and loving and patient and forgiving? Are you nuts, woman?"

"You're shouting."

"I'm not shouting. I'm screaming. He didn't find out about your father. If he had, he would have said so. He's a no-good son-of-a-bitch. And what was your apology about?"

Why did I mention that? "I just said . . . I was sorry I left to go meet you when he didn't want me to go."

Rudy plopped back into his chair. "Oh, God."

"What?"

"Nothing. What else?"

She omitted that Cliff's tone became warm and loving after her apology. "By the end of the call he said he missed me, how to reach him and that . . . he loved me."

Rudy leaned forward. "How did his dear, sweet change make you feel?"

She looked at Rudy squarely. "I thought I'd be elated afterwards, but I felt numb."

Rudy looked straight into her eyes. "And how do you feel now?"

"He's so complicated, so mysterious."

"So self-engrossed, so unfeeling," Rudy added. "Get rid of the bum."

"I knew you'd say that."

"Answer the question, love. Not for me, for yourself. How do you feel now?"

It's useless to lie to Rudy. "The truth? I feel like I've just jumped out of a plane and praying my parachute will open."

The sadness in Rudy's eyes startled her.

"If the parachute doesn't open, pigeon, you'll be crushed."

CHAPTER 8

Trunk shows were over. Runway shows began. And still no concrete news from Cliff. His travel schedule was erratic. He'd try to squeeze in another trip to Omaha. No mention of her coming to LA.

"I love you and miss you," he wrote. "Be patient with me. I'm trying to build a future for us." Those words that so elated her at first gave her little comfort after weeks of neglect. When the weeks turned into three months, she grew weary of clinging to hollow words.

So, fighting emptiness and longing, she succumbed to Emeralds and Michelle.

"Runway modeling is far different from showrooms," an Emeralds model told Georgia. "On stage you're giving a performance. I'll help you."

At a runway show set in the Hotel Blackstone ballroom, Michelle's narration droned on slow and tedious, as usual. Georgia noticed guests talking among themselves, looking at the models only now and then.

After the show, Michelle stomped into the dressing room. "Why are you girls in such a hurry to get off the runway when I haven't finished?"

When Michelle left, one model complained, "She hasn't a clue about how to do a show."

Another model confided, "We only keep working for her because Emeralds provides the most work."

The models left in a hurry, leaving Michelle and Georgia to ride down in the elevator together.

"I've asked the doorman to bring our car," Michelle said.

They stepped into the lobby and as they neared the exit, Georgia froze. Her father came out of Blackstone's gourmet restaurant, the Orleans Room. He was with another man—a white man. Her father opened the exit door for Michelle.

"Thank you," she said in a condescending tone.

Georgia held her breath. *My God, does Michelle think he's the doorman?*

Georgia looked at her father as he held the door for her too. His look told her to just keep moving.

Michelle said, "Our driver's waiting. Here, give this dollar to the doorman."

I don't dare. He'll explode right here in front of the hotel, and I'll be fired.

Her father saw the transaction and approached his numb daughter. He positioned himself so Michelle could not see him take the dollar from Georgia's hand. "Thank you. Miss. Good day."

Today her father was mistaken for a doorman. She was terrified he might respond as he had in a similar situation when they lived in Mississippi. She had vowed long ago to put that all behind her, but as she and Michelle rode back to Emeralds in silence, her relentless memory had preserved every detail.

From day one at the exclusive Jefferson Davis High School Academy in Landing, Mississippi, Georgia was shunned. Girls condescended to smile—sweet but cool—and that was all. The stares from the boys were chilling. They wanted only to distance themselves from this tall, lanky girl, who, in most cases, towered over them.

For months she was their Damn Yankee, who walked to classes alone, ate lunch alone and endured nicknames, like Georgia the Giant or Nanook of the North.

Then, a miracle happened. Sally Jo Barton, the most prominent girl in school, was failing math and asked Georgia to help her. Thanks to Georgia's laborious tutoring, Sally Jo passed. Slowly, other girls in the class began to say hello, and, once in awhile, invited her to sit with them at lunch. One day, Sally Jo casually tossed Georgia an invitation to her sweet-sixteen party, the event of the year. "It's formal. Come if you like

Georgia ran all the way home from school. She found Olympia, her father's housekeeper, in the kitchen polishing silver. "Olympia, get the car. We're going shopping!"

Georgia was still breathless when they arrived at her favorite store, The Satin Bonnet, Landing's most exclusive specialty shop. Georgia received a bubbly greeting from Poppy, the shop's manager.

Poppy was all the more gushy when Georgia revealed the dress was for Sally Jo's party. She showed Georgia several gowns, all fluffy, puffy things endowed with endless steps of organdy ruffles. Not her style. Georgia finally selected a slim-fitting gown of white eyelet with a modest flare from hip to floor.

When she walked out of the dressing room, Poppy gasped. "My gracious. You look like a regular movie star."

Georgia must have made a similar impression when she arrived at the Barton's spacious home. One of the Petrie twins, a popular upperclassman, asked her to save the first dance for him. He glided her skillfully around the dance floor, and soon shoulder taps came from others wanting to dance with her.

When the music ended, she darted into the powder room to retouch her lips and cheeks. When she came out she found everyone assembled in the living room where the birthday cake was being served.

Georgia scanned the large room, aglow with crystal chandeliers and windows graced with lace valances. The floor was covered with the young guests. The girls' gowns looked like pastel flowers among the stem-like tuxedos of the boys. Youth Dew fragrance permeated the air. Cake being passed overhead, hand over hand, brought waves of giggles and laughter.

"Georgia! Over here," came invitations from everywhere, but when the Petrie twins stood up—in the middle of the room—she headed in their direction. She had to step over several people, who greeted her with warmth and up-raised arms to help her along her precarious path. One twin handed her his cake plate. She thought she'd burst with happiness.

Then it happened. The doorbell rang and Mrs. Barton was summoned by a servant. She left and quickly returned. "Georgia," she sang out in a strong voice, clearly heard over the animated chatter. "Your driver is here. I told him to wait by the car."

But he didn't wait outside. Mrs. Barton and Georgia saw him almost at the same time, standing just inside the room. His usual choice of suit and tie were as black as his mood.

"I'm not her driver," he announced in his deep, booming voice. "I'm her father." He spotted her. "Georgia? Ready, dear?"

If death could be summoned, she would have welcomed it. All the happy chatter stopped. Plates and forks hung immobilized in midair.

And there she was. In the middle of the room, unable to escape anyone's eyes. Earlier, the lighting in the room had seemed soft. But when she stood up, the light seemed like a bright spotlight, focused only on her.

Classmates, who, just moments earlier were so friendly, averted their eyes as she tried to step over those in her path. At one point, she stepped on the hem of her dress and reached for a boy's shoulder to steady herself. He jerked away. She fell. Standing up, she saw strawberry frosting smeared down the front of her beautiful white gown. In a shaky voice, she mumbled a pitiful "excuse me" and stumbled on.

Her father reached out to help her, but she pretended not to notice.

Georgia called her father the moment she reached home. "So now you're a doorman?"

"I was just being polite."

"Really? Would the gentleman with you be mistaken for a doorman? No way. He would have been thanked with a broad smile and a gushy 'Well, aren't you sweet? Thank you so much.' Do you agree?"

"No doubt, but don't worry, dear. My career as a doorman is over. It doesn't pay enough."

As soon as their conversation ended, she decided to call him back.

"Dad, one more thing. When and how do you plan to end this charade?"

"I thought you wanted to live as white?"

"Yes, but I'm torn between when to tell or not to tell." *I shouldn't have brought it up. I want to be white, but I don't want my proud father, who is silently funding research on diabetes. At the same time, he's working at Heartland Medical Research Center—forty miles from Lincoln— and they don't seem to care what color he is. His remarkable achievements have distinguished the firm and his associates.*

"Let's leave things as they are and talk later. Right now isn't the time."

The day Georgia was helping Michelle unpack show merchandise, Rudy called. "Guess where Jesse is from?"

"I don't dare."

"From Landing, Mississippi."

"Are you sure?"

"Yep. He doesn't especially like Omaha, but there's nothing for him in Landing. His mother is dead and his father is in prison."

"Sad." Nothing that Rudy revealed about Jesse triggered a memory. It did, however, reinforce her belief that they had met before.

At home that evening, she changed into jeans and white shirt, grabbed a few chocolate nonpareils, and went to her study with the mail.

Among the bills and junk mail, she found several postcards from Cliff, with brief messages from all over Europe. One read, "I'm looking up at Notre Dame, thinking what a wonderful place for a wedding. I miss you." *Then why don't you ask me to come over?* Still nothing about returning to the States.

Georgia had little appetite for dinner. She sought out an old movie on television and found one in progress. The scene was a plush hotel lobby. A pageboy, dressed in a red jacket with brass buttons and white gloves, carried a small silver tray and approached the leading man with a message. Georgia never heard the dialogue. "The red jacket. Good lord," she said aloud.

She called Rudy. "I remember where I met Jesse."

"Tell me."

"Too long a story. I'll tell you this weekend while we're shopping for my apartment accessories."

"No. Now. I'm coming over."

Rudy arrived in jeans and an Emeralds softball sweatshirt. He ceremoniously presented an apple pie. "You never have anything to eat, so I bought this to go with your wonderful coffee."

She served them in the study. "The first month we were in Landing, my father wanted to take me to see *To Kill a Mockingbird,* but it wasn't shown in Landing."

"Not surprising."

"So we saw *Music Man.* Inside was a young ticket taker, looking really snazzy in a waist-high red jacket with brass buttons and white gloves. That was Jesse Wiggins."

"You're kidding!"

"He wasn't very tall then, kind of skinny and his hair—let me think—not as light as it is now."

"Are you sure it was Jesse?"

"Positive. He was, I'd say, about fourteen." Georgia closed her eyes. "I can see my father handing him our tickets, and Jesse was appalled to see a dark-skinned man with a young white girl."

"Was that the time your father had to show his birth certificate and driver's license to prove he wasn't black?"

"Yes. When Jesse chased us out of the main floor seating, my dad produced proof that both his parents were Caucasian. How much more did I tell you before?"

"Nothing."

"Well, the theatre manager walked by and recognized my father. The man's mother had severe diabetes. My father was asked to confer with her doctors. You should have seen Jesse's face when the manager and my father shook hands."

"Wow."

"Jesse said that it was our fault he was quitting his job."

"Why?"

"The theatre manager told him to escort us to the main floor—an area reserved for whites only. Earlier, Jesse had directed us to the balcony, seating for 'coloreds', as he put it."

Rudy sipped his coffee. "So he quit."

"Yes, because, in his own words: 'I ain't escorting no niggers nowhere, and I don't belong in a place that lets coloreds mix with whites.' I never forgot those words. That's when he threatened us."

Georgia took Rudy's plate. "I know you want more." She brought him apple pie topped with vanilla ice cream.

"Thanks, love. What was the threat?"

Georgia sat cross-legged on the floor. "Jesse said, in effect, 'You'd better pray our paths never cross. I'll get even.' He's probably forgotten it. He's grown up now."

Rudy looked doubtful. "Having heard his bigoted blabbering, I'm not sure he's grown up."

"Well, don't worry. I'm at Emeralds only temporarily. Our paths are unlikely to cross."

"Meanwhile I intend to keep him too busy to get in trouble. Besides, most of the time he'll be setting up the new store in Lincoln."

CHAPTER 9

Georgia and Rudy arrived together for the monthly dinner with her father at Nebraska Steak Barn. He was already at his usual table and stood as he saw them approach.

"Good evening, Dr. Parker," Rudy greeted.

Parker did not speak. He was staring at Georgia.

Her hand went to her hair. "Well, Dad, what do you think?"

No response.

"I know it's a big change, but do you like it?"

"Yes. You look beautiful but—"

"But?"

"You look so much like your mother," he said, unsmiling, "it's . . . startling."

He opened a menu—something he never used—and fanned through the pages. "Is everybody hungry?"

The tantalizing aroma and sound of sizzling steaks heightened Georgia's appetite. The food was always good and she was counting on Rudy's animated patter to keep the conversation light.

When Charlie, their regular waiter approached, Georgia and her father ordered their usual filets with ranch fries and Rudy chose prime rib.

Georgia watched her father eat with a healthy appetite. He looked wonderful. His black intelligent eyes gleamed against his satin caramel-colored skin. He was tall and sat elegantly erect. A woman walked by, glanced at her father, then at Georgia and Rudy sitting across from him. Judging from her perplexed, yet pleasant smile, she seemed more curious about this attractive black man than concerned about a young white couple dining with him. Her gaze on Parker lingered.

Georgia often wondered if her father had a woman in his life. She never asked. She knew that he adored her mother and grieves for her still. Throughout dinner, when she looked up from her plate, he was looking at her.

She dared not discuss her hair again. She stayed with his favorite subjects—current events or his work. "How was the Canada medical conference?"

"Stimulating. Important strides are being made in diabetes research. I'm anxious to go to work every day."

"Sounds as though," Rudy said, "you're more passionate than ever about your work."

Parker nodded. "Glad I chose research over private practice as an endocrinologist."

Georgia concurred. A research lab. Best place for a man who doesn't enjoy interacting with people.

"I've always wondered why you chose research," Rudy said.

Dr. Parker smiled. "Because of Vernon Endowsky."

"An inspiring teacher?" Rudy asked.

"No. A high school classmate. We met on the basketball team. Vernon had skill and speed beyond belief. He was equally outstanding in track and football. He received offers of full scholarships from more than one notable university."

Rudy asked, "Which school did he choose?"

"He hadn't decided. After graduation we promised to write. I did. He didn't. I tried calling, but there was no listing."

"How did his story end?" Rudy asked.

"It doesn't have an end. Only a beginning and middle."

Charlie brought coffee and left.

"One time, on spring break, I went to Vernon's home."

"Did you find him?" Rudy asked.

"Yes. He answered the door. Vernon invited me in. He had accepted *none* of the scholarships. He stayed home to take care of his father."

"Why?"

"His father came into the room in a wheel chair. He had lost both legs from diabetes."

"Couldn't he afford proper care?" Georgia asked.

"Yes, but back then insulin had problems with purity and inconsistency of potency. A lack of proper diet, exercise, weight control, along with patients' fear of the pain of injection, there were many failures.

Not until the last two decades was there much progress." Parker sighed. "Vernon now has diabetes. It's often hereditary. His father died from the disease. I don't want Vernon to lose limbs or life."

"Which of us," Rudy asked, "needs to worry about becoming a statistic?"

"Obese people, folks over sixty. Negroes are seventy percent more susceptible than whites, to name a few."

Georgia wondered if he was including himself. Even though both of his biological parents were white, his color wasn't. Her mother had mentioned something about a gene in his family background that had surfaced, but Georgia knew very little about that background.

A wave of courage engulfed her. "Dad, why have you never discussed your background with me?"

Rudy looked with alarm at Georgia. He made a move to get up.

"It's alright, son. Sit down. Why have I never told you? Cowardice."

"If you'd rather not—"

"No. It's time. It's quite a story, but tough to tell." As he leaned forward, poised to begin, a burst of laughter exploded behind him. A waiter carrying a large decorated cake blazing with candles was followed by the off-key chorus of off-key singing waiters.

"We can't talk here," Parker said. "Let's have dinner next Tuesday at my house."

The three walked to the parking lot together, but Parker stopped before they reached their cars, extended his hand to Rudy. "It was a pleasure, as always, young man." Then he kissed his daughter on the cheek. "I'll look forward to next Tuesday."

"Wait a minute, Dr. Parker; we'll walk you to your car."

"We want to see your new Chrysler Imperial, Dad."

In silence, he led the way.

"What a beauty," Rudy exclaimed, as he walked around both sides. "Oh my God. What's this?"

Georgia ran to where Rudy stood. "What?"

Rudy indicated a long, thick scratch that ran the length of the car.

"I didn't want you to see it, Georgia. It's not unusual for a new car to get keyed."

Rudy touched the scar. "When did this happen?"

"Yesterday. I saw it when I reached my parking space after work."

Georgia felt old pain that quickly translated into anger. "Damn them."

Rudy put an arm around her. "Just some prankster."

Georgia leaned against the car to steady herself. His car attacked at the research center? An act of violence at the place her father helped build, where he worked tirelessly. "Is there no safe place? Your Cadillac in Landing and now this?"

"Someone just took joy in keying a new car. In Landing it was an act of hate," Parker said. "Not the same reason."

Georgia remembered the reason. *Niggers not welcome here.*

When Parker drove away, Georgia and Rudy walked to her car. "My father's just trying to gloss this over. He knows how traumatic the Landing car incident was for me."

"Why can't you accept it was just some jealous jerk?"

Georgia stopped walking. "Why can't you understand that I'm more aware of the dangers we face than you are."

Rudy looked confused. "Georgia, let it go."

She placed her hands on her hips. "I know what I'm saying, but I don't know what you're hearing."

Rudy sighed. "What in hell are you talking about?"

"The attack on my father's car," she shouted, "was an attack on *him.*"

An elderly couple, walking by, slowed and turned to listen.

"Just a lover's quarrel," Rudy said, with a sheepish grin. "We always make up."

They seemed relieved, smiled and moved on.

"Shall we kiss and make up?" he asked, as he opened her car door.

"Are you going to listen to me or do you want to walk home?"

"I'll listen."

"My father always parks in his reserved space at work. His name is painted on the wall. Whoever did this knew it was his car."

She gestured to Rudy to follow her as she walked around her car, checking it carefully. "My car is a new Mercedes. No one seems to be after mine."

Rudy shrugged. "You've been lucky."

"And you know what, Ascot? If we weren't with him, do you think he'd be welcome here?"

Neither spoke. They got into the car. Georgia turned the key, then turned it off. "One more thing. Remember what you said when I wanted to quit modeling for Michelle—that if I intended to help change things I shouldn't walk away?"

"I remember."

"Well, I keep thinking of the woman in the orange dress that Michelle wanted to get rid of. My father chose diabetes research because of Vernon. I'm staying with Michelle for the lady in orange."

Rudy smiled. "Want ice cream? I'm buying."

CHAPTER 10

Along with her concern about her father's damaged car, Georgia felt somewhat fearful about the proposed dinner at his house. Why had he not told her before why he, who had Caucasian parents, had the skin color of a black man?

Gratefully, she was consumed by Michelle's decree that Georgia give the black-tie benefit show a completely new look.

"I've dreaded this Windsor Country Club event, Michelle had said. "Too much pressure." Michelle had looked into her coffee cup as if she was reading tea leaves. "I'll admit I'm jealous, but I see you finding better things than modeling."

Georgia's enthusiasm grew after she booked fourteen female models and seven males. She changed the runway's shape, replaced the tired old pool-table green with silver gray carpeting and skirting. Georgia's greatest thrill was designing a double-level stage. She divided all the fashion looks into specific scenes—by color or life style. Now, if Michelle arranges a good rehearsal, Georgia hoped, and doesn't make long speeches during the show, all should go well.

Saturday morning, Georgia was awakened by a phone call from Rudy.

"What time is it?" she asked.

"About five. I wanted to call an hour ago, but decided to let you sleep late. Get up, love."

"I'm up. What's the problem?"

"Michelle's in the hospital for an emergency appendectomy. You'll have to do the show tonight."

"Oh, no. I can't."

"Oh, yes you can. My crew is already at the club. I'll get Michelle's script from her office. By the time your models arrive we'll be ready for rehearsal. Drink black coffee."

From the moment Georgia arrived at the Windsor Country Club, the show had disaster written all over it. She spent an agonizing half hour going over Michelle's script. "This is deadly," she told Rudy. "Same old routine—single model appearances and long commentary."

"Trash it. Michelle asked you to give the show a new look. Do it."

"Commentary and staging were not included."

"The show is in your hands now. Do it Georgia Parker style."

By the time the models arrived her plan was firm. The models exclaimed with delight about the eight-foot wide runway and elegant new color.

She explained about Michelle. "Since one model called in sick, I can't eliminate myself from the lineup. There will be an introduction to each scene, but nothing else."

During rehearsal Georgia's voice became hoarse trying to talk over the din of models all talking at once.

"Two shirts are missing and there are no ties," one man announced.

"I don't have shoes for the gown you switched to me," another model complained.

Georgia took a deep breath. "Call Darlene in accessories. She's bringing other things. She'll bring yours too." Georgia fell into a chair. *I haven't enough time to pull this all together.* It was obvious that Michelle had not arranged a proper rehearsal schedule.

When the light and sound operators arrived, Georgia gave them scripts and cues. One of the new models came to her in tears. "I can't do this. I'm sorry. I'm going home."

"Oh, no, please. I picked you as our only size six because you're a wonderful model. I know what you're feeling, but, believe me, once you're out there, you'll love it." She prayed the girl's anxiety wouldn't stir up more tension than was already brewing.

The orchestra arrived late and when the club's manager announced that the doors were opening, Georgia had to end the rehearsal without finalizing the light and orchestra cues. Her head felt hot and her hands ice cold.

All was ready for the first scene. Georgia heard the master of ceremonies introduce her and she made her way to the stage. The room was packed. In a brief statement she explained the theme of the show, then added, "There will be no commentary, but Michelle's fashion choices are so remarkable they speak for themselves."

At first, everything went well. The audience applauded after every thematic scene and the models made their changes on time, even though they were pushing hard.

Georgia gave the dressers a hand by zipping up clothes and clasping necklaces, until she realized she'd better get into her own next change. She grabbed a beautiful black number. Unable to get close to a mirror, she dressed without one. She realized too late that something was wrong. She had put the dress on backwards. Terrified, she walked out with her arms forming an X across her chest. The dress was designed as a deep back plunge. The dress now plunged in front—wide and deep. She was braless.

As Georgia approached the stage the lights went out. A missed light cue. A chance to run off? As she started to leave, the lights came on. The confused orchestra leader undoubtedly assumed something special was about to happen, so he called for a drum roll. With her back to the audience, and her arms still crossed over her breasts, she slowly turned to face them.

All the way down the long runway, Georgia pondered what to do. She couldn't remove her arms. The puzzled guests began to whisper. Georgia heard one man ask, "Why is that girl hugging herself?"

Finally, in desperation, she walked to the microphone. "Ladies and gentlemen, in my rush to get out here, I put this dress on backward."

The audience laughed.

Georgia was surprised by the cheerful response. She added, "And if you visit Emeralds Designer Salon to try it on . . . you can decide which way you like it best."

The audience responded with resounding applause.

After the show, Georgia was met with friendly teasing in the dressing room. "It's amazing what some people will do to steal the show," one model teased.

Georgia changed and stepped out of the dressing room. She saw Emeralds president, Aaron Hoffman. Her heart fell.

"I'm so sorry, sir. I didn't set the proper light and music cues and . . ."

"This is my wife, Karen," Mr. Hoffman said. "We both enjoyed the show a great deal."

"Thank you. Michelle will be delighted to hear that."

Mr. Hoffman smiled. "I'm impressed with the way you stepped in at the last minute and pulled this off. Would you be kind enough to stop by my office tomorrow?"

"Yes, sir. What time?"

"My secretary will call you."

Karen Hoffman approached Georgia and whispered. "Frankly, my dear, the women drag the men to fashion shows, but tonight they thoroughly enjoyed it."

After the Hoffmans left, a waiter approached Georgia with an envelope. "A gentleman asked me to deliver this to you."

Eagerly, Georgia opened the envelope and read a message written on the back of a white business card. "If you will model the dress for me the way you did in the show, I'll buy it for you. H."

Infuriated, Georgia tore up the card and tossed it into the nearest trash receptacle.

CHAPTER 11

By seven the next morning, Georgia had already showered, poured her coffee, and watched the kitchen clock for Mr. Hoffman's secretary to call. *What if he is the author of that insulting note? If I had only turned that business card over. I had the answer and threw it away.*

She pulled her terry cloth robe tighter around her and clutched her coffee mug. Hoffman had asked her to meet with him today in the presence of his wife. Was that a clever man's ploy to be above suspicion? Everything she had heard about the man was in praise of his integrity and high principles.

But then, all this praise was from Rudy. *Rudy's perceptive, but I'd trust my intuition over a man's any day.* The club's ballroom could have been full of men with the initial "H".

Why did Mr. Hoffman want to see her? To ask her to work full time helping Michelle? Hardly. A matter so trivial wouldn't be handled by the store's president.

The ringing of the phone so startled her she spilled coffee on her robe.

"Miss Parker? This is Faith. Mr. Hoffman is going to New York this afternoon. Could you come in this morning?"

Say no. But maybe it wasn't Hoffman's card. Her need to know won out.

Georgia's appointment was at ten. From her collection of fall clothes she opted to play it safe with an Anne Klein suit. Understated. Quality. Businesslike.

Mr. Hoffman was on the phone when she arrived and he waved her into his inner office. "Coffee's on the conference table,"

Faith, a small, smiling woman, told Georgia. "Mr. Hoffman asked me to run some errands, so help yourself."

While he was talking, Georgia sauntered over to his wall of windows. Not much to see—just a quiet morning in downtown Omaha with patient automobile traffic and unhurried pedestrians. None of the build-ings were as high or as handsome as Emeralds. Some new structures nestled among the old indicated Omaha's intention to grow but wasn't in a hurry to do so.

Georgia could easily spot out-of-towners. They'd slow down and point as they passed the ten-story flagship of Emeralds. Shopping here—the biggest and most admired store of the Midlands—was a must when visiting Omaha.

Georgia noticed Mr. Hoffman's gray suit matched his hair and eyes and he seemed as unpretentious as his surroundings. The office wasn't very large considering his position, but tastefully furnished with two light brown leather chairs, a couch, dark mahogany desk, and a small conference table. The air smelled fresh—undoubtedly a no-smoking zone.

"Sorry to keep you waiting. Coffee?" He poured two cups, and closed his office door.

Georgia's internal alarm went off. Secretary gone. Door closed.

He gestured to a chair at the conference table and sat across from her.

"You were a hit at the show last night, young lady. Do you enjoy working here?"

She glanced at the closed door. "Yes, sir."

"What do you think of our store?"

"My mother used to bring me here when I was a child to see your animated Christmas windows and Toyland. Amazing that people still meet under the clock on the main floor."

Mr. Hoffman chuckled. "Old man Emeralds was a customer rela-tions genius. Who wouldn't love a store whose return policy was to cheerfully grant refunds and credits, with or without a receipt? He was famous for saying 'the customer is always right; even when she's wrong, she's right.'"

Georgia nodded. "Customers feel special here."

His friendly face glowed. "You're saying all the right things, Miss Parker. So, let's get down to business." He stood up and Georgia flinched. He walked past her to his desk and picked up a leather folder. She held her breath until he returned to his seat at the conference table.

"I'm adding a new area in this company—a fashion office. We need a strong, talented fashion coordinator. Right now, we have a youth coordinator. She works with children and teenagers. She will report to the fashion coordinator and also serve as her secretary."

"The fashion coordinator's duties would include," he read from notes in his folder, "handling all fashion shows, coordinating the fashion calendar with Special Events and Advertising, advising Display on fashion choices for mannequins, windows, etc. Occasionally we have celebrities come in for personal appearances. Special Events books such people and when they're fashion-related, the Fashion office will participate. For example, we recently had Marlo Thomas here for a fashion event in conjunction with a benefit for St. Jude Children's Research Hospital."

"How exciting."

"Yes, but that's a job for the fashion coordinator, not a buyer. Later, a big part of the job will involve covering the markets in New York, California, and abroad with our buying staff." He leaned back and twisted his silver pen. "How does it sound so far?"

In spite of his all-business tone, the words of Judy, Michelle's maid, came to mind. Some husbands have mistresses, Judy had said. "It sounds . . . interesting."

"I'm going to New York this afternoon and will be consulting with our new buying office on further details about this position."

"You're telling me all this because . . .?"

"I'm offering you the position of fashion coordinator."

Georgia was stunned. "I'm flattered, but I wonder if I'm qualified."

"I have no doubt of that. Michelle and her people have told me that you're a very hard worker, well organized, a self-starter with good follow-through. What I saw was a good rapport with an audience, a sense of humor, and a remarkable sense of style."

"I'm all of that?"

"There's more. Rudy Ascot has been dropping your name to me for some time. He tells me you graduated from Vassar with honors, that you're not only a bright young woman, but a *loyal* one."

Loyal? As in being grateful?

"This is a great opportunity. It can be whatever you make it, because we've never had a full-scale fashion coordinator before. So, what do you think?"

"It sounds . . . interesting, but such a surprise. I hadn't thought about fashion as a career."

"What kind of career had you envisioned?"

To marry Cliff and maybe write. "I'm not sure."

"I guess I can't blame you for hesitating, but I would like to know if you have enough interest to consider this position. We prefer to promote from within, but if I don't have a choice candidate here, I'll need to interview someone in New York. Our buying office is urging me to act."

"There's so much I need to learn about this business."

"We prefer to train qualified people. Experience will teach you, and my door will always be open. Think it over. Is there a chance you could give me an answer while I'm still in New York, say, tomorrow?"

All the way home she felt the elation of such a compliment from Emeralds' president. True, she loved fashion, even the girls at Vassar had exclaimed how she had a unique fashion flare, but as a career? Am I really qualified? Working with merchandisers and buyers, traveling, seeing the trends before the public sees them. What a challenge.

On her apartment elevator, she fanned through her mail and came upon a letter from Cliff. Inside her apartment, she ripped open the envelope and read his message.

"Georgia, I've been thinking. It's not good for us to be separated like this. I sometimes get too involved with my work, but no matter what I'm doing I'm always thinking of you. I don't expect you to respond to this immediately. I'm going to try to arrange a trip to Omaha. I hope you will listen to what I have to say. P. S. I love you. Cliff."

P. S.? An afterthought? Besides, I hate P.S. under any circumstances. Those are Paul Stratley's initials. Rudy assured me Stratley had moved to New York and would never return. Forget it, girl. He's gone.

Georgia needed to think. Maybe in a bath—with bubbles and wine. A quiet place to reflect. She put on a Sinatra album, lit a candle and turned off her bathroom light. Carrying a glass of wine, she slipped into the frothy water, closed her eyes. Eventually the chatter in her head slowed.

She pictured herself among the beautiful people, viewing Paris collections, then on to Milan and London. Maybe she'd run into Cliff on one of his assignments. She opened her eyes. Here comes his letter today after seven weeks of silence.

Am I considering this job because it's a sure thing and a future with Cliff is not? And yet, it sounds as though he has solid plans for us.

She obsessed over every word in his letter until her tub water had cooled.

Out of the tub, she wrapped herself in a pink robe and poured another glass of wine. And there's her father. He thought her job as a model was a temporary lark, but a *career* at Emeralds? She drained her glass and opened another bottle. She selected it from the temperature-controlled wine closet her father had installed off the kitchen. Even though she told him she didn't drink, he assured her that every good hostess needs good wine when entertaining. "So now I'm entertaining—me," she said aloud.

Georgia carried the bottle and two glasses into her study. After placing a small table in front of her chair, she filled both glasses, and stood them side by side. "Now, guys, we're going to do a little role playing. You, on the left, are YES, and you on the right, are NO. Consider this: I am the first fashion coordinator of Emeralds. It has a nice ring to it, doesn't it?" She picked up YES, took a sip. "That's one for you."

"Now, about my father . . . staying here means worrying about . . . what color am I? That's one for NO."

"This might be a chance to do something more challenging while waiting for Cliff to remember that he asked me to marry him." Her eyes grew moist. She stared at the two wine glasses. "Would that be YES to a challenging career? Or NO to waiting for Cliff?"

"I think I need a drink to decide." She took a long swig out of the bottle, and glanced at the NO glass. "Sorry, Cliff, but this one goes to YES." She saluted the glass and drank.

Sinatra's voice floated towards her. She began to dance.

"Maybe, down the line Mr. Hoffman may want me to show my gratitude. Sure, he's playing it cool now. Was 'H' you, Mr. Hoffman?" She sighed. "Damn my stupidity. Why didn't I turn that card over?" She picked up the wine glass on the right. "Got to go with NO."

She refilled the glasses. "What if Cliff comes back and wants me to come to California? Hooray! Here's to you, YES, so, why even consider this job? You don't want to stay here." She smiled at glass NO and drained another glass.

Sinatra was singing *Come Fly with Me,* a song from which she always hoped Cliff would take a cue. Tears now dropped into the wine.

YES or NO hadn't helped a tinker's damn.

"Mr. Hoffman wants an answer tomorrow. Cliff, call me."

Georgia closed her eyes. She thought of how much time they had spent apart. Precious time. She recalled how she had told him about the jeweled clock in Emeralds and its meaning.

"Stupidity," he had said. "Jewels on a wall clock? Stupid." She tried to explain the meaning of the precious stones and precious time, but his answer was a disapproving laugh.

She picked up the phone, and set it back down. She picked it up again. "Should I call him? Rudy would scream NO. I guess I better ask my experts. Is it YES or NO?" She looked with blurred vision from one glass to the other. NO held more wine. "I guess that's a NO." She drained the glass, giggled and fell to the floor.

CHAPTER 12

Georgia opened her eyes. The phone was ringing. Slowly, she lifted herself up off the floor, eyed the two empty glasses and remembered. She staggered to the phone. "Hello?"

"Good morning, sunshine. It's ten o'clock your time, isn't it?"

"Ten? Who is this?"

"Cliff. Are you okay?"

Cliff! *An answered prayer.* "Yes, yes, I'm fine. Where are you?"

"Italy. I'm covering the earthquake. Great break for me. I was nearby."

She took a deep breath, trying to clear her aching head. "When are you coming back?"

"No idea."

Georgia dropped her head. "Emeralds has offered me an executive position."

"No kidding? Doing what?"

"As fashion coordinator. Someone to pull together the store's fashion direction, I guess."

"Sounds weird."

"I wasn't sure whether . . . to take it or not."

"That's up to you. Pick up a copy of my paper. You'll see my story."

Had he heard what she said? *"*I will." Her voice felt as weak as her total being. "So, should I consider this job offer?"

"Why not? What have you got to lose?"

Why not, indeed. "I miss you, Cliff."

"I miss you, too. You're the first I called about this story. I love you."

As soon as they said goodbye, she called Mr. Hoffman's secretary and asked how to reach him in New York.

"Georgia. So glad you called. I hope you have good news for us. I discussed you with our New York office and they agreed you're a good choice."

Make a decision, girl. "If you have that much faith in me, I'd be honored."

"Congratulations, young lady," he said. "I promise you, the rewards will come in proportion to your contributions. Report to personnel today if you can."

Driving to Emeralds she reviewed every word of her conversation with Cliff, and the revelation left her limp and hollow. Reporting to Personnel was a blur. None of her senses seemed to awaken until the personnel director shook hands with her and handed her a book on the store's history: *Emeralds, the Retail Jewel of the Midwest.* "You're a first in this position. I envy you." *Wise up, girl. This opportunity is special.* Georgia felt a tinge of excitement.

Rudy's door was open. Walls were covered with bulletin boards, heavily endowed with blue prints, fabric swatches, pictures and notes. His desk was covered with piles of paper almost a foot high.

"Georgia. What brings you here?"

"When was the last time you saw the top of that desk?"

"About . . . two or three years ago. Why?"

"How do you find anything?"

"Easy. I never look for anything. You didn't come here to critique my office."

"I have some news you'll love."

"Tell me."

"You are looking at Emeralds first fashion coordinator."

"Fantastic! Rudy hugged her. "Do you know what a plum of an opportunity this is? With your talent, you can make it all the way up to the seventh floor." He removed a stack of trade papers from a chair so Georgia could sit.

"The seventh floor?"

"That's where all the executive offices are. How do you feel?"

"Like I followed the yellow brick road and found Emerald City."

Rudy chuckled. "Well, don't be surprised if you meet a wicked witch or two. Like all big companies, we have our share."

"I'm excited," Georgia said. "We'll be working together."

"And do I need you. We change all the windows and in-store displays constantly. We need fashion direction. I've been bugging Mr.

Hoffman for some time. He's been all for it, but—"

"But, what?"

"His myopic merchandisers can't see the need for a fashion coordinator. That's why he's handling this himself. Our New York buying office told him that every major store in the country has a Fashion office, and it's time Emeralds got with the program."

Georgia saw two young men standing in the doorway.

"Sorry. The door was open." It was Jesse, followed by another young man.

"Come in," Rudy said. "Jesse Wiggins, Steve Burdette, say hello to our new fashion coordinator."

Jesse smiled sweetly and shook her hand. "You sure look like the perfect choice, Miss . . .?"

"Parker. Georgia Parker."

At the sound of her name, he seemed to become rigid. He stood holding her hand, then slowly pulled away. His bright blue eyes dulled, as though shades had been pulled over them.

Georgia noticed it instantly. She glanced at Rudy. He had noticed it too.

Jesse remembered her.

CHAPTER 13

"Where the hell have you been? The phone hasn't stopped ringing." Holding a bottle of beer, Jesse's co-worker and roommate, Steve Burdette closed their apartment door and retreated to a green recliner.

"Who called?"

Steve smirked. "Some of those chippies you've been bedding down. Note's on the kitchen table."

Jesse hated the smell of beer. "How many of those have you had since you came home?"

Steve didn't answer, just focused on a *Gunsmoke* episode on TV.

In their Pullman-sized kitchen he found Steve's note. Three calls. Three girls. Jesse smiled. That was one of Omaha's virtues—plenty of girls. He was amused by the girls' fascination with his southern accent, and how they came across wet and eager.

Jesse looked in the kitchen trash can. Four beer cans. Some day, Jesse vowed, he'd separate from Steve and get his own apartment, better than this four-room pit. He returned to their living room with a cold bottle of Orange Crush, placed it on a table, and stretched out on the beige corduroy couch. With his hands folded behind his head, he examined the ceiling, as though he'd find the answer he was looking for up there. "Georgia. Georgia Parker. I wonder . . ."

"You wonder what? You planning on hitting on that new fashion coordinator?"

Jesse reflected. "I met another Georgia Parker once, back in Landing. I wonder if it's the same Georgia."

Steve laughed. "Where would the likes of you meet a classy lady like that?"

Jesse didn't respond. "I met a Dr. Benjamin Fredrick Parker in Landing when I was a ticket taker at a movie theatre. I'll never forget that man's name."

"Why not?"

"I'll tell you if you shut off that damn TV."

Steve obliged. "Okay."

"That was my first job—a ticket taker at the Grande Movie Theatre. And I lost it because of the Parkers."

"No shit."

"You want to hear this story or not?"

"Sure. Wait 'til I get another beer." He returned quickly.

"I had a snazzy uniform for that job," Jesse began, and then looked at Steve wiping his mouth with his undershirt. "You're a slob. Just like my pa."

"How's that?"

"He had a faded Lay-Z-Boy chair, patched up with duct tape, and he would sit in that damn chair drinking beer for hours." Jesse sat up. "He wore a stinking undershirt and always wiped his mouth on it. He drank so much he blew up like a balloon. His shirt barely covered that bloated belly."

Steve looked down at himself. "I don't have a big belly."

"Give yourself time." Jesse opened the bottle of Orange Crush. "I remember everything about that night. That was the only time my father was proud of me—for a while."

"What happened?"

"He looked me over just before I left for the theatre. 'Dammed if you don't look like you're from West Point. Nifty jacket. Brass buttons and all.' He told me to stand up straight and act with authority."

Steve nodded. "Yeah, so?"

"He told me if you want to get any place, you need to take charge, and never let anyone push you around."

"Then what?"

"Then he popped the cap off his beer with his teeth."

"Here's to your old man."

"I was about fourteen and really proud of that red jacket. I even had white gloves."

"No shit?"

The mind-picture made Jesse smile. "I tell you, that uniform had power. Girls smiled at me. Old broads gave me that, you know, such-a-nice-boy look. But, best of all, nobody gave me any lip about my seating directions."

Steve sounded incredulous. "You told people where to sit?"

"Damn right. Whites downstairs, colored to the balcony. That is, until a black guy with a young white girl came in. Boy, was I careful not to let my white glove touch that darky's hand."

"Are you kidding me?"

"You know damn well I'm not. I directed them to the balcony, but they went right into main floor seating."

Steve chuckled. "Guess that was the end of your authority."

"No way. I ran after them, told them they had to go upstairs."

"Did they go?"

Jesse felt his face flush. "No, damn it. That uppity nigger tried to pull a fast one by showing me a bogus birth certificate saying he was white."

Steve finished his beer. "How black was he?"

Jesse reflected a moment. "Kind of light-skinned. No matter. Black is black."

"You think that was Georgia Parker's old man?"

"When the theatre manager came by, Parker introduced his daughter to him. Georgia. I think she'd be about the same age as our new fashion coordinator."

"Holy shit."

"Instead of taking my side, the manager—he was from North Carolina—asked me to show them to seats on the main floor. He knew Parker was a doctor. Met him at a hospital or something."

"Did you? Escort them to the main floor?"

"Hell, no. I quit."

"What the fuck for?"

"You think I'd work for a place that allowed coloreds and whites to sit together? I told the Parkers straight out—I was losing my job because of them. And if I ever saw them again, it would be payback time."

"You're a nut cake," Steve said. "I've gotta go pee."

And I've got to get laid. Jesse headed for the phone to call one of the girls who had called him. Instead, he picked up the phone book. With eager fingers he turned to "Park . . . Parker. Hell, there's so many.

Benjamin? B. Fredrick? No. Damn." He looked up Georgia Parker. No listing. Then, he had an idea. He dialed information. He requested listings for Dr. Parker or Georgia.

"One moment, please," the operator sang. She returned quickly. "I'm sorry. I find only one and that party prefers to be unlisted."

Steve walked in and saw Jesse sitting by the phone, smiling. "You lined up a hot piece of ass?"

"Something much better."

CHAPTER 14

Georgia arrived at Michelle's hospital room with flowers, candy, lunch and no small measure of discomfort. Michelle liked to keep her distance. Maybe a hospital visit was an invasion of privacy.

That's why my father kept me out of a hospital after I was attacked by Paul Stratley. Protection of privacy.

Michelle's private room had a sweet fragrance from two bouquets of flowers on the window sill and another on her beside table. Wearing a blue satin robe, Michelle was sitting in a chair with a fashion magazine on her lap.

"Hope it isn't too soon for company. I called and a nurse said you were doing well."

"I am doing well, and I'm happy to have visitors, especially if they bring presents. Flowers, candy, and what's this?"

"I heard you didn't like hospital food, so I brought you soup, salad and a sandwich."

She responded with such a strange look Georgia felt she had overstepped Michelle's boundaries.

"Of course, you don't have to eat it if you're not hungry."

"I've complained to enough people but no one responded but you. Sit down."

Good lord, she's pleased. Georgia pointed to her lavish bouquets. "Looks as though some people care a great deal."

"Those two are from Mr. Hoffman and Larry Lasondo. The other is from Rudy. I hear congratulations are in order. Thank goodness I won't be responsible for another fashion show. When do you start?"

"Monday. Today I filled out the employment forms, got my discount card, page number, and learned no office space was available for me."

"Not surprising. Scott's secretary is a bitch. She pulls that stuff all the time. Loves to have people crawl back to her, pleading." Michelle gestured to Georgia to pull up a chair.

"Sit. Relax. This may be the last chance you'll have for years."

"Thanks," Georgia chuckled. "I owe you a lot for this opportunity. And I know I'm going to need your advice."

"The best advice I can give you is who to trust and who to watch out for."

"I thought this was one big happy family."

Michelle laughed. "Oh, yes, when you consider our president, Mr. Hoffman and Larry Lasondo, after that drop your voice."

"What does Larry Lasondo do?"

"Larry's Vice President and Divisional Merchandise Manager of all ready-to-wear. My boss. He's as dear a man as you'll ever find in this business. And you'll work with him a lot."

"Good."

"But don't believe too much in the tooth fairy. Not with the likes of Harry Ralston around. He's one wolf who doesn't even disguise himself in sheep's clothing."

"Will I have to work with him?"

"Oh, yes. He's V.P. and Divisional for accessories and cosmetics. Sidestep him when you can."

"Anyone else?"

"Mortimer Scott. I need only two words to describe Scott: devout tyrant. His secretary failed to find your office space because she thought that would please her boss. Not a good sign. It's amazing how that man can imitate a human being."

"Do I have to work with him?"

Michelle closed her magazine. "Dear girl, you report directly to Scott. All fashion and promotional heads do. He's the GMM—General Merchandise Manager and Senior Vice President. Your boss."

"I thought Mr. Hoffman was my boss."

"He's the President. Everyone loves Hoffman, but his lieutenants run the day-to-day business.

Georgia flinched. "Well, thanks for all those encouraging words."

"I didn't intend to scare you off, but you've got your work cut out for you. If you know what to expect you'll do fine. Now I'm ready for lunch."

I'll do fine? Until they meet my father.

CHAPTER 15

Rudy offered Georgia his arm. "We're going to look at your new office. That is, if you can stomach a look before the interior decorators arrive."

Georgia grinned. "Who are the interior decorators?"

Rudy batted his eyes. "Me. And maybe a couple of display guys."

With a gallant gesture, Rudy motioned Georgia into the proposed office space. It was a pit.

Dark, musty, no window and only one anemic light bulb in the center of the gray ceiling. The room was stacked with dusty, outdated glass display cases and disassembled clothes racks. Broken mannequins were laid to rest on the cement floor.

"But don't worry, love," Rudy said. "It's only temporary."

"How temporary?"

"Only about three months. Maybe three years. Not long."

A few days later, when Georgia hit the light switch, one long strip of fluorescent lighting sprung into action. "It's amazing, Rudy, how you've transformed this God-forsaken space."

He beamed. "A coat of white paint, carpeting and a couple of pictures on the walls go a long way."

No bigger than a long walk-in closet, the space looked as though it might work. The best addition was a large bay window painted on the wall.

"Whose idea was this? How clever. And a painted tree to look as though we're actually looking through that window."

"It was Jesse Wiggins idea. He heard of your lament over the lack of a window, so he painted one, complete with an outdoor view. Nice touch, huh?"

Georgia stepped back and looked at the make-believe window, so incredibly realistic. "He's a good artist."

The furnishings included two gray metal desks, two folding chairs, a rolling clothes rack, and a file cabinet. The two desks were to accommodate her and the youth coordinator, Jean Ashley.

Jean arrived soon after the furniture. "I'm so relieved to still have this job," she told Georgia. "It doesn't pay much but I love it, and it keeps me off the streets."

"Good. And we'd better like each other because our elbows will be touching when we're sitting at our desks."

Jean looked around. "I think I'll see if Display can build a window-sill on that window. I can put some live plants on it. Live plants need to be near a window, you know."

I'm going to like this girl. A radiant redhead, Jean Ashley's green eyes flashed with mischief and warmth. Her slim figure was embraced with a multi-colored skirt and orange jacket. Even with her brown spike heels she wasn't more than five six. "I love your red hair."

"Thanks. I was a blonde, but when I heard you were blonde, I thought a variety in the Fashion office would be fun. I hear you went to Vassar. I bet I'll learn a lot from you. I never went to college. My folks felt it was only important that my brothers went."

Jean was true to her word, the next day we not only got a board attached as a window sill, she brought in three hardy philodendron plants and placed them on the "window sill" Jesse had attached to his painting. Jean was a great help, having been at Emeralds two years before Georgia. "Don't count on management. They haven't a clue."

"Ordinary employees are your best help. If you need a rolling rack, just call a stock boy. If you need a show piece altered in a hurry, the seamstress is your only friend." Jean nudged Georgia. "Here comes someone you can count on."

"Miss Parker?" He smiled and extended his hand. "I'm Larry Lasondo. Can't tell you how great it is to have a fashion coordinator on our team."

His brown eyes were as warm as his smile. This man, Georgia felt, had a manner that invited trust.

"If you need anything," he said as he left, "let me know."

"Having Larry Lasondo in charge of ladies ready-to-wear is a blessing," Jean told Georgia. "That's where you'll spend most of your time."

On the way out of the store, Jean had someone else for Georgia to meet. At a rear door, where all employees were required to exit, stood a smiling guard, who checked all packages carried out by employees.

"That's Coach," Jean said. "He comes on duty at closing time and stays on as night watchman. A real sweet guy. He was nicknamed Coach because he's always offering strategies for how to run this business."

Coach acknowledged the introduction by singing "Georgia . . . Georgia . . . la la la."

Outside the store, Jean told her, "Coach once was a CPA and had his own accounting firm."

"What happened?"

"He had some set backs, started drinking, hit bottom. He dropped out of sight, and then one day, after he stopped drinking, he showed up here. He seems to like the job. Everybody likes Coach."

A few weeks later, as they approached Coach, he spotted Georgia and started singing again. "Georgia, Georgia . . . always on my mind . . ."

She smiled at the kindly old man. "When are you going to learn the lyrics?"

"I'll work on it," he said while checking sales tickets stapled on employees' packages.

Another singing voice came from their right. It was Jesse. He waved as he walked out the door singing "Sweet Georgia Brown."

"He's trying to outdo me," Coach said. "Bet he's sweet on you, like all of us."

Georgia had seen Jesse a few times from a distance. However, once she got caught up in her busy schedule, she thought less about him. She did send him a thank-you note for his art work. "If I spend too much time looking out that charming window you painted I'll never get any work done."

If he remembered her, would he be likely to follow through on the threat "should our paths ever cross" made so long ago? He's a grown man now. Besides, what could he do to her?

CHAPTER 16

"Good morning, Georgia. This is Faith. I have news that will make a memorable addition to your first New York trip for Emeralds."

"What New York trip?"

"Didn't Mr. Scott's office contact you about the upcoming fashion directors meeting?" Pause. "I suppose there was . . . an oversight. As soon as I hang up, call Mr. Scott."

Georgia hadn't heard word one from her new boss.

"Mr. and Mrs. Hoffman are hosting an engagement party for their daughter Lyndy and her fiancé in New York and they would very much like you to attend."

"I would be honored. What's the dress?"

"Black tie. Cocktails and dinner. The party will be in the Hotel Plaza ballroom. Sunday evening. Seven o'clock."

"Thank you, Faith. I'll call Mr. Scott."

After three phone conversations with Scott's caustic secretary, Georgia finally was granted a meeting with Mortimer Scott.

The smoke in his secretary's office was stifling. Without a smile or eye contact, the rail-thin woman ushered Georgia into Scott's office.

His office—also smoke-filled—was much larger and more pretentious than Hoffman's. His guest seating area included five beige chairs in elegant suede.

Scott motioned for her to a straight chair opposite his massive mahogany desk. A filled ashtray, directly in front of Georgia, signaling a deadly warning—this isn't a healthy spot to be in.

Although a large, imposing man, grossly overweight, he was impeccably dressed in a dark blue suit, gold silk tie, and white shirt with handsome gold cufflinks. At their first brief meeting in Hoffman's office, Scott had been cordial but distant. "After you get settled, I'll call you." He had not called.

Scott picked up a paper. "This is a request to attend a fashion directors meeting in New York next week. Did you make this request through Mr. Hoffman?"

She could sense resentment oozing out of his pores. "No sir, I heard nothing until I received a call from his secretary."

"For future reference, everything pertaining to your office comes out of *this* office. I have no provision for you in my budget. I'll okay it this time, but never again if it hasn't originated here." He stood up. "I'll look forward to a written report when you get back."

No advice? Nothing about who to see, where to start? He swung his chair around, leaving her looking at his back.

CHAPTER 17

Her father wasn't the one to postpone their dinner engagement on Tuesday. It was Georgia. Because of her New York trip they moved the date to the following Tuesday. Though the postponement was unavoidable, she wondered what element of fate was keeping her from learning about her father's background.

At the Hotel St. Moritz, she was fortunate to get a room with a view of Central Park. She showered and leisurely dressed for the Hoffman party scheduled at seven.

A surge of apprehension seized her. Each time she was on her way to a large event, the memory of Sally Jo's party in Landing—the first big party she had ever attended—tainted every one thereafter. For a moment she entertained not going. Nonsense. What could happen to her at an engagement party?

At the Plaza, she stood transfixed at the ballroom's entrance. It was sparkling with massive chandeliers, elegantly dressed guests, lilting music, and happy chatter. In spite of the confidence she felt in a sleek, black halter-top dress and her mother's diamond earrings, uneasiness was her escort. In addition to her dread of big parties, a high-powered gathering such as this presented too much unbridled energy.

My engagement to Cliff is one I can't share with anyone. A veil of sadness fell over her. She wanted to leave.

"There you are. We're delighted you could come," Aaron Hoffman said. "I want you to meet my daughter." He guided her over to a small brunette in an emerald off-shoulder dress of silk crepe.

She was far from beautiful, Georgia felt, but the moment Lyndy smiled she radiated a kind of beauty that would never fade.

"My best wishes," Georgia said. "Is it traditional for an Emerald family member to wear green?"

"No, I just wanted my dress to match my ring," she said, holding out her hand.

Georgia admired the emerald engagement ring. "Beautiful. And with your green eyes everything matches."

Smiles and laughter flowed easily between them.

"My father says I could take lessons from you, Georgia, I'm not very savvy about clothes. I have an errand tomorrow morning, near Emeralds' office, any chance we could have breakfast together? There's a good cafeteria in the building."

"I have a fashion director's meeting at nine thirty. How about eight-thirty?"

As Lyndy was pulled away to greet other guests, a waiter approached Georgia with a tray of champagne. She declined. She looked around. Not a single familiar face. None of Emeralds' people were scheduled for New York this week, except Michelle, who was due in tomorrow. Still, strangers acknowledged her with smiles and friendly nods. Time she put away those childish fears.

Then she saw him. Across the room, at the bar was Paul Stratley. He was more handsome than she had remembered. In a tuxedo he was elegant beyond words. He had to be about twenty-five now. She hadn't seen him since she was fifteen. Her arms went limp.

He whispered in the ear of a redhead. She must be his girlfriend, Georgia figured, but quickly changed her mind. Another young beauty snuggled up to him, and he welcomed *her* with an arm around her waist and an exploring hand moving down her backside. Georgia turned away, closed her eyes, hoping it was an illusion.

My father had consented to my having a birthday party at home as long as Sarah, our new housekeeper was there to chaperon. He would be out of town.

"I hope you don't mind an extra man. This is Paul Stratley, on a weekend pass from Masters Military Academy."

Why would I mind? He was the handsomest boy I had ever seen. In full dress uniform, he stood tall and displayed remarkable manners all evening.

Later, my girlfriend had whispered to me, "Paul's father sent him to Masters for discipline Paul had become kind of unmanageable."

During the party, held in our lower level, complete with music for

dancing, a luscious buffet table prepared by Sarah and a real soda foun-
tain, available for malts and ice cream sundaes.

"Thank you," he had said, "for allowing me to join your birthday
party."

I wasn't surprised when every girl boldly campaigned to dance with
him. Later, he had disappeared.

"He went upstairs," someone announced.

Maybe he left. I went upstairs to see. The door to my father's study,
always locked, was partly open. I heard the voices of Paul and Sarah.

"May I help you, sir?" Sarah had asked.

"I was looking for a bathroom."

"There are two downstairs, sir."

"Sorry. This door was open. What room is this?"

"Dr. Parker's study and off limits. I was so busy with the party I
forgot to lock it after cleaning."

"Great house. That picture on his desk. I recognize Georgia. Who's
the lady and colored man?"

I held my breath. Sarah's new. Did my father instruct her?"

"That's her mother. Passed away."

"And the man?"

"That's Dr. Parker, Georgia's father. He's out of town this week.
Now, I need to lock this room."

I felt faint. None of my friends, except Rudy Ascot had ever met my
father. Now, everyone in Lincoln, Nebraska would know.

Before Paul returned, I managed to get downstairs first. He joined
others at the buffet table. He looked at me, no scrutinized. After a strange
smile, he winked.

Too young and naïve then to understand, when he came back two
days later, I let him in.

When Georgia opened her eyes, glanced around the Plaza ballroom,
she knew it wasn't an illusion. Paul Stratley was at the bar, laughing
with the girls. Before she could move, he was looking at her. She sped
in search of an escape—a staircase, a powder room, but as she rounded
a corner, she bumped into him.

"Please forgive me," he said, "but I couldn't help noticing you.
You're the most beautiful woman I've ever seen." He sounded so

sincere; she might have believed him, if it weren't that she knew his ugly, lustful side.

"I'm Paul Stratley. May I get you a drink?"

He doesn't remember me. "No, thank you." She started to move on. He touched her arm to detain her. She cringed.

"Hey, Paul," shouted a man about Paul's age. "Say, who's this? Introduce me."

"Sure," Paul said. "Miss . . .?"

If I tell him my name he'll remember.

A drum roll filled the ballroom. "Oh," Georgia smiled. "I think there's going to be an announcement. Excuse me." And she rushed towards the bandstand.

All the guests turned their attention to Mr. and Mrs. Hoffman at the microphone in front of the band. "Ladies and gentlemen," Aaron Hoffman began, "this is a very happy occasion for us. Our only child, Lyndy, the light of our life, has found the love of her life." Applause. "Like her mother, she has impeccable taste."

Laughter and more applause. "This is my wife Karen, and we want to welcome the parents of the groom-to-be." He gestured for them to step up to the microphone.

What a lovely way to share this happy moment, Georgia thought, all parents smiling and proud. *Could I ever have that?*

A musical fanfare announced the entrance of the engaged couple.

Georgia's hand went to her mouth to muffle the words that almost escaped. "Oh, no." That innocent Lyndy. How could this happen? Georgia grew cold as she watched Lyndy place a kiss on the cheek of her betrothed, Paul Stratley.

Georgia rushed back to her hotel and called Rudy. "Rudy, oh God. You won't believe who Lyndy Hoffman is going to marry. Paul Stratley!"

"Good God! Did he see you?"

"Yes, but he didn't recognize me. Can you believe what's happening to me? First I cross paths with Jesse now Paul. Two men from my teenage years. What are the chances of that ever happening?"

"Pretty slim, but don't be so quick to expect traumatic consequences. I'm sure Jesse won't stay here very long. And Stratley's parents own

People's Savings & Loan in Omaha. That's where he'll end up, I guarantee it."

"I'll miss you, old buddy, but my career at Emeralds is over. In fact, so is my stay in Omaha. Whether it's California or wherever, I'm not staying."

CHAPTER 18

"Good morning, Georgia," Lyndy greeted, at the Cafeteria entrance. "You look sharp. Everyone should have a navy suit like that."

"I think everyone does. It's the working girl's new uniform." Visualizing Lyndy with Paul, made it difficult for Georgia to look her in the eye. "Hungry?"

"Very. We just get in line here," Lyndy insisted that Georgia go first. "It's not fancy but the food's good."

Customers barked at servers and servers answered in kind. It took Georgia a few minutes, and a smile of amusement from Lyndy, to realize this was the norm, done in good humor.

The woman in front of Georgia shouted. "Sammy, I wanted cream cheese on an onion bagel. Where's the cream cheese? You call that a serving? That's not a full serving. Put some on I can see without a magnifying glass." This chubby woman, with thinning hair dyed an astonishing flame red, turned to Georgia. "Every day they cut the portions. I like cream cheese. That's why I look like this."

The woman left and Sammy turned to Georgia. Noticing the growing line behind her, she decided quickly. "Black coffee and same as the cream cheese lady. Only not too much cream cheese."

"There you go," he said, putting her order up on the counter. "You a model? I bet you're a model."

"No, I'm a fashion coordinator."

"Oh, an executive. Well, you've got your hands full with all those egomaniac buyers. I know about that stuff. My daughter sells hosiery at Macy's. She goes to those meetings the fashion person has about what's new."

Amazing. The man who cuts bagels and scoops cream cheese knows more about my job than I do.

Lyndy ordered the same and they found a small table in a corner.

"I love New York," Lyndy said. "The people are so colorful and everything in the world is here. Paul and I are going to live here."

"Really?" They removed their orders from the trays. "That was a lovely party last night, Lyndy."

"But you didn't stay for dinner."

"Well, I . . . had a bit of a headache."

"I'm sorry. Paul made a wonderful speech. He had everybody in stitches."

Georgia managed a bogus smile. *I have to tell her about Paul.*

"I was about to be engaged to someone else. I had known Paul for ages, but we never dated. I had a crush on him once, but he never looked at me. Probably because our parents are friends. It wasn't until we both went to the Wharton School of Business at Penn. We sometimes studied together. Then, out of the blue, he began a pursuit that overwhelmed me."

I bet. "You studied together?"

"Yes, we had a lot of the same classes."

Unable to eat, Georgia sipped coffee. "You graduated together? He seems older than you."

"He is. He went to West Point, toughed it out for awhile. It wasn't for him. The topper was when he had to salute a Negro officer."

"He quit?"

"He did. He traveled for a while, not sure what he wanted to do. His parents suggested he go to Wharton. Both our parents felt we needed good business backgrounds so we could someday join the family business."

A young man stopped by to refill their cups.

Lyndy attacked her bagel with a happy appetite. She told Georgia she hadn't dated a great deal—her studies came first. "Paul and I had often talked about how we loved the financial world and wanted to work on Wall Street. I told him that might be out of the question for me, because I was my family's only heir. Then, I don't know, he began to pursue me. I mean he snowed me."

Georgia recalled how he pawed the two girls at the bar last night. He hadn't changed. Looking at Lyndy, her heart ached. The girl was over-the-top with happiness. How could she tear Lyndy down from that euphoric place? Lyndy wouldn't believe her, anyway.

Georgia looked at her watch and jumped up. "It's nine-thirty. My meeting. I'm sorry, Lyndy."

"We never got to my fashion problem."

"Perhaps another time."

"I'll call you."

On the fifth floor, the fashion directors' meeting was easy to find. Animated conversation and laughter floated out into the hall, sounding like an orchestra tuning up for a performance.

Inside, were dozens of handsomely-dressed women—some young, some not so young—standing in groups. It was obvious they were not all in agreement with whatever was being discussed.

Georgia noted conflicting fashion statements. Most were in knee-length dresses or suits, but a few were in long skirts. Those seemed to be the center of the discussion. One woman, in a tweed jacket, flannel trousers, and silk blouse stood out. A great look for Lyndy, Georgia thought.

Minutes later, the women drifted over to two oblong tables facing each other. Each place was identified with a store name in bold letters.

A young woman in a long skirt approached Georgia. "I'm Roni Rosen. And, you are . . .?"

"Georgia Parker. I'm here for Emeralds in Omaha."

Roni extended her hand. "I'm the fashion director for UMA— United Merchandising Association. We're happy to have your store as a new affiliate. Sit over there, where your store name is. If you have any questions, see me after the meeting."

Georgia found she was sitting with Bloomingdale's New York on one side and Dayton's of Minneapolis on the other. The lady in trousers was Bloomingdale's. One of the long-skirted mavericks was Dayton's. Georgia tugged at her own short skirt to cover her knees.

Roni first offered a slide presentation of the new trends for spring '70. "England's Mary Quant and her mini skirts have had their day." Roni announced. "After a long run it's time for change."

With slides of street scenes in Paris—illustrating new looks French women were already wearing, plus pictures of creations by noted European designers—change was imminent.

"Ever since the 1967 movie *Bonnie and Clyde,*" Roni Rosen said,

"Young fashionables have been experimenting with Bonnie's long skirt."

Everyone received a packet of new color charts, fabric samples, and suggested new color combinations, all of which were identified with creative names. Santa Fe Sunset, Blue Berry, and Wall Street Gray were touted as leadership colors.

"And each of you will take back a copy of our slide presentation to show to your management, buyers, and sales associates."

During a mid-morning break, coffee and gourmet pastries were wheeled in. The debate continued. Opinions ran the gamut from "It's about time we had a change" to "It's too dumpy looking. Our customers won't go for it."

The meeting resumed, and Roni looked so serious the chatty group became silent.

"The American fashion business—from manufacturing to retailing—is a giant industry, extremely important to our economy. And how fashion becomes a support system for our lifestyles depends upon people like you. Stores are beginning to see how your input can have a positive affect on their bottom line."

Applause erupted. "But remember, if you're not first in your area, your competition will be, and you may lose your chance for fashion leadership."

Heavy stuff, Georgia thought all the way back to her hotel. Unsure of her judgment at this point, she hoped she wouldn't destroy Mr. Hoffman's faith in her.

After a sandwich at Rumplemeyer's, a small, chic restaurant attached to the St. Moritz, she went to her room and carefully reviewed all the new fashion information. Rudy could do wonders with these innovations in display.

She felt duty bound to share all this with management before submitting her resignation.

To wind down, Georgia watched Johnny Carson's *Tonight Show* until she fell asleep.

Starting well after midnight, the phone rang three times. Each time she answered, the caller hung up. The hotel must have rung the wrong room. She called the hotel operator.

"No, Miss Parker, it wasn't a wrong number. They asked for you by name. We never give out room numbers."

"Was it a man or a woman?"

"A man and I believe the same man every time. Would you prefer no more late calls?"

"I'd appreciate that."

Was this Paul's way of telling her he finally remembered her and to keep her mouth shut?

CHAPTER 19

At Club 21 Georgia gave her name to the maitre d', and he escorted her to Lyndy Hoffman's table.

"You're really glowing today," Georgia said.

"I love fall. Know where I was this morning? At Elizabeth Arden's Red Door. I submitted to the makeup. Like it?"

"Very much."

"They sold me a lot of stuff. Hope I remember how to use it."

At the party Lyndy's brown hair had been swept up. Today it fell to her shoulders like a gleaming waterfall. "Did they do your hair?"

"No. They wanted to cut it."

"Long hair suits you."

Lyndy's face brightened. "Paul loves it long." Her smile was as honest as her friendly green eyes. Like her father, Georgia thought.

"Did you have an exciting morning covering the market with Michelle?"

"Some of it was exciting," Georgia said.

Michelle had commented—her voice dripping with envy—that lunch with Lyndy Hoffman was a clever connection. Hardly, since today Georgia needed to reveal the sordid side of Paul. "We saw Lauren Bacall at Oscar de la Renta, and Juliet Prowse, the famous dancer, at another designer show. Photographers were all over them. Michelle said they give the designers a lot of clout."

"Naturally. So, what has the fashion industry cooked up for us?"

"A big change. Hemlines are dropping."

"Why?"

"It seems that women who were twenty when the mini came in, are almost thirty now. Soon they'd look like middle-aged cheerleaders."

"Interesting."

Georgia was bracing herself to plunge into the subject of Paul. *I have to tell her. Today.* "So, what's this about you and fashion?"

Lyndy buttered a roll. "Well, I like shorts in the summer, and jeans in the winter. Not much else interests me."

"So?"

"Lyndy Hoffman? A member of the Emeralds family—fashion retailers from the beginning of time?" Lyndy chuckled. "My mother feels I need to be a better example."

Lyndy was wearing a camel-colored cashmere sweater, matching skirt, and pearl earrings. She looked wonderful. Georgia admired Lyndy's relaxed, cheerful attitude.

To change anything about this tranquil young woman would be like tampering with the natural color of a flower. "I'm very new at this business. I can only tell you how I've dealt with myself. Once, I bought a dress because I wanted to look like the popular girls in my class. It was yellow organdy."

"Wrong for you?"

"Very wrong. It taught me never to imitate. If you can't be a good original, at least be true to yourself."

Lyndy seemed relieved. "I like tailored clothes."

"Perfect for you."

"I wish the day would come when anything goes." Lyndy looked at her watch. "Paul is meeting us here for dessert."

Dessert? *With Paul Stratley?*

"Thank you, Lyndy, but I'm running late. Thank you for lunch. I'll be on the lookout for clothes you might like."

Seized with panic, Georgia rushed out of Club 21 and asked the doorman to hail a taxi. One drove up immediately. How lucky. The passenger stepped out and she almost stopped breathing. Stratley.

"Well, if this isn't serendipity," he said. "I looked everywhere for you at our party."

"I . . . had to leave early. Excuse me, I'm in a great hurry. "She darted around him and slid into the cab. Her short skirt moved up even shorter, and before she could pull in the second leg, he was leaning into the cab.

"I have never seen such a beautiful leg."

Oh, yes, you have, you bastard. You've seen both my legs and tried to force them apart. "I'm very late."

"Where can I call you? I don't even know your name."

Thank God she was now a blonde, taller and looked very different than she did at fifteen. "We met at your engagement party. You're spoken for."

"I'm not married yet. What's the harm in having a drink together?"

"Driver!" Georgia finally shouted in desperation.

The cab slowly moved. Paul stepped back enough for Georgia to grab the door. She gave the driver the address on Seventh Avenue and dropped her head into her hands. She felt at any second she'd lose her lunch.

"You alright, miss?"

Georgia saw the driver looking in his rear view mirror. "Yes. No."

"Did I hear right—you met that guy at his engagement party?"

Georgia couldn't lift her head. "Yes."

"Are you going to tell his girl?"

"I don't know. She deserves better. And she's my boss's daughter."

"A no-good heel like that would blame you, you know what I mean?"

"Yes."

"Bums like that never change."

Georgia looked at the driver's identification on his dashboard. "His girl is a sweetheart, Mr. Epstein. I'm afraid for her."

Where Georgia was to meet Michelle, the driver stopped and ignored the people waving for cabs.

"Miss, you got a tough choice. If this louse marries that nice girl and you don't say anything, well, put yourself in her shoes, know what I mean?"

Georgia smiled at the kind man. "I know what you mean. Thank you, Mr. Epstein."

"Good luck, kid."

CHAPTER 20

On her return from New York, Georgia noticed that her office looked different.

"Welcome to the executive suite, boss," greeted Jean. "I'll take you on a tour." She walked to Georgia's desk. "Over here, is the art gallery. The contributor was Rudy Ascot."

On the wall hung three oblong pictures in gold frames. Each Erte' figure was modeling a magnificent costume, like a star in Broadway's Ziegfeld Follies.

"Rudy said you'd like these."

"He was so right." Georgia noticed a small bouquet of white daisies.

"The flowers are from me. Rudy said it's your favorite flower."

Georgia smiled. "A sweet young man named Jon Roberts used to bring them to me. He said daisies represent purity, gentleness and loyal love. I was in high school. He was my first love." *And my hero. We might have had a future, if it hadn't been for my father.*

Georgia turned around, pointed to a light focused on three live plants on the shelf under the painted window. "What's that?"

"A grow light." Jean's voice dripped with joy. "I came back from lunch one day and there it was. Jesse did it."

Georgia felt a sudden chill. *Will Jesse remember me? He has total access to my office, and an ally in Jean.* "Seems he's made a big impression."

Jean blushed. "Well, we went on a coffee break, and . . ."

"And?"

"He asked me out. We went to a movie and ice cream at Dairy Queen. He kissed me once . . . or twice." Jean giggled like a teenager.

"I think we'll be getting more than a grow light." Georgia hoped her voice didn't telegraph her concern. She surveyed Jean. "Your hair looks different."

"It's frosted. Like it?"

"Interesting."

Jean left to go to Central High School, to speak to students about fashion as a career, and how to qualify for Emerald's Teen Board.

For Georgia the first order of business was to prepare her report for Scott, but she kept hearing Jean's loving tale about Jesse. *Let it go for now. Get to work.*

In New York she had learned that it was her responsibility to advise the store of new trends. By seven that evening, her neatly bound report was ready to deliver to Scott first thing in the morning.

Before leaving her office, Georgia looked around. Even with the improvements, it was a sorry-looking place. Her father—and everyone who regarded her job as glamorous—envisioned a movie-set office.

The store had been closed since five-thirty, so she had to walk down in the dark on the stationary escalator to the second floor. She saw light at the exit. Coach wasn't there. On his chair was his after-hours checkout book. Georgia waited a good twenty minutes. Finally, she picked up the book so she could sit. She noticed that Scott and Jesse had signed out at six. *Scott and Jesse together? Why?*

"And who's been sitting in my chair," came a deep voice out of the dark. It was Coach, carrying a ring of keys and a huge flashlight. "Ah, Goldilocks," he exclaimed. "Sorry you had to wait, but I was making my rounds."

"I'm glad you're here. This is a scary place after hours." She signed out below Scott and Jesse. *I'm beginning to feel it's a scary place anytime.*

First thing Tuesday morning, Georgia was in Scott's office with her market report.

Without looking up, Scott's secretary continued typing. "Just leave it with me. He'll call you when he's read it."

Reluctantly, Georgia handed over her report and left.

Back at her office, Georgia checked the model list she had inherited from Michelle.

"Jean, has the store ever used black models?"

"Never. And since you brought it up, I'm getting a lot of applications for our teen board from colored girls."

"Black girls."

"Oh? Okay. And I wonder how many *black* girls I should accept?"

"How many?"

"Yeah. What do you think?"

"Select people on the basis of merit."

Georgia felt Jean had reservations. "What is your concern?"

"The truth? Most of our girls are from prominent families or are leaders in school. I just wonder if that would create . . . something of a problem."

Georgia frowned. "Work it out."

Right now clothes had to be selected for the next show. She and Jean divided the chores and hurried off in different directions. They both skipped lunch and worked without interruption until almost closing time.

Georgia heard her page. "Eighteen . . . eighteen." She ran to the closest phone.

"Mr. Scott wants to see you at five-twenty," his secretary told Georgia.

What a lousy time for a meeting. She had hoped to leave for Lincoln at five-thirty. If she arrived too late, her father might be out of the mood to tell his story. *I can't miss this chance.*

When Georgia arrived at Scott's office, he motioned her in.

"I've read your report. It's well done."

"Thank you." *His first words of approval, but he's frowning.*

"There's one line calling the new trend a drastic change."

"In New York they say it's time for a major change, but some feel the new long length may be slow to take off."

"Nonsense. Women will love it. Their closets are filled with the same mini looks they've worn for years." He closed her report. "Customers look through our racks and see more of the same. Change will be a boon to our business."

Being so new, who was she to question the General Merchandise Manager?

"I'm taking out that word *drastic* and sending a copy of your report to all concerned." He looked at his watch. "I've kept you long enough."

At the door, she stopped. "Mr. Scott, when may I hold a forecast meeting? I brought back a slide presentation and have written handouts and—"

"We have too many meetings now. This report will suffice."

"But Roni Rosen, the Fashion Director of UMA said each store's fashion person should—"

"Roni Rosen is not running this store, Miss Parker, I am. Thank you for stopping by."

CHAPTER 21

Georgia hoped her father's revelation about their family background would bring clarity and peace to her life. He greeted her with his version of a smile—restrained and no hug included.

"Rudy called. He said this evening should be for the two of us alone," he said, leading her to the dining room.

From the dining room, Georgia could hear Ginny the cook singing and smell her famous pot roast. After dinner, Ginny delivered a tray of coffee and apple bread pudding to Dr. Parker's study.

Georgia served and then settled into a wing-back chair facing his.

Bread pudding was his favorite but he hardly touched it.

"If talking about our family is too difficult, Dad—"

"No, no. I just don't know where to begin.""

At the beginning she hoped.

"As you know, both sides of my family were English. My paternal great-great grandfather came to America in 1852. His profession was engineering and his goal was to accumulate land. His intelligence and vision eventually translated into wealth."

"And your great-great grandmother?"

"She gave birth to three sons. Only one lived long enough to marry. They had one daughter—Victoria."

"That was your great-grandmother?"

"Yes. Victoria was fourteen when she met Joshua, the son of a black woman who worked in my great grandparents' household. Joshua was exceptionally bright. He'd spend hours in the kitchen, thumbing through books. My grandmother told me for a long time he wouldn't dare look at her. Finally, she urged him to tell her about the books he liked.

"Did he learn to read?"

"He did. Victoria's father was so impressed with him he hired a tutor. And all this time, he and my grandmother were friends. Only—"

"Only what?"

"Victoria and Joshua fell in love. They defied convention." He paused. "She got pregnant. My great grandmother died of heart failure a month after she learned of Victoria's unforgivable sin."

"How sad." Georgia put her coffee aside. "Did they get married?"

"Oh, good heavens, no. Such a marriage was against the law." He paused again. "Victoria's father quickly married her off to an Englishman who worked for him as a bookkeeper. He was ten years older than she was, a rather rigid guy. All meals at a specified time, regular bedtime, and always first at church."

Georgia was puzzled. "How did he convince that man to marry his daughter?"

Parker reflected. "I heard he told the man he should settle down. 'I have only one child and I want grandchildren. I would like to see her with someone solid . . . like you.' Victoria was a beauty and the only heir of a wealthy family. It wasn't difficult to get them together."

Georgia asked, "Did she have a voice in this?"

"No."

Georgia's heart ached for her. "Did she have the baby?"

"She did. It was to be her only child—a boy. That was my father. They named him Jeremy."

"What did your father look like? I never saw any pictures."

"Never had any. He had an olive complexion and brown hair, but aside from that he looked like his mother. Definitely white. Jeremy went into medicine. He married a Swedish girl and they had one child—me."

"Your father and mother were both Caucasian."

"Yes. My birth certificate reads Caucasian. Producing it when my race was challenged was the only way to prove it."

"Did your father wonder about your color?"

"He asked questions. He was told that way back there was some Spanish blood, or maybe they said American Indian, I'm not sure. Not until my English grandfather died did my grandmother share her secret about my *real* grandfather, Joshua. All through her loveless marriage her memory of Joshua kept her going."

I wonder if she ever saw Joshua again. My romantic soul tells me she did. Maybe even with their son.

Parker's first smile of the evening finally appeared. "I was fond of Grandmother Victoria. She liked the way I looked." He grew pensive. "She left me her money and her land, most inherited from her wealthy father, plus considerable assets from her enterprising husband. She made me a wealthy man."

"And powerful."

He grinned. "In my case, not at all. I have control over my investments and my charitable foundation. I enjoy that. But even wealth can't help my being taken for a driver or doorman. I couldn't buy the land on which I built my home, or where I built Regal Towers."

"How did you acquire the land for both those endeavors?"

"More coffee?" He refilled both cups.

"Acquiring land was a big problem. Being black, none of the land owners would sell to me."

"But you bought the land."

"With the help of my friend and lawyer, Abe Burstein."

Georgia sat upright. "Abe? A Jew was welcome?"

"Hell, no. He had to solicit a buddy who was highly regarded and with a name like Peter Johnson to buy everything for me. I had hoped things would get better in the Sixties" He stopped talking.

"Now what are you thinking, Dad?"

"About you. You're a white woman concerned about having children. No one can advise you. It's something you and the man you marry must decide."

"I didn't come here to ask for advice."

"I know, my biological parents were white. I've always been adamant about explaining my color. Even when I learned the whole story, maybe I was in denial or maybe even ashamed."

"And now?"

"I'm ashamed that I was ashamed."

I wonder if that's what I'm feeling.

"Why didn't you tell me all this before?"

"I wasn't ready. And I wasn't sure you were ready to hear it. Now that you know, does it change anything?"

CHAPTER 22

When Georgia returned from New York, she counted three, four—no, five letters from Cliff. All postmarked in London, but written in France or Italy.

"It's a damn nuisance finding a stamp," one read, "so I carried your letters with me until I found a post office."

Even though every letter was about his work, she cherished his words at the end. "I miss you" or "I love you." The last letter ended with "I can't wait to see you."

See me? When? She scrambled through her mail, and found a postcard.

"Trick or treat, my love. I'll be there by Halloween."

"That's in two weeks," she said aloud. "He's coming!"

This time I have to tell him about my background. Joshua. He was at the base of all this. What could my father's great grandmother have been thinking? She wasn't thinking. She was in love. Georgia wondered how they managed to be alone in those days. Love finds a way, she decided.

Love finds a way? If Notre Dame made Cliff think of me, why didn't he ask me to join him? He knew I would come.

And five letters all at once? He carried them from country to country, satisfied that he had written them, but did it not occur to him that weeks and weeks went by without a single word from him?

Georgia wondered what Joshua looked like. She visualized him reading in the kitchen, where his mother worked. Victoria visited the kitchen often, gazing at the handsome, copper-skinned Joshua, who dared not look at her. One day she insisted he tell her about his books, and soon they were talking, laughing and looking longingly at each other. In time, they vowed to love each other forever. Joshua must have felt great pain, knowing that Victoria and their child could never be his.

Victoria loved Georgia's father's resemblance to Joshua. There was love attached to all of this, Georgia felt, deep, unapologetic love.

If Cliff felt that kind of love for her, news of her background couldn't destroy it.

She called her father. "You remember me telling you about Cliff Hudson?"

"I remember. The brilliant giant. What about him?"

"He'll be here October thirty-first. Could you join us for dinner or something?"

She was sure she sensed a smile in her father's voice. "I'll look forward to it." He paused. "Georgia, are you sure you want us to meet?"

"Very sure." As soon as she hung up, she wasn't at all sure.

The phone rang. "Don't make dinner tonight." Rudy instructed. "I'm bringing over gourmet Chinese. I'll be there at seven."

She assumed he was coming to hear her father's heritage story.

At seven-forty Rudy arrived with a large bag of Chinese take-out. "Follow me to the kitchen. I'm serving."

She watched him set the table with flourish, as though he were serving caviar and champagne with sterling silverware instead of food in paper cartons with chopsticks.

Rudy looked around the kitchen. "This blue and white dining furniture gives your kitchen a happy look."

"This kitchen is just happy to have company. Why this glamorous dinner?"

He put on a pot for tea. "Have you seen the current issue of *Specialty Shops Journal?*"

"No. I don't subscribe to it."

He laid the tabloid-size paper on the table. "There's a story about The Satin Bonnet. Page sixteen."

He passed the paper across the table and she shoved it back.

He cleared his throat. "I wanted to be around when you read it, just in case you wanted to . . . share your thoughts or something."

"Or cry on your shoulder?"

"Maybe."

She placed her nose close to her carton of curry chicken. "Love the smell of this. Please don't ruin my dinner. I'm done with Mississippi." The silence that followed wasn't one Georgia wanted to break.

Rudy sliced a lemon and poured the tea." I haven't taken a vow of silence, so let's talk."

"I promised to tell you my father's story. I'm ready."

"You're dodging." He lifted the *Specialty Shop Journal.* "What say we do this first?"

"Okay, if you promise never to ask me about The Bonnet again."

"I only make promises with my fingers crossed. What happened there?"

Georgia drew a deep breath. "On the day we left Landing, Olympia, our housekeeper was driving my father and me to the airport. We passed The Satin Bonnet. I asked to stop and buy one last thing from my favorite store."

"So you stopped."

"Yes. I loved that store. Even as a fifteen-year-old, I found The Bonnet a fairyland. It was the one place in all of Landing where I felt welcomed. Being a northerner didn't bother them."

Rudy laughed. "As long as you were white and rich, they wouldn't care where you were from."

"So I've learned. Anyway, I entered the store with a bright hello to Poppy, the bubbly store manager who always served me. But this time she wasn't bubbly. She stood frozen, as though she had never seen me before."

"Ouch!"

"That day, like always, the store smelled of gardenias. Loved that. I told Poppy I wanted to buy one last thing before I left town. I looked around and found a white cashmere sweater. I told Poppy I'd take it.

"Then behind me, I heard this icy voice say, 'I'm sorry, Miss Parker. We're closing.' That was Abigail Stone, the owner. I looked up at the wall clock. 'It's only four-thirty. You don't close until five-thirty.'

"Abigail walked to the front door. 'I said we're closing.' If she had pointed a gun at me it couldn't have been more frightening."

"How did you handle that?"

"Well, as I recall, I glanced from Poppy to Abigail and back again. I asked, 'What's changed, Poppy? You always said I was your favorite customer."

"What had changed?"

Georgia twisted her napkin. "Word about my black father's appearance at Sally Jo's birthday party had spread like brush fire."

"Then what?"

"I was holding that darling sweater, really upset over having to put it back. I saw rigid Abigail standing at the door, with eyes glaring and teeth clenched. That woman's look was motivation enough for me to walk to the fine gift and china area and sweep the sweater over a magnificent display of delicate porcelain statuary and pricey imported gift pieces. Sounded like an explosion when they crashed to the floor. Then I walked to the expensive stemware and crystal. With a strong sweep of my hand, I reduced it all to trash."

"Wow."

"Abigail turned gray-white and ran to where Poppy was standing. Then, you know what? I walked to the door, and told them with icky-sticky sweetness, 'You're right to close early. You have a lot of cleaning up to do."

"Pretty gutsy there, miss." He picked up the *Journal* and turned to page sixteen. "It says here that arson was the cause of the store burning to the ground. When was the fire?"

"The same day I was in the store. I was the prime suspect."

"You? They charged you with arson?"

"At first I was glad the store burned down. Then I felt sad. It was a landmark with a remarkable history."

"I read something about that . . . here it is; 'The store started out as a millinery shop, and they never changed the name, even when it grew into a full-scale fashion store. The Satin Bonnet became nationally known in the industry as a forerunner of the upscale specialty shop." Rudy folded the paper. "Why were you accused?"

"Because of Abigail. She was at her country club when news reached her about the fire. The dining room was full, and her first words were 'that Parker girl. She did it for revenge. Georgia Parker did it.' Her words were repeated by everyone."

"A lynching."

Georgia held her twisted napkin tighter. "My father and his attorney went to Landing. They had solid proof of our boarding the plane long before the fire."

"So that was the end of it?"

"No. Even though my father had paid her far in excess of the damage I did, Abigail continued to blame me. She talked about my display of anger. She even suggested that my father had hired someone to burn her store."

"But that was, what, seven years ago? People certainly don't dwell on old rumors."

"I hope not. But why do I expect it all to resurface?" A long sigh. "Can I tell you my father's story now?"

"Let's open our fortune cookies first. You know how I depend on them to guide my life."

She rolled her eyes. "I'll open yours and you open mine." Georgia pulled out the little printed slip. "It says: 'There will be a major change in your career and you'll realize a long-time dream.' How about that?" She laid the paper fortune on the table.

"Now, here's yours." He read the fortune to himself. He looked grim.

"It's only a fortune cookie, Rudy. Read it."

The phone rang. "Go answer. I'll read it when you come back."

When she returned, she saw him tuck her fortune into his jacket pocket.

"I just turned down my last chance to buy siding at a once-in-a-lifetime low price. Okay. Read my fortune."

"Well, well. It's the same as mine. Save it, it'll bring you luck." He handed it to her.

"May I see the one you put in your pocket?"

Reluctantly, he handed it to her. "Beware of enemies wearing friendly faces." She smiled.

"Guess I'd better start suspecting . . . people like you."

"You can't be too careful. So, tell me your father's story."

"Too much of an emotional swing. Another time."

"Tomorrow night?" Rudy asked. "By the way, why hadn't you ever told me The Satin Bonnet story before?"

"Because I was sure you'd accuse me of blaming my father for that too."

"Do you?"

"Good night, Rudy."

CHAPTER 23

Two days before Halloween, while Georgia and Jean were returning show merchandise to their departments, she passed the lingerie area. On display was a short black lace nightgown and matching peignoir. She saw herself wearing it with sexy stiletto heels. *Cliff is lying on her bed, his massive bare shoulders against her pillows when she slinks in, carrying two glasses and his favorite wine.*

She heard her page. "Eighteen . . . eighteen." She picked up the closest phone. "Cliff? You're here?"

"Not yet. Are you as beautiful as you sound?"

"Of course. I was just thinking about you. Can't wait to see you."

"Same here, darling."

I'm going back and buy that black lingerie. Perfect Halloween costume.

"I'll pick you up at the airport. What time?"

"Don't know the time, but I'll be there early December thirty-first."

Georgia laughed. "You mean October thirty-first." She looked around. "Are you in the store?"

An ominous pause. "No, I'm in New York." His voice was far from playful. "I've just been interviewed by Hearst Newspapers and have to fly to Los Angeles for another interview tomorrow. Georgia?"

She couldn't answer.

"Look, sweetheart, I'm damn sorry. This is important to both of us. It's just rotten timing."

"And will you be interviewing all of November and December and through Christmas?"

"Of course not, but even if I get the job my contract with *The Register* isn't over until the end of the year. I have to fulfill that obligation. I have no idea where I'll end up, but the prospects are excellent."

Georgia was silent.

"Please hang in there with me. I'll be in Omaha for New Year's Eve. I promise."

This delay must be as painful for him as it is for me. "New Year's Eve it is."

Moments after Cliff's call, she heard her page again. Scott summoned her to his office. Before she reported, she called Rudy.

"Cliff's not coming."

"What happened?"

Still stunned, she could only manage, "A job interview."

Rudy growled. "Couldn't he come afterwards?"

"Not until New Year's Eve."

"What? Probably because you botched your love potion recipe. That's what you get for being a lousy cook." No response.

"Sorry, love. Just trying to make you laugh. See you at my Halloween party tonight?"

"Need Halloween decorations? I bought a carload."

"Sure. You okay?"

"Yes." *I have to stop laying my hurts on him.* She took a deep breath to find a new voice. "I'm bringing my famous dip and chips tonight. Made with Lipton's onion soup mix."

He groaned. "How unique."

"Only the best for you, love. Gotta go. The Goblin's waiting."

The moment she reached Scott's office he motioned for her to sit. "As you know, I was in New York last week for the General Merchandise Managers' meeting."

"Yes, sir."

"They showed us a very effective slide presentation on new trends."

"Yes, sir."

"And, I understand you have a copy."

"Yes, sir."

"Well, I think we should share it with our people, don't you?"

Am I in the Twilight Zone? I told you about this, and you said we have too many meetings already.

"Yes, sir." Georgia's stomach was churning.

"I'll set up a meeting. He looked at his calendar. "Let's say . . . Friday."

"This Friday? That doesn't give me a lot of time to prepare."

"This is a business of immediacy, Miss Parker. I'm sure you can manage. Thank you for your cooperation."

She fumed all the way back to her office. "You bastard. Immediacy, my ass."

Georgia dialed Rudy's office. "I can't come to your party tonight."

"Does that mean I don't get your famous dip?"

She told him about her meeting with Scott.

"The presentation you wanted to do weeks ago?"

"The very one."

Friday morning, Rudy was seated in the audience with the other department heads. Georgia caught his eye and he winked at her.

Scott approached the microphone. "After my recent New York trip, I feel that all of you, the really important arm of our business, should be informed early about what's new for the coming season. This is a presentation I saw in New York and Georgia Parker, our fashion coordinator, will present it. Will someone turn out the lights, please?"

She stood up in the dark. She wasn't given a chance for opening remarks or setup. And even though her entire being throbbed with anger, she managed to keep her voice pleasant. "Mr. Scott was kind enough to send you all a copy of my market report. If you have any questions, please call me."

Jean operated the slide projector. Georgia explained the fashion importance of everything shown on the screen. Each time pictures of the long skirts came up, a buzz of comments and groans swept over the room.

At the end of the presentation, the lights came on. Hands were up everywhere. Before Georgia could respond to anyone, Scott was on his feet. "I know what your concerns are, but we need a change, and it must be big enough to make everything in a woman's closet obsolete."

There were a few more groans. One hand continued to wave and annoyed Scott finally acknowledged the persistent better sportswear buyer. "What's your question, Barb?"

Barb stood up. "I'd like to ask Miss Parker if, in the face of such radical change, can she suggest any alternative to the long skirt?"

Georgia looked to her boss for permission to answer.

"Go ahead," Scott said. "I'm anxious to hear what you have to say."

Georgia surmised from Scott's amused grin that she was trapped. She was one heartbeat away from allowing him to be right. A wrong answer could put an indelible, negative stamp on her. "This is far from an observation based on experience, because, as you know, I've had very little. However, judging by what I learned in New York and what I know so far about the average Emeralds customer, there'll be enough confusion around to push some women towards an alternative. In lieu of the long skirt, she might expand what she already enjoys in leisure and casual wear to her daytime wardrobe. I'm referring to . . . pants."

"Pants?" Scott was on his feet.

There were whispers and a smattering of applause.

With a swift and stern declaration, Scott announced that the meeting was over. He moved quickly to Georgia's side. "I want to see you in my office. Now." As he walked out, Georgia could hear his anger in every hard step.

Before she could follow Scott, both Rudy and Barb rushed up to her.

"That was gorgeous," Rudy said.

"You're prejudiced, but thanks."

Barb approached. "I knew there had to be an alternative."

"Thank you," Georgia said. "But did you like the answer?"

"I liked the answer. I'm not going to put all my open-to-buy money into long skirts. I'm going to sample pants as well. The customer will tell us."

Georgia agreed. How buyers spend allotted dollars, she had learned, makes the difference between a good or bad season. Too many incorrect decisions could end their careers. I must remember to carefully weigh everything I say, Georgia decided. Even with what I said today—though I strongly believe it—who really knows?

When Georgia reached Scott's office, he stood up. "Your job is to report fashion forecasts. Our job—mine and the buyers—is to make all the buying decisions. Is that clear?"

"Yes, sir."

"That comment about pants was irresponsible. You could influence big dollars with such words."

"Yes, sir. I believe I qualified my statement. But I agree. I'll follow your advice."

"That's not good enough," he said through clenched teeth. "I will not tolerate such arrogance from what—a former model? Have you ever held a regular job before this one?"

"No."

His voice had been gradually turning into a shout. "From here on, you say nothing at your presentations without getting permission from me."

She hesitated, and then nodded.

"Creating your position was not my idea, but it may be mine to eliminate."

CHAPTER 24

The painted window in the fashion office had changed. Instead of autumn leaves on the tree, snow gracefully traced every branch and covered the ground.

"Isn't Jesse clever?" Jean said. "Doesn't that snow look real?"

Georgia admitted it did. "When was he here?"

"I have no idea." Jean poked her finger in her live plants. "Freshly watered too."

Georgia tried to hide her disapproval of his unauthorized trips to her office. She'd have to delicately handle this problem, maybe through Jean.

"Jesse has no family here, so I invited him to join my family for Christmas."

She and Jesse are getting even closer than I suspected.

Rudy's family wouldn't include him for anything—not since they learned he was homosexual—so, Georgia invited him to share Christmas dinner, and other holidays, at her father's house.

I wonder when I'll have the joy of sharing Christmas with Cliff?

Lyndy Hoffman came back to Omaha for the holidays and they exchanged gifts at lunch. Now would be a good time to tell Lyndy about Paul Stratley. She'd say, "The best gift I can give you would be to tell you the truth."

"My parents like my clothes these days and my friends say I look chic. Good work, Georgia."

Two of Lyndy's friends stopped by their table. "So happy for you, Lyndy. And you snagged the handsomest man around. Lucky girl."

Lyndy beamed. "I was the onion among those roses," she said, nodding towards her departing friends. "I'm blessed."

Seeing Lyndy's sweet, innocent smile was heart-wrenching. The girl was overflowing with the miracle of love. Tear away this rare happiness Lyndy was given? Not today.

The night after her lunch with Lyndy, Georgia was awakened at two in the morning by her phone ringing. She answered. No answer. She hung up.

On December thirty-first, Georgia was up at six and singing in the shower. Cliff's plane wasn't due in until twelve fifty-five, but she was too excited to sleep. She decided on a wool skirt with a matching jacket in light blue, his favorite color.

Cliff's flight was on time. All of passengers deplaned. No Cliff. Had he missed his flight?

It was apparent he wasn't aboard when the gate closed. The very sound of it slamming shut—with a final, solid clang of heavy steel— uncovered feelings of another door that was slammed shut on her—in Mississippi at The Satin Bonnet.

The only passengers left at the arrival gate were an old couple, a short man in a business suit and a shaggy-haired, bearded man with a backpack. Cliff wasn't here.

Rejection of such proportions was minimal before Mississippi, before Cliff, but now it seemed to breed with vengeance. She left.

At first, she didn't respond to the tap on her shoulder.

"Georgia?"

She turned and looked at the smiling face of the man with shaggy black hair, mustache and short-cropped beard. In a black leather jacket and large backpack, it took her a second to recognize him. "Cliff?"

Without answering, he swept her into his arms.

"You never mentioned that you let your hair grow. And a beard!"

"You never told me you changed hair color. How could I have stayed away so long?" he whispered, between ardent kisses.

She wondered too.

The moment they stepped into her apartment, he gasped. "Holy cow. Looks like the movie set of a palace."

"Nonsense."

"You did all this since I was here?" He dropped his backpack on the marble foyer floor.

"My father did. Hungry?"

"Hungry for you." He pulled her into his arms and kissed her so passionately she could hardly breathe. He held her out with extended arms. "God, you're beautiful."

She walked with him to a guest room in the separate wing of the apartment, where he had stayed before. "Notice anything different?"

He looked around. "Yes. This desk wasn't here before."

"That's for you. A place for your typewriter and supplies."

"You're too much," he said.

"While you unpack—take a shower if you'd like—I'll make lunch."

She put on a pot of coffee, made turkey sandwiches and tossed a green salad.

Cliff joined her with hair still damp from his shower. He had changed into clean jeans and white sweatshirt. He was barefooted. Georgia's gaze scanned every inch of his broad shoulders, slim waist and hips. *God, he's gorgeous.*

He took the salad tongs out of her hand, pulled her into his arms, and spoke in a breathy whisper. "I've traveled all over Europe and never have seen anything as beautiful as you." As his lips reached her neck, he added, "You don't really mean for me to sleep in the guest room again, do you?"

She whispered back. "I don't sleep with strangers." *Does he sense this is not my final answer?*

"What? We've known each other over two years."

"We *met* over two years ago. The time we've spent together has been pretty sparse."

He took her hand, sat in a chair at the table, and pulled her down on his lap. "I'll try to do better. Okay?"

More than okay. Imagine me, Georgia the Giant finding a man so tall and muscular he makes me feel small and huggable. Why didn't I buy that black lace lingerie?

He held her in his arms. "There's so much I want to tell you."

"Me too."

He talked nonstop throughout lunch and all afternoon about his travels. He shared details about what he had written and planned to write. He showed her magazine articles and newspaper tear sheets of his published work.

"My father will love to hear all this tonight." She felt anxious. "It's time you two met. He's invited us for cocktails at his house—his only chance to meet you. He leaves tomorrow for a conference in Washington. Afterwards, you and I will come back to Omaha for dinner at my Club."

"I'm looking forward to meeting your father."

Now. Tell him now. For a moment she thought she couldn't breathe. She needed air, flung open a kitchen window. The cold Nebraska wind slapped her with an awakening gust. "Cliff . . . I have something important to tell you."

"Okay. I know you're not pregnant," he chuckled. "What's up?"

She turned slowly towards him. "What say, we open a bottle of wine, then go into the study and build a fire?"

He looked quizzical. "Sounds good. I'll start the fire. You bring the wine."

The moment he left she grabbed hold of a chair for support. Anxiety and fear poured over her.

Holding the stems of two wine glasses in one hand and the wine bottle with the other, she managed a weak smile as she reached the study. The fire was getting underway and Cliff was sitting on the hearth encouraging it with a poker.

She was about to pour the wine, but her hands shook. "Cliff, would you like to pour?"

He obliged. The glow from the fire added a shimmer of gold to the rich ruby vintage. When they lifted their glasses, he said, "To the most beautiful woman in the world." He leaned over and kissed her tenderly on the lips. "Now, what was it you wanted to tell me?"

"It's about my father." There. She had started.

"He disapproves of me?"

"No. I hope you won't disapprove of him."

Cliff put down his glass. "This sounds serious."

"Cliff. My father is a wonderful man. In more ways than I can tell you. We had some differences after he took me to Landing, Mississippi for a year. It was a year of hell."

"Because you were northerners?"

"At first, I was shunned at school because I was a northerner, but eventually, I made a friend or two and was welcomed."

"So, what was the problem?"

She disposed of her glass. "I was so intent upon being accepted, I feared telling anyone about my father."

"Tell them what? That he was a Republican?"

"My father is black."

He looked at her, his eyes wide, scrutinizing. "Are you kidding?"

"No."

"Stepfather?"

"Biological."

He stared at her as though searching for clues. "I'll be damned."

Her courage increased. "Surprising, isn't it? My mother was white. I resemble her. My father adored her, worked hard to prove himself worthy of her."

He looked around the luxurious apartment. "Seems his hard work paid off."

"He was wealthy before he started to work. His white grandmother endowed him with her wealth. Her lover was black."

"Holy cow."

Georgia watched Cliff. He drained his glass, rubbed the back of his neck. Shook his head. Rubbed his chin. Poured more wine.

"I haven't been forthcoming with the truth ever since Mississippi." She drained her glass, then launched into the story of her friend's formal birthday party. "Boys and girls alike treated me as if I were a real southern girl. Until my dad arrived. It was instant rejection."

"What year was that party?"

Spoken like a true investigative reporter. "It was 1962."

"A very tense time."

"I'm partly to blame. I hid the truth. The pain of being branded black was overwhelming. It was new to me. While I was going to school in Lincoln, my father never went to PTA meetings or any school event. Only my mother. My father encouraged me not to disclose. Even years later, when I suggested it might be better to tell, he said the time wasn't right. Wait, he'd say. In fact, that's what he did most of his own life. Both his biological parents were Caucasian. His birth certificate named him white. I'm white, but society considers the 'one drop of black blood' theory the deciding factor."

"He's Caucasian but he's black?"

"That's right." Georgia swallowed hard. "What I need to know is— does my father being black change things between us?"

She examined his unsmiling face and downcast eyes. Little fists of fear pounded against the wall of her body.

Finally, he walked over and kissed her forehead. "Nothing's changed."

Oh, dear God. She pulled him toward her and kissed him with a passion she had never expressed before.

"Your room or mine?" he breathed with a playful chuckle.

She spotted the wall clock. "Both. To dress. We're already late getting to my father's house. Lincoln is an hour away."

As she rushed to her room, she called out, "I can't wait for you and Dad to meet."

Slipping quickly into a royal blue cocktail dress, with matching satin pumps, she grabbed her gold evening bag and mink jacket and walked into the study. Cliff was dressed in black jeans and black shirt, reading her *New York Times.*

"This is the newspaper I hope to work for some day," he said, folding the paper. "Wow! Aren't you something."

Georgia starred at him. "I've made a terrible blunder. New Year's Eve at my Club is always black-tie. How stupid not to have told you."

Cliff laughed. "I wouldn't wear a tuxedo if you gave me one. Let's go."

"Wait." She turned his face around. "You've shaved off all your facial hair! Were you afraid my father would disapprove?"

"No. Too much upkeep."

Dr. Parker greeted them warmly at his door. "Is that the new look in tuxedos?" Parker asked, reviewing Cliff's attire.

"I travel with a backpack, sir. I had to leave my tuxedo in Istanbul."

"In that case, why don't you both humor an old man and have dinner here with me?"

"I'd hardly call you old, Dad. You're only fifty-two."

His cook was already preparing a special dinner for the doctor, so he asked her to increase the guest list to three.

Georgia watched the body language between the two men. She knew her father had a heightened sense about any resistance to him, so when Cliff smiled and participated in a warm handshake she knew no pretense had taken place. *They seem to like each other.*

She couldn't help smiling at how attractive her father looked in a white turtleneck sweater. She reviewed his facial features. Nose, not broad. Lips, not full. Skin color—light caramel. Nappy hair, very short and becoming. She liked inheriting his eyes. Large, shiny black. Well, almost black. And perfect teeth.

"Is this your mother?" Cliff was standing in front of a life-size portrait in the living room.

Georgia had always regarded the seated woman as a study in elegance. So feminine in a pale pink gown, with a waterfall of pearls held by long, graceful fingers.

"My, God, I could swear this was a painting of Georgia," Cliff said.

Georgia walked up beside him. "Thank you."

"Your mother was a blonde? I mean, a real blonde?"

"Yes."

"Is that why you got rid of your dark brown?"

Georgia hesitated. "I don't know. Maybe she was the reason."

Parker joined them, looked up at the painting. "Gretchen and I were both natives of Chicago. We met in college there. We didn't move to Lincoln until Georgia was what . . . six or seven?"

"Six", Georgia said, "When you joined Heartland Research here."

"That painting could be of Georgia," Cliff said.

Parker agreed. "If you'll excuse me, I'll go check on dinner."

Georgia gazed up at the portrait again. "I was thirteen when she was killed."

"How? You never told me."

"My father was packing his tuxedo. He was to be guest speaker at a medical conference. He discovered his bow tie was missing. My mother said the hotel had a men's shop and could supply one. But what if they couldn't? So, my mother drove to the men's shop, parked her car, and as she walked across the street, was hit by a drunk driver." *She'd still be alive if it weren't for that bow tie.* "The irony was that soon after she left for the store, he found the bow tie in his tux pants pocket."

Dinner was called. The prime rib was excellent and when Parker opened champagne, they toasted each other and reflected on 1969.

"We put a man on the moon," Georgia said with pride.

"We're still in Vietnam," Cliff grumbled.

"Joe Namath led the New York Jets to the Superbowl," Dr. Parker recalled.

Cliff frowned. "Charles Manson led the druggies to a new low—murder."

All three were silent, until Georgia lifted her glass again. "Well, we're heading for 1970, a new decade. Next year will be better."

"Worse," Cliff said. "All over the world. Here at home people are fed up with being lied to about Vietnam. What's going to make next year better?"

Parker's only answer was that he didn't have a crystal ball, only faith, and let it go at that. The two men talked world affairs for a time, but the texture of the conversation continued to disintegrate.

About ten, when they bid Parker goodnight, Georgia noticed her father was less than cheerful. At the door, Parker was unsmiling and the two lines between his eyebrows deepened.

CHAPTER 25

As soon as they reached her apartment, Georgia changed into a robe and found Cliff on the couch in the study. His legs were stretched out on the ottoman, his arms folded and his eyes fixed on the fireplace. She was pleased he had a good fire going. She snuggled beside him. He didn't move. Just stared. They sat in silence, watching the dancing flames perform.

Georgia wasn't comfortable with the silence. His being wordless and starring out the window most of the drive home telegraphed his inner conflict. Was it the talk of politics and his focus on the negative side of the human condition that made him so glum? Or was it the realization that marrying her meant he'd have a black man for a father-in-law?

Georgia looked up at the wall clock. Eleven-forty.

She had a chilled bottle of champagne in the kitchen, ready to be uncorked at midnight. But what were they celebrating? Barely turning her head, she took a side glance at Cliff. The reflection from the fire threw a warm glow over his remarkable face. She was aware of the trend towards long hair, but this was the first time she found it appealing. He kept it impeccably clean, smoothly combed, and with his majestic height and build, his total look was right off the screen of a Hollywood western. She was happy he shaved off his facial hair. Nothing should hide that remarkable face.

"Would you like to hear about my job?"

"Sure," he said, still looking at the fire.

She told him about her wonderful assistant, Jean, and her rigid boss, Scott, about the fashion shows, the trip to New York, and her first fashion forecast meeting. She even told him about how Jesse Wiggins from Landing had reappeared.

"What are the odds of that ever happening? Is he giving you any problems?"

"Not really, only the ones I'm creating for myself, I guess. I keep looking over my shoulder expecting trouble."

"Good plan. Be watchful," he said, drawing her close to him. They sat cuddled with their feet on the ottoman, cherishing the luxury of the long, loving stillness. Only the voice of the fire continued to chatter.

"I was going to wait until after the stroke of twelve, but I can't wait," Cliff finally said. He reached into his pocket and pulled out a ring box and handed it to her.

She was stunned. His constant unpredictability added an unfamiliar kind of excitement. Rudy had classified Cliff's unpredictability as immature. "Is this my Christmas present?"

"Partly. Open it."

She did. "I love it." It was a blue sapphire solitaire. She kissed his cheek. "Thank you."

"So, what do you say?"

"Say?"

"That's an engagement ring. If you take it that means you'll marry me. So, what do you say?"

Georgia emitted a nervous little laugh. She was waiting for him to slip it on her finger, but he just sat there with his arms outstretched on the back of the couch. "Is this a proposal?"

"Damn right." He pulled her closer to him. "You'll love California. You won't have to put up with these awful Nebraska winters, nor that egocentric boss of yours."

She sat up. "Sounds like you've got this all worked out."

"I've found a great apartment for us. It belongs to a friend who got transferred to San Francisco. When I get back tomorrow, I'll tell him I'm ready to sign the lease and then when you're there, we'll go furniture shopping."

"Wait. Wait a minute. Back up a little. You're leaving *tomorrow*? I haven't seen you in months and you're staying *one* day?"

"I have to report for work January second, sweetheart."

"But you said—"

"I said I'd see you New Year's Eve, but I didn't say I could stay. Look, baby, we can get married, say next month and we'll be together forever."

At this moment, it was difficult for her to recapture the delicious dream she had held onto, waiting for the day he would say just that— 'we'll be together forever'. *Why am I not elated?*

Georgia stood up and walked to the fireplace. She was annoyed with the cheerful sounding fire, crackling happily.

She looked at Cliff with astonishment. "Did you say get married next month?"

He sat up. "Yes. What's wrong with that? You're not going to hold out for a long white dress and all that fuss, are you? God, Georgia, I couldn't deal with all that."

She was standing in front of the fireplace, but she felt chilled. "I'm trying to follow you. With such short notice what should I do about my job and my apartment?"

"I thought your father was furnishing it for sale. So he'll sell it."

I forgot I told him that. How do I tell him the truth?

"Your job? You've only been there a short time. It isn't as though you were giving up an established career. Plenty of places in California would kill to have someone like you."

Perhaps he was right, but the rush troubled her. "We're almost like strangers, Cliff. We need a little time together. So much has changed in both of our lives. I feel that I'm just beginning to grow up. I've dealt with situations I used to run away from. There's so much I need to learn."

"Oh, God, you're not going to give me that crap about finding yourself."

"That wasn't what I meant. I got into this fashion business by accident. Everything about it isn't perfect, so what? Right now it's like . . . reading a good novel. I've gotten far enough into it and can't put it down. I need to know what happens."

Cliff was on his feet. "I'll tell you what happens. Nothing. You'll go on doing those dumb shows. You'll lock horns with that jerk of a boss. You'll never get credit for what you contribute."

"I'm not looking for credit, only accomplishment."

"Accomplishment? Telling a bunch of silly women what stocking looks best with what shoe? If you want accomplishment, follow me around the world for a while. Men are dying on battlefields. Children are starving in depressed countries. People are fighting for equal rights—you and your father should relate to that—and not one of them, I guarantee you, gives a damn about the length of next year's hemline."

The fire's crackle was barely audible now. All its strength and warmth faded away. They stood in silence, until Georgia spoke in a voice so soft and deep she hardly recognized it as her own. "Maybe that's true, but man cannot live by problems alone."

"And what the hell does that mean?"

"I guess it means that we still want ice cream and baseball and love songs and walks in the park."

"And fashion?" Cliff snickered.

"Yes. We have to wear clothes. Why shouldn't clothes be supportive of who we are? And what's wrong with clothes being pleasant and even fun?"

"My jeans are pleasant and fun. I don't need fashion."

"And where do you think your jeans came from? Jean sprouts? If it weren't for the Levis, Ralph Laurens and Calvin Kleins of the world, you wouldn't have that sleek styling and great fit."

Cliff stuck his thumbs in his pockets and blew exasperated air through his lips. "Well, in the total scheme of things, I'd put fashion on the bottom of the list."

Georgia shrugged. "At least it's on the list."

Cliff ran his fingers through his hair. "Maybe this will all look different to us in the morning."

"Maybe."

At that moment, the Regulator clock in her study struck twelve midnight. It was 1970. Tears made a path down her cheek.

"Oh, baby," he said, moving quickly to her and taking her in his arms. He kissed her tears. "I'm not sure I know how to explain this, but I've seen so much pain everywhere, I want to grab my happiness now."

"What do you think is going to happen? You used to be so positive. When you spoke to my class at Vassar, you urged us to regard knowledge as a banquet. Consume it with passion, you said. Watch. Listen. Absorb. Read. Then write."

He took her hand and walked back to the couch. "I've sobered a great deal since then. The dynamics of living are reshaping fast and recklessly. We're moving into severe change."

"I know about change. Even in the fashion business people are threatened by it."

"I love you and I want you now, not next year or next month. Now. All we have is now."

She was trying to understand, but his overwhelming urgency was something she couldn't share. Strange. If he had said all this when he was in Omaha in June she might have jumped, relishing the thrill of it all. "I guess I'm in a different place."

His face was tainted with annoyance. He flung his head back and closed his eyes. "Please don't turn philosopher on me."

"Maybe you're right. Things may look different in the morning." She glanced back at him. He looked deflated.

"I love you," he said.

She was careful not to walk past him now. If he touched her again she'd forget how she felt just moments ago. *He's leaving tomorrow. He's throwing me a bone of one day and I'm supposed to fold my life and follow him?* She wished him a Happy New Year and said good night.

As she turned towards her bedroom, she could see that he had watched her leave, then he turned and looked at the ring she had left on the table.

For a long time she sat propped up in bed, with the lights out, gazing out her window. Soft moonlight turned the gentle snowfall into strips of silver.

Why had she defended the fashion industry with such vigor . . . and made Cliff's lack of time spent with her such an issue? Wasn't it enough that he was alright with her father's color? He not only brought a ring, but proposed. He not only proposed but wanted to marry her right away. *So, why am I so uncomfortable?* Maybe because he had been gone for months with so little communication? And he's leaving after one day. Not just that. There's something else.

Moonlight had changed to sunlight when Georgia opened her eyes. It was eight-fifteen. She listened. No sound of movement in the apartment. Then a new thought surfaced—Cliff didn't knock at her door last night or this morning because . . . he's gone.

She grabbed her robe and headed down the hall. His bedroom door was open. He wasn't there. She started toward the study, but a sound coming from the kitchen diverted her.

"Good morning," Cliff said, as she reached the kitchen doorway. "I hope you don't mind drinking coffee out of a paper cup and eating breakfast rolls off of a paper plate. I went to the bakery I saw yesterday on the way over here. If that's okay, breakfast is ready."

She smiled and climbed onto a breakfast bar stool. "Did you sleep well?" she asked, uncertain about what to say.

"Fitful. And you?"

"Same."

He uncapped the coffee cups and handed one to her. "We didn't exactly kiss goodnight, did we?"

"No. And I'm sorry."

Cliff smiled. "I think you just stole part of my speech."

"Which part?"

"I'm sorry." He cut off a piece of an apple turnover. "Have a bite. It's delicious, although not as delicious as you look this morning."

"Thank you." She leaned over the bar and kissed him. In dark blue jeans, blue denim shirt, and freshly shampooed hair he was irresistible. "What was the rest of your speech?"

"All night I replayed that stuff you said about the fashion business."

"And?"

"I wished you loved me as much as you love that stupid store."

Her smile faded. "How can you compare what I feel for you to a store? And Emeralds is not stupid."

"There. You see? Look at the passion you show when I dare say something about your store."

"You're misunderstanding."

He folded his arms. "Okay. Explain what I don't understand."

The moment seemed unreal, like looking into a carnival mirror where everything is distorted. "I think…I'll hop in the shower and get dressed, then we can talk. Okay?"

After her shower, she got into jeans and a blue turtleneck sweater. She found him in the study.

"Now, that's the Georgia I love. Do you know how sexy you look in jeans?"

She always thought that about him.

When she came close, he pulled her down beside him, held her tightly in his arms and kissed her with escalating passion. "Isn't this better than arguing?"

"Far better."

He kissed her again. "Then you'll marry me and come to California?" She hesitated a moment and he held her by her shoulders. "Georgia, listen to me. I'm far from perfect, and being married to me won't be easy, but I love you and want no one in my life but you."

She kissed him with the longing she had felt during all the months she didn't see or hear from him.

"Baby, take all the time you need. Okay?" He kissed her cheek, then moved slowly to her lips.

Her reply was a breathy whisper. "Okay."

"So the answer is yes?"

"Not until you slip that ring on my finger."

He did. "Will you marry me?"

"Yes."

CHAPTER 26

At her office Monday, the ringing phone interrupted Georgia's work on the January bridal shows. Jean was on vacation so she had to answer. Maybe it was Cliff. She hadn't heard from him since he left.

This was the third call of its kind—a woman asking for fashion guidance.

"Is it too late to wear holiday pastels?"

Wear anything, for all I care, Georgia wanted to say. "Don't be too intimidated by the calendar," she told the caller. "With the streets covered with dirty snow, I'd pick darker colors." Maybe Cliff was right. Doling out insignificant information was a bore.

She found a communication on her desk from New York, advising her of an upcoming fashion directors meeting in six days. Scott's approval was attached.

"Damn him," she said aloud. "This meeting notice is dated November first. Why has he waited until January to notify me?" Oh, well. Her days here were numbered, thanks to Cliff.

She dialed the St. Moritz and United Airlines for reservations. She would leave this coming Sunday, attend the meeting Monday, see some recommended fashion houses, and be home Wednesday night. She wouldn't be seeing Jean until Thursday. That reminded her. Jean's plants need watering.

She found everything had been watered. Jesse.

She noticed something different about the painted window. On the lovely mound of snow beneath the snow-covered tree was a sizable spot of red. Beside it was a dead bird. Blood. The red was the bird's blood. Georgia stared at the limp little bird. Why would Jesse mar his charming painting with this gruesome addition? She shuddered.

The phone rang. It was Jesse. "Jean gave me a key to your office so I could water the plants. Is that okay?"

No, it was not okay. "That was kind of you, but I'm here now. I can take care of them, so drop off the key." Silence. Georgia knew he was waiting for reaction to the dead bird. "The plants are fine. Thanks for your help." She hung up.

What's Jesse up to? She looked back at the white snow marred with the bird's blood. The phone rang. Jesse again? She let it ring four times before she picked up.

"How would you like to buy me lunch at Northrup's?" It was Rudy.

"Love to. What time?"

They agreed on 11:30 to beat the noon rush. She walked through Northrup's cafeteria line and took her tray to a table in a far corner.

Twenty minutes later, Rudy mounted the stool next to her and announced, "I got dumped New Year's Eve. But don't feel sorry for me. I wish I'd dumped him first. I was home by eleven."

"I'm sorry."

"Don't be. I did what I always do when I hit a rock or a hard place. I clean closets. What about you?"

"Just a proposal and a ring."

"Who from?"

"Very funny. Cliff asked me to marry him." She scrutinized Rudy for some sign of pleasure.

"Did you accept?"

"Yes. It was a short visit. Actually, one day."

"One day? What the hell?"

"He couldn't help it. Its job related."

"Well, when a man's six foot six I guess a woman might feel he's a lot of man."

"I'll explain it some day when you've grown up." Georgia started to bristle, but this was her best friend talking. She sighed. "Come on, Rudy. Don't be so judgmental."

"If you used good judgment I wouldn't appear judgmental."

They walked back to the store in silence. Outside the entrance, Georgia stopped. "Rudy, you don't understand what it's like to love someone and long for him to commit to you."

Rudy's face reddened. "I don't huh? Do you think it's different for me? You think I don't know what longing is? What loving is? What rejection is? I also know what it is to give and give and not get back. That's what I see happening to you."

She couldn't find adequate words to erase her careless comment. "I'm sorry, Rudy."

He shrugged. "I think I know more about women than Cliff does."

She sighed. "Sometimes you behave like a parent. No one would be good enough."

He said nothing and left. She ran after him. "Wait. Don't tell anyone about my engagement yet."

"My pleasure."

She wanted to tell him about the bird Jesse had painted but decided to wait. Rudy was headed for huge responsibilities on new stores and depended upon Jesse to watch the Omaha store. Friction between the two men would only hurt Rudy.

That night, Georgia called Lyndy regarding her meeting in New York.

Lyndy sounded thrilled. "Great. How about Tuesday?"

Georgia looked down at her ring. Better not let management know she was engaged. Scott would jump at the chance to look for an immediate replacement. Later, Georgia put Cliff's ring back in its box. Then the phone rang. "Hello?" She hoped it was Cliff.

No answer.

"Hello?"

No answer. She hung up, then took the phone off the hook.

CHAPTER 27

Jesse watched Georgia Parker walk towards the Designer Salon. Graceful as a swan, with a body so tantalizing it made him shudder from the warmth in his groin. And that face—so lovely, always smiling. Thinking of how he'd wipe away that smile gave him a rush.

He passed a mirror and stopped to pick a thread off his navy blazer. He smoothed his blond hair and grinned with approval at his image.

In his pocket, Jesse jingled his key ring. With hungry fingers, he sought out the key he had made to Georgia's office. He might have had time to get in and out before she returned, but he heard his page. He picked up the nearest phone and dialed the operator.

"Here's a number for you to call. I was told it was urgent."

Jesse called the number. "Steve? Where the hell are you?"

"In jail. Come get me."

Cold rain added to Jesse's foul mood as he walked Steve to the car parked three blocks away from the jail. "This is the third and last time, pal. Next time, you rot."

"Don't I always pay you back?" Steve said as they drove off. "And where do you get off being such a saint? Boys Town is no finishing school. You were in trouble with the law."

"So? I was a kid."

Steve opened the window to spit. "That's what I think of your excuse. You're always so secretive. What were you? A burglar?"

"Hell, no."

"So tell me."

"My mom was dead. My old man was in prison. Some wise guys talked me into taking them for a ride in my pa's pickup truck."

"Did you have a license?"

"No. I didn't even know how to drive."

"So the cops caught you."

"Not at first. My old man's truck was full of tools, wood, nails, you name it. He was a handyman. So, one of the guys suggested we build a cross and burn it in some nigger's front yard."

Steve shook his head. "You southern guys are really creepy."

"Yeah? You haven't lived in the south, so don't talk."

Jesse chuckled.

"We built this cross, tore a drop cloth into strips, soaked them in kerosene, wrapped them around the cross, and headed out for Dr. Parker's house."

"No, shit? Georgia's house?"

"Yeah. Jesse chuckled. We got the cross into the ground." Jesse's laughter escalated.

"Let me in on the joke. What happened?"

"We were ready to light the cross and—"

"The cops came?"

"No. We forgot the matches."

Steve joined him in what progressed into hysterical yelps.

"I was the only one caught. The judge said that my father hadn't been in jail three weeks and here I was already in trouble. Like father like son, he said, up to no good. So, it was Boys Town or reform school."

The laughter was short lived. Not only because the heavy rain made driving difficult, but because Jesse had broken out into a cold sweat. "I don't like visiting jails."

"Because of your dad?"

"Yeah. I always felt kind of responsible for his being there. He told his drinking buddies in a bar that I quit my theatre job because I was told to escort some niggers to main seating. One guy said that was bullshit. I must have gotten fired. My dad knocked the man's head against the bar. He died three days later. My dad went to prison."

"Tough."

"I went to see him once. On my sixteenth birthday. Never went back."

"You went there for your birthday?"

"He didn't know it was my birthday. When I asked him what day it was he said Thursday. He never remembered my birthday. My mom always did. When I said I missed her, he said some awful things."

"Like what?

"He said I killed the only good thing in his life. I asked him what happened, and he said '*You* happened. She labored for three days and when I finally came, I tore her apart as sure as if I'd taken a knife and cut her in two."

"Holy shit."

"He said she was bad off from then on, couldn't even fix him a decent meal. I knew she felt poorly a lot but I never knew why."

Jesse looked out at the heavy downpour. Just like it was the day he visited his father in jail. He didn't feel like telling Steve the rest, but he couldn't help remembering. He had walked all the way home. The rain slapped his face, and as brutal as it was, Jesse hoped the pure rain would wash away his sin.

A half mile from his house, sidewalks were nonexistent, only dirt roads. To salvage his shoes, he walked the rest of the way in quicksand-like mud up to his ankles.

At home, he dropped his clothes beside his bed—a mattress on the floor—and slipped naked under a thin blanket. He fell asleep to the sound of rain, dripping into the bucket that always stood in the corner of his room. He slept for two days.

"I think the rain is stopping," Steve said.

Jesse sat immobilized. The nagging thought that his father was in jail because of a fight over his son's lost job, brought the blame back to where it all began—with the Parkers. Because of them he had to lose his theatre job, and his life went downhill from there.

Finally, Steve nudged Jesse. "Look alive, man. Traffic's moving. The rain's stopped."

"I'll drop you at home, but I'm going back to the store. Got to take care of some unfinished business."

CHAPTER 28

After Georgia's Fashion Directors' meeting, she and Lyndy opted for tea late in the afternoon at the Plaza Hotel's Palm Court. Here they enjoyed soothing, live music; ordered fruit tarts, and pulled away from New York's high energy. The fragrance of elegantly perfumed women at tables nearby, together with the gentle violins, provided serenity.

"I brought some sketches of wedding dresses," Lyndy said. "Help me decide."

They came up with a composite of the best features of each sketch. Lyndy was delighted. "I knew you'd support me on the idea of simplicity. Paul might prefer something more glamorous, but I don't relate to that stuff."

Georgia knew what they had selected was right for Lyndy. The urge to reveal the dark side of Stratley surfaced again. "Since you haven't ordered the dress yet," Georgia said, trying not to sound facetious, "you can still back out."

Lyndy smiled and shook her head.

"You said you wanted a career on Wall Street."

"That's the beauty of our relationship. We both love the same field. Paul's proud of my knowledge of finance."

I wish Cliff was proud of what I do.

Lyndy pressed her hands together. "I can't believe I could have found someone so perfect."

So perfect? How could she prove what Stratley would surely deny? Lyndy would believe him, not her.

Georgia was glad that she hadn't revealed that she was engaged. She had no inclination to bubble about how wonderful it is to love and be loved. *My feelings are so lackluster compared to hers. Even though I feel Cliff is perfect for me? What's missing?*

On the plane back home, Georgia hit on a promotion plan. Color. Since fashion changes were so radical and acceptance so iffy, color could help sell the new trends. Blue was touted as the leading color. She envisioned a store-wide fashion story. She scribbled several ideas. Leading color: blue. Most positive association with blue? The sky. "Blue Above All," she said. "Perfect."

She had her plan on color well refined by the time she arrived home, but the first thing she wanted to address at the office was Jesse's ugly art work on his window painting.

Jean greeted Georgia with a smile and a new hair color.

"Strawberry blonde they call it." Jean announced with pride. "Like it?"

Georgia smiled. But she was more intrigued with Jean's approach to the versatility of scarves. Ignoring the conventional use, she had tied a small matching scarf on each cuff of her blouse.

"Don't wear that around soup." Georgia said, nodding at the dangling tails. "Think that will catch on?

"Hell, no. Not unless you wear it. Want coffee?"

Georgia gestured behind her. "What do you think of our new addition?"

"Which one?" Jean asked.

"This one." Georgia walked over to the painting, awaiting Jean's reaction to the dead bird. Georgia gulped. The snow heap beneath the tree was smooth and white. The blood and dead bird were gone. Jesse had painted them out. Now Georgia knew. He had intended that horrid sight for her only.

"What addition?" Jean asked. "This new plant?"

"Uh . . . yes."

"I love it. Jesse bought it to surprise me when I returned from vacation. Wasn't that sweet?"

Georgia turned quickly to her desk, grabbed some mail and pretended to read. Her vision was like a camera out of focus. Damn Jesse. She had a strong feeling more jabs were coming.

Scott called for Georgia to come to his office. She responded in seconds.

"We're getting short of time before most of our people go to New York. I thought I'd set up a small meeting tomorrow, to get information for advanced planning. Do you have anything for a total store promotion?"

"Yes, sir. A color story. It could be very effective."

"Good. You have the rest of today to prepare."

When Georgia arrived at the meeting Scott was already there, and so were the fashion buyers, divisional merchandise managers, advertising director, and special events director. When Jesse came in, she knew Rudy wasn't coming.

"Rudy Ascot is in Des Moines," Scott told the group. "The new store there will take his undivided attention for the next two months, so Jesse will be sitting in for him. Georgia, you sit down at that end, please."

Scott was at the head of the table at the other end. The only empty seat was at Scott's right and Jesse took that.

"My first concern is our customer," Scott began. "Women spend eighty percent of the money here, so be sure they love us. Cater patiently to the rich broads, coddle the moderate-price customers and smother the low-end, bargain-hunting crowd with kindness. There's more money made in the moderate to low end than in all the designer departments put together. Every customer counts. Thank her as though she had just purchased the Hope diamond. Any questions?"

None.

"Good. Next point. We need to be more promotional-minded than ever. Georgia will make a detailed spring presentation about her New York meeting next Thursday, but I want you all to have some advance information."

This was the first she had heard of the Thursday meeting.

Scott asked her to present her idea of a total store color story.

"If we make a strong statement with the coming season's top color story—blue—maybe the glorified color will make new trends more tempting."

Everyone nodded.

Jesse lifted his hand. "I think that's a great idea and I have a name or theme that might tie it all together."

Scott encouraged him to share it.

"Since blue is the top color, how about Blue Above All? I can see putting up blue sky backdrops in the windows, bluebirds perched on displays, signs, etc."

Everyone responded. "Great idea. . . love it . . . good work, Jesse."

Georgia glared at Jesse. You son-of-a-bitch. The thought was so strong in her head she was afraid she had said it aloud. He was even wearing a pale blue shirt and blue tie. Bastard!

"Well, what do you think, Georgia?" Scott asked.

She looked down at her open folder in front of her. I'm glad everyone thinks it's a great idea, because it's mine and that bastard stole it, she wanted to say. She'd sound like a cry-baby, and she knew Scott was death on whining. "It's . . . the perfect theme."

"Excellent," Scott said. "Then let's run with it."

Jesse turned on a two-thousand-watt smile.

After the meeting, Georgia followed him. "Wait a minute, Jesse."

He stopped. "Yes, Miss Parker?"

"What the hell are you doing?"

"Whatever do you mean?"

"You know damn well what I mean. How did you get your hands on my blue theme?"

"Well, now, Miss Georgia *Brown*, this must be one of those times when two people have the same idea." His tone was coated with mockery. "It's going to be fun working with you during the next two months." He walked away, stopped, and turned back.

She was still standing there, glaring at him.

"By the way," he said," how's your fucking father?"

All the way back to her office, Georgia's anger escalated—and that included Jean. She wanted to grab Jean by the shoulders, shake her, and say, "How dare you share my privileged information with that louse?"

Oh, how she wished she could. She knew she couldn't accuse anyone without proof. She wasn't going to risk having Jean tell Jesse that Georgia returned totally unglued. What a rotten, unjust, impossible, agonizing position to be in, she screamed inwardly. She was trapped.

"How did the meeting go?" Jean asked when Georgia returned.

"Did you know Jesse was going to be there?"

"Yes. He was so excited. Did he do okay?"

"Oh, yes. He did extremely well."

"Great. He was worried about being with so many high-level executives. Want to go to lunch?"

Georgia turned and looked squarely at Jean. "Did Jesse ever return the key you gave him?"

"Oh, yes."

"Key or no key, he comes in here any time he damn well pleases, doesn't he?"

Jean stirred in her chair. "I . . . don't know."

"And maybe you don't know that he stole my spring theme right off my desk. He presented it at the meeting as *his* idea."

Jean didn't answer, but her bewildered look told Georgia that she really didn't know.

"In the future, no one comes into this office without an appointment and approval from me. Understood?"

"Yes."

"I wish that painted window had a real glass pane, because, right now, I'd like nothing better than to take one of your flower pots and throw it through that window!"

Jean didn't move. Georgia looked away from her and back at the wall. She reflected on the absurdity of her words and began to grin." I really wouldn't smash the window with one of your plants." Her grin turned into a chuckle "I'd throw a paperweight."

CHAPTER 29

On Thursdays, Georgia checked the fashion windows. Today, like before, nothing was changed. Jesse claimed he never received directives from her, directives she always sent far in advance.

Two Emeralds employees were looking at the windows. "Not changed since last week. If you ask me, we were better off before that fashion coordinator came."

Jesse never missed an opportunity to undermine her credibility. For one show, he didn't build the set promised. Another time, one hamper with the most important show pieces never arrived. When she approached Jesse about the missing clothes, he was all smiles.

"Seems you tagged the hamper wrong. It got on a truck to Lincoln."

Not possible. All tags were printed at the same time. Same date. Same destination.

It was useless to say anything to Jean; she'd only feed it back to Jesse. Management was not a consideration. Scott would never support her. Besides, if there were personality conflicts within the company, management expected strong, mature people to work these things out for themselves. The only person she could talk to was Rudy, but he was in Des Moines working on a new store opening. "I hope you're coming back soon," she told him on the phone.

"Looks like I'll be here another two, three weeks. Everything going okay for you? Jesse says you've been a great help to him. I was afraid for awhile that you two might clash."

"Well, to tell you the truth—"

Rudy was shouting at someone. Then, into the phone, he said, "Georgia, hold on a minute."

Georgia decided to tell him about Jesse.

"I'm back," he said. "I lost a couple of good men, and breaking in new people is a drag. Thank goodness I don't have to worry about Omaha. You were saying?"

She didn't have the heart to burden him with her Jesse problem. He could straighten it out when he came back.

She did tell him about the hang-up phone calls she had received.

"You should change your home phone number and don't give it to anyone except those close to you. By the way, what do you hear from Cliff?"

She was relieved that she had some good news. "He called this morning. He got the job he wanted."

Rudy paused. "And is he getting the girl he wanted?"

"I'll let you know."

She gave her new, unlisted number to her father, Rudy, Cliff, and Scott—in case of emergency. She didn't dare give it to Lyndy, in case Paul should get his hands on it, nor to Jean, as long as she was close to Jesse.

CHAPTER 30

Georgia helped Lyndy Hoffman dress for her wedding. Maybe this was fate. Georgia's heart quivered like a trapped butterfly. She'd been given one last chance to tell Lyndy about Paul.

With trembling fingers, she closed up the tiny satin buttons on Lyndy's wedding gown. *Remember what Sam Epstein, the New York taxi driver told you—put yourself in her shoes.*

Lyndy stood motionless while Georgia arranged every fold of the gown. "Imagine me marrying a wonderful man like Paul?"

How can I tell you what a rotten bastard he is? Would it be better to hurt her now or leave her to a lifetime of hurt?

In response to a knock at Lyndy's dressing room door, Georgia offered to answer. The moment she touched the door handle, she was pulled back to the day she opened the door to Paul Stratley. She was fifteen and living in Lincoln with her father.

Paul Stratley stood there—his face flushed, his eyes shifting. "Hi, Georgia," he said, "aren't you going to ask me in?"

For a split second—she wasn't sure why—she hesitated. Then, with a weak smile, she stepped aside for him to enter.

He looked around. "Where's your housekeeper?"

"She went to pick up my father at his research lab. He had car trouble."

Paul looked different today. His smile was there, but it had none of the charm that so enchanted her just three days ago when her girl friend brought him to her party. "Would you like some lemonade?"

"No, thanks." His gaze left her face and surveyed her body. "Come here."

She didn't move, so he walked over to her. "You sure look pretty. Not many people know you've got a colored father, do they?" He laughed and stroked her hair. His hand traveled slowly down to her shoulders.

Why had she tingled so when they first met? His touch today made her shudder.

His lips touched her neck. She pulled away. "You'd better go."

"I'm just getting started."

His voice, low and lusty, frightened her. The phone rang and she repeated. "Please, go." She started towards the phone. He blocked her path. Georgia bristled. "What are you doing?"

"Let it ring." He gripped her arm with one hand and unbuttoned his white shirt with the other, pulled it off. "Want to touch me?" He reached for the zipper of his pants.

Terror sealed her lungs. For a moment, she felt as though she was someone else, standing on the sidelines, watching, unable to help.

He reached for the buttons at the neck of her dress. Then, seized with impatience, he ripped the dress down to her waist and grabbed her breasts.

Now, she wasn't on the sidelines. She was there—hating his touch, his breath, his sweat—as he tore off her dress. She pushed him. "Get out of here!"

Panting like a crazed animal, he bit her throat and unhooked her bra. "You know you want me."

"No! I hate you! Let me go . . . please."

Holding her firmly against a wall, he ripped her petticoat. "Where shall we do it, sweetheart? On the floor or the dining room table?"

Georgia screamed. He covered her mouth with his rough hand. "I don't want to hear that noise again, understand?"

He pulled her down on the floor. The weight of his powerful body rendered her motionless. She dug her nails into his flesh.

"Ohhh, I like that. You're a real tiger, aren't you? I knew you would be. Black blood is hot."

Those words drained all of her remaining strength. She could only whimper like a child.

"Just relax and enjoy it. And look what I've got for you." He lifted her head to look at his throbbing penis.

Georgia screamed. She bit his hand and drew blood.

He slapped her hard. "You black bitch. I'm going to teach you a lesson you'll never forget. This is for you, nigger baby."

The phone rang again. No. It wasn't the phone. It was the doorbell. The ringing stopped, then started again.

Paul listened, lifted his head, jumped up. He grabbed his clothes and ran out the back. The ringing began again.

Lyndy's phone was ringing, and she answered it. After a short, loving conversation, she hung up. "It was my father with last minute best wishes. Who was at the door?"

"Someone who said she had the wrong room."

"Are you okay?" Lyndy touched Georgia's cheek. "You're cold as ice."

Georgia took a deep breath. "I'm fine. My thoughts were floating back to some . . . old memories."

"You've been working too hard."

Georgia stepped back to survey Lyndy. "You look like an angel."

Lyndy examined her reflection in the full-length mirror. "I'm scared."

Now is the time to speak up. Georgia held back tears as she looked at Lyndy in her magnificent peau de soie wedding dress and frothy floor-length veil of French tulle. *How should I say this?*

"Well," Georgia began, trying not to cross the line too fast, "you could leave him at the altar."

Lyndy laughed. "I guess everyone gets cold feet at the last minute. I wonder if Paul is feeling the same way." She laughed again. "Maybe he'll leave me at the altar."

You should be so lucky. "Lyndy, there's something you need to know—"

Karen Hoffman walked in and gasped. "Oh, Lyndy. You're a dream. Thank you for your help, Georgia." Karen stretched out a hand to her daughter. "Well, dear, they're ready for us."

Lyndy looked back at Georgia "You were saying . . . there's something I need to know?"

Georgia's throat tightened and breathing became laborious. *Now. I have to tell her now.*

Georgia looked at the radiant faces of both women. "You need . . . you need . . . something borrowed, something blue."

Lyndy smiled. "Thanks, dear friend. I have it all."

The weather was perfect for a garden wedding. Rudy and his staff had decorated the garden at the Hoffmans' home. White tents with graceful chandeliers created elegance to dining areas and dance floor. When the florist had moved in with his magic, the main tent was breathtaking.

Indescribable sadness gripped Georgia as she dutifully stood in line to congratulate the couple. With a kiss and hug Lyndy thanked Georgia profusely. Paul extended his hand. With Lyndy watching, she couldn't refuse to extend hers. His smile seemed strange. And he held her hand in his much too long.

During dinner, she saw Jesse and Rudy taking pictures of their creative decor. After dinner, Rudy asked Georgia to dance. "I assume you never told Lyndy."

"I tried." Tears clouded her vision. "I always cry at weddings."

"I could cry at this one myself." Rudy held her tight to comfort her.

A tap on Rudy's shoulder destroyed her momentary comfort. It was Paul. "May I?"

Rudy didn't move, but at that moment Mrs. Hoffman danced by with her partner and eyed them. Rudy stepped aside.

"I was shocked when I learned who you were," Paul said, "And I want to apologize."

Georgia couldn't answer. She was about to walk off when she saw Mr. Hoffman smiling and waving at her. She smiled back, only God knows how she managed it. *Will that damn music never stop?* He had danced her to one of the tent's exits and led her outside into the garden, where three or four other couples were dancing. She turned to leave and he blocked her path. She considered shoving him, but other couples were too close.

He drew her to him again—nodding towards the others—and continued dancing. "Please hear me out. I was a young and foolish kid. It was a terrible thing I did, and I'm truly sorry."

Sorry! And are you sorry for coming on to me at your engagement party?

"Can't we be friends?"

She glared at him. *Friends? When I laid beneath you and envisioned death?* Georgia looked around. The music had stopped and the other couples had returned to the tent. No one was in sight. In fact, he had maneuvered her to a dark spot, dense with trees. "Just be good to Lyndy. She's a wonderful girl," Georgia said, again starting to leave.

"I will, I promise." He held her arm. His voice was soft. "Please accept my apology."

Anything to get away. She jerked her arm away and forced an affirmative nod.

"Good." He smiled and stepped back, holding each of her outstretched hands. "What a woman you've become."

Gradually, she pulled her hands away. "I'm going in now and don't try to stop me."

He smiled. But instead of escorting her back, he moved closer. "Can we kiss and make up?"

"No!" she shot back, but his arms were already around her.

"I've been aching to kiss you ever since I saw you in New York."

She tried desperately to push him away but those steel arms held her firmly and his lips imprisoned hers. "You dirty, rotten—" The horrific scene of his tearing off her clothes, forcing her to the floor, threatening to rape her appeared now, all too real.

She dug her heel into his foot but he dislodged it quickly.

He uttered a small laugh. "I just can't resist a beautiful woman."

She shook her head in disbelief. "Aren't you afraid I'll tell Lyndy?"

"About what? That you kissed the groom, like everyone kisses the bride?"

"You really are the king of creeps. What if I told her about what you did to me when I was fifteen?"

Now his smile was broad and ugly. "I don't think so, lady. Why didn't you say something before? Because you knew she wouldn't believe you. Right? You won't say anything. You're too good a friend of hers."

She thought she heard something in the bushes. Once again she pushed away from him and slapped him across the face. He seemed more intrigued than wounded.

Just as she had from the engagement party in New York, Georgia ran away from another Hoffman event because of Paul Stratley.

CHAPTER 31

"How many years have I've known you? Fifteen? And how many times have I told you to call me Ben?" Dr. Parker was at his favorite table at the Nebraska Steak Barn, sitting across from his guest, Rudy Ascot.

"Yes, sir. Ben. Where's Georgia? Here I am on time and she's not here to witness this miracle."

"I asked her to come a half hour later. That would give us some time to talk."

Rudy looked puzzled.

"I've got a scotch and water here. What would you like?"

"I'm still a Coca Cola man."

Parker waved to Charlie, his regular waiter and placed the order. Parker had to smile seeing Rudy straighten his navy dot tie and his camel sport jacket. *I know he dresses up to please me. Nice kid.*

Rudy poked at the ice in his drink. "How's the research business?"

"With over two thousand diabetic cases reported in this country every day, we have plenty of incentive to work hard." Parker looked squarely at Rudy. "Georgia didn't tell me Paul Stratley had surfaced. I read about his wedding in the newspaper. I'm concerned about her working in a company where that man exists."

"He's in New York, working on Wall Street. Lyndy too. They like it there."

"Are you sure?"

"That's what I hear." Rudy's gaze shifted.

"That's not what you believe, is it?"

"Well. I believe they like New York, but I also believe that sooner or later, the family will want Lyndy involved in Emeralds. After all, it's all going to be hers some day."

"And Stratley?"

Rudy stirred in his chair. "Stratley's family owns Peoples Savings and Loan. I would guess they want him to carry on there."

Parker regarded Rudy's eye shifting. "Something else you want to say, son?"

"Georgia is highly regarded at Emeralds, sir, uh, Ben, and has a remarkable future there. I'm all for not crossing bridges."

It was a pleasure for Parker to look upon the face of his daughter's long-time friend. It was a face full of warmth and optimism. His head of thick red hair had a shine as healthy as his attentive hazel eyes. Aside from a rich, energetic voice, Rudy hadn't changed all that much since he and Georgia were classmates. "Has Georgia ever said anything . . . derogatory about me?"

Rudy answered too quickly. "No. Why?"

Parker sighed. "I feel Georgia hasn't forgiven me for what I did to his hand. Jon was a classmate of hers in Lincoln. Had a big crush on her. She never told you about his heroism and how I beat him up?"

"Some."

"That day, when I reached my house, the front door was wide open and broken glass was all over the porch."

Rudy nodded. "Georgia told me that's how Jon hurt his hand— struck his fist through the glass pane to unlock the door."

"Right. I found her on the dining room floor covered with blood." Parker's eyes grew moist. "When I asked Georgia who did this to her, she pointed towards the kitchen. Then I saw this boy. I grabbed him by the neck, shouted something like . . . what did you do to her, then slammed him against the wall with one hand and hit him with the other." Parker wiped his forehead with a handkerchief. "I had never met him. If it hadn't been for Sarah, then Jon's parents, who arrived seconds later, I might have killed him. I gave him a severe concussion."

Parker grabbed for his drink. "Rudy, I'm not trying to make excuses for what I did to Jon, but we had recently returned from Mississippi where Georgia suffered emotional scars. We're now safe at home in Lincoln, Nebraska and what do I see? My daughter on the floor in a bloody, incoherent state. I had stored enough revenge-coated fungus in my gut to kill the man I thought violated her."

Parker could feel veins bulge in his neck, and judging from Rudy's face, he knew he saw them too.

"Take it easy, Ben. I know it was bad, but it's over."

"It's not over."

"Because you feel Georgia hasn't forgiven you?"

Parker nodded.

The waiter brought menus.

Rudy set his aside. "I don't mind waiting. I'd like to hear what happened."

Parker agreed and the waiter left.

"When I called that day for Sarah, our housekeeper, to come pick me up because my car was damaged, Jon was there and he left at the same time as Sarah. Said he was going to the Peppermint Malt Shop."

"Now Georgia was alone," Rudy said.

"Yes, but at the malt shop, we later learned, Stratley overheard Jon say that Georgia was home alone. Stratley left suddenly, and being aware of Paul's reputation, Jon came back to our house. He found her on the floor, covered her with the torn dress he found beside her and held her."

They stopped talking while Charlie refilled their water glasses and glanced at the unopened menus.

"My other guest will be along soon," Parker said. "We'll wait for her." Parker noticed a fleeting reaction from Rudy when he said guest instead of daughter.

As the waiter left, Parker leaned in closer. "Jon was bleeding profusely from the glass cuts. That's how he got blood all over Georgia. When I saw him coming out of the kitchen, bare to the waist I—"

Rudy interrupted. "Why was he bare to the waist?"

"I later learned he had gone into the kitchen to call his parents for help and wash off the blood. He tore his shirt into strips for a tourniquet and bandage. I tried hard to make amends for harm done to Jon. All my checks were returned."

"Were you able to see him in the hospital?"

"No calls or visitors were allowed."

Rudy nodded. "That must have been tough on Georgia."

"It was. She called Mrs. Roberts several times but was always told she was unavailable. Finally, Mr. Roberts called Georgia."

"And?"

"He told Georgia 'the only thing you people can do is never contact us again. We want you and that crazy black father of yours out of our lives.' That hit Georgia hard." Dr. Parker took a deep breath. "How about answering my earlier question. Do you think she holds a grudge against me?"

"Well, I don't think she has sorted out her feelings. She's said things like . . . Jon will never become the surgeon he'd planned to be, because of his hand injury. I think she feels more pain about Jon's parents forbidding their ever seeing each other again."

Could Rudy be right? Maybe she remembers the days I sat at her bedside after the Stratley assault, trying to reach my traumatized daughter, who cried all day and screamed in the night.

Charlie came back with a tray of hot appetizers. "You might enjoy these while waiting. Compliments of the management."

Rudy gazed with undisguised hunger at the generously laden platter.

Parker motioned to Rudy to help himself. Rudy sampled three baby-back ribs. When he finished he tapped his plate with one of the naked bones. "Seems Stratley caused a lot of pain all around. Why didn't you sue the son-of-a-bitch?"

"Because my lawyer advised me not to."

"Why?"

"Sure you want to hear?"

"Yes."

Parker took another slug of his drink. "My lawyer literally played out the likely trial for me."

Rudy leaned forward.

"They would put Georgia on the witness stand. Stratley's defense attorney would approach. 'You claim Paul Stratley assaulted you. Did he rape you?'

'No.'

'Did you let him in the house?'

'Yes.'

'He didn't force his way in.'

'No.'

"And you were alone." Parker inhaled. "Here comes the worst part.

The attorney would walk up close to her and smile. 'You really dig that kind of guy—in a military uniform, with polished good manners, from one of our finest families. Pretty sexy, huh?'

"No, she would say, but any further comment from her would be blocked."

'Would you stand up, Miss Parker?'

"She stands."

'Now, could anyone in this courtroom regard this tall young woman as defenseless?'

Parker rubbed his temples. "My lawyer said it wouldn't surprise him if every man in the courtroom would laugh or snicker. Then, the defense attorney would continue. 'The truth is, Miss Parker, you wanted him to make love to you, but he refused to take advantage of you, so you want to get even. And you say he assaulted you? You testified earlier you hadn't seen a doctor. That's because it never happened. You lied about the whole thing. Any decent young man should be wary of you.'" Parker didn't try to hide his tears.

"Good God," Rudy breathed, "That would make her look like a . . . tramp."

"Exactly. It was her word against his. Remember, that was 1962. My lawyer convinced me that Georgia would be the one on trial. He said we wouldn't have a chance."

Charlie returned, leading Georgia to the table.

The men stood.

She sat down slowly, averting eye contact with either of them.

"Something wrong?" her father asked.

Her eyes were blazing and her mouth was held tight, as though she were holding back a flood of obscenities.

"What is it, dear?"

"Your car, Dad. I saw it in the parking lot. Someone has smeared 'nigger' all over it."

CHAPTER 32

After a lackluster meeting in New York, Georgia started towards her gate at Chicago's O'Hare Airport, where she changed planes. She caught a glimpse of what seemed like a familiar face. He was walking in the opposite direction, stopped to look at his watch. Yes! It was him. Jon Roberts, looking very elegant in a dark suit and carrying a black attaché case. The curl in his brown hair seemed more tamed. The same, serious look was still there. It was the expression he had worn when he brought her his first bouquet of daisies. Even though the last time she saw him was a blur—the day he saved her from Stratley's assault—his gentle manner and compassionate eyes had been burned into her memory.

She called out his name, but with all the noise she knew he didn't hear her. She ran towards him, but a rushing crowd of travelers darted between them. Among so many dark suits, she lost him, spotted him again moving quickly ahead of her. She had to catch him. Just when she felt close enough to shout his name, a trio of wheel chairs appeared. She turned long enough to get out of their way. She looked back and he was out of sight again. No, there he was. "Jon." she shouted.

He stopped. Turned and looked back. His quizzical look indicated he wondered if he heard right. Then, she knew he remembered.

When he started to walk back towards her, she moved towards him. "Georgia?" His voice was halting and cautious.

"Hello, Jon. Yes, Georgia Parker."

"Georgia!" He set down his attaché case and held out his arms. "My God. What a surprise. What a wonderful surprise."

She rushed into his arms and held him tight. Holding onto the memory of daisies, and funny notes and bike rides and daily phone calls.

He stood back and smiled down at her. "You're amazing. Every bit as wonderful as I knew you would be. Are you okay?"

"Yes. I'm fine. Thanks to you. And you?"

"I'm fine too. I'm practicing medicine here in Chicago."

"And your hand, Jon?" She lifted his right hand and saw the scar was still there.

"It's okay. Being a surgeon was more my father's idea than mine. I love being an endocrinologist."

"I'm so pleased you remembered me," she said, touching his cheek. "You were . . . very special to me."

He looked away, then back to her. "And you to me, Georgia. You were my first love."

It was there. That sweet, gentle glint in his eyes.

"I've often wondered why you never tried to contact me. Because of your parents?"

He nodded. "My mother made me promise when she was dying. A deathbed promise, Georgia, is very powerful." He paused. "So, I guess you're married?" He looked at her gloved hand.

"No. Still single and available," she said, not hiding her eagerness for his reply.

A voice behind him called out. "Jon. Over here." A woman's voice. He waved.

A pretty young woman holding a little boy approached. "Sorry, I'm late. Traffic was unbelievable."

Jon kissed her and took the little boy from her. "Joan, this is Georgia Parker. Georgia, my wife Joan, and this is Grant, our son."

"So nice to meet you, Georgia. Jon has spoken of you."

Georgia heard the page for final boarding of her flight, but couldn't move. *He wouldn't have considered me. Not after the beating he took from my black father.*

"Where are you living?" Jon asked.

"Omaha," she mumbled, "That page's for me."

"Can we exchange cards?" he asked.

She hurriedly obliged. And as she ran she heard Joan shout, "Come visit us."

Out of breath, she arrived at the gate after they had closed the door. Looking over her shoulder, tears rimmed her eyes. *I'm . . . too late.*

CHAPTER 33

Georgia came up with an idea she was eager to share with management, but her energy level was wanting. Thoughts of Jon Roberts clung with an unrelenting grip. Gratitude, that's all it was. She would always remember him for his heroism. *Why should I care that he's married? I'm engaged to Cliff, for heaven's sake.*

Still, disturbing thoughts surfaced. If her father hadn't mistaken Jon for the man who assaulted her and beaten him up so badly, his parents wouldn't have turned against her. Or, was it because her father was black?

After three days, she knew she had to let go. They both had sweet memories, but he had moved on. She must too.

She scheduled a meeting with Scott and spelled out the details of her idea. "The proposed fashion look for fall certainly has a better chance than the maxi, but still, the average woman may be slow to take to it. So, if this below-the-knee trend was associated with something she likes, it might help."

Scott's eyes were focused on advertising tear sheets. "And what would that be?"

"Young marrieds these days play bridge." She paused, hoping he'd look up.

He did not. "So?"

She was about to launch into her explanation when Mr. Hoffman appeared in the doorway. "Am I interrupting something important?"

"No, sir. Come in. Georgia was just about to share some thoughts about her trip, but it can wait."

"I'd like to hear what she has to say. Would you mind if I listen in?"

Scott frowned and gestured to Georgia to proceed.

She repeated her introductory comments. "Using bridge as a vehicle to attract women to the new look would go like this: run a fall ad with an illustration of the new hemline, and in the background a fanned-out

142

bridge hand, with the phrase: *Play Your Long Suit.* Then, for continuity, do a replica of the idea in our windows, with mannequins in long-skirted suits, with the bridge hand backdrop and the same phrase."

Hoffman took out a pen and a small note pad. "Go on."

Georgia let her enthusiasm fly. "To further enhance the idea, we could have a sign beside every in-store mannequin touting the theme."

"Like what?" Scott asked.

"Signs could read, Take this to HEART . . . Join the CLUB . . . Fashion in SPADES . . . Elegant as DIAMONDS. And in each case using the corresponding playing card. And I bet Special Events could line up a bridge tournament in our auditorium and give a complete fall wardrobe to the winner. I'm sure one of our venders would provide that wardrobe for the credit. And, of course, I'd tie in my fashion shows."

Both men were silent. Georgia wished she had the power of Elizabeth Montgomery's TV "Bewitched" character—to twitch her nose and disappear.

Hoffman spoke first. "I hate that new look. I like to see women's legs, but if that's what we'll have to sell, I can't think of anything that would be more fun and make it more palatable. What do you think, Mort?"

Scott lifted his shoulders. "Could work."

Hoffman smiled. "Good. I'll look forward to seeing it all put together. Good work, Georgia."

The Fashion office vibrated with tension and excitement. "I feel we have a winner, Jean."

With meticulous care, they rehearsed the new slide presentation twice the night before and synchronized every step.

Jean had even changed her hair color for the occasion. "Deep auburn for fall. What do you think, Georgia?"

"Charming."

The meeting room was packed. Everyone on the merchandising side was there, plus Advertising, Display, and Special Events.

Georgia came up to the microphone. "Our business is in a period of transition, not unlike what the rest of the country's facing." She mentioned that new voices were being heard regarding the plight of the environment, and television broadcasts by satellite brought Americans intimate updates on the continuing conflict in Vietnam. Viewers were confused by what they heard and so it might be for the fashion customer."

She asked for the lights to be turned out. Jean ran the slide projector and Georgia narrated. In minutes, however, they both knew, as did the entire audience, that something was very wrong. What Georgia was saying had nothing to do with what was on the screen.

At first, Georgia was bewildered, then horrified. It would have been easy enough to ad-lib about what was being shown, but slides of sportswear were mixed up with evening wear, slides from last season— swimwear and straw hats—popped up next to fall coats. How could this be? She and Jean had arranged each and every slide and thoroughly rehearsed the entire presentation.

Georgia asked for the lights. "Jean and I were extremely careful with this presentation." There was dead silence. "We rehearsed and rehearsed. Perhaps if you refer to the handouts—" Most of the top brass were already walking out, following Scott. "The only explanation— someone tampered with the slides." Half the room had cleared. Her voice was raspy and weak. "I'm . . . sorry."

When the room was empty, she turned to Jean. "Where did you leave these slides last night?"

"In the office. On my desk." Her voice shook.

"Where on your desk?"

"I think . . . next to the phone."

"How can you be sure?"

"Because I called Coach when we were leaving, and I remember tapping my nails on the slide case, waiting for him to answer."

"And where were they this morning? Think before you answer."

Jean grew pale. "They were . . ."

"They were where?"

"On . . . your desk."

"Don't you think that's strange, since we both left at the same time last night and you arrived when I did this morning? We walked into the office together."

Jean's words were hesitant and shaky. "Very strange."

"And those slides from last season . . . where were they?"

Jean didn't answer, but looked frightened.

"What did you do with them?"

Jean was in tears. "I . . . gave them to Display."

"Who in Display?"

"They needed them for reference."

"Who needed them? Who did you give them to?"

Jean whispered between sobs. "Jesse. I gave them to Jesse." Now the distraught girl was crying as though her heart would break. "I'm sorry, Georgia, I'm so sorry."

Georgia was torn between wanting to comfort Jean or shake her. Instead, she headed for Display.

"Rudy?" Georgia shouted, bursting into his office. It was time she told him everything about Jesse. Rudy's office was empty.

"Damn." She turned around and headed for Jesse's office. He was sitting at his drawing board. The sleeves of his white shirt were rolled up to his elbows.

"What the hell are you trying to do?" she shouted.

He turned around and smiled. "Well, how do, Miss Parker. Interesting presentation this morning."

"Yes, wasn't it? Listen, you fink. I've had it up to here with your crap."

He didn't answer.

"Enough is enough! I'm going to tell management all about you and why you're carrying on this stupid vendetta. And if you want to save your job, you'd better stop this nonsense. Understand?"

He tilted his head the way a puppy might.

"Don't try being cute with me," she screamed.

He left the drawing board, walked to his desk, and reached into the belly drawer. He drew out an envelope and offered it to Georgia. "I don't think you're going to tell anybody anything, Miss Parker. I was going to send this to you for Christmas, but why not now? Here."

"What is it?"

"Open it."

She drew herself up to regain composure. "Nothing that you have would be of interest to me."

"Wrong. I'll open it for you." He handed her a photograph.

She gasped. He had taken a picture of Paul kissing her in the garden at his wedding. She looked at Jesse with a hate she had never felt before, and tore the photo into little pieces.

His laugh sounded almost obscene. "I can provide you with a dozen billfold sizes, an eight-by-ten glossy, or make you an original oil painting."

"Jesse, don't do this. You'd only hurt Lyndy and Mr. Hoffman."

He folded his arms and leaned casually against his desk. "No one will get hurt, as long as you behave yourself. One complaint about me to anyone—and I mean anyone—and the picture goes into circulation."

"You're sick."

"Not as sick as you're going to be when I get through with you, Sweet Georgia . . . Brown."

Dealing with Jesse, as enormous as it was, presented only part of what she had yet to face about the tarnished slide presentation. She hadn't heard from Scott. Her original plan was to march up to Scott's office and tell him exactly what Jesse had done. After Jesse's threat, she wondered if she dared mention his name.

At four o'clock, Scott still hadn't contacted her. Instead of his cryptic silence, she would have welcomed a scathing call. At five o'clock, she headed for his office.

"I don't have an appointment," Georgia told his grim-faced secretary, "but I'd appreciate seeing Mr. Scott."

"Sorry. He's on the phone." She pointed to the light buttons on her phone. "And when he's finished, he has another call on hold."

"I'll wait."

"I wouldn't if I were you."

Georgia ignored the brittle woman. Scott's phone conversation was long and so was the second one. Several times Scott's secretary looked at her with disdain. Georgia pretended not to notice.

It was five-thirty when Scott walked out of his office. Georgia stood up. "Mr. Scott, may I see you?"

"What about?"

"Could I see you in your office?"

Scott looked at his watch. "It's five-thirty."

How many times have you called me for a meeting to start at 5:30? "I know."

Whether he sensed that she would not be easily dismissed, or wanted to get it over with, he nodded and returned to his inner office. Georgia followed and asked permission to close his door.

He sat behind his desk. "Is this about your presentation this morning?"

"Yes."

He stood up again. "I heard your excuse at the meeting. I don't need to hear more."

"It was sabotage, sir."

"Really? By whom?"

Oh, how she longed to tell him, but Jesse's blackmail was working. "I . . . don't know."

"Miss Parker, this meeting is over."

"We worked hard on that presentation. Even if we had mixed up slides, which we didn't, certainly you can understand that we would never insert last season's slides. Somebody—"

He slammed a hand down on his desk. "You are responsible for whatever comes out of your office. Excuses are useless, and I might say, unprofessional. Goodnight."

CHAPTER 34

Each day Georgia came to work she was surprised she still had a job. Each ring of the phone was jarring. Jean worked wordlessly every day. Rudy was out of town. No calls from Cliff. Scott hadn't summoned her. She felt invisible.

Seeing Jon at the airport with a wife and child, the failure of her slide presentation, and Jesse's threat with the incriminating picture, left her reeling.

The silence seemed to scream trouble. *I need to know what's going on.*

Maybe she'd talk to Mr. Hoffman. She could count on him to talk straight. When she reached his office, the door was open.

"Georgia. Come in and say hello to Paul Stratley."

Anxiety grabbed her chest.

"You remember Paul."

Paul put out his hand. "Miss Parker. How nice to see you again."

It was all she could do to shake his hand and force a half smile.

"Paul and Lyndy are in Omaha to stay. Karen and I are so glad to have our family close by. Paul's working for Peoples Savings & Loan for now. It'll help him get reacquainted with local finance before he comes over to Emeralds."

Inwardly, Georgia screamed, but she nodded politely.

Stratley took a step towards her. He was impeccably dressed and she noticed a large diamond ring on his right hand. "You gave wonderful fashion advice to Lyndy, and I hope I can count on you to help me when I join your team."

"You have the best teacher standing beside you." She nodded towards Mr. Hoffman.

"I'll need all the help I can get," Paul said. Then, in a voice with a sultry undertone, he added, "I'll be in touch."

She turned to Hoffman. "How long will he be at People's?" *Why did*

148

I ask that? Did it make me sound anxious?

"About two years, more or less."

I'll be long gone before that.

On her way back to her office she was halted with a new thought. *Has Stratley told anyone about my black father? Or . . . is he also going to blackmail me?*

The following Monday, Jean tip-toed in with mail. She started to leave, but Georgia called her back.

"Will you stop acting like I'm the warden or something? Sit down."

Jean slid into a chair and moved a small vase of fresh daisies for a clearer view of Georgia.

"Thank you for the daisies, Jean. And your note was wonderful."

"Then my apology is accepted?"

"Completely. When you gave those slides to Jesse you couldn't know what he had planned."

Georgia looked around her office, where the air was stale and the décor nonexistent. "Do you ever feel as though the work we do here is useless . . . insignificant?"

"What?"

"I mean. Does this job seem important to you, besides the paycheck?"

Jean hesitated. "Sometimes. But when I see the great results with the kids on our teen boards . . . how they become aware of their potential and gain confidence . . . and—"

"And?"

"Working with you. I'm trying to do what you do—keep on doing my best—even when the chips are down."

"Do I do that?"

"Hell, yes."

Georgia grinned. "You're just saying that because I didn't fire you over the slide mess up."

"Pure luck." Jean crossed her fingers.

"I'm lucky Scott didn't fire *me*. He refused to listen to my explanation. He's keeping score."

"You mean like . . . building a case against you?"

"I sense he has more than just a reprimand in mind."

Jean looked concerned.

"I feel Cliff's right. How many bruises should I accept from this silly job?"

"Silly job? You can't mean that."

"It's hard being silent about unjust abuse."

"Really?" Jean cocked her head. "How do you rank Cliff's behavior? When did you hear from him last? Weeks ago?"

"No. I received a package of stories he had published recently. And I called him afterwards. We're planning to be together when I go to LA to cover California sportswear."

"Do you get letters or notes with those clippings?"

"No."

Jean sighed. "When I saw Jesse's true colors I was through with him. I was heartbroken, but I know I deserve better."

Georgia flinched. *Jean doesn't understand the newspaper business. Constant pressure. He loves me. Cliff is not Jesse.*

In September, Georgia's "Play Your Long Suit" campaign was launched. The newspaper ads, windows, and bridge tournament brought crowds of people into the store and sales were good.

Two days later, Georgia received a call from Faith, Mr. Hoffman's secretary.

"Good morning, Georgia. We just received a call from *The Omaha Post*. They want some information about fashion in the new century. Mr. Hoffman referred them to you."

The Omaha Post interviewed Georgia on the new decade's fashion attitude. Omaha's NBC television affiliate came by to include her in their evening news. Was it true if hemlines drop so does the stock market? Were women actually "playing their long suit?"

All this seemed to be the springboard for other requests for Georgia Parker's fashion opinions. Her name appeared repeatedly with quotes in newspaper fashion pages. She was invited to host a monthly fashion segment on TV and often as guest speaker at women's charity events.

Mr. Hoffman called her. "You're putting our name out there in a most effective way. Congratulations, Georgia."

A new thought grabbed her. *I'm having fun. I love the feeling of making things work.*

Rudy called. "Your celebrity is being launched, kiddo."

"Nonsense. Emeralds is the celebrity."

A month after Georgia's Long Suit promotion, Scott called a special meeting, He stood up in front of a packed room of employees. He pulled out the cuffs of his white shirt until his huge gold cuff links showed. He lifted a trophy. "This is a special day for us. The 'Play Your Long Suit' campaign has made a grand slam." He chuckled at his little joke and employees politely responded. "Pictures of our theme windows and displays were taken by Jesse Wiggins and submitted in competition to the *National Visual Presentation Journal* and won the national award for the best original idea of the year."

He held up the gleaming trophy and asked Jesse to come forward. "Congratulations, young man. Well done." Not a word was said about the original concept and step-by-step planning coming from Georgia.

That wasn't just an oversight. It was almost as though he and Jesse shared something about me. Watch out, girl. Paranoia setting in.

What would Cliff say about all this? Too much fuss about the length of a skirt.

CHAPTER 35

The ringing telephone awakened Georgia from a deep sleep. Her bedside clock read one a.m. Another crank call? "Hello."

"Georgia? Did I wake you? I'm sorry. I forgot about the time difference. It's Cliff."

She sat up now wide awake. "Cliff? Where are you?"

"California. How are you, sweetheart?"

"I'm fine. And you?"

"Great. They're working me to death, but I love every minute of it. I miss you something fierce. Have you been getting my clippings?"

"Oh, yes. They're on the bulletin board in my home office. That piece you wrote on the student uprising at Kent State earlier this year? It's so powerful I've read it over and over."

"That was a lucky break."

"Seems you've been getting one high profile assignment after another. I'm proud of you."

"Thanks. You know the plans we made for you coming out here for a weekend?"

"How could I forget? Just two weeks away."

"Honey, I can't imagine anything better, but— "

"But what?" *Is he going to do this to me again?*

"I'm going abroad tomorrow to work on a story about the fifty hostages being held in the Jordanian desert. I hope you'll forgive me," he stammered. "I have to go."

She couldn't answer.

"Please hang in there with me. Okay?"

It wasn't okay, but she said, "Okay."

She dropped her head into her hands. *Is being sensitive making me insensitive? Of course he has to go.*

Georgia also had a byline. Emeralds advertising director was responsible. She told Georgia that she had alerted management to the fact that Georgia had become very visible through TV and newspaper fashion pages. Why not utilize that visibility in a fashion column? The *Omaha Post* loved the idea. And so it was agreed. Georgia's column would appear every Sunday with her picture and byline.

A residual of the column's success came from Emeralds advertising agency, requesting that she become the store's spokesperson on all TV fashion commercials.

"I love these challenges," she told Rudy. "I never dreamed this job could be so diversified."

Other things changed. She was given the title of fashion director, received an increase in salary, and, best of all, her office was moved to spacious quarters and her staff was increased by one. Jean was promoted to fashion coordinator and the new girl, Jennifer, was assistant to both of them.

Jean celebrated her promotion by changing her hair color.

Georgia blinked. "Is that red or brown?"

"It's both. It's called Wild Berry. Like it?"

"You look lovely in all of your colors." With her hot pink dress Jean wore hose to match. Georgia shook her head. "You look like you got caught in the rain and the color faded down to your shoes."

"The whole thing only cost 49.99. If it had cost $50 I might have passed," Jean giggled. "Who thought up using ninety-nine cents instead of a dollar?"

"John D. Rockefeller. Brilliant, wasn't it?"

Rudy called for lunch. "And I won't be late. Got news."

She grabbed a letter she had just received and rushed to Emeralds Tea Room.

"I have news too," she told him as soon as they were seated. She handed him her letter.

"From Scott, huh? Wow. A promotion, salary increase, and what's this? A new office?"

"Can you believe it?"

"I was delighted when I read about it yesterday."

The waitress brought their BLTs and Cokes. "Don't you people ever eat anything else?"

"Once. In 1969. Thanks, love."

Georgia grabbed his arm. "What do you mean you read about it yesterday?"

"If you'll let go of my arm I'll tell you. Got a note from Scott instructing me to decorate and furnish the new Fashion Office. Congratulations."

"Did Scott suddenly have a vision?"

"He couldn't hold out. You make him look good."

She had a different twist on it. "How would Emeralds look if customers saw our current hellhole? What confuses me is the promotion and salary increase."

"The reason for all of this. Mr. Hoffman." Rudy expressed his idea for the new Fashion office. "Glamour."

"I don't want to appear presumptuous."

"Your office needs to look different. That's where the store's fashion image is reinforced. You're an image maker or breaker, baby."

She told him she liked gray, so the walls were painted silver-gray to match the carpeting. She was high on purple at the moment. He had a small couch upholstered in purple velvet and added two floral easy chairs.

As a personal gift, Rudy bought her a small leather armchair in light pearl-gray. She placed it with pride beside her new mahogany desk. The list of celebrities she had met or worked with had grown. Now she had the perfect wall on which to hang their autographed pictures.

Georgia was delighted with the finished look. "Did you have an unlimited budget?"

Rudy smiled. "It didn't come out of my budget. Mr. Hoffman said he wanted to be proud of the image if he sent important customers here. He knows there's always a committee calling for a benefit show or guest appearance."

"Add the parade of model applicants and reps from fashion companies looking for fashion office support. Traffic is growing."

"And no need to worry about Scott," Rudy assured her. "He'll never step foot in here."

Four weeks after Cliff had left to cover the American hostage situation, she received a letter from him, advising her he'd be back in time to connect with her when she had a California fashion directors meeting. "We'll communicate through my LA office."

She called his office the moment she arrived in Los Angles.

"We thought he'd be back today, but haven't seen him yet," his office told her. "I'll have him call your hotel, Miss Parker, as soon as he arrives." No call came.

What could be keeping him?

The day she returned to Omaha Cliff called. He had a bad case of the flu and was in a hospital in New York.

Why had she not been notified earlier? The fault of his office, he said.

An agonizing thought gripped her. Could it be possible . . . he's having a rendezvous with someone else? Nonsense. He had often mentioned he traveled and worked with his buddy Joe Collins, who regarded him as a mentor. Certainly he wouldn't risk losing face with a guy who looked up to him.

"So what's it going to take to wake you up?" Rudy scolded, one day during coffee break. "He's thoughtless. If he cared he'd have given firm instructions to his office to get in touch with you *immediately.* Was he so sick he couldn't call you personally?"

Georgia laid her head on her friend's shoulder. "Shut up. I can't stand it when you're right."

She vowed she was through. Even if Cliff didn't realize he had mishandled things, his being well meaning was not enough. It was over.

Two days after her talk with Rudy, Cliff called. "Sorry how things worked out, baby, but illness is unpredictable. The next time you're here I'll cancel everything. I promise."

"Even unpredictable flu?"

She didn't hear his answer. She had hung up.

The following day she received flowers. And the day after that.

He called. She hung up.

"Nice going, kid. I'm proud of you," Rudy said.

Soon letters appeared. One every day declaring his love. Flowers continued. She read the letters, tossed them aside. She had to admit they were masterpieces. Why hadn't she been privy to his amorous talent before?

Weeks later she had to schedule a California trip to cover the sportswear market.

Cliff called. "Please don't hang up. I called your office and learned you're coming to California tomorrow. Please let me see you. If you're not pleased with what I have to say, slam the door in my face."

When she reached her hotel room, more flowers accompanied with ardent, pleading notes.

She gave in and met him on Sunday.

Throughout the day, she went along with whatever he had planned— swimming, walking the beach, and dinner in a restaurant overlooking the water. They had a window table. A full moon dropped silver highlights on the dark waters.

He reached across the table and took her hand. "I love you."

She pulled away. "I'm an old fashioned show and tell person. I can't believe in words spoken without showing."

"I'm sorry, baby. Establishing a career is the hardest part. I want to provide a lifestyle worthy of you, a home you can show with pride and a husband you can be proud of."

"Are you trying to compete with my father?"

"No." He lifted his wine. "I can't settle for less than the finest wine, being at the top of my game, marrying the most beautiful woman in the world."

In that order of importance?

"I've understood working hard," she said. "It's the lack of communication and consideration I can't understand."

"I know. I'll do better. I promise."

After dinner, they walked out on the restaurant's balcony. He reached up to a large bougainvillea plant, plucked a stem with two bright red blossoms and handed it to her. "They're paled next to you," he said, kissing her hand. He looked out into the iridescent water. "I plan to become indispensable and famous in my field. Write a best seller." He turned to her. "And I want you by my side. I won't always be away this much. I may even become a syndicated columnist."

"Is that something that would make you happy? I mean, as happy as you are with foreign assignments?"

"I guess so. I'd have you." He held her face between his palms. "Why aren't you smiling?"

Slowly, she removed his hands from her face. "Be honest with me, Cliff. With such ambitious plans, are you sure marriage is right for you?"

"Because I don't want children—we both agreed on that—doesn't mean I don't want marriage. I do. I want no one but you." He looked down at her hand, without his engagement ring. "I don't blame you. But please put it back on. I want to put a wedding band with it. Any time you say."

She didn't tell him she had the ring in her handbag. *Why did I bring it?*

He held her head firmly between his hands, kissed each cheek. Then cautiously, moved to her mouth.

His lips touched hers with ultimate tenderness. Moving his hands down to her shoulders, she was sure he could feel her tremble. She longed to respond to his touch.

Remember. Try to remember why you said it was over.

His arms now surrounded her. His lips capturing her completely. The intensity of his kisses was so tantalizing she was losing touch with her defenses.

He whispered, "Don't go back to your hotel tonight. Come home with me."

For a delicious moment she wanted to agree. She loved how he towered over her.

She caught a glimpse of waves rushing up to the shore, snuggling into the warm sand, depositing its cool moisture, and then pulling back into the black waters. The tall, strong waves returned again to the sand, only to pull away again. She stepped out of his arms. Took a deep, reviving breath. "I'm sorry, Cliff. I need to get back to the hotel. All my things are there. My clothes and papers for tomorrow's appointments at the Mart."

At four the next day he picked her up at the Mart, but he had to go to his office. "I'll only be an hour," he said.

At her request, he dropped her at Rodeo Drive so she could review the elite shops. He was thirty minutes late picking her up.

"I'm taking you to a fabulous place for dinner tonight. The favorite of Hollywood stars. Mind if we stop at my apartment? And, I promise, I have nothing in mind but to show you some of my latest work."

"But I need to change," she protested.

"We'll have time."

During moments of silence he'd look over at her and smile. "It's such a joy to have you near me," he said. "Thank you for being patient with me."

She became aware that when they were together he was sweet and attentive, except that time in Omaha, when he spent most of the day at his typewriter, and left her with nothing but an unexplained note. When they were apart his contact with her was almost nonexistent. She looked over at him. He was the personification of tall, dark and handsome. And smart. *What more do I want?*

His apartment was in a handsome resident hotel. Beige walls and flooring were filled with colorless male furnishings— matching couch and chairs, built-in TV and shelves filled with souvenirs from his travels. In what might have been a second bedroom was a fully equipped office.

"I don't need much," he said. "I'm seldom here. I need you to get me out of here and into a decent place we can call home."

She looked down at her handbag. *Now I know why I brought my engagement ring along. Maybe at dinner?*

They sat on the beige couch. He opened a file.

"This is the latest batch of clippings I've had my office send to you."

So that's why there was never a note enclosed. I was on a mailing list.

The phone rang. "I'll just be a minute."

It wasn't a minute. It was a rather long conversation, sparked with laughter.

"Sorry, baby. That was Collins. She had some news to share with me. Now, I'm really proud of these stories. This one was—"

"Wait a minute. That was Joe Collins? The buddy you travel and work with?"

"Right."

"Joe Collins? You said *she*?"

"Yes. Now, this was a tip from—"

"Your teammate Joe Collins is a she."

"Yes. Oh. You thought . . . Joe?" His laugh seemed a bit nervous. "Her name is Josephine but we call her Jo."

He opened his folder and reached for her hand. "No one's opinion is more important to me than yours."

He had an elongated tale to tell about each printed story. She listened and was generous with praise, although concentration was difficult, thinking about Jo Collins. They traveled and worked together. He was her mentor. That can be very attractive to a man, Georgia thought.

Later, she drew out a small folder from her brief case. "Of course, this isn't in your class of journalism, but these columns of mine have been a great aid for business at Emeralds."

He read part of one and skimmed the others. "Cute."

Georgia felt she had been punched in the stomach.

"Why don't you come out here and write something worthwhile?" He tossed her folder to the floor, pulled her into his arms and kissed her with unbridled hunger. "When we were swimming and I saw your gorgeous long legs, it drove me wild." His embrace was solid iron and his kiss was fierce. "I want you, Georgia. Here. Now."

Georgia's heart stumbled, trying to keep mind and body in balance. She pulled away and walked to a window. She stared out and saw nothing. Her vision was as blurred as her thoughts.

Cliff didn't move off the couch. "Georgia. I'm sorry."

While still at Vassar, she felt everything this glamorous newspaper man did was perfect. When they were together in New York, he picked the Broadway shows, the museums, the restaurants. A man who could take charge. Very enchanting for a twenty year old college girl. *But I'm not in college now.*

On the street below. She noticed a young woman coming out of a shop with a small bunch of flowers. The last time she held a small bunch of flowers was when she was fifteen. Jon Roberts brought her daisies, with such sweetness in his face, and adoration in his eyes. What had she felt then? Special. Cherished.

That was it. *Oh, how I loved that feeling. That's what I'm missing.*

"Cliff, it's been a long day, I think I'll be going." She picked up her briefcase, handbag and her folder from the floor. Suddenly, Jean's words, regarding her breakup with Jesse—'I was heartbroken, but I deserve better'—loomed up like a billboard.

Then another gripping thought appeared. That unexplained note on her pillow when he suddenly left. She had buried that incident, not wanting to remember the agony of that horrendous time. *Now I don't care to know what the note meant.*

Georgia looked at Cliff. "Actually, it's been a long three years."

"Huh?"

"You're a great writer, Cliff, but that's not enough for me."

"I said I was sorry."

She looked at her folder. "I don't believe I'll ever forget being so trivialized by a man who claims to love me. Yours is not a *giving* love. Maybe I'm too needful. But if I'm happy to *give,* I need a man who knows how to give back."

"What don't I give you? Gifts? That's not my style. Affection? I don't think I've failed there."

"Actually, I'm somewhat to blame. You gave me plenty of signals, but I didn't recognize them as being thoughtless and self-absorbed. My friend Rudy knew it."

"That fag? You listen to him?"

Georgia bristled. "He's a far, far better man than many I've met."

"Now, wait a minute, didn't I accept the fact that you have a black father? How many guys would do that?"

She took a deep breath.

He moved to the door and closed it. "Don't go, Georgia. I need you."

"You don't need me. All you need is a press pass. You have a brilliant career ahead of you. I wish you well." She reached for the door knob, stood firm. He stepped aside. She didn't wait for the elevator, but ran down the stairs. She heard him running after her.

"Georgia. Let's talk. We can resolve this. I know I've been absorbed in my work. Competition is fierce. I had to be the best. The best!"

She hailed a cab. She opened her handbag. "Your ring."

He leaned into the cab window, holding the ring. "No. I want you to keep it. Look, Georgia—"

"To remember you? No thanks. I need to forget."

CHAPTER 36

On her fifth anniversary with Emeralds, Georgia received roses from Mr. Hoffman. Rudy sent her a basket of goodies and gift certificate for Chinese take-out. Jean commemorated the event by becoming a golden blonde. "On your tenth anniversary I'll go platinum."

After their chance encounter two weeks ago, Georgia wasn't surprised by what Jesse wrote on his greeting card. They had been alone in a store elevator and Jesse said, "I can't tell you how pleased I am to see you become so well known. I read your column every week. Love your TV commercials. And all those quotes in the newspaper. 'According to fashion expert Georgia Parker'. They say you're fast becoming the leading fashion authority in the area. Yes, indeedee. The higher you climb the harder you'll fall—if my photo ever falls into the wrong hands."

He got off on his floor and said goodbye with a smirk and a salute. Jesse's card said on the cover, "Congratulations" and on the inside he had written "You're moving up." She tore the card and tossed it into her wastebasket, but the words uttered in the elevator were not forgotten.

Rudy also sent an invitation for dinner. They dined at one of Omaha's finest French restaurants.

"Look at you," he said, lifting his glass of wine, "an elegant fashion diva, a shining example of what a well-dressed woman can add to a community's landscape."

Georgia poked him in the chest. "Who writes your material? A comedian?"

"Just buttering you up. I told the waiter to give you the bill."

She chuckled. "I remember you actually did that when we were teens. At the ice cream fountain at Larry's drug store. When the bill came, you said you didn't have any money. Freeloader."

He blew out his chest. "I paid you back big time. I took you to a prom because you didn't have a date."

Georgia laughed. "That was one of my better ideas. All my girl friends thought you were the cutest. They flirted and you wouldn't give them a tumble."

"I only had eyes for you."

"Yeah, right. I had a hard time keeping your eyes off of Willy Jettson." Georgia also reminded Rudy about the time they tried to smoke a cigarette for the first time behind his parents' garage. She knew then she could always trust him with a secret.

Rudy's title had been upgraded to Corporate Visual Merchandising Director, with a notable salary increase. Georgia's title became Corporate Fashion Merchandising Director—both titles recommended by Emeralds New York buying office.

They toasted each other and the bright future they would share.

"Georgia girl, I do believe you've grown to love this business. In fact, you had a strong attachment to it from the beginning. Right?"

True. Something clutched her even while she was planning to leave and marry Cliff.

Tears suddenly rimmed her eyes. She grabbed a handkerchief and tried unsuccessfully to regain her composer.

"What's the matter?"

"Oh Rudy. I've got a five-year anniversary with Emeralds, and what do I have? I lost Cliff. I lost Jon. I'm not a winner. I'm a loser. What do I have? Paul Stratley's back, the bastard. I have Scott, the chauvinist and bully, and after enduring all this, I'm through if they find out about my father, and…" *I almost said Jesse, but I want to spare Rudy.* "Do I want to end up like Michelle, a bitter and brittle old maid? I should have gotten my MRS degree like my classmates and serve on fifteen charitable boards like my mother. The workplace is hostile towards women in high positions. Where will I be in another five years?"

The anniversary flowers on Georgia's desk were wilting, a reflection of her mood. Jean popped in, and said "Georgia, Mr. Hoffman just called and asked if it was convenient to come to his office?"

Georgia nodded, and headed to the seventh floor.

Cheer up, girl. I can't walk into the president's office looking despondent.

But she needn't have worried. His warm smile gave her the strength to respond.

"Thank you for coming. I need your help. Can you think of any customer block where we aren't getting our share of their fashion business?" Mr. Hoffman asked Georgia.

"Yes. The military. We have this huge Offutt Air Force Base here—the famous Strategic Air Command—and only a small portion of their personnel shops with us."

"I think we've overlooked them because they get such great price breaks at their base commissary."

"Definitely," she said, "when it comes to jeans, hosiery, sweatshirts, and windbreakers, but I bet they can't compete with us on a fashion level. I can't imagine, with officers' wives and the constant flow of new personnel coming to the Base, that somebody's not getting their fashion dollar."

Mr. Hoffman's eyes reflected interest. "Any suggestions?"

It warmed her heart to have the president ask her for advice. Scott never had.

Within a week she called Mr. Hoffman, but knowing Scott's touchy ego, she asked if she could share the meeting with both men together.

"I called the base and learned that the Officers Club has an annual formal dinner coming up. They're looking for entertainment, but want it free. So, I offered to provide them with a smashing fashion show. I told them we'd not only pick up the tab for the show, but would provide favors and door prizes."

They both liked the plan, but Georgia had one other idea. "If we showed how much we value our service men and women by extending some special privilege when they shop with us, I think they'd respond."

Scott grunted. "Give away the store and they will come."

Georgia ignored his comment. "If we gave them, a discount on all purchases, just by showing their military ID, we might be pleasantly surprised. I'd like to offer it at the show and see what happens."

"Sounds great," Hoffman said. "What do you think, Mort?"

Scott agreed.

Hot damn! Are they actually welcoming me on the team? Georgia went back to her office and shared all details with her staff. "The show will be in three weeks. The evening starts with our show at five-thirty, with dinner and dancing following. Let's give them a dandy."

Georgia was introduced to Capt. Matt Fields by the colonel's wife, who was chairman of the event. "Capt. Fields will be our MC tonight and he'll introduce you. I've given him your bio. It's five-thirty. We're ready if you are."

After the introduction, which he delivered eloquently, Capt. Fields joined the Colonel and his wife at a front table. Georgia was aware of his eyes on her throughout the show. The room was sparkling with military brass and formally-dressed women. The applause was thunderous and when they received a standing ovation, she noticed Capt. Fields was the first on his feet.

As she left the stage, a service man wearing white gloves handed her an envelope. "I'm to wait, ma'am," he said.

It was from Capt. Fields. "Wonderful show, Miss Parker, and I was very impressed with your bio," his note began. "Here's mine. I'm single, never been married, I'm an Air Force pilot, I'm good to my mother, and if you don't have dinner with me tonight, you could undermine the morale of a very good soldier."

Even though her immediate inclination was to say no, she couldn't resist smiling. *Another man in uniform, blue like Stratley's.* Uniforms should be avoided, she had long ago decided. And he has blue eyes and dark hair, similar to Cliff's coloring, not as tall, maybe six two. She had worn high heels. Damn. Oh, well, if he can't deal with it, so be it. *It's just dinner and I'm hungry.* "Tell him yes."

His good looks were enhanced by his totally relaxed manner, and a sense of humor heavily tinged with mischief. He kept her laughing all evening.

"I love your laugh," he told her. "It's so . . . melodic—like soft music. Can you sing?"

"No. And you?"

"Oh, yes. Off key is my specialty. How about dancing?"

"Love to."

He took her hand and led her to the dance floor. "This is the finest dinner dance our Officers Club has ever had. Your show made it special."

"Thank you. What entertainment have you had in the past?"

"No idea. I've never attended before."

She laughed as he spun her around. Fast or slow numbers, he executed with style. "Where did you learn to dance so well?"

"Watched Arthur Murray on television."

They danced until the band played *Goodnight Sweetheart.*

"I'm flying out in the morning," he said before they parted, "But I'll return Friday. Will you have dinner with me Friday?" He asked to take her home, but she had her car. "I'll see you Friday," he said while walking to her car. And Saturday? And Sunday?"

"Can we just start with Friday?" she said, shifting her car into drive.

"Sure," he shouted, waving goodnight. "But save Saturday and Sunday for me."

On Friday, about four, he called her at the store.

"I just touched down. How's your day going?"

Georgia was pleased that he asked. "Very well, thank you. How was your trip?"

"Uneventful. Which in my business is good news. Where would you like to have dinner tonight?"

It was nice to be asked, but she didn't have a clue.

"Would dinner and a movie interest you? I hear *Jaws* and *The Great Gatsby* are playing. Any interest?"

"I'd love to see either."

"Then you shall see both. "How about *Jaws* tonight and *Gatsby* Sunday afternoon?"

She agreed before she realized she had committed for the whole weekend without seeing how tonight worked out.

He was to pick her up at six and was at her door at five fifty-five. With a handful of flowers, he handed her a note.

She liked his smile. It not only revealed fine white teeth but something more. Contentment? She read the note aloud. "I picked these from your front yard."

She chuckled. "I don't have a front yard."

He took her to Mario's, a new Italian restaurant. Soft lighting, string music and excellent food. "I don't know Omaha very well, but the colonel's wife recommended this. Hope you like it."

His consideration in every aspect of the evening enchanted her. Everything she selected, he ordered the same. He was gracious to the waiters, asked what song she would like the musicians to play. And added delicious helpings of laughter with every course.

They reached the theatre just as *Jaws* was starting. At a tense moment in the film, she grabbed his hand. Slowly, he put his free hand over hers. Not a clutch, just a gentle touch. She felt a twinge of something new. Certainly a touch of protection, but more like a sign of caring.

When they reached her apartment, he stopped at her door. "Would you like to go dancing tomorrow night?"

She nodded.

He lifted her hand to his lips. "I have to work all day tomorrow. Okay if I pick you up at seven?"

Georgia nodded.

He kissed her quickly on the cheek and was gone.

Sunday they had brunch at the Officers Club before going to see *The Great Gatsby*. She was enchanted with the period costuming. She hoped the fashion changes for the late seventies wouldn't continue putting women in severe career clothes. Let us be women, she hoped.

Georgia was so grateful she had that full weekend with Matt. His flight schedules, conflicting with her market trips made their time together sparse. She became aware of how empty she felt when they were apart and how the ecstasy of his touch and the loving message in his kiss filled her with longing until they were together again.

"I don't want you to think I'm just smart and handsome," Matt said after a dinner date. "I'm also a very good cook. How about my making breakfast tomorrow?"

"How wonderful. I'm a non-cook."

"My kind of woman. I'll be at your door tomorrow at what? Nine?"

"Perfect. What do I need to provide?"

"A good appetite. I come fully equipped."

He arrived with a large grocery bag, leaned over to kiss her cheek. "Mmm, you smell good."

"Just got out of the shower. Need any help?"

"Nope. Just eat and ask for seconds. By the way, I cook in quantity, so if you'd like to invite Rudy over that would be fine. I enjoyed him at lunch the other day. Good guy."

With amazement Georgia watched Matt make fresh-squeezed orange juice, bacon on the grill, stir cinnamon, nutmeg and chopped pecans into his pancake batter. He arranged a picture-perfect platter of fresh fruit and made his personally flavored coffee.

She took a sip. "This is fabulous. What's in it?"

"Secret. Breakfast is ready." He placed a full plate in front of her with a small pitcher of warm syrup. "Bon appetit."

After one bite, Georgia exclaimed, "Delicious. Will you marry me?"

"This is so sudden. But not until I ask your father, hear how many children you want, and if you'll promise to stay out of the kitchen."

Georgia flinched. How many children? "How can two people who travel so much have a family?"

He sat across from her at the table. "I didn't mean a large family— maybe just three or four. Not more than five . . . six."

"Are you serious?"

He tilted his head. "Was your proposal serious?"

She took a bite. Forced a smile. "If I could count on you always cooking." Then, playfully added, "Did you want it to be?" *What if a child of ours was born black? I'd better introduce him to my father soon.*

After six months, she called her father about Matt.

"You really like this guy?"

"I really like this guy. My life couldn't be better."

CHAPTER 37

"Your place or mine, sweetheart?" Rudy asked, in his best Bogart voice.

"Mine. What's up?"

"I feel like cooking tonight and this recipe is too good not to share. What time?"

"Whenever you get here. I'll keep busy until you arrive."

"I'll be there by six."

He arrived after seven. "I had to pick up some fixings. Now, stay out of my kitchen."

He made chicken breasts with apricot glaze and wild rice with mushrooms and almonds.

"Delicious," Georgia exclaimed. "I'll cook for you some time."

"No, please," he begged. "Just make coffee."

While having coffee in the study, Georgia wondered why Rudy really came over. She still hadn't told him anything about Jesse. Every time she thought of it, she heard Jesse's threat 'If you tell anybody, and I mean anybody', she put the idea aside. Too risky. Rudy would want to kill Jesse. Besides, Jesse was no longer working with the Omaha stores. Rudy needed a strong team in Lincoln so he sent Jesse to take over.

"Matt likes you. He's away for awhile, but we'll all have lunch again when he gets back."

"He's a good guy. But are you sure you're not getting involved with another man who's constantly traveling?"

"You mean because he's a pilot?"

"Yeah. He has one travel schedule and you have another. Wasn't that the way it was with you and Cliff?"

"No. Matt is nothing like Cliff. He's optimistic, very sweet, and is as interested in my work as I am in his. He calls me from wherever he is and the minute he touches down. Believe me, he's special."

"You said Cliff Hudson was special."

She didn't answer.

"Okay. Is he as special as Jon Roberts?"

"I will always love Jon the hero. We were just dear friends. Besides, he's married. I told you that." She watched him twist and untwist his napkin. "You didn't come here just to make dinner."

Rudy looked sheepish. "Did you know that People's Savings & Loan is in financial trouble?"

"I'd heard they're on shaky ground, and his father hoped Paul would straighten things out. Why do you ask?"

"Just wondered."

"No, you didn't just wonder. Why did you ask?"

"Well . . . I came to tell you . . . it's kind of a good news/bad news thing."

"What do you mean—kind of?"

"Well, Scott may be retiring one of these days."

"That's got to be the good news."

Rudy gulped. "The bad news is that Paul Stratley will be leaving People's for a new career."

Georgia nodded. "At Emeralds, of course."

"Stratley will be groomed for a high position."

"How high?"

"Replacing Scott as the next GMM. Your boss."

CHAPTER 38

Georgia, Jean and Barb, the better sportswear buyer, left the store together on Valentine's Day. Jean carried a heart-shaped candy box and a card signed by all three of them.

At the exit, Coach was checking Jean's package when she pulled out the candy and card. "Happy Valentine's Day."

"Good Lord," he exclaimed, "nobody has ever remembered me like this."

Georgia was sure he was blushing, a charming contrast to his thinning white hair.

"It's a day for love," Georgia said, "and we all love you."

"If Coach is the only man in our lives, we're in big trouble," Barb said, as they entered the prestigious Imperial Hotel cocktail lounge. The three women were seated in the center of the room.

"Three beautiful women alone on Valentine's Day?" the waiter said, as he took their orders. "What's this world coming to?"

"I don't see a lot of good men these days," Jean said, looking around the room.

A moment later, Matt arrived in dress uniform and paused at the entrance. Georgia winked at her friends. "I wouldn't say that." Georgia motioned towards the entrance. "Now that's what I call a man."

They watched the Air Force officer survey the room until he spotted their table. He smiled and walked over.

The waiter lingered, perhaps waiting for another drink order.

"Excuse me, ladies," the officer said to Jean and Barb, then turned to Georgia. "Care to dance?"

"Dance?" she chuckled, looking around. "There's no dance floor here. Waiter, do you have dancing here?"

"No, ma'am."

"You see, no dancing. There's not even any music."

"That's strange," Matt said. "The moment I saw you I heard beautiful music."

He pulled out the one empty chair at their table. "Do you play chess?"

Georgia nodded.

"How about a game?"

Georgia felt sure her eyes widened almost as broad as her smile. "You want to play chess?"

He nodded.

"And where would we do this?"

He pulled a key out of his pocket and laid it on the table. "My place."

The waiter, still holding his order pad, didn't move.

"What happens if I lose?"

In a deep, intimate tone he said, "Winner takes all."

She reached for the key, examined it, then slowly tucked it into her bra. She lifted one long leg, slid it sensuously over his lap, and kissed him on the lips.

The waiter blinked. People watching at tables around them grew quiet. While Georgia's friends covered their mouths to stifle laughter, they pretended to be shocked.

Matt took out his money clip and tossed several bills on the waiter's tray. "Bring the ladies anything they want and a tip for you." Then, to the waiter, and within earshot of the next table, he said, "Some women can't resist a uniform."

Georgia was aware that people watched them walk out with their arms around their waists.

They laughed most of the way to Mario's, the Italian restaurant where Matt had taken her on their first date.

At their table, Georgia retrieved his key from her bra and waved it at Matt. "What does this key unlock, sir?"

He leaned forward and whispered. "What's your guess?"

She whispered back. "Your apartment?"

"No. Much more important than that."

She fluttered her eyes lids. "Is it the key to your heart?"

"No. Top secret."

She winked. "You can trust me, Captain."

He looked both ways, leaned in closer, whispered, "It's the key . . . to my gym locker."

She threw her head back with laughter and tossed the key at him. "There goes my chance to beat you at chess." She opened her menu. "You knew I was taking you to dinner tonight for Valentine's Day. Clever of you to pick the most pricey restaurant in town. I was kind of thinking of Godfather's Pizza."

He grinned, opened the menu. "Meat balls are cheaper, but I'm in the mood for veal."

She adored his fun-loving spirit, his constant smile and eyes that gleamed with mischief. And that strong jaw. How it intensified his masculinity. Still, his playful manner was put aside when talk was serious. Like the time she told him about Cliff, or described Scott's chauvinist treatment. He had pulled her into his protective arms.

They ordered drinks, toasted each other. Her feeling of joy put a perpetual smile on her face.

Caressed with gentle lighting, each table held a small bouquet of roses. Live music, offering one romantic song after another, inspired Georgia to challenge Matt to a contest of song titles and artists who made them famous.

"*First Time Ever I Saw Your Face* Roberta Flack," Matt announced, sending her an air kiss and taking out a pen and paper. "I'm keeping score. What's the winner's prize?"

"What I learned from you—winner takes all."

"I think I've died and gone to heaven." He identified the next song. "*You are so Beautiful,* Joe Cocker."

"Darn. I'll catch up."

"A delicious tingle enveloped Georgia. "*I Honestly Love You.*" She said, with more feeling than she meant to show, "Olivia Newton-John."

The musicians took a break.

After entrée plates were removed Georgia noticed Matt loosen his tie, stir in his chair. "Something wrong?"

"No. Well, yes. Tomorrow I'm off for another tour of duty. I may be gone . . . awhile."

"How long is awhile?"

"One to three months."

A flash of fear overtook her. Was traveling and flying his life, in the same way traveling and writing was Cliff's?

"When I get back," he said, "maybe we can talk about where we're heading."

She questioned now where they were headed. Would Matt's work or her father's color be the deciding factor?

The waiter brought a small platter covered with a silver dome. "Your dessert, Miss Parker."

"I didn't order dessert."

Matt grinned. "I did."

The waiter lifted the dome cover and left.

On the plate was a beautifully wrapped package. About the size of a ring box.

"How did the waiter know my name?"

"He's seen your picture at the top of your weekly newspaper column. He said his wife reads you faithfully."

Indecision grabbed her. Was she ready for another ring?

"Aren't you going to open it?" Matt asked.

She slowly untied the satin ribbon, and opened the silver box. Relief came first, then a tinge of disappointment.

On a chain was a gold medallion with a diamond in the center. "It's beautiful, Matt. I love it." She reached across the table and his hand met hers. "Thank you. It's exquisite."

"I'd like it if you'd put it on and never take it off."

Those words spoke volumes to her and almost brought tears. "I'll go to the ladies room and have the maid help put it on."

On her way back, Georgia' felt her heart seemed to sing and she along with it. She looked down at the necklace that now hung close to her heart. *Am I afraid of being hurt again. Why? He's nothing like Cliff. I was obsessed with Cliff. With Matt it's different. I feel safe. Cherished. Admit it. You love the man. I do. I do. And I'm going to tell him. Now.*

Georgia lifted the medallion to her lips. It had been a long time since she felt so alive. The orchestra was back and playing *Everything is Beautiful*, Ray Stevens. As she quickened her steps back to Matt, her heart was dancing. That is, until she saw a lovely redhead standing next to Matt, plus a middle-aged couple. Georgia stopped while still beyond their sight.

They all three were well dressed and tanned.

"You look wonderful, Diana," Matt said to the redhead.

"Remember this gold bracelet you gave me?" Diana indicated. "I've never taken it off."

Georgia gasped, examined Matt. She understood that look. His smile was warm, glowing with pride.

Matt never mentioned Diana. What else hasn't he told me?

"We miss you coming over and cooking with us, Matt," the older woman said. "Come to dinner. For old times."

"I'd love to, Maria, but I'm leaving tomorrow and will be gone awhile."

"Then when you come back. I'll only accept a yes."

The pretty redhead linked her arm into Matt's and laid her head on his shoulder. "Say, yes."

Georgia had seen enough. "Hello," she said, going directly to her chair.

Everyone looked to Matt for explanation. "Georgia, these are old friends. Diana Castino and her parents, Maria and Sergio. This is Georgia Parker."

They all mumbled something of a greeting. Diana turned to Matt and kissed his cheek. "Don't forget. Dinner when you get back. Nice to meet you, Georgia."

The Castinos waved and threw kisses as they left. When Diana lifted her arm to wave, the bracelet slipped down and Georgia saw where the suntan line stopped; she had indeed not taken it off.

The orchestra was playing. Matt tapped his forehead. "Uh . . . *I'll Never Love This Way Again,* Diane Warwick."

Georgia touched his necklace. *Never take it off, he had said. And Diana had never taken off his bracelet. An expensive gift as thanks for a great time, here's a little something to remember me by?*

"That was an interesting scene," Georgia said.

"Yes. Surprising. They were walking by and saw me."

Georgia nodded.

"Let's sit down." He pulled out her chair.

"We're leaving."

He looked puzzled. "Okay. I'll get the check."

"It's taken care of. Let's go." Georgia recognized the song being played as they left, but didn't want to identify it.

Matt drove for several minutes before speaking. "I haven't seen the Castinos in over three years. I used to date Diana."

"Very pretty girl." Pause. "And a very pretty bracelet. Seems it meant a lot to her."

Matt pulled over to the side of the road and stopped. "Diana and I had been dating a few months and for her birthday I gave her the bracelet."

"So it was serious."

Matt's sighed. When he glanced at Georgia, she turned away. He sighed again, then started the car. "It's getting damn chilly sitting here." He skidded onto the road, driving faster than usual. "What do you want to know?"

"A damn lot more than you've told me. I shared everything with you, Matt. Why did I never hear about Diana?"

"I didn't think it was important."

A light snow had begun and the swish of the windshield wipers seemed like a mockery to their cold silence.

"I loved spending evenings with her family," Matt finally said. "They were gracious, fun to be around. I learned a lot about Italian cooking." He smiled. "Sergio used to say, "When there's love in the house, the pasta sauce comes out better."

"What in the hell are you talking about? Cooking skills? Is this a slap at my failure as a cook?"

"Georgia, stop it! We've been going together for almost two years. I haven't seen or heard from the Castinos for over three years, so why care about a girl I knew long before we met?"

"You think I'm stupid?" She touched his pendant. "Put this on and never take it off? Those words meant so much to me. I heard her say she never took off your bracelet. Do you say that to all the girls you give gifts to? So they always remember you?"

He stared straight ahead, said nothing. When they reached her apartment, she jumped out of the car. She felt snow hit her face, mixing with tears.

Matt followed. "Will you simmer down so we can talk?"

"Not unless you have something worthwhile to say."

He tried to take her hand. She pulled away. When they reached the elevator inside, she pushed the Up button.

"Why did you break up with her?"

"Can we talk about this another time?

He doesn't want to talk about it because I'm the next casualty. A parting gift softens the guilt. "Just an honest answer would be nice."

His eyes shifted. "She . . . broke up with me."

This unexpected answer left her shaken. *I suppose that's where I came in.* Georgia longed for a stabilizing breath. "Are you over her?"

His eyes widened. He looked as though that hadn't occurred to him until now.

The elevator door opened.

"You didn't answer my question."

He stared at her, his lips tightening.

She waited. No words came. His silence was answer enough. The last song they played at the restaurant now screamed in her ears. *How Can You Mend a Broken Heart*, Bee Gees.

She stepped inside the elevator. The door closed.

CHAPTER 39

As usual, working with Scott resulted in negative reactions to everything Georgia said. Take your job and shove it, she longed to say, but she didn't have the stamina to change anything in her life right now. She needed work to distract her from thoughts about Matt. She hadn't heard from him since Valentine's Day. Three weeks. He'd be gone for months. Soon he'd forget her. But her longing for him intensified every day.

"Large-size women," Georgia told Scott, "are weary of seldom seeing models their size."

Scott shrugged. "Our large-size department is a small part of our business."

"I know, but it could be much more. Besides, these women also buy accessories, cosmetics and house wares."

He leaned back in his chair and gave her an unmistakable okay-but-this-better-be-good look.

"I'd like to create a semi-annual event—spring and fall—with models size fourteen to twenty-four."

Scott snorted. "Where in hell are you going to get models in those sizes?"

"Easy. We put out a call. I need about fourteen women."

"Large women don't want to be segregated. They're uncomfortable enough about their size. I think they'd be insulted."

Georgia was surprised. "I'd think they'd feel cherished. It would show that we care."

Scott leaned forward. "Mrs. Scott wouldn't feel cherished. She'd be embarrassed."

She forgot about Mrs. Scott, a good size eighteen or twenty. Georgia felt Mrs. Scott was an attractive woman with a good sense of style. She never bought clothes at Emeralds. She shopped in Chicago and New York. "Mrs. Scott would be a shining example of how beautiful a woman can look if she wears the correct clothes."

"I have no budget for such speculation. If you're determined to take on this project, every dime will have to come out of your budget. Where are you going to get enough money to advertise for models? And what about an ad for the show? Without publicity, who would come?"

Georgia didn't reply, but pressed on. "We should have refreshments . . . like a party."

"Well, I suppose carrot and celery sticks—low calorie stuff like that shouldn't cost too much." He paused and shook his head. "I've seldom seen well-dressed large women around here."

If designers created more fashionable clothes and we carried a better selection, Georgia thought, we'd see a lot of happier women. "Even with limitations, I think we can make friends."

"Good luck." He stood up. "But, remember, no more budget until the first of the year."

Riding down the escalator, she reviewed her idea. Could she be mistaken?

Why didn't I ask myself that when I confronted Matt about Diana? But something else plagued her more—Matt hadn't told her why Diana broke up with him.

By the time she called her staff into her office, she had decided the event was a go. "Call our regular models—Jackie, Valerie, Dotty, and Suzanne. I need their help."

And help she got. Within a week, Georgia had selected fourteen inexperienced, but very enthusiastic women.

When the media learned that her idea was the first of its kind, Georgia obtained free time on interview shows. Rudy ran off signs for the "Big City Woman Spring Fashion Show" and had them placed in all their Nebraska and Iowa stores. Georgia got tag lines in all Emeralds fashion ads at no cost.

Rudy's crew decorated the auditorium's stage and runway with spring colors and set up two hundred chairs.

"If we fill those seats I'll be amazed," Georgia told Rudy.

The morning of the show started with a downpour.

"A weather whammy," Jean moaned.

Terror struck at one-thirty when only a half dozen women were seated for the two o'clock show.

During the planning stage, Georgia had asked the advice of her full-figured models about the menu.

"Celery and carrot sticks? That's an insinuation that we should lose weight."

One woman said. "If you really want it to be a party, I have a better idea."

Georgia followed her advice. Long, spring-decorated serving tables were set up on either side of the auditorium entrance with attendants serving vanilla ice cream, together with chocolate, butterscotch, and strawberry toppings, plus nuts and whipping cream. Georgia enlisted the help of Ginny, her father's cook, who made platters of homemade cookies.

At one-forty the attendance increased somewhat, but not enough to be encouraging. By one-fifty a slow stream of guests walked in with their custom-made sundaes. During the last five minutes, the crowd had turned into a mob. Every seat was taken.

Top management stood against the back wall like a jury.

The show was delayed for several minutes to accommodate the late arrivals. At two-twenty Georgia walked onto the stage and was overwhelmed. Rudy's crew had set up all available chairs, every inch of floor space was filled. Even standing room was at a premium.

The Omaha Post's fashion editor arrived with a photographer and sat on the floor next to the runway. The television personality who had interviewed Georgia, arrived with her cameraman.

The models forgot everything they had rehearsed. They waved at the crowd, kicked up their heels, and winked at the cameras. The audience responded with screams and wild applause. Movements that would have been prohibited for high-fashion models—wiggling their ample behinds or striking Marilyn Monroe poses—brought delighted squeals. As the models pranced to the beat of the recorded music, the audience clapped in tempo.

Georgia knew that management recognized the value of such a captive audience. She saw Mr. Hoffman whisper to Scott. Scott scribbled on a note and Rudy delivered it to her on stage.

"Ladies, good news," she announced," as a special gift, our management says you will be given a fifteen percent discount at the register for anything you buy today."

A cheer erupted.

After the show, Georgia watched the audience file out. They were smiling, laughing, and bubbling with chatter.

One large woman was approached by a reporter, who asked what she thought of the event.

"This is the first time I've come out of a fashion show and felt good about myself." She put her hands on her hips. "I don't consider myself fat now; just more of me to love." She shook with laughter, as a cameraman focused on her.

Georgia wanted to hug the woman.

"They're buying up a storm in all departments," Rudy later told Georgia. "It's amazing."

The following day, a story appeared in *The Omaha Post*. The wire services picked it up, which led to a phone interview with *Time*. As soon as the story came out, Emeralds was showered with praise from manufacturers of large size apparel, and fellow merchants in their New York buying group who wanted to follow the example.

I wish I could have shared this with Matt.

A few days later, on their way to Hoffman's office for a recap meeting on the Big City Woman show, Georgia whispered to Rudy. "Do you suppose that event will gain some points for the Fashion Office?"

"Hell, yes! More than points."

Just as the meeting started, Georgia and Rudy slipped into two seats behind Scott and Hoffman. Georgia noted that Scott bristled when Hoffman and merchandisers heaped praise on her.

At his sarcastic best, Scott quipped, "Next thing we know she'll want to be a vice president."

"Not a bad idea," said Hoffman.

Georgia and Rudy exchanged glances and smiled, until they heard Scott vow half aloud, "Over my dead body. Women belong on their backs not on boards."

CHAPTER 40

When Georgia and Rudy were seated on a plane to New York, she asked him if Scott knew she heard what he said about women in management.

"It's possible he wanted you to hear it."

"Why?"

"To keep you in your place. And let you know he'd never support you as a vice president."

She sighed. "I'm glad your buying trip coincides with mine. I'll need a friendly shoulder to lean on. I'll be working with our large-size buyer for more stylish designs. Also, help find new designers for Michelle. Her business is sagging."

"Those are tough assignments."

"Enough about business," Georgia decided. "What say we have dinner tonight at your favorite restaurant in the Village?"

"Should a celebrity like you be seen with a lowly display guy like me?"

"Are you kidding? How many stores does Emeralds own now? Nine?"

"Ten next year."

"And you've designed remarkable ambiance for each. And how many people do you have working for you? An army. If I'm such a celebrity, how come I serve the same number of stores and I still have a staff of—count them—three."

"Because yours is a department of brains and mine is a department of brawn. But I hear you've been okayed to increase your staff."

"By how many?"

"One. Maybe two."

"How do you know all this before I do?"

"Instinct."

"Well, what's your instinct about Paul Stratley? When's he leaving People's Savings & Loan?"

"Soon. Hoffman wanted to see Paul implement his business know-how."

"And?"

"People's profit margin improved. I hate to say it, but Paul's a smart son-of-a-bitch."

"So why doesn't he stay there?"

Rudy snickered. "Paul and his father never got along. Besides, Emeralds is a much bigger fish."

"But how can Paul step into the top job with no retail experience?"

"Mr. Hoffman's planned every step."

"And Lyndy?" Georgia leaned her head back on her pillow.

"With two sons? Mr. Hoffman has been heard saying she loves being a full-time mom. Hoffman feels Paul has the brains and charisma for this business."

Georgia sighed. "I sent baby gifts. Lyndy responded with printed notes. I sent her a birthday card, said I'd love to see the children. Never heard from her."

"That's a puzzlement." He closed his magazine. "What does your father think about Stratley joining Emeralds?"

Georgia squeezed her eyes closed. "I haven't told him. He'd demand that I quit."

"You wouldn't quit, would you? Give up everything you've accomplished during the past eight years? And just when you're likely to become the first woman vice president?"

Georgia sat up. "What?"

"Mr. Hoffman is pushing for it. Now it's up to the executive board."

Georgia looked at Rudy in awe. "You're a regular pipeline,"

"I do what I can."

They shared a long silence, the kind that only people who are comfortable with each other can enjoy.

"Georgia? You know how I've been nagging you to stop your masquerade about your father's color?"

"Yes."

Rudy leaned closer to her. "Listen closely. I still want you to free yourself of deception, but postpone it until after the board votes on your vice presidency. They can handle only one shock wave at a time. The first woman vice president? But wait until you're canonized, then let 'em have it."

The beverage cart arrived. They requested Cokes.

"How's your dashing Capt. Fields? You've been dating how long?"

"Two years."

"He sure is a good looking hunk, especially in that Air Force uniform. What do you hear?"

"Nothing. Not for five weeks. I don't know if he's back or still away."

"Did you fight?"

"Yes." She told him what happened Valentine's Day.

Rudy shook his head, said nothing.

In the morning, Rudy escorted Georgia through his display houses. He bought some items—huge, inflatable Christmas characters, to be suspended and suitable for floating from store ceilings. "Steve can create some of this other stuff in our workshop."

"You seem to be very high on Steve. And has Jesse the Jerk had a name change?"

Rudy hailed a taxi. "Steve has emerged as a big talent, but he's such a party boy. He's an idea guy and Jesse can translate ideas like magic. A good team." Rudy gave the cab driver the address. "I stopped calling him Jesse the Jerk when he stopped being a jerk. However, I could do without his hang-up about blacks."

Georgia decided this was the moment to tell Rudy. "Would Mr. Hoffman want a man like that working for Emeralds?"

Rudy shook his head. "Maybe not, but unless Jesse does something illegal, he can't be fired for his beliefs."

"Certainly there are other talented guys to replace Jesse."

Rudy disagreed. "The years of training we've invested in Jesse makes him valuable. If he continues to be an asset and commits no crime, he stays."

I can give you grounds for dismissal. Isn't blackmail a crime?

"I bet among all the thousands of people Emeralds employs there are plenty who don't like blacks, Jews, gays or women. What should we do? Fire them all?"

I'll handle this Jesse problem myself.

Rudy took Georgia to a mannequin company. "Here's where I need your help."

"There's so many," Georgia said. "How do you decide?"

"Choose those that help sell and add to our fashion image."

She gazed at both sides of a long aisle. "They look so life-like. A couple look like people I know."

"Some are inspired by fashion models you've seen on runways or magazines."

They selected one that could stretch out on a chaise lounge in lingerie, another with a young, mischievous-look and slouchy stance for the junior department, and one very elegant for designer clothes.

They couldn't resist one more—a mannequin that leaned with her elbows on a banister. "I've seen such a mannequin in a high-fashion store. She looked so real customers walked up to the banister to see what she was looking at below."

With the perks offered to Georgia and Rudy, they were invited to dinners, theatre, and cocktail parties with the industry's beautiful people.

On the third day, Georgia and Rudy joined Michelle to view a couple of fashion collections.

At one stop, Michelle, Georgia and Rudy were escorted to seats in the front row. Michelle and Georgia exchanged surprised glances. Front row?

The music for the show was more upbeat than usual for designer collections and so were the fashions.

"What do you think?" Georgia asked Michelle.

Michelle shrugged.

On the way out of the showroom a reporter from *Women's Wear Daily* approached Georgia. "What is your opinion of this collection?"

Georgia looked around. Did the reporter mean her? Quotes of this kind were usually obtained from big names in retail.

"What did you think of the collection, Miss Parker?" the young woman repeated.

How does she know my name? Oh, yes. It was taped to my chair.
"I feel the designer captured what today's woman really wants, and I loved the innovative mixture of fabrics—silk with wool or smooth with texture."

"What do you think is the customer block for this collection?"

"All savvy young women. Especially working women. The ambitious ones wanting to move up will dress for the job they *want* not the job they *have*." Those words sparked an idea Georgia was anxious to explore when she returned home.

The reporter seemed pleased with Georgia's remarks. She also complemented Georgia on her elegant pantsuit by Yves Saint Laurent. "You'd make a great model, Miss Parker." After getting confirmation on Georgia's exact title she mentioned that she had seen the story about Big City Woman. "Let me know if you have anything else like that coming along." She handed Georgia her card.

"That's why we were seated in the front row," Michelle said, frowning. "That big woman show got national attention."

The next appointment was with an up-and-coming young designer, Alfredo, recommended by Emeralds New York buying office.

"I hear Alfredo has great choices for the younger, up-scale customer," Georgia told Michelle.

They ran across the street packed with retailers, and merchandise on rolling racks being moved from warehouses—all dodging heavy motor traffic.

Inside the building, the crowd was even greater. After a long wait, they squeezed into a packed elevator.

The Alfredo showroom was crowded, but when they were seated, they were offered lunch. Alfredo himself came by to welcome them. Michelle introduced her party by name and title.

In slim-fitting charcoal-gray slacks, an even tighter light gray turtleneck, and golden Florida tan, Alfredo was a show-stopper. His gray-green eyes focused firmly on Rudy, who was blushing.

"We're not usually visited by display directors," Alfredo said, in a low voice. "We're flattered."

The sparks that ignited between the two men were so powerful Georgia could hardly concentrate on the merchandise being shown.

"You all staying at the same hotel?" Alfredo asked.

"No," Rudy answered, "they're at the St. Moritz. I'm at the Algonquin."

After that exchange, Georgia wasn't at all surprised when Rudy called her later at her hotel and begged off having dinner with her.

"Something's come up?" she teased. "Like . . . Alfredo?" Georgia felt his excitement coming over the phone line.

"Yes," Rudy said. "Can you imagine? He's taking me to dinner."

After that night, Rudy was no longer available.

CHAPTER 41

The moment Georgia reached her office, she asked Jean if she had any calls. Maybe from Matt? Six weeks, no word.

"No, but a gorgeous new model came in this morning. I was blown away. She'll come back soon, if you're available."

Her phone rang. "This is Faith, Georgia. Welcome home. Since George Hamilton is going to be our guest celebrity at Saturday night's benefit show, Mr. and Mrs. Hoffman wish you to attend a dinner party in his honor. Friday at their home."

"Thank you. I'll be there," After she hung up, Jean escorted in the drop-dead model she had seen earlier.

The model handed Georgia her photo composite—close-ups, full shots in various poses and attitudes. Gwen Val Wray's beauty was unique. Tall, slim, and graceful—attributes of most good models—but Gwen presented herself like royalty. From her pulled back black hair, to her high cheekbones and large black eyes, she was a stunner. Her light brown skin was as warm as her smile. After Georgia saw Gwen walk, she booked her for the Country Club benefit. "George Hamilton will be our guest celebrity," Georgia mentioned.

"The handsome movie star?" Gwen exclaimed.

"The very one."

"She reminds me of you," Jean told Georgia after Gwen left.

Georgia laughed. "You're kidding."

"I think so, too," Jennifer, the newest staff member said. "She walks like you, similar high cheek bones and same dark eyes."

"Honestly," Jean said, "she's a black version of Georgia Parker."

Those words fell on Georgia like a physical blow. Certainly she should have been flattered. Instead, she was shaken. Back in her office she looked at Gwen's pictures, then examined herself in a mirror. *"We're nothing alike. She's black, I'm . . ."*

188

Georgia looked again in the mirror. She couldn't resist imagining, as she had so often in her dreams, what she'd look like if her skin was actually dark. How many times had she feared that others saw more than her black eyes? Maybe that was enough to see her as black. Her own staff saw it.

Maybe she should have taken this occasion to tell her staff. *No, I can't. Rudy said now's not the time.*

Georgia tried to concentrate on her report for Scott, but Jean's observation haunted her. *Gwen's a black version of me?*

The night of the party, Karen Hoffman greeted Georgia warmly and guided her into the living room, furnished in traditional elegance. The guests were Emeralds management and their wives. Because George Hamilton would be coming directly from the airport the suggested dress was business attire.

Georgia looked around for George Hamilton, who, apparently, had not yet arrived. And to her relief, Lyndy and Paul Stratley were not there.

A waiter approached Georgia with a tray of drinks and she selected red wine. Aaron Hoffman came into the room, and announced, "I've just received a call from Mr. Hamilton. His plane is socked in at O'Hare Airport in Chicago. Heavy fog. He doubts he'll make it to Omaha before midnight, so let's have dinner."

At the table, Georgia found that on her right was Mortimer Scott and on her left was a place card for Paul Stratley. When everyone was seated, and Paul's seat was empty she sighed with relief.

"Sorry I'm late," Stratley said, strutting in and stroking his hair. "I was helping Lyndy get our boys to bed." He kissed his mother-in-law, who pointed to his place.

"It's hard to imagine," he whispered to Georgia, "you're more beautiful than ever."

Georgia tightened. "Where's Lyndy?"

"Both boys have a fever. She didn't want to leave them."

Sitting between Scott and Stratley. Could this evening get any worse?

Mrs. Hoffman's dinner table was a lovely array of gold embellished china and Bacharach stemware. Georgia had to smile as she looked at the other guests. Most of the board members and department heads of Emeralds were present. With the exception of three or four, few looked as though they had any association with the fashion business. Harry Ralston looked more like a used car salesman than the Divisional Vice President of accessories and cosmetics. His plaid jacket and garish tie made her want to laugh. From his well-known elevator shoes and mail-order reddish toupee, he was an enigma.

"Hey, Georgia," he shouted across the table. "I got one hell of an idea for your shows. Call me next week and we'll talk. Okay?" So far, she had successfully avoided this man whom Michelle had warned. "He's a wolf, and beware."

And then Georgia glanced at Larry Lasondo, Divisional Vice President of all ladies ready-to-wear. What a prince. His attire was always as impeccable as his word.

"Looking forward to your show tomorrow night," Lasondo said.

Whenever she saw Larry Lasondo she marveled at his even, calm persona. He never seemed ruffled, and was quick to give credit to others. The man is ego-free, Georgia decided. "I'm so grateful for the special show pieces you obtained for us, Larry."

At the far end of the table, Mr. Hoffman had been talking with Mrs. Scott on his right and Mrs. Ralston on his left. When dessert was served, Mr. Hoffman addressed the group. "Since we don't have Hamilton here, we might as well talk shop. Any volunteers? None? Well, then, Georgia, tell us what new ideas you've brought back from New York."

Georgia's first instinct was to look at Scott, even though she was less intimidated by him lately. She was understanding the game she had to play to best serve the store. She felt Scott would try to kill her proposal for merchandising to career women. She had heard him say, "Who cares how file clerks or secretaries dress?"

The president has just asked me to tell what I've learned, and I don't need Scott's permission to answer.

All the guests were entirely too quiet. Hoffman nodded towards Georgia.

She turned away from Scott and looked at Mr. Hoffman.

"The working woman segment is growing stronger. Ever since John T. Malloy came out with his *Dress for Success* book, she has been eager to follow specific guidelines. She really needed a Malloy-type direction then, but that was a couple of years ago. Lord knows we sold racks and racks of navy blazers, white shirts, and those little ribbon neck bows. Today, we could take hold of our rightful role—directors of suitable fashion for serious career women." She paused. Was the silence judgmental?

Hoffman nodded. "Go on."

"We could establish special departments for career dressing. We could train our sales people to show this customer how to assemble her working wardrobe, if she wanted help. I would like to establish a career board made up of representatives from the major companies in the area. We could pick their brains on company dress codes and see that our stocks reflected their needs. We could have special fashion shows with career board members as models. We could have even greater success with this customer block than we did with the Big City Woman effort."

Now, everyone was talking, until Hoffman spoke. Georgia didn't hear a word he said. She felt something on her leg. Slowly, she looked down and saw Paul's hand. How could she stop him? She thought of knocking over her water glass, but the fear of breaking one of those lovely goblets halted her. When she felt his hand slip between her knees, a loud gasp escaped her throat. It sounded like a violent hiccup, so she repeated the sound, as she ran from the room, faking hiccups all the way.

CHAPTER 42

George Hamilton arrived in time for the black-tie benefit at the Windsor Country Club. The models begged Georgia, "Do you think he'll let us get a picture with him? . . . my, God, he's gorgeous . . . ask him to autograph the show's program for me." Georgia asked and he obliged. Georgia could feel the electric effect on the models. Tonight they would strut their very best. Surely, nothing could go wrong.

The orchestra began and lights came up on the total black and white scene. Ten-foot tall white letters, spelling out the word *CHANGE* stood against a black background. Fourteen models frozen in fashionable poses drew huge applause. It was an elegant beginning for the fast-paced show.

Everything clicked. Georgia was on one side of the stage and Hamilton on the other. She gladly relinquished her comments so that he could share his charm.

Each time Gwen-Val Wray, the black model appeared, she dazzled the audience. In the finale, she wore a long, white beaded gown, slit up the side, revealing her beautiful legs. The audience was stunned. Scott should love this show.

Mr. and Mrs. Hoffman came backstage afterwards with congratulations. "Georgia," Hoffman said. "It was the best." However, his kind words were uttered without a smile. What was wrong? Was it something about Lyndy and Paul? During the show she could see them at the Hoffman table. Hoffman's sober compliment wasn't the only one. Rudy gave her a hug and whispered "Fabulous." But he, too, was unsmiling.

After all the guests had left, several models stayed behind to help Georgia and her staff pack up the clothes.

"Did I do alright?" Gwen asked.

"You were great. You're on my A list."

The following Tuesday, Georgia hurried to unlock her office door. The phone had rung several times and sounded angry, she thought, as though it resented not being answered.

It was Scott, requesting that she come to his office immediately. She obeyed.

"Sit down," Scott said, holding up a fistful of papers. "These are the most devastating complaints this company has ever received. All about your show Saturday night."

Georgia's heart was pounding as though she had run up ten flights of stairs. "Why? The lingerie scene?"

"We had a couple about that, but the big complaint is much more serious."

"Which is?"

"That Negro model. Where do you get off bringing her to our most exclusive country club?"

"You said you wanted a professional show."

"Don't you challenge me, Georgia Parker. We have a big problem on our hands because of your bad judgment."

"She's the finest model I've ever seen. I thought the show warranted the best."

He passed over her comment and picked up more letters. "Know what these say? They demand that you be fired."

"On what grounds?"

Scott leaned forward and shook the letters in her face. "You're in hot water, young lady. You'd better do as I say or these women might get their wish."

And don't you threaten me, you bigoted ass.

"What you need to do is call each one of these customers and tell them you acted on your own, and that management had no knowledge of your decision to use a Negro model."

"That's true."

"Alright. Tell them you're sorry, that you made a mistake and will never do it again." He folded the letters and held them out to her when his secretary knocked.

"Mr. Hoffman would like you to come to his office."

"As soon as Miss Parker leaves."

"He wants to see both of you. Now."

Scott looked at the letters in his hand. "I'm taking these along," he told Georgia. "You know Hoffman's creed: the customer comes first."

My staff called Gwen a black version of me. I wonder if Scott thinks the same. Georgia, stop it. Out damn thoughts, out I say.

Not until she and Scott were well inside Mr. Hoffman's office did Georgia see that Michelle was present.

"We have a problem that I believe will take all of us to solve." Hoffman produced a long letter from its envelope. "This is from Tiffany Farnsworth. In her words, 'a colored model is unacceptable at the Club.' She demands the model and Miss Parker be fired. And, if this isn't done'—he turned the envelope upside down—this shredded Emeralds charge account will represent the end of her relationship with Emeralds."

Hoffman's voice was even and his body language difficult to read. "Mr. and Mrs. Farnsworth are co-chairmen of the Windsor Country Club's board. And David Farnsworth is president of MidAmerica Bank, with whom we do business. Now, I'll let Michelle tell you her problem."

Rigid and tight-lipped, Michelle spat her words directly at Georgia. "Mrs. Farnsworth is my best customer. She spends thousands of dollars at a crack. She's done that for years. What's more, she's so powerful, many of my present customers came into my department because of her. If she leaves, we might as well close the Designer Salon."

Scott held up one letter from those he brought. "I think we all need to hear this one. 'I loved that white beaded gown and would have bought it on the spot but not after that colored person had it on her body and paraded it around in front of everyone I know.'"

Scott waved the letter. "We have fashion shows to make sales not lose them." Scott handed Hoffman the other letters he had received.

Georgia's heart throbbed as Hoffman silently read each one. She felt bent and shattered.

Hoffman leaned back in his chair and folded his arms. "The question is, what's the best way to handle this?"

"Have Georgia call the protesting customers and apologize," said Scott.

Michelle snapped, "Not good enough."

Hoffman raised his hand. "Everyone, settle down. Georgia, how do you feel we should handle this?"

Too flustered, too angry, too outnumbered, Georgia felt besieged. "Do whatever you need to do, Mr. Hoffman." She looked at Michelle. "I'm sorry this caused you pain. I had so hoped the show would bring you more . . ."

She couldn't finish. Better to leave.

CHAPTER 43

Rudy grabbed Steve Burdette, stoned again, and plopped his young assistant into his office chair.

"Wipe that silly grin off your face, Burdette. What in hell is going on?"

"Nothing," Steve answered with slow-motion speech. "Same old shit."

"What are you on?"

Steve smirked. "What do you mean?"

"You heard me." Rudy pulled up a chair and sat in front of him. "You're going to screw up a good career, Steve."

Steve didn't respond, just slumped back in the chair and grinned. His hooded eyes and sallow skin were not compatible with his customary intelligent face and winsome smile. His wrinkled blue slacks and shirt looked and smelled as though he had slept in them for days.

Rudy got up and walked to the window. What to do? He knew Steve's parents had divorced when he started high school. From then on he lived with an aunt, then a grandmother, now deceased. If Rudy had to contact a family member he wouldn't know who it would be.

A family member. Funny. *I never did anything to cause my parents any grief. I went to church with them, did my chores, got good grades in school. After three daughters, my father was ecstatic about having a son. We did everything together—fishing, ball games, golf. All was well until they learned about my 'unmanliness' they called it. 'You're a disgrace,' they screamed, threw me out and slammed the door. They said they had no son.*

Rudy turned back to Steve. "Where are you getting that stuff?"

Steve giggled. "Why, you want some?"

Propelled by anger, Rudy lunged at Steve, pulled him up out of the chair. "You stupid shithead, are you listening to me? I'm trying to help you. If I let you walk out of here like this, you'll get fired." Rudy shoved him back in the chair. If he called the police or took him to a hospital, management would find out. He had the operator page Jesse.

Jesse answered in seconds and Rudy asked him to come to his office. "Any ideas about what we can do without throwing him to the wolves? I'd like to get him straightened out."

Jesse seemed undaunted. "He's been going down this road for some time. I guess the thing to do is take him home and let him sleep it off." Jesse said he'd drive to the loading dock and pick Steve up there. "No one will see us this time of day."

Rudy put him in a desk chair with wheels and rolled him across the display storage area and out to the dock.

"Did he tell you anything?" Jesse asked as they transferred him into the backseat of his car.

"Nothing. He's on the moon. Can you handle him?"

"Sure. I'll take it from here."

"I'd rather no one knows about this. I want to do a little investigating first. Okay?"

"Sure, boss," Jesse grinned, "this is just between us."

CHAPTER 44

"I've been calling Rudy every minute on the minute," Jean told Georgia. "He's not in his office and doesn't answer his page."

"Keep trying. Anything else?"

"Besides the usual parade of model hopefuls? Yes. Advertising says your newspaper column's due this morning. I'll get back to you about Rudy."

If I'm still working here.

In minutes, Jean was back, closed the door. "Gwen-Val Wray is here."

Georgia dropped her head. "Oh lord, bad news travels fast. Send her in."

Stunning in a moss green dress, Gwen came in clutching a tote bag. "Hope I'm not interrupting."

"No, no." Georgia guided her to the purple couch, eyed Gwen's tote bag. Has she received a bundle of hate mail too?

Gwen opened the bag. Georgia's chest tightened.

"I couldn't believe this," Gwen began, pulling out a large hardcover book. "*Emeralds: The Retail Jewel of the Midwest.* My folks gave it to me as a gift last week and I've read it cover to cover."

Georgia smiled. "An inspiring story. Reads like a novel, doesn't it?"

Gwen turned some pages. "This is what I wanted to show you. It's on . . . page 17." It was a group picture of young black men dressed in dark suits and white gloves. "Up here, in the second row, that's my great grandfather. He worked here as a porter. About 1913. Porters were assigned to carry ladies' packages to their carriage or trolley."

"Your great grandfather was handsome."

"Thank you." She turned more pages. "I liked this story about the jeweled clock. That's the one at the front entrance, right?"

"Right."

"My favorite story was about the organ during World War I, love this part: 'The store's founder had an organ put on the balcony overlooking the main floor, and every morning before the store opened, employees met there, and accompanied by the organ, sang the national anthem.' Sounds like this company has a lot of heart."

Both Angels and devils are hired here. Equal opportunity employer.

A shy tap on Georgia's door preceded Jean's entrance. "Mr. Hoffman called. He'd like to see you."

For three days since the black model ignominy, Georgia had dreaded this call. She didn't need this job to pay her rent, but she did need it. For what? To work under the scrutiny of Scott? To always fear the next move of Jesse or Stratley? To be shunned by the resentful Michelle? Or could it be that she was afraid of leaving the lady in orange and other Gwen-Val Wrays in their hands?

"Sorry, Gwen. Mr. Hoffman's the top brass."

At the door, Gwen paused. "Any shows coming up?"

Georgia hid her internal ache. "Sooner or later." She smiled at the lovely Gwen. "I'll keep in touch. Maybe we could have lunch one day."

"I'd love that."

On her way to Hoffman's office, Georgia bumped into Jesse Wiggins.

"Howdy, Miss Parker," he said with exaggerated graciousness. "Been hearing about the new model. Employing one of your own kind? Got your resume updated?"

She turned on her best synthetic smile. "Wouldn't you hate to see me leave? Think of all the fun you'd miss needling me."

"Maybe," he said, mounting the escalator. "Maybe not."

Struggling over whether to tell Rudy about Jesse's blackmail scheme, she decided not until the new stores were all opened. Rudy would have developed new talent. And, if not, he still had Steve to fall back on.

She stopped outside Hoffman's door. If enough pressure was put on management to fire her, even Mr. Hoffman would be forced to bend. So, who would prevail? The customer, of course.

"Mr. Hoffman will see you now, Georgia," Faith said. "I'll bring in coffee."

Hoffman greeted her warmly. *Maybe the news isn't too bad.* But when his secretary came in with a box of Kleenex, along with the coffee, her spirits fell. Did they expect she'd flood the room with tears after she was asked to resign?

"I might as well get right to the point," Hoffman said, gesturing to Georgia to sit. "The black model in the Windsor Country Club show ruffled a lot of feathers. I've been bombarded by customers, the Club, and my board of directors. A time-consuming mish-mosh. One, frankly, I could have done without."

"I'm sorry, sir."

"I've been reminded that Windsor is a private club and can set any rules it wants. I talked with Mrs. Farnsworth's husband. He suggested that we send his wife flowers, tell her we cherish her as a customer, and he'd take care of the rest. Oh, yes, he said, and I quote: 'Tell Miss Parker that the show was outstanding.' Any questions?" Hoffman reached for a tissue and blew his nose. "I think I've developed an allergy; I'm allergic to stupid controversy."

"I'm not fired?"

"Fired? When you dashed out of here the other day, I thought you were going to fire *us*. And that would be sad. You've been good for us, young lady. Your prediction that pants and pantsuits for women would be big was right on target, and we were well ahead of our competition. The hate mail we got regarding the black model was small compared to the positive response we got on your Big City Woman promotion. Your weekly newspaper column has developed a large readership and grow-ing. We also get good results from your television commercials. So our astute board needs to simmer down and weigh the facts."

"Your executive board is . . . upset?"

"Expected. Keep in mind that this is a business of big egos and aggressive personalities. These can be positive virtues in this competi-tive arena, but when they face someone who threatens their control, they'll do anything to eliminate the threat."

In other words, watch my back. "How can I be a threat? All my efforts are designed to help build their business."

"Absolutely, and in time they'll recognize the value of the Fashion office."

She knew it was Hoffman's policy not to pull rank if he could avoid it. "I'm glad Mrs. Farnsworth will be pacified."

Mr. Hoffman stood up. "And let's not upset the likes of her again."

"Yes, sir." At the door she stopped. She remembered when she was refused service at The Satin Bonnet. That's how Gwen-Val Wray would feel if we never used her again. "No."

"What?"

"I love my job and I love this store, but none of that is enough to make me be part of something in which I do not believe."

"Oh?"

"If I continue to use black models in places other than the Club,— and I intend to—will I have to be chastised every time?"

"You'll have to fight for what you believe."

"Fair enough."

Hoffman smiled. He held out his hand. "Welcome to the corporate world."

As she opened the door, Hoffman called after her. "I'd like to ask a favor—one I'm asking every department head. My son-in-law Paul will be leaving Peoples soon and coming to Emeralds. I'd appreciate your giving him as much help as possible while he's learning the business." Hoffman smiled. "He told me he was impressed with what you said at our dinner party about career dressing. He's looking forward to working with you."

CHAPTER 45

Georgia waved good morning to Jean. "Your hair is really getting long. Another two weeks and you'll look like Farrah Fawcett."

"That's my plan. Gwen Val-Wray called. She's on her way to Paris. Got a chance for a modeling job there. She promised to let you know her address."

"Wow. On my next trip abroad I'll make it a point to see her."

"Oh, Harry Ralston called twice. The accessory and cosmetic departments are on the brink of disaster if you don't call right away."

Georgia forgot her promise to call Ralston. He had indicated support for her career women's program. If she was to accomplish what Hoffman suggested, she should start lining up allies.

Georgia called. He wasn't in. She asked his secretary to set up a meeting at his convenience.

An hour later, Jean popped in again. "Want to go to lunch?"

"You betcha. I'm starved."

"Sorry," came a brash voice from the doorway. "Georgia has an appointment with me and I'm starved too." It was Ralston, in one of his glaring plaid jackets. "We'll have lunch and talk business. My car's right outside." He boldly led her out by the arm.

She felt uncomfortable being seen with him outside the store. He was well known as a "player" and his wife, Georgia had heard, turned the other way.

"Ever been to Madison's Lake? New place. Great food and overlooks a man-made lake. Fresh fish is flown in every day. He started the car. So, how are things going, gorgeous?"

"Fine."

"Like hell," he laughed. "Hear you got raked over the coals for using a nigger model. Bet you'll never do that again."

Bet I will.

At the restaurant, they were seated by a window with a pleasant view of the lake. She'd love to come here with Matt. She touched the necklace he gave her. Seven weeks and no word. She longed for his strong arms around her. *What if Matt came in here and saw me with this man?*

She ordered grilled salmon and went quickly to the subject of business. "You have ideas that would work with my plan for career women?"

"I do. Want a drink? I'm having one."

"No, thank you. What's your idea?"

He turned to the waiter. "Scotch and water." Ralston folded his arms on the table. "When you get that career board, how's about my hosiery department providing each member with a gift certificate for three pairs of hose, compliments of Harry?"

"You would do that?"

"Damn right. Who do you think buys my hosiery? Housewives? Hell, they wear a pair to church and out on Saturday night. I like that working girl." He winked. "And you know what else? I can get perfume gifts from my vendors. Could you use those?"

"Oh, yes. How many are we talking about?"

"How many do you want? Hundreds? And I'm not talking about those little vials on cards. I mean real purse-size perfume bottles. Maybe I can get a fragrance company to serve as a sponsor—pay for some advertising, supply gifts, and major door prizes in exchange for the exposure."

"That would be fabulous." His ideas were sound.

They talked with growing enthusiasm about merchandising for working women.

"Could one of your cosmetic companies provide experts to demonstrate proper makeup for the office?"

He took out a notebook. "Good idea."

"Like you, Scott heard my thoughts for the first time at Mr. Hoffman's dinner. It's on hold until I get Scott's approval."

"Just let me know."

All the way home he insisted on telling her about his illustrious retail career. "I was a toy buyer in Detroit, a coat buyer in Chicago, a hosiery buyer in Cleveland. And here I am—merchandising accessories and cosmetics in Omaha. I know retail inside and out."

Back at the store, they shook hands and Georgia thanked him for his support.

"Don't mention it, sweetheart. Call me anytime."

At home, Georgia's phone rang. She touched the receiver and sent up a little prayer that it was Matt. *This is what I used to do with Cliff.*

"Hello?"

It was Rudy. "Doing anything?"

"No, what are you doing?"

"Cleaning closets."

"Oh, oh. Something's bugging you. Want to come over?"

"Be there in a jiffy." He arrived in less than thirty minutes.

"What's up?" she asked.

"Wish I knew."

"Interesting answer. Hungry?"

"No. Yes. What have you got?"

"I can make a turkey sandwich and give you a piece of sweet potato pie. My father's cook, brings me something whenever she visits Omaha. It's fabulous."

Georgia watched him eat. He looked great in his royal blue sweatshirt. His usually serene face, however, looked drawn tonight.

Rudy sighed. "Display things are disappearing."

"What kind of things?"

"Well, for one, the giant Raggedy Andy doll."

"Any clues?"

"None. We've checked all the stores. No one's seen Andy."

"Just like a guy to wander off. What else?"

"Two artificial palm trees. Gone."

"Not things someone can stuff into a pocket."

"Exactly," he said. "Good sandwich."

She cut the pie. "Somebody's stealing them."

"Absolutely. But who? And why?" Rudy got off of his stool at the kitchen bar and walked to the pie. "I'll help myself. Join me?"

"Sure."

"Can't accuse anyone without proof." He took a bite. "This is fabulous."

"I told you. So, what's next?"

"Not sure. Plenty of losses from shoplifting, but our greatest losses, Security says, are from internal thievery."

"You suspect anyone?"

"Lots of people work in display, in stockrooms, on the dock, but I'm having problems with Steve's drinking or getting stoned. I wonder where he's getting money for his high living. He just bought an expensive watch and some high-end stereo equipment."

"Who told you that?"

"Jesse."

"Have you seen those things?"

"No."

"You have proof Steve bought that stuff?

Rudy grew thoughtful. "No. But where would he hock that stuff?"

"Let's go sit in comfortable chairs." Georgia lead the way with the pie and served him another hefty slice.

"Thanks, love. What's new with the Captain?"

Georgia slumped down into her chair. "Nothing. You were right. I've gotten involved with another man with unpredictable traveling schedules."

"I wonder . . ." He took a hefty bite.

"You wonder?"

"It didn't take me long to see the selfish side of Cliff. And just as quickly, I saw Matt as a standup guy. Matt's not the type that would give gifts to women and break up, like you said."

"Maybe not. After Matt said Diana broke up with *him*, I had a different fear."

"Like what?"

"That he's not over Diana. He never told me about her. I had told him everything about me."

"Everything? How is it you guys dated for two years and he's not met your father?"

"I don't owe you an explanation," she snapped.

"No you don't, but you sure do owe yourself one."

"Damn you, Ascot. You came here to talk about your missing merchandise. Let's stick with that."

She rushed to the kitchen and came back with a large sheet of foil, wrapped the remaining pie and handed it to him. "Go." She pushed him towards the front door. "Go stuff your face and leave me to think."

"Why are you kicking me out?"

"I want to think things through."

"Really? Maybe you feared he'd reject you after he met your father, so you grabbed onto this Diana nonsense as an excuse to avoid that humiliation?"

"What?" She nudged him. "Go home."

He threw his head back and laughed.

"What's so funny?"

"This is the first time I've ever been thrown out of a woman's apartment."

In seconds she joined him in laughter. "You nut." She kissed his cheek and shut the door.

Can Rudy be right? I love Matt. So, why did I behave as I did? She replayed what her life had been like with Matt—a constant source of humor, sweetness, consideration. Would such a sensitive man be so insensitive as to reject her because of her father?

After three days, she called the base. "May I leave a message for Captain Matt Fields?"

"Hold on, please." He returned. "Diana? His aide said to tell you he's running late but is on his way."

CHAPTER 46

Georgia stood, barely breathing. Matt was back in town and on his way to Diana. "Oh, God. I've lost him."

The phone rang.

By now Matt's with Diana. Still dazed, and ignoring the ringing phone, she retreated to her bedroom suite. She glanced towards her veranda, and recalled standing out there for hours, agonizing about Cliff. *I'm not going to do that again.*

The phone rang again. Stopped.

She dropped into a chair and put her hand over Matt's Valentine necklace. *I love him. I can't lose him.*

The phone rang. She answered. "Hello?"

It was Rudy. "I've called three times. Why didn't you answer?"

"What do you want?"

"Alfredo called." Rudy sounded euphoric. "Alfredo said he can't wait to get here. He gave me a shopping list of groceries. He's going to cook dinner for me."

That's probably what Matt is doing right now—cooking dinner with the Castinos. Tears now were unstoppable.

"Georgia? You crying?"

"Oh, Rudy. . . ." Somehow she managed to tell him about her call to Matt's base.

"Oh, lord. Shall I come over?"

"No. I'm shattered. Why did this happen? How can I go to work tomorrow?"

Rudy sighed. "Things are not always what they seem. I read something once I never forgot. 'Don't despair. But if you must, work on in despair.' That's helped me through some tough stuff. Did you hear me?"

"Yes. And I think it's stupid."

"I did too at first. It works. Just try it."

Alfredo's appearance at Emeralds garnered huge attention. It reinforced what Georgia had been urging Scott to consider—a young designer department. Michelle's Designer Salon continued to cater to the older woman of leisure, and their numbers were diminishing.

The local press gave a great deal of space to Alfredo. He was fashion's new glamour boy—attractive and eloquent. But most notable, he was turning out creations loved by famous young women—socialites and entertainment celebrities were wearing Alfredo.

Rudy called. "Georgia, get down here. These customers are meeting a fashion star for the first time and are going nuts."

She walked into the packed Salon unnoticed.

One customer after another requested, "Alfredo, would you select the pieces best suited for me? Alfredo, will you autograph my sales slip?" And one sultry redhead snuggled up to him asking, "Am I more appealing in an Alfredo?" She reminded Georgia of Diana snuggling up to Matt.

"Michelle," another young customer called out from a dressing room. "Ask Alfredo to come in here? I need his advice."

"Brazen hussy," Michelle mumbled, but obliged

Alfredo was gracious to everyone, and visibly pleased when he recognized Georgia wearing one of his favorite pieces. "Look at you," he exclaimed, spinning her around, then insisted that she model her pink Alfredo suit for the customers present.

The formidable Michelle watched Georgia model with the coolness she had shown when they first met. Even worse, Michelle grew rigid as Georgia approached her to say hello.

Later, Georgia whispered to Rudy, who had been hanging around for most of the day. "Michelle won't speak to me."

"She's harboring misplaced anger. Her business, aside from today, has been lousy. She blames you and the country club issue. She was on a downslide long before that."

"Nevertheless," Georgia whispered, "I'll try to help if she'll let me."

"While we're whispering, when are you going to call Matt?"

"Are you crazy?"

"Tell me you don't love him."

She glared. "Stop it, Rudy."

"Which is it, lady? Yes or no?"

"Let go of my arm."

"Okay. Can you let go?"

She looked away.

"You've given up smiling, and started slumping, kid. Go after your man, Georgia. He's worth it."

The next stop for Alfredo was Kansas City, and Rudy took off a couple of days to accompany him.

When Rudy returned, he came over for dinner, and together, they made a cheese fondue. They initiated the new glass-top table and turquoise upholstered chairs Rudy had selected for her kitchen. Later Georgia served chocolate fondue with fruit in her study.

At dinner they had chatted about the successful Kansas City reaction to Alfredo's creations. "What's next for you and Alfredo?"

Rudy squirmed. "First things first, love. The store's executive board has put the vote for your vice presidency back on the agenda."

"I didn't know it was ever actually on."

"Well, it was. Then it was off—after BC, Black Controversy—they tabled it. But noting your remarkable successes, they had no excuse, and Hoffman told them, in his most charming way, stop screwing around."

Georgia smiled. "You don't suppose they learned Sears was looking for a national fashion director and contacted me?"

"Of course."

Georgia shook her head. "I can't imagine Emeralds board accepting me."

"They can't afford to lose you to Sears. They'll vote on you at next month's meeting. It'll go well."

"And with Alfredo? Did that go well?"

"Very well. This is highly confidential."

"Cross my heart," Georgia promised with gesture.

"You know I've always wanted to go to New York and design school. Alfredo wants me to move in with him and he'll arrange for me to attend Parson's School of Design. I'm not planning to become a fashion designer, per se, but Alfredo feels I need to know about garment construction, fabric manipulation, things like that. So when I'm working with him I'll be knowledgeable."

She wanted to be happy for Rudy, but something was holding her back. "You're right at the top of your field here, Rudy. Everyone loves you, respects your talent. You're going to walk away on the chance you'll get to work with Alfredo?" After having said that, she felt ashamed, but couldn't dispel her fear that Rudy and Alfredo were worlds apart, and that might make Rudy's dream crumble.

Rudy shook his head. "I've thought this through carefully. Alfredo wouldn't ask me if he didn't really want me."

Georgia sighed. "Why don't you just take a leave of absence?"

"I'm going. Mr. Hoffman is out of town, but next Monday I'll tell him. I'll stay to organize things, turn over the reins, and leave by the end of the year."

"Who will take over?"

"Jesse. He's proved he can do the job."

"But what about all that missing merchandise?"

Rudy shrugged. "Scott said not to worry about it."

That didn't smell right to Georgia.

Rudy took a sip of coffee. "Tell me, what's what with Matt?"

"So many times I went to the phone to call him and stopped."

"Understandable. Got another slogan for you. Be a risk taker."

"Who wrote that one?"

"I did. That's what I'm doing. Nothing comes with a guarantee, love. If you take a calculated risk, at least you're giving yourself a chance."

She ruffled his curly hair. "What's going on in that fiery-red head of yours?"

"I can't believe Matt is out of your life. You still wear his necklace. You've never taken it off, have you?"

"No."

"You love him, Georgia. Tell him."

CHAPTER 47

While in the shower, Georgia looked down at Matt's necklace, gleaming like crystal. The water sounded like music as it bounced against the tile walls. Matt loved music, loved to dance, and she recalled how deeply touched he was by the love songs played at their Valentine dinner. Water mingled with tears. Not with sorrow this time, but a revelation.

What's been holding me back? Pride? Fear of rejection? Win or lose. I need to know. And if I have to grovel, I'll do that too.

Still wet, she slipped into a terry cloth robe and dialed Matt's apartment. She let it ring six times. No answer. She'd try later.

She dialed her father's office.

"This is a surprise. Anything wrong?"

"No, Dad. Got a minute?"

"Yes."

"You told me once how Mom came to you in tears after you broke up with her. She said she didn't care what people thought."

"Right. Because she loved me."

"How did you feel about her coming to you?"

"I had never been so happy in my life. Giving her up was torture. If she hadn't come, I might have been stupid enough to let her slip away."

"Oh, Dad. That's just what I needed to hear. Wish me luck."

Georgia called Matt's apartment again. No answer. She tried the Base at the special number he had given her. "Would you ask Captain Matthew Fields to call Georgia? It's important."

She waited for two days. No call.

Georgia called Rudy for help. She walked around her bedroom as far as her phone cord permitted. "Matt's not at home. My messages left at the base haven't been returned. You said I should call him."

A long silence.

"Rudy?"

"I'm thinking."

"Well, think out loud."

"I think . . . I have a thought. Give me time. Okay?"

The following day, after a long, tedious meeting with Scott, fraught with bitter resistance, he finally granted Georgia the go-ahead for a career board.

Georgia recognized a rare opportunity. "Mr. Scott, we need the support of our area's leading firms, and no one has more clout than you to reach them."

Don't despair. But if you must, work on in despair. Rudy and his ridiculous slogan. And here I am doing it.

Rudy walked into her office. "How was your meeting with Scott?"

"Got a go ahead for the Career Board."

"Fabulous." He found a Tootsie Roll. "Regarding Matt, I made one call, but a good one. It'll take a little time. But it's doable."

She hugged him. "What will I do without you?"

"Damn well. You'll have Matt. Hold that thought."

For the spring Career Night, the board members received modeling lessons from the Fashion Office. For the show, each member was fitted in fashions guided by their desired price points and company's dress code.

Three board members from the leading twenty companies Scott had contacted, were black women. *How about that, Mr. Scott? Did you tell those three prominent companies that you don't like their choices?*

The turnout for Career Night was spectacular. With live music and special lighting the energetic show was magic. During a major scene with new ideas for office attire—still career correct, but a bit more feminine—Georgia's commentary asked, "Where is it written that a woman can't make a good executive decision unless she's dressed like a man?" The audience cheered.

Management joined the applause. They seemed convinced that major change was eminent, bringing potential rewards for the savvy fashion retailer.

The enthusiastic crowd voted not only with their applause but with their wallets. The final sales tally indicated a thirty percent increase over any comparable Saturday.

Georgia received notes of congratulations from buyers, merchandisers, and even clerks. Nothing from Scott.

Jean came into Georgia's office. "Got a minute?"

"Sure. What's up?"

"Our new girl."

"Hollie's not working out?"

"She wants to take her lunch hour when General Hospital's on. And she gets upset if she doesn't get home in time for Wheel of Fortune."

Georgia chuckled. "So, what's your wish?"

"We desperately need a competent person or two in this office—and quick."

"Scott says no budget increase. To take anything more out of our existing budget will cripple us."

Jean groaned. "Like walking with one crutch for two broken legs."

Rudy dropped in. Georgia couldn't remember when he had looked so gloomy.

"What's wrong? Alfredo?"

"No. Everything's fine with us. Got some news about Matt."

"He hasn't been hurt?"

"No. He's fine. I think." He looked away. "My source said he's on leave."

"Where?"

"He's out of the country. And . . ."

"And?"

"Now, this is hardly fact, the call I got was almost inaudible. Static. Terrible connection."

"I'm going to kill you."

"I could barely hear but it sounded like somebody's ill, and then—it didn't make sense—something about . . . a wedding."

CHAPTER 48

Saturday morning, Georgia unlocked her office door and turned on the lights. A soothing stillness greeted her. She was alone. Rudy said he'd get more information regarding that inaudible message about Matt and call her at noon. Better to be here working than at home watching the clock.

What will life be without my best friend? And without Matt, this is no life at all.

"I saw you come in." It was Harry Ralston. "How you doing, babe?" He dropped into Rudy's gift chair. "What do you say we go tip a few?"

"Do what?"

"Go have a few drinks. And talk about your next big event. I did a good job for your last one, didn't I? What do you say?"

She wanted to give him a flat-out no, except she needed to be diplomatic. Ralston was an executive board member. He had definitely been helpful with the Career event. Still, title or no title, she wasn't going anywhere with this man. "Thanks, but I can't. Tons of work"

"Bullshit," he said, picking up one of her folders. "What's this? 'Window recommendations for August'? It's only May."

"We have to plan ahead."

"Listen, kid, you and I could do some exciting things around here." Georgia faked patience. "Harry, I need to work."

"One day it'll be yes. Know how I know? Remember when I sent you that note after your first big show?"

He had Georgia's attention. "The show where I put a dress on backwards?"

"Right. Next time I saw you, you gave me a nice smile. If not a yes, that was a maybe."

"I didn't know it was from you." *H for Harry. Damn. Why didn't I turn that card over?*

She stood up to show him out, but he grabbed her and kissed her hard on the mouth. She pressed her hands against his chest, but he was immovable.

Michelle was standing in the doorway. "I see you two are tied up."

Ralston made a quick exit. He left a shaken Georgia facing a disgusted-looking Michelle.

"I didn't expect to find you here," Michelle began, "I came to slip this note under your door."

"Please come in," Georgia urged.

"No," she said, all ice.

"Let me explain—"

Michelle was gone.

Desperate to explain, she headed for the Designer Salon.

A blank-faced woman, with arms folded, was leaning against the walnut arch to the Designer Salon.

"Is Michelle here?"

"No," the blank face said, with complete indifference. "She went to the stockroom or somewhere."

Georgia searched the stockroom, then back to the Designer Salon. She hadn't returned.

Georgia went back to her office and picked up the phone. "Please page Michelle."

"What for? I'm right here." Michelle entered Georgia's office.

"What you saw, Michelle, wasn't at all-"

Michelle stopped her. "I know what I saw. And I know what happened. I didn't realize it until later."

"Realize . . . what?"

"I know that louse's reputation, and it's plain to see it wasn't your doing."

"How did you know?"

Michelle pointed. "For one thing, your outside door wasn't locked and this door to your office was wide open. Both would have been locked if you were involved in any hanky-panky."

Georgia smiled. "You'd make a good detective."

"I'd better make a good something." Michelle handed her an envelope. "I meant to leave this, but the little scene I happened on stopped me. It's . . . an apology. My behavior when Alfredo was here was unfair.

I guess . . . seeing you look so smashing in your Alfredo suit and all those sparkling young women clambering for his things made me, well, realize how out of step I am."

"Oh, Michelle."

"It frightens me that things are changing and maybe I'm too old to keep up."

"That's nonsense. I remember you buying specific things for specific customers and it worked. You can do the same thing for that younger, upscale customer. You found Alfredo, I didn't."

"I just went there to see what everyone was talking about. I wouldn't have brought in his trunk show if you and Rudy hadn't urged me. I didn't think he was for my department."

"Well, now you know."

Michelle's eyes brightened. "Did you take charm lessons from Vassar or from me?"

"From you, of course." Georgia had to restrain herself from hugging Michelle, who wasn't the hugging type. In her heart, Georgia hugged her anyway.

Michelle started to leave.

"Wait. This Harry Ralston thing might continue to be a nuisance. Any suggestions?"

"Everyone knows he squeezes his vendors for kickbacks. If they want more space, he'll go along—provided they grease his dirty palm. Same with women—if he does them a favor he expects payment. Be careful."

Georgia waited for Rudy's call. Noon moved into one before the phone rang.

"Got any Tootsie Rolls?"

"Gobs."

The moment Rudy arrived, she shut both doors. "Did you locate Matt?"

"Not putting out yet. Feed me first."

She pulled out a new bag of Tootsie Rolls and tossed it to him. "Knock yourself out."

"Thanks, love. Matt was out of town until last night."

"He's back?"

He opened the bag. "He's at his apartment."

"Rudy, you're wonderful," she exclaimed, as she grabbed her handbag and started for the door.

"Georgia. Wait. Call first."

She threw him a kiss and rushed to her car.

Outside Matt's apartment door, she hesitated, sent up a prayer, then knocked. No answer. She knocked again. This time she heard the click of a lock. A grey-haired woman stood there with a basket of cleaning supplies.

"I'm Bertha. The housekeeper. Captain Fields left. A bit late, but he'll make it."

"Late? Will he . . . make it?"

"To St. Margaret Mary's? Oh sure. It's only fifteen minutes away. Gonna be a fancy wedding. He was all spiffed up." She stepped outside the apartment and reached for her keys. "You a relative?"

"No . . . friend. Georgia Parker. He was in full-dress uniform?"

"No, ma'am. A tuxedo."

Georgia could only manage a nod and left.

She drove aimlessly. Back home? The office? For either, she was headed in the wrong direction. Didn't matter. Seems she had lost her way a long time ago.

How was it with Cliff? Feeling so unworthy she'd endured neglect and humiliation? And with Matt? She was the recipient of consideration, laughter and endearing gestures of love. Yet, what did she do? At what she deemed a misstep, she lashed out at the man she loved.

But perfect me kept the truth from people I pretended to trust.

As she approached a stop sign, she saw it. St. Margaret Mary's Church. The parking lot was packed. Several cars resorted to parking on the street. Georgia spotted an empty space and pulled in. She examined license plates for a clue about the bride and groom. Matt had Air Force buddies in Colorado. The Castinos spent time in warm climates. Nothing. Most plates were from Nebraska.

In a hypnotic state, she followed the others inside.

"Aren't you going to sign the book?" a formally dressed usher asked.

Georgia looked over her shoulder. "Oh . . . guess I missed it." She signed the book "Jackie Onassis" and was escorted to a seat in the last row.

The chapel's aisle was lavishly decorated with red roses, frothy tulle and satin streamers. She noted that the male guests wore dark business suits. But Matt, the housekeeper said, wore a tuxedo. Of course. It's his wedding.

Was that Diana's mother being seated in the front row? In a lavender lace gown and radiant suntan, Georgia recognized Mrs. Castino.

The organ's ethereal sound announced the bridal procession—bridesmaids with groomsmen, flower girls, ring bearer. The guests stood for the bride's entrance.

Escorted by her father, it was Diana Castino.

Georgia contemplated escape. No way was she going to see this marriage performed. By the time everyone was seated again, she noted the wedding attendants were below the alter—bridesmaids set apart from the maid-of-honor, groomsmen from the best man. The redheaded bride and *blond* groom were on the alter.

Something between a squeal and a yelp escaped Georgia's throat and tears touched her flushed face. More than a dozen people looked in her direction. A woman sitting next to her provided a handkerchief, put her arm around Georgia and whispered. "I cry at weddings too."

"He's the best man! The best man!"

The bewildered woman shrugged. "Well, yes, dear, I'm sure he is."

Georgia sniffled and smiled all through the wedding mass. The moment the recessional began, unable to halt her noisy sobs, she needed to get out. As Matt approached with the maid of honor on his arm, Georgia plunged to the floor.

The woman looked down. "Lose something?"

"Huh? I . . . dropped my watch." Georgia sat up, empty handed.

The woman blinked. "It's on your wrist."

"Oh." Georgia emitted a high-pitched giggle. "Well, I tried to wear it on the other wrist, and must have switched back. Silly me. Here's your hankie. Thanks so much. Sorry I'm so emotional. It's such a happy day. Excuse me." She climbed over legs and laps, with breathless apologies all the way.

Matt would be at the reception late, Georgia felt, so, she reached his apartment about eleven the next morning, Bertha the housekeeper was knocking on his door.

"Good morning, Miss Georgia. Nice to see you again." She nodded towards the tray she held. "Coffee. Black."

"May I deliver it? He loves surprises."

"Fine with me. Here." Bertha stepped aside.

Georgia touched his apartment door with a meek tap. Again.

"Bertha?" His voice sounded hoarse.

The lock clicked. Georgia shook.

Matt opened the door, rubbing his eyes. His hair was disheveled, as was his navy robe. With half-opened eyes, he looked at Georgia. "Oh, my God," he gurgled and kicked the door shut with a bare foot.

Georgia felt so limp she almost dropped the tray. She looked for Bertha and saw her at another door with her key. "Bertha. Help. He slammed the door on me."

Bertha took the tray, and looked at Georgia's moist eyes. "You wait here."

A snail minute after Bertha knocked, Matt responded. Georgia saw him look at Bertha and squint. "A minute ago you looked like . . . someone else."

"I was someone else. Why did you slam the door on that pretty girl?"

He blinked. "Who?"

"Georgia."

He groaned. "I thought I was hallucinating." He walked away.

Bertha signaled Georgia to follow her. She placed the tray on an end table, then whispered, "You take over from here, deary."

He had slumped into a living room chair. "You better go. I'm hung over."

She handed him a cup of coffee. "You must have had a great time last night."

"Yeah. Great. I had to dance with aunts and cousins and grandmothers. My feet are killing me. And stand back—my head is going to explode."

She wanted to laugh but resisted. He looked so pathetic she longed to crawl into his lap and kiss his dark-ringed eyes.

"Why are you here?"

She moved to the coffee pot. "I was in the neighborhood. Tell me about the wedding."

He watched her pour another cup. "A reunion of two longtime friends. Marty and I met during flight training. I had introduced him to Diana." He rubbed his forehead. "How did you know I was at a wedding?"

"Uh . . . Bertha told me. Matt. I've missed you."

He looked at her with a stern glare.

Georgia leaned against a table for support. "You were . . . gone so long."

"Tell me something I don't know."

She had never heard such a cold response from him. "You don't know . . . how sorry I am."

"About what?"

"I'm trying to tell you, but you sound as though you're ready to throw me out."

"I was considering it."

Georgia felt defeated. "Okay, but not until you hear me out."

He leaned back. Waited.

Faint heart never won . . . best man.

"I was hoping . . . when your tour of duty was over—"

"I called. You didn't call back."

Georgia's eyes widened. "You called?"

"Your home, your office. The girl said you were out."

"What girl?"

"Not Jean. Molly or Dolly, something like that."

Hollie. Damn her. "I never received your message."

"I left the following morning for Canada to see my mother. I called again when I came back. Same routine. Got Holly or Molly again. She said you were out of town. It began to sound as though—if *he* calls tell him I'm not available."

"You called twice?"

"I'm going to bed."

"Matt, wait. Please. Why did you call?"

He shot her an astonished glance. "Why indeed." He walked into his kitchen and poured a glass of water.

She followed. "I've made a mess of things. I had never been so happy as I was that Valentine's Day. That is, until I heard Diana say she never removed the bracelet you gave her. You had asked me to never take off the gift you gave me."

"After two years I thought you knew me. I guess I shouldn't be surprised. There was always a kind of barrier between us. You dodged discussing our future, avoided making a commitment, avoided introducing me to your father. Not sure I was good enough? Remember what I said that Valentine night? When I got back we needed to talk about where we're heading?"

"I remember. I know now, my world is nothing without you. Nothing."

"Really." He put his glass down. "You think you can hit me with a few sweet words and everything is okay? I can live without you, Georgia."

Her heart seemed to forget its job—to keep her breathing.

"But I'd rather not. I got drunk last night because of you."

"What?"

"I had wanted to take you to the wedding."

"Why?"

"Because I wouldn't have had to dance with all those non-dancers."

"What?"

"Will you stop with the whats and the whys? Because I wanted to be with the woman I loved."

"Oh, Matt. All I want is one lifetime to prove to you how much I love you." She rushed into his arms.

"That's not enough. What I had in mind was an eternity." He stepped back and held her in front of him.

"You're wearing it."

She touched his necklace. "I've never taken it off."

She moved back into his arms. "Thank you for loving me."

He took her hand and kissed her fingertips. "Now I need to meet your father. I'm an old fashioned guy and I want to ask him for your hand."

She froze. *I can't taint this beautiful moment. Tomorrow. I'll tell him tomorrow.*

CHAPTER 49

Because this was the morning Rudy was up in Mr. Hoffman's office submitting his resignation, Georgia was riddled with anxiety. The friend with whom she had shared every important aspect of her life since grade school would soon be gone.

Her gaze focused on the dish of Tootsie Rolls she always kept for him.

Like a curtain, her moist eyes blurred her vision. Sure, he had promised to keep in touch, but distance and life changes often smother promises.

Rudy said he'd call her immediately after the meeting. If her prayers reached the seventh floor, Mr. Hoffman would offer him a big incentive to stay.

"Georgia, line one," Jean said.

It was Matt. "Hi, gorgeous."

"Hi, handsome," she cooed. This call was a surprise since he had called her at six this morning to tell her he loved her and wished her a happy day. "Everything okay?"

"Never better. Just wanted to set up a dinner date with your father. I'll be off this weekend. How about going to our favorite restaurant? Would he like that?"

This weekend? And Sunday I leave for New York.

"That sounds . . . lovely. Will I get the pleasure of your company before this weekend?"

"Afraid not. I've been on leave for so long, I'm relieving the guys who covered for me."

"Why don't we save Friday night just for us, and meet with my dad Saturday?"

"Fine. And we have Sunday too."

"I leave for New York Sunday. The Fashion Directors meeting and I'm making a presentation."

"Damn. Well, we'll have to deal with separations. I love you."

After they said goodbye, she sat smiling, grateful that he had always looked upon her work with respect. And thankful she could tell Matt everything Friday night.

Jean buzzed again. "Georgia, line two."

It was Harry Ralston. "Hey, Georgia, I'm having a meeting in my office on how to improve our fashion mix and presentation. Could I trouble you to drop by? Sure could use your help."

No, you bastard. Not today or any day. Still, she knew she was trapped. Assisting all management was part of her job. And Ralston knew it. Refusing would give Scott good reason to vote against her. But, this might be a way to give the kick-back king a return on investment, since he was such a proponent of "I do you a favor, you do me one."

"What time's your meeting?"

"Two-thirty this afternoon."

"Okay. Your office, two-thirty."

At one o'clock Rudy called. "Meet me in ten minutes at Northrup's."

"Well? Tell me. Tell me."

"Every word at lunch."

Georgia was on time. Rudy wasn't.

"I sent Steve home in a cab, stoned again," Rudy grumbled when he joined her. "I saw in this morning's paper that street drugs coming into Omaha have escalated. Steve's obviously one of their good customers. Let's eat."

"Tell me quick," she urged. "What did Hoffman say?

"When we sit down. What did Matt say?"

"He loves me."

"Didn't I tell you? Bravo."

As soon as they took their lunch trays to a corner table, Rudy began his story. "Hoffman is a class act. He wished me well then offered me a fabulous raise. Even when I said no, he offered me a generous bonus— a going-away gift, he said."

Georgia sighed. "I hate to think of what happens to Emeralds when he retires."

"Ditto. I'll stay until December twenty-second. I want to spend Christmas with Alfredo. Time enough to train my replacement."

Georgia knew that one word about Jesse's harassment would eliminate him.

Rudy tapped her hand. "What are you thinking? You keep biting your lip as though you're telling your mouth not to say something."

She wasn't surprised that he noticed. Hadn't he always been able to read her? "I was thinking . . . of what might keep you from leaving."

"Give up, kiddo. I'm going."

Of course. And how dare she interfere with his life—something he wants so much. Jesse was her problem, not his.

She looked at her watch. "We've got a meeting with Ralston's division. You've been invited, haven't you?"

"No. Should I have been?"

"Yes, he wants to get his departments' fashion message out more effectively. That includes display."

"If I can get away, I'll drop by."

Georgia arrived at Ralston's office on time. She was the first one there.

"Come in, doll," he greeted, almost as loud as his plaid jacket and yellow dot tie.

Georgia blinked. Where in hell does he get those clothes? Not at Emeralds.

He pulled up a chair for her at a small table. It was covered with stacks of papers, totally in keeping with the rest of his messy office.

"Let me ask you something," he began. "If you say purple is going to be an important color, should we have every classification loaded with purple?"

"Heavens no. There should be a representation of purple. The customer should be able to go through the store and find choices of an important color or trend. It sends a strong message of what we believe in, and makes it easy for her to coordinate or update her wardrobe."

"And how will all the buyers know at the same time what the big color is going to be?"

His questions surprised her. "I address this at every fashion forecast meeting. All buyers and you get a copy of the information. The

Fashion office makes a recommendation of what the leading trend or color should be, then, buyers go to market, and make selections to support the store's fashion direction."

Georgia was getting impatient with questions about things he must already know. She looked at her watch. No one had arrived. "Where is everybody?"

He moved his chair closer to hers. "Look, doll, we're both grownups. I'm really turned on by you and we could have a lot of fun together." His husky voice was growing more intimate. "I'd do anything for you. I'm not going to mince words. I want to have a thing with you."

His seduction style was as offensive as his wardrobe. "You're not having a meeting, are you?"

"Sure I am," he said, with a crooked smile, "between you and me."

Georgia stood up. "Well, mister, meeting is adjourned." She pushed him aside. As she walked out, she ran into Rudy.

"Is the meeting over?"

"It's *all* over. I just lost one vote for vice president."

CHAPTER 50

Soon after Georgia left Ralston's office and returned to her own, Jean walked in looking bewildered. "Our support from the Accessory and Cosmetics Departments has dried up."

"Harry Ralston called you?"

"Yes. He said he'd have no more gifts or door prizes. What do you think's going on?"

"Never mind, we'll do fine without his support. Only this presents a problem regarding the report I've prepared on his division."

"Like what?"

"You know how tough it's been to accessorize a show?"

"All the time."

"A store that carries upscale ready-to-wear must have accessories to complement those clothes."

"Amen," Jean said. "Who wants a dumb handbag with an elegant suit."

"Emeralds has been upgrading to meet the growing demand for quality, but not accessories."

"And why don't we have more major fragrance and cosmetic lines?"

Because so many dollars, Georgia had learned, go where Ralston can buy cheap or get kick-backs. She couldn't tell this to Jean. Inside information was for management only.

Georgia looked at Jean's hair. "What do you call that color?"

"Autumn. It's a blend of brown, orange and gold. Interesting, isn't it?"

"When winter comes will Icicle Silver be the color of choice?"

Sharing her report with Scott wasn't easy. "Major labels in accessories and cosmetics are going to our competition," she said, "but I know they would love to be in Emeralds. We're strong in budget and moderate, but the better customer, whose numbers are growing, will soon go elsewhere."

"Just because they can't find expensive accessories here?" Scott barked.

"I didn't say expensive. I said better. Better quality. Better styling. The career woman wants to carry a gold pen, but doesn't want to take it out of a dowdy handbag."

Mr. Scott's secretary came into the office, handed him a file folder and left. He opened the door to his file room—a long, narrow area with a regiment of steel file cabinets along both walls. He was a meticulous pack rat, she had learned. Saved everything. He slipped the file into a drawer and returned to his desk.

Scott looked at the pages Georgia had given him about Ralston's area. "I'll review all this with Ralston."

As she walked out of Scott's office, Paul Stratley appeared. The sight of him produced a flash of nausea.

"Georgia! What a nice surprise. I've resigned my position at Peoples Savings & Loan and—"

"I've heard."

"I'm here to work with Scott. He's plotting out my training program." Paul leaned closer. "Can't wait to work with you. I know you can teach me a lot."

On Friday Rudy called Georgia to join him for lunch.

"Haven't got time to go out, but if you'd bring in some sandwiches I'll buy."

"No way. My treat. Thanks are not necessary. I know. I'm an angel."

The angel arrived with BLTs and Cokes, their favorite lunch.

"I'm leaving earlier than originally planned," Rudy announced. "Alfredo has found a larger apartment and wants me to help decorate."

"Oh, no. How much earlier?" Her original fear that this was a dangerous move loomed up again. *Keep your silly fears to yourself.* "How am I going to get inside information without you?"

"I'm not moving to Mars, just to New York. I brought you extra tomato for your sandwich, and if you eat it all gone I have chocolate chip cookies."

"These are the moments I'll miss the most."

His smile told her he shared her feelings.

Georgia looked into her Coke, as though she were reading tea leaves. "I saw Stratley today."

"Well, relax. He's going to work in Lincoln and then be assistant manager for our Lincoln stores. He won't be in Omaha much."

"Are you sure?"

"Have I ever given you wrong information? They plan to move him around—giving him a hands-on view of the business." Rudy looked at Georgia's untouched sandwich. "No cookies for you, young lady. By the way, the executive board will definitely cast their vote on your vice presidency next month. I'll still be here to celebrate with you."

"It doesn't matter. I'm dead. Harry Ralston will never vote yes."

"Ho, ho," he yelped, setting down his Coke. "You haven't heard. Ralston resigned this morning."

Georgia looked at Rudy with disbelief.

"If he hadn't resigned, he would have been fired."

"Resigned? Fired?" *Because of my report to Scott?*

"He had vendors send expensive gifts to his home plus fattening up his bank account. Scott keeps every document in a file room regarding his divisions." Rudy sipped his Coke. "Scott noticed reorders were given to unproductive vendors. Flashy-Jacket Ralston was caught. Ready for a cookie?"

"No, thanks, you just gave me a better dessert. Wait. The vote for board membership has to be unanimous, right?"

"Right."

"There's Scott. Nothing will change his mind."

Rudy shrugged. "We'll worry about that later. When is your New York Fashion Directors Meeting?"

"Monday. I'll be back Wednesday."

"Tonight's your date with Matt?"

"Yes, and I'm going to tell him about Dad. Tonight."

Friday evening, while waiting for Matt to arrive, Georgia caught a glimpse of herself in her hall mirror. Sparks of guilt ignited. Matt had often said he loved the gold in her hair and gleam in her black eyes.

"I get my eyes from my father. My mother was a blonde," she avoided mentioning her natural hair color. Half-truths had become the norm for her. "My father's parents were English," she had told Matt, with no mention of his black ancestor Joshua.

She had never lied to Matt. But the sin of omission loomed up now as an even greater lie. Tonight, the truth.

Do I deserve him? That I love him may be my only truth.

She had suggested that they dress casually and not do anything too pretentious.

"Got the perfect plan," he announced after a greeting kiss. "How about a drive-in movie with cold hot dogs and greasy popcorn? We won't like any of it, so there's nothing left to do but neck."

"I thought we weren't going to do anything pretentious."

"Got a better idea—a new little restaurant, family owned, excellent home-cooked food. And its only about two miles from here."

"Let's walk," Georgia suggested. "These sneakers were made for walking." They were both dressed in jeans—she with a short denim jacket, he in a blue shirt with rolled up sleeves.

They walked a mile, hand in hand. No need for words. The feel of his strong hand filled her heart. An occasional comment was shared about a beautiful linden tree, beds of red begonias, or white and pink impatiens encircling trees.

Matt was unusually quiet for most of the walk.

Suddenly, in hopes of provoking a response, Georgia took off her shoes and walked into the dew-kissed grass. It cooled her toes and tickled her soles. "Jump in, Captain. The grass's fine."

He smiled, seemingly enchanted with her child-like romp. "Too deep for me."

By the time she returned to his side, and hobbled along replacing her shoes, he took her arm and guided her across the street. "Just around the corner and we're there."

The place was dimly lighted. Quiet prevailed while diners chatted in intimate tones. From the menu pasted on a piece of board, Matt ordered beef stew for two, served in a soup terrain. Matt served. "This place is like a flashback to early American Salem. Like a set from *The Crucible.*"

Rustic wood furnishings, and waitresses in long dresses, white caps and aprons. Georgia could envision herself being dragged out to have her head and hands imprisoned in a public stockade for lying and deceiving.

She moved the stew around on her plate, only taking an occasional bite, forcing a smile and trying to find a way to discuss her father.

Matt put down his fork. "I had a short phone conversation with your father. He graciously accepted my invitation for dinner but I'm apprehensive."

"'Why?"

"He came across as having the same kind of veiled manner when I spoke of you as you had when you spoke of him."

"Really?"

"Yeah. Felt strange," then added, "but I think I've got a handle on this."

I better speak up. Now.

"I've been reviewing all the reasons we couldn't meet with him. He was out of town . . . working late . . had the flu. . . unexpected company. All convincing, at the time. But, during two years, did you ever mention that we were getting serious?"

"Of course I did."

"And what did you tell him about me?"

"Everything." She tilted her head. "I told him you were handsome, and tall. And loving. And funny. That you were a captain in the Air Force." Pause. "And that I love you." She dropped her gaze. "Matt. I'd like to explain—"

"No need. I already know."

"You . . . *know*?

He turned towards the fireplace surrounded by wooden rockers.

"Matt, look at me. I need for you to know—"

"I told you. I know." He took a bite. "Know how I figured out about your father? You had told him about how you felt about me. Right?"

"Right."

"Yet he's been too occupied to meet me. You, his only child, and he's not interested to meet the man in your life?"

"Oh, no. It wasn't like that."

"Not totally. There was a greater reason. Right?"

She clasped her hands, as though in prayer. "Please. Listen to me. I was afraid to tell you . . . I was afraid . . . I'd lose you."

He seemed surprised. "You'll only lose me if you don't stand by me."

"What?"

"If your father didn't think an officer in the Air Force was right for his daughter, would you or wouldn't you stand by me?"

"I don't understand."

"I think your father is a pacifist."

"A what?"

"Pacifist. You know how the hippie anti-war activists convinced even intelligent professionals, like your father, to embrace their ideology. Do you have any idea how harmful that was to the military and America's security? What's wrong with loving my country and committing to protect it?"

Georgia held her head in her hands. "Is that what you thought?"

"Yes. Am I right?"

She placed her napkin on the table. "Can we leave?"

He regarded her for a moment. "Sure."

The daylight was gone. And so was her courage. The air had cooled, and, seemingly, so had Matt. He hadn't taken her hand.

The boulevard was devoid of traffic. She pulled a blossom off a drooping branch, handed it to him. "Your boutonnière."

He sniffed the lilac blossom, then tucked it into his shirt's breast pocket.

She linked her arm in his. She tried to ignore that he felt rigid. She wished they were already at her apartment. Patience. Just a few blocks more.

"Matt, what you thought about my father was dead wrong." She stopped walking so she could see his eyes. "All those excuses about my elusive father were fabricated. Will you stand by *me*, when I tell you the real reason?"

"*Real* reason?"

Now she could see the lights tracing the curved driveway to her apartment building. "Do I look like Grace Kelly?"

"What in the hell are you talking about?"

"Well, do I?"

He stopped. "Georgia. You're scaring me."

"Do I look like Grace Kelly?"

He looked away. Looked back. "Well. Somewhat."

She was shaking. "My mother looked like Grace Kelly. I look like my mother. But, you know what? It's a miracle." She had planned to wait until they were in her apartment. But she couldn't stop. Hysteria had crept into her trembling voice. "Know why it's a miracle?" She felt tears were streaking her face like scars.

"My father's black." She watched Matt. Was that a stare or a glare? "Did you hear me? I'm black. I'm a fraud, Matt. A liar. A cheat. All smoke and mirrors. And I'm sorry, so sorry."

His gaze seemed beyond surprise. It was obviously shock and disbelief. And anger? If only she had waited as she had originally planned—sitting together on the comfortable couch in her study. She pulled away from him, ran to her apartment's walk, and looked over her shoulder. He hadn't followed her. She reached the elevator and looked back. He wasn't there. *I've done it again. Turned away from a problem before it was solved.*

The elevator came and the door opened. She stepped in. The door only half closed; Matt's foot stopped it. "You going to shut the elevator on me again?"

She gasped. "No. No, I just felt . . . I had to leave. I couldn't bear to watch you leave me."

As he stepped in, pushed the Up button, a man approached.

"Sorry, sir," Matt said, "this elevator is out of service." The door closed.

"You've forgiven me?"

"Hell no. I'm mad as hell."

"Then . . . why—"

"Because I need to tell you what's on my mind."

The elevator reached her floor and she pulled the key out of her pocket.

"No. I'm not coming in. We can talk out here."

"Why?"

"Because I'm not staying."

Georgia leaned against her door. If there was such a thing as a bleeding heart, hers seemed to be draining.

"We're on the threshold of being married, and at this late date you hit me with this about your father? Why in God's name hadn't you told me this long ago? What's more, when I think of your reaction to Diana and that damn bracelet I gave her. I didn't tell her to always wear it. She said it brought her luck—I introduced her to Marty."

"I'm . . . sorry."

"Sorry? Trust comes with the love territory, Georgia. Why don't you trust me?"

"I do. I do."

"Like hell. You thought I gave gifts to girls as a kiss-off. You didn't tell me about your father being black because, why? You were afraid I'd turn my back on you? Where's the trust, Georgia?"

Tears rimmed her eyes. Trust? After the brutal rejection in Mississippi, after Paul Stratley's assault, after her father's fears and denial about color? All this got buried deep inside her. And Cliff? But she's a grown woman now, blessed with the love of a good man. Why can't she trust?

"I guess one deception led to another. I've gotten so far away from the truth, I couldn't find my way back." *And all I do is cry.*

Matt lifted her chin, encouraging her to look straight at him. "My father was a major in the Air Force, my mother was a military nurse. I've been an Air Force brat from day one. I was raised with kids of every color in the rainbow. Your father being black doesn't shake me up. Your façade and lack of trust in me does."

He looked at her, as though waiting for her to speak.

She couldn't. *I've trusted where I shouldn't and failed to trust where I should.*

"Well, then. Goodnight."

Early Saturday morning Georgia paced around her bedroom. "Last night Matt didn't say goodbye," she said aloud. "He said goodnight. Okay then. Why shouldn't I call him?"

The moment he answered she blurted out, "Well? Where do we stand?"

"What?" He sounded drowsy.

"You left rather abruptly last night."

"So I did."

"Why?"

"Look, Georgia. It's only six a.m. I had a rough night trying to sort out things. I need sleep. I'll call you in a couple of hours."

"You need more than a couple. I'll see you at dinner tonight."

"No."

"No?" Breathing became laborious. He doesn't want to meet her father. He's walking away.

"I'll call and explain later." He hung up.

Georgia lost count of the number of cups of coffee she had. Still she poured another. She turned on the radio. Nothing on—it's Saturday. She walked out on her balcony. Perched on the railing was a cardinal, the first she had seen in ages. She stood very still, enchanted by its regal beauty. Amazing, she thought, how such a perfect creature exists in an imperfect world. She moved a bit closer. The bird tilted its head but didn't leave. *It trusts me. I wonder. What did it sense that created trust?*

The instant the doorbell rang, the bird flew away.

Georgia dashed to the door.

"Well, don't look so disappointed." It was Rudy. Remaining outside the door, he peaked in. "I'm sorry to interrupt, but—"

"Matt's not here."

"Then, may I come in?"

She stepped forward and hugged him. "How did you know I needed to see you?"

"Intuitive. Got coffee?"

"If there's any left."

"It's kind of fun seeing the elegant Georgia Parker in a tee, shorts and barefooted."

"You've seen me worse." She knew he would riddle her with questions about Matt, so as soon as she poured his coffee, she explained as best she could. "So, it seems that my delayed revelation about my father ended things for us."

Rudy looked stunned. "I can't believe I was that wrong about Matt. I could have sworn—"

"Me too. He cancelled dinner for tonight. He said he'd call me back to explain, but that was over three hours ago."

Rudy blinked. "Then who were you talking to? I tried to call you for hours and your line was busy. That's why I'm here. I need to talk to you." Pause. "Could a phone be off the hook?"

She ran to her bedroom. Rudy followed. "You were right, Rudy. Look. Oh, bless you. Her lips smacked his cheek. "Go finish your coffee. I'll call Matt and explain the phone problem."

Rudy set the receiver right, then took her hand. "First, let's go back to the kitchen. I'll tell you why I'm here, then leave."

They mounted the breakfast bar stools. Georgia waited, growing anxious while he refilled their cups.

"You leave for New York tomorrow morning and you'll be back Wednesday morning, right?"

"You didn't come here to tell me that."

"No, I came to tell you that I'm going too. I'll pick you up at seven tomorrow morning, unless you have other plans."

"That'll be great, but why are you going?" He's not leaving for good, she prayed. Not yet.

"I'm going to introduce Emeralds new display director to our resources and show him the ropes."

"Is it Jesse?"

"Yes. Nobody I interviewed held a candle to him. He's coming to New York Monday."

Georgia bit her lip. "So that's your big news?"

"No. The vote on your vice presidency has been moved up to this coming Wednesday. Hoffman had a conflict with the original date."

"Wait a minute, ole buddy. One shock wave at a time."

Rudy leaned over and kissed her cheek. "Go call Matt. I'm leaving."

She grabbed his arm. "I'll never understand how you get inside information. Will you ever tell me the name of your source?"

He tilted his head, and a puckish smile lit up his hazel eyes. "Some day."

The moment he left she rushed to the phone and dialed Matt. The line was busy. Ten minutes later she tried again. No answer. She walked out on the balcony to see if the cardinal had returned. No. The phone rang and she bumped into the glass door. She fumbled with the reluctant lock. By the time she reached the phone the ringing had stopped.

Why fall in love? Too much pain. But that silly thought disappeared the moment the phone rang and she heard Matt's voice.

"Who have you been talking to? Or did you take your receiver off the hook so I couldn't reach you? I know I was rude this morning, but it was a tough night for me. I apologize. Are you okay?"

"Now. Yes. Are you okay?"

"Now. Yes. I want to explain about tonight. I called your father last night."

"Why?"

"I wasn't sure if I did the right thing but as we talked I felt it was a good idea. We decided we needed to do some in-depth talking. Alone."

"Without me?"

"Yes. I'm going to Lincoln in a few minutes. We're having dinner at his house."

These two are going to decide my fate—without me?

"Remember, I leave tomorrow for New York."

"Do you need a ride to the airport?"

"No. Rudy is taking me."

"Oh. Okay. I'll call you after I get back tonight."

"Matt. I don't care how late it is. I'll wait for your call."

"I'll call."

Georgia packed for her trip, went for a walk, watched a movie, the news, another movie. When she pulled an afghan over her on the couch in her study, it was after midnight. The phone was on the end table. She checked the receiver twice to be sure it was secure. No call.

The need for sleep was pushing her eyelids shut. She dreamed Matt had taken her hand, brushed hair away from her face, and kissed her oh, so gently. "Georgia, I love you."

The sweetness of the dream made her smile. She dreamed he placed her arm across her waist, then kissed her hand. "You're the ultimate sleeping beauty," he whispered. "I want to remember you like this forever."

"Don't leave," she wanted to say, but no words came. Only a pleading moan-like sound. Slowly, she opened her eyes. He was here. Matt was kneeling beside the couch, stroking her hair, smiling down at her.

"Matt? You're here?"

"I'm here."

She touched him to be sure. Not a dream. The sweetness on his face made her heart seem to levitate. As he bent over her, she moved a strand of hair away from his eye, kissed him.

He lifted her and held her close.

"Oh, Matt. You're here."

"I needed to see you. After dinner, your father and I walked and talked almost to midnight, then I drove straight here."

"How did you get in?"

He reached in his pocket. "You gave me this key six months ago. Never needed to use it until now." He kissed the tip of her nose. "How beautiful you are. I'll miss you."

She held his face in her hands. "I'll only be gone a couple of days. How did things go with you and my father?"

His smile seemed forced. "Good. Good."

She sensed a reservation in his tone.

"At first glance," Matt said, "he kind of reminded me of Harry Belafonte He told me all about himself, his background, about your mother, about you."

"What about me?"

"Mississippi. Stratley. I understand a lot now."

"And my dad. How do you feel about . . . his being black?"

"Black? I didn't notice. He's a great guy. Anyone who gets a father-in-law like Dr. Parker—he made me call him Ben—is damn lucky."

Georgia's intuitive side was churning. "What does that mean? Did you ask him? I mean, like you wanted to?"

"Ask for his permission to marry you? I did."

"Oh, Matt. I knew you'd like him. When I get back we'll talk and make plans." She turned to the wall clock. "Six fifteen. Oh, Rudy's picking me up at seven."

"Go get ready. I'll wait and see you off."

CHAPTER 51

Georgia was glad to be home. Compared to the stores in New York, Emeralds looked almost as sophisticated. Riding down the escalator, and admiring the store's handsome displays, Georgia became aware of a man on the step behind her.

You know you want me. Paul Stratley's long-ago voice thundered in her mind.

"Hi, Georgia," the man said. "You look elegant as always."

She turned and faced Larry Lasondo, who merchandised all female fashions. "You startled me."

"I'm sorry. How was New York?

"Routine."

"Where you headed?"

"Store walk-through. I'll send you a report."

"Good. I value your input." He got off on the second floor and waved goodbye.

A sigh brought her back to center, but she needed fresh air. She got off on the main floor and stepped outside, alive with lunchtime shoppers. The rain had stopped, but customers' gear bore the refreshing fragrance of cool rain.

Two teen-aged black boys rushed out of the store, and right behind them were two store security guards. One guard bumped into Georgia and almost knocked her down.

The burly officers grabbed the boys and ordered them to open their jackets. The smallest boy hesitated, so the officer yanked the jacket's zipper and went through all the pockets. They also searched the other boy, found nothing.

A crowd had gathered. Georgia heard whispers and snickers, even laughter. She cringed. The boys' humiliation aroused her own, as though it had happened yesterday.

One officer escorted the boys back inside. The other, the one who had bumped into Georgia, approached her. "Hope I didn't hurt you, Miss Parker. Shoplifting is getting worse. Whenever we see colored kids in the store, we try to watch them, but hell, they're everywhere today. School's out for some teacher conference. You okay?"

"I'm fine." But she wasn't fine. Far from it. She feared incidents like this would escalate with Paul Stratley bringing his prejudice to the executive board. For such a scoundrel to have a high place with this fine company would be like a felon sitting on a judge's bench.

She followed them inside. "Wait."

"Yes, Miss Parker?" It was chief officer Hank Bladerton, often referred to as "The Blade" because of his harsh judgments.

She had no idea what she intended to say. Small, indecisive sounds emerged before she could translate them into words. "I wondered . . . what are you going to do with these boys?"

"Search them. Why do you ask?"

"You've already searched them."

"You have no idea how clever these people can be. They stuff merchandise in their clothes in ways you couldn't imagine."

Perhaps Bladerton was right. She shouldn't interfere. She apologized for detaining them.

Looking into the boys' faces, she saw the taller one was sweating and the smaller one had tears in his eyes. To avoid saying more, she hurried away, all the time looking back until they disappeared behind a door marked Private.

She made her walk-through of the fashion areas, taking note of what customers were looking for and what they were buying. Before she reached her floor, she spotted a young man below her on the Up escalator. He wore the store's security badge, traditional navy uniform, and a serious expression on his face. She got off and waited for him.

"Hi, I'm Georgia Parker, could you tell me—"

"I know who you are. My girl friend models for you sometimes. She says she's learning a lot from you."

"That's nice to hear."

"You started to ask me something?"

"The two young boys who were just brought in to be searched. Do you know anything about the outcome?"

He nodded. "I just stopped in there. They found nothing. They're clean."

Georgia sighed with relief. "Good. So they've been released."

He shrugged. "No, they're still there. Just between you and me, The Blade thinks he's an interrogator for homicide."

Without hesitation, she took the Down escalator, knocked once on the Private door, and walked in.

Bladerton, the older, larger man, was sitting behind the desk. The guard who had bumped into her was slouched in a chair clipping his fingernails. They were not only astonished to see her, but visibly annoyed.

Bladerton frowned. "You forget something, Miss Parker?"

She looked to her right and saw the two black boys sitting on folding chairs, clutching their jackets.

She walked up to Bladerton's desk. "You must be pleased that nothing was stolen."

"Tickled pink."

"Then they're free to go."

The officer's button eyes narrowed. "As soon as we finish the paper work."

Not a single sheet of paper was visible on his desk. In fact, there was nothing on it but a copy of Playboy, a jar of pencils and a small, cheap replica of the sculpture *The Thinker*, seated on a toilet.

"Why paperwork when they aren't guilty?"

Bladerton leaned back and folded his arms. "I've headed up this department for ten years. Would you say that gives me the right to tell you how to run your fashion office?"

"I think you owe these boys an apology."

Both officers snapped upright. "What?"

"You humiliated them outside in front of a crowd without provocation. You should apologize."

The two officers looked at each other and laughed. Bladerton tapped a pencil on the desk. "You sure are full of surprises, Miss Parker. Who would guess, after seeing you floating around here and on television, looking so pretty and lady-like, that you'd meddle into things that don't concern you."

The taller boy jumped up. "We don't need an apology, ma'am. We just want to go home. I made my high school basketball team. One bad mark and I'm out. I'm staying clean."

"I ain't never took nothin'," the smaller boy added. "We just came in to get out of the rain." Like a frightened little animal, his tear-filled eyes darted from one officer to the other. "We don't need no apology."

Bladerton smirked. "You see, Miss Parker, your interference is unwanted by everyone."

Georgia fixed her eyes hard on the senior officer. "Are they free to go?"

Bladerton's resentment contaminated the air like a smoke bomb. He broke his pencil in two, and turned towards the boys. "Get the hell out of here."

A magician couldn't have made them disappear faster.

Bladerton glared at Georgia. "Hard to figure why a classy lady like you is such a nigger lover." He picked up the phone. "If you'll excuse me, I'd like to be the first to tell the vice president of Operations my side of this story."

The Blade's boss is on the executive board. I'm dead.

CHAPTER 52

Wednesday morning Georgia told Jean to hold all calls. Except one from Matt. He had called her in New York, advising her he was TDY, but would definitely call Wednesday and wished her luck.

If Rudy had been correct, today she would be voted the first female vice president of Emeralds. That could make her a driving force in the Midwest's fastest growing chain of fashion department stores. Having arrived unscathed at this high place without undisclosed facts about her being discovered was nothing short of a miracle.

A barrage of "what ifs" stomped around in her head. Residuals of buried haunts gave power to her greatest fear. The first woman on the board, but a *black* woman?

Gratitude filled her being. Matt loved her. He had asked for her hand. They would make plans for their future. Isn't that what he said? Or was it I who said that? Georgia walked to the window. The day was as cloudy as her thoughts. After Matt's dinner with her father, hadn't he driven back to her, found her asleep on a couch, held her, kissed her, spoke of his deep love for her? *So, why do I doubt that we have a future together?*

She turned back to her spacious office. So different from her first dingy little office. When she joined the company, only the downtown flagship and Omaha's first major shopping mall were Emeralds. Today, eight years later, Emeralds had spread to five states with a total of thirteen stores. But expansion was occurring faster on the outside than on the inside, she had lamented. Management lagged when it came to fashion leadership. Oh, what a vision she had for Emeralds, if given the chance.

The phone rang. Hello?"

"It's just me," Jean said. "Rudy Ascot says he must see you right away."

"Good, tell him—" Georgia's office door flew open. "—to come right in." Rudy sauntered in and plopped down in the grey leather chair. "Morning, love," he grinned, digging into the silver candy dish on her desk. "All out of Tootsie Rolls?"

"Completely out," she said.

"Okay. I'll take my Tootsie Roll business elsewhere." He settled for her chocolate nonpareils.

Soon he would move to New York. *Maybe Rudy or Alfredo will have second thoughts?* She watched him pick up *Celeb* magazine and aimlessly thumb through the pages.

"What's up?"

"Huh? Well . . . hey, look at this—about celebrities we've lost so far in '77. Another version of how Elvis Presley died . . . why Maria Callas had a heart attack—"

She pulled the magazine away. "You know something. Tell me."

"I just learned that your tight-ass boss ordered a background check on you. I thought you ought to know."

"Thanks . . . I think." She sat and cupped her eyes with her palms. "I knew this was too good to be true."

Rudy pulled her hands away from her face. "You deserve a seat on that board, kiddo."

"After that background check, *kiddo*, deserving won't mean a thing." She picked up a pen, needing something to hold onto. "How did you find out about the background check? You're the display director, for God's sake. Your closest friends are plaster dummies."

"Please!" A patently false look of injury creased his face. "Mannequins, not dummies."

"Whatever. But those mute dolls don't tell you what's going on here."

Rudy softened his tone. "How do you feel?"

"Scared." Putting a label on her reaction to Rudy's news made Georgia realize how firmly the cold fingers of fear were clutching her. It wasn't that she might be denied the vice presidency, it was the reason she might not get it. "If they needed a background check, why not months ago, when they were considering me for the board? Why down at the wire?"

Rudy walked to the wall covered with glossy celebrity pictures, each autographed to Georgia. He straightened one frame. "Maybe they wanted to know more about you." He straightened another. "When did you get this one from Johnny Carson?"

"Are you changing the subject?"

"Sorry, love."

"I've been here eight years and they don't know me?"

"Who cared about your background when you were a model?"

His casually tossed hair and shy grin made him appear younger than his thirty years. Although they were the same age, she felt older.

"It's Mortimer Scott's last-ditch effort to keep women out of top management."

Georgia threw the pen across the desk. "How did I fall into such a great job and inherit such a paranoid boss?"

Rudy reflected. "Even if Scott learns about you, he wouldn't go near anything that smacks of color discrimination, not with the EEOC watching."

"The what?"

"The Equal Employment Opportunities Commission."

She emitted a deep groan. "Get real, boy. What Scott learns will intensify his plan to disqualify me."

"When is Georgia going to stand up for Georgia?"

"You advised me not to tell about my father until after the vote. Remember? Now when they find out they'll brand me a liar."

"How could you be a liar if no one asked you?" Rudy cleared his throat. "There's something else I'd better tell you."

"About the background check?"

"No, about Paul Stratley." Rudy shifted his eyes. "Nepotism has lifted its ugly head. He's up for the executive board."

Georgia stared at Rudy without seeing him. She saw only an apparition of Paul Stratley. She heard only Paul's voice. *Stop fighting, sweetheart, relax and enjoy it.* She shook her head. "But he's had so little retail training. How can he be qualified for Emeralds board? And, why now?"

"You're as pale as a ghost." Rudy put his arms around her. "I thought it best that you heard all this from me."

"I might as well face it, Rudy. I'm not going to make it." She moved to her couch.

Rudy followed. "If I may quote the great sage Yogi Berra 'It's not over until it's over.' Smart man."

"I had a confrontation with Bladerton." She revealed the story about the two black boys.

Rudy jumped up. "You didn't! Just before the board's vote? Jesus. Let me think." He paced. "Gotta go. Stay here. Don't talk to anyone."

The call from Hoffman's office didn't come until almost three. She'd miss Matt's call. "Jean, when Matt calls tell him I'll call him as soon as I return."

She stood outside the door of Hoffman's office, unable to open it. By chance, Faith appeared and beckoned her inside. Hoffman didn't wait for his secretary to bring Georgia into his inner office; he came out himself and escorted her in.

She felt encouraged by this gesture. Then, just as quickly, she was deflated. Scott was also there. He sat erect at Hoffman's conference table. Even though the other chairs were empty, Georgia envisioned them all filled with Mortimer Scott, each looking offensively smug.

On the table in front of Scott was a large manila envelope. The fact that he didn't smile meant nothing; he seldom smiled.

Hoffman pulled out a chair for her across from Scott and then took his place at the head. "Georgia, you know that the vote for a place on the Executive Board must be unanimous?"

She nodded.

"Well, I cancelled the vote when Mort here had a question he'd like answered. The final vote on your membership on our board will be next Friday."

He turned to Scott, indicating that the floor was his.

"I received this article in the mail," Scott said, pulling it out of the envelope. "This is the *Landing Courier* in Mississippi. Have you seen this?"

"Yes."

"This story vividly laments the loss of an important landmark." Scott's voice took on a dramatic tone. "Touching quotes from Landing citizens recalled generations of family members who owned keepsakes purchased from The Satin Bonnet."

Georgia made no comment.

"It also noted that the store's owner, Abigail Stone, following the merchandising strategy started by her grandmother, became famous for creating a prototype for the upscale specialty shop."

Georgia noted Hoffman looked pensive.

Scott turned to the second page. "This story also mentions that the culprit who set the fire and destroyed this fine store was never found." Scott adjusted his glasses. "It goes on to note the persistent rumor that a northern black girl passing as white destroyed valuable merchandise and then fled to the Midwest on the night of the fire." His words, cold and sharp, pierced her like icicles. "Remember any of that, Miss Parker?"

She pushed the pages of the newspaper article back towards him. "Stop," Georgia said, getting to her feet. "I've carried enough scars from all the things that happened to me when I was fifteen years old in Landing—things that have followed me around like I was . . . Jean Valjean in *Les Miserables*. And I didn't even steal a loaf of bread." She leaned across the table at Scott and glared down at him until he leaned backward, as though he feared she might strike him.

"I'm white. I have a father with dark skin, even though both of his parents were Caucasian. His skin color comes from a black great grand-father." Georgia straightened up. "Now, if that's a problem for you, Mr. Scott, you'll have to deal with it." She turned away from both of them and looked towards the windows. Don't cry, girl, she cautioned. Vice presidents don't cry. She sat down. "I can't remain silent about things I feel aren't right."

"Nor can I," Scott came back, expanding his chest.

Hoffman raised his hand as though he feared a fight would escalate. "Georgia, tell us your side of the story."

Without hesitation, she answered.

"They refused to serve me because of a rumor that I was black, I trashed some of the store's merchandise the day I left Landing."

"Go on," Hoffman said.

"My behavior was the irresponsible act of a sensitive fifteen-year-old. My father sent a check to Abigail—a very, very generous check—to cover the damage and cleanup and to apologize for my behavior."

"I've met Abigail Stone a time or two over the years," Hoffman began, moving from the conference table to a large leather chair. He motioned Scott and Georgia to move to the couch facing him.

They followed and sat rigidly at opposite ends.

Hoffman went on, "I remember Mrs. Stone as an elegant lady. Highly respected in the industry." He formed a steeple with his fingers. His eyes focused hard, first on Georgia, then Scott. "If Mrs. Stone did spread the rumor of Georgia's involvement in the fire, how did she explain Georgia accomplishing such a feat from an airplane bound for Nebraska? Mort?"

Georgia felt some relief. How could Scott have a valid response to that question? Maybe he'd regard this as a good try and let it go.

"That question came to my mind when Abigail told me the story," Scott responded smugly. "She agreed a fifteen-year old might not have acted alone." He turned towards Georgia with a gleeful look. Scott opened his manila envelope again and pulled out another document. "Abigail and I, wishing to get to the bottom of this, did some checking."

"What kind of checking?" Hoffman asked.

"A private investigator. We learned that Georgia's father, Dr. Benjamin Fredrick Parker, was offended by the treatment he received from a theatre employee and had him fired."

Had Jesse Wiggins fired? That's a lie.

"Also, Dr. Parker got so angry with Mrs. . . . ." He referred to his papers. "Mrs. Claude Barton for not allowing him in her house during her daughter's birthday party, he broke in and threatened to strike her. Also, we learned that he beat up Jon Roberts, son of Lincoln's leading surgeon, in fact, he almost killed him. We were told that a man as rich as Dr. Parker—and prone to temper outbursts—could pick up a phone and order a job of arson for a price."

"All lies! How dare you accuse my father of such things?"

"Now, calm down, Georgia," Hoffman urged.

Scott was undaunted. "Did your father not have a confrontation with a young usher at a movie theatre?"

"Yes, but he didn't—"

"Did your father enter the Barton residence uninvited?"

"Yes, but it wasn't—"

"Did your father beat up Dr. Roberts' son Jon?"

"Yes, but he didn't know—"

Interrupting her again, Scott turned to Hoffman. "Unless Miss Parker proves that she had no connection to The Satin Bonnet's fire, I cannot cast the confirming vote."

Georgia returned to her office and left a note on Jean's desk. "Gone for the day. Will call you at home to explain."

On her desk were two messages from Matt. One said he'd call her tonight. Just as she was leaving her office the phone rang. It was Rudy.

"Got some news. Not good. The V.P. of Operations heard from Bladerton about your interfering with the two black kids. Bladeton's boss is furious. Might be a lost vote. Anyway, we have until next Friday."

How does he already know that?

Georgia reached her apartment with thoughts so muddled she barely remembered the trip home. But once inside, her thoughts began to untangle. "Screw the vice presidency," she said aloud while changing into jeans. "I've got to do something."

She moved restlessly from room to room, turning over one idea after another and discarding them. A new resolve appeared. "Dammed if I'm going to walk away from the chance to be Emeralds first female vice president. Give Scott the satisfaction of shutting me out? Or that bigot Bladerton? And ditto Jesse Wiggins. And that degenerate Paul Stratley? Or forget about the disgraceful response to the beautiful black model at the country club show? And the lady in orange? How many women after me? No, damn it. No!"

Then, suddenly, a valid thought surfaced. With renewed energy, she made a phone call. It rang four times. No answer. "Pick up, please, pick up." She hung up. Waited ten minutes and tried again. This time he answered.

"Dad? I need your help."

CHAPTER 53

Georgia called Jean at home. "I need a favor."

"Sure. Shoot."

"This is personal so none of this can be done on company time. Here are a couple of calls I'd appreciate your making."

"Of course."

She felt no need to add that this was confidential. She knew she could trust Jean. "I won't be back until Monday."

"Okay, but be sure to be here Monday. Remember, Arthur Ashe will be here for Catalina. Mr. Hoffman wants you, and only you to handle this. What do I say about your absence?"

"I went home sick. And that's no lie."

Georgia and her father had talked strategy on the phone well after midnight. "Your idea's remarkable, Georgia. We'll find out what we can, and go with logic on the rest."

In the morning, Parker drove Georgia to the airport. At the departure gate, he handed her a small packet. "Everything I could find is in here. Review it during your flight. I'm proud of you."

Say you love me. "I want to succeed for . . . both of us."

He nodded, then came a smile so warm and loving and eyes gleaming with pride it was all she could do not to put her arms around him. *Why don't I?*

He hesitated, then left. Georgia didn't enter the plane until he was out of sight.

She also wanted to ask him more about his meeting with Matt. During the cab ride all their energies were focused on her mission. All he had time to say was that Matt was a fine man, so open and honest. They had a great man-to-man talk. He promised to tell her everything on her return.

She had sworn she'd never go back, but here she was—on her way to Landing, Mississippi. Too bad she hadn't thought of this plan long ago. Now time was against her.

If Georgia's flight had arrived on time, she would have had plenty of time to get to the county courthouse before the five o'clock closing. This was the only business day she had to accomplish her mission. Next week was the board's final vote on her, and she had to be back for Arthur Ashe on Monday. It was today or never.

I'll still be okay, she told herself, as she waited her turn at the car rental counter. "Georgia Parker. My secretary ordered a two-door. And I'm in a great hurry."

"Parker? Yes, here it is. We're all out of two-doors, but we have a four-door Buick. It'll cost more but—"

"Fine. I'll take it."

The counter girl wasn't sure she could make the change on the same contract and opted to start all over again.

Georgia screamed inwardly. It was three fifty-five when she drove out of the airport. "How far is it to downtown Oak Street?" she shouted to a car beside her at a stoplight.

"About thirty minutes. This is Friday traffic," a young man called out.

Thirty minutes! That would put her at the courthouse about four-twenty five. *I'll make it.*

Landing had grown considerably in the last fifteen years. She didn't remember much traffic back then, but, now traffic slowed to a maddening pace when she reached downtown.

"There's Oak Street," she noted. "But do I turn left or right?" Another glance at her watch. Four-forty. When the light turned green, she was in a left lane so she had to turn left. Scrutinizing the buildings on both sides of the street, she quickly realized—no courthouse here. As soon as she saw a break, she made a sweeping, illegal U-turn.

Back at the intersection, the light had turned red again. Four forty five. When she crossed the intersection, she saw the courthouse a block away on her right. The traffic crawled. She still had fifteen minutes before they closed the doors. If she got in under the wire, she might still be able to get the pertinent information she needed. Without it, this trip was wasted.

Four-fifty. Ten minutes might work if she could have pulled right into a parking spot. Cars lined the street on both sides. *Just leave the damn car and pay the traffic ticket.* A car pulled out right in front of the building, and she pulled in so fast, she barely missed hitting the car coming out. Four fifty-two.

The steps leading to the entrance were as steep as those climbed by Sylvester Stallone in *Rocky* and Georgia Parker climbed them almost as fast—propelled by her goal to stop Abigail Stone. Breathless, she asked a gray-haired man at the information desk where to find Permits and Inspections.

"Afternoon, ma'am. Take the elevator to the third floor. It's the second door on your right."

The elevator moved up so slowly, she feared it would stall. She checked her watch. Three minutes left. She jumped off at the third floor and, to her surprise, the door marked "Permits and Inspections" was open. She rushed in and quickly produced two documents from the packet her father had given her. "Could you help me with these? We obtained the lot, block, and addition of the property by phone this morning."

The young man behind the counter scratched his nose. "Yes, ma'am. This is fine. I'll have it all ready for you first thing Monday morning."

"No, no. I'm leaving Sunday. I've got to have it today."

He looked up at the big round clock on the wall. "We're closing, ma'am."

"Please," she begged. She touched his hand and looked pleadingly into his shy eyes. "I bet you could accomplish this little chore in no time."

He looked at her, mouth half opened. "I guess I can."

"Oh, thank you, thank you. Now, where is the County Assessor's office?"

"Across the hall."

"Thank you. I'll be right back." She dashed across the hall and opened the door as an elderly man with white hair and mustache, in a wrinkled white suit, and walking with a cane was approaching with his key in hand. "Sir, I know it's late, but I'm desperate. Could I delay you long enough to check the taxes on this property?" He hesitated.

"I need this information now. If you say no I don't know what I'll do."

He looked at her with scrutinizing silence. "I don't believe a word of that," he grunted, "but I have nowhere special to go. Have a seat."

CHAPTER 54

On Saturday morning, elegantly dressed in her latest taupe and peach Armani suit and carrying a taupe suede briefcase to match, Georgia walked into The Satin Bonnet.

"Good morning," a pretty young woman sang out. "I'm Jessica. Is there something special you'd like to see?"

"Yes. Abigail Stone." Just the sound of that name made Georgia's heart feel it might falter.

"Mrs. Stone stepped out for a few minutes. She should be back soon. Is she expecting you?"

"No. It's a surprise."

Jessica evidently approved of surprises. Besides, after scrutinizing Georgia from head to toe, she led her to Stone's office. Before Jessica left, she provided a porcelain pot of sweet tea.

Georgia glanced around the cozy room. The desk was antique white French provincial. Where Georgia was seated, two facing couches repeated the period look with white wood frames and pastel yellow linen upholstery. With the delicate fragrance of gardenias, and sunlight pouring in from French doors, the room looked more like a boudoir than an office.

Stay calm. Remember what the success of this mission will mean.

"Good morning." Abigail floated into the room with a glowing smile. She looked smaller than Georgia had remembered. Perfectly coiffed titian-brown hair framed an ageless face with milk-white skin and piercing blue eyes. Like many southern ladies, she chose a soft dress instead of a suit. In pale green floral print, her image was one of feminine elegance.

"Jessica told me a beautiful young woman was here to see me, and, I might add, beautifully dressed. Armani?"

"Yes."

"I'm Abigail Stone. And you are—?"

"Georgia Parker." Her heart felt like it was trying to beat its way out of a tortured place.

Abigail had extended her hand but pulled back. Her hospitality smile snapped into a frown. Abigail's tightened lips and glaring eyes hardly matched her delicate lady persona. Yet, when she spoke, her voice was the ultimate of poise. "What brings you here, Miss Parker?"

Watching Abigail calmly pouring and handing her a cup of tea was infuriating. "I have a business proposition for you," Georgia began, opening her briefcase.

"Really?" Stone lifted her teacup from the antique-white table between them.

"Your new store is beautiful. Clever of you to retain much of its old charm." Georgia pulled out an official-looking folder.

"Thank you. And what have you there?"

Georgia opened the folder. "According to the Permits and Inspections records, Worthington Construction applied for your building permit twice. The first was in the amount of three million dollars, to refurbish some of your store."

Stone smiled. "So? That's a matter of public record."

"Of course," Georgia said. "That permit, issued in 1961, was never acted upon." Georgia knew her information was sketchy. The rest would have to come from logic, as her father had said. *Can I do this?*

"Another permit was applied for six months later. This time for two million dollars."

"Smart business to get a better price," Abigail said, smiling sweetly.

"Very smart," Georgia responded, "if the reason wasn't because your debts exceeded your assets."

"I beg your pardon?"

"The repairs were never made because of lack of funds."

"What are you getting at?" Abigail's voice remained soft and even.

Time to take the big leap. "The building had fallen into disrepair," Georgia said, looking down at her folder as though it was filled with revealing documentation. "What if fire-inspection codes were not met?"

Abigail stood up. "This visit is over, Miss Parker."

"Are you going to show me the door again? I wouldn't do that if I were you."

"That's exactly what I'm going to do." She started for her office door.

"Anthony Worthington."

"What?" She turned back to face Georgia.

Did I see her flinch? "The president of Worthington Construction. He noted that it would be a better business move to tear down the old building and rebuild."

"You're hallucinating. There would be no such comment on record."

How do I cover my tracks with that? "Never mind where I got my information. It's a fact. Georgia opened another folder. "I had a nice chat with the County Assessor and it seems that taxes on the old building had been in arrears in 1959 and 1960 and had not been satisfied as of spring 1961. In fact, Mrs. Stone, not another grace period would be forthcoming. You were down to the wire."

"I am not going to dignify this situation by granting you another minute." Abigail continued to the door. "Good day, Miss Parker."

Georgia ignored the woman and began talking faster. "Then, suddenly, one night The Satin Bonnet goes up in flames and the fire department detects arson."

"That's right. You, Miss Parker, you and your black father sought revenge. It's amazing that you got away with it."

"No, Mrs. Stone, it's amazing that *you* got away with it," Georgia said, returning the folders to her briefcase. "Wasn't it fortunate that my little temper tantrum occurred in the presence of witnesses? Now you could blame your desperate act on someone else." Georgia had moved to the door and saw Abigail's face flush. "You burned down your own store."

Abigail laughed. "You're out of control."

"I'd say you were. You had it burned down for the insurance. And insurance paid you well for the building, merchandise, and business interruption."

"You're bluffing. What do you hope to gain by all this?"

"I want very little, actually," Georgia said, peering down at the woman who seemed totally unshaken. "I want you to tell Mortimer Scott that you had spread the rumor about me and my father being responsible for your fire, and that it was absolutely untrue."

"Never."

Georgia was undaunted. "I'm staying at the Barrington. I'll be there until noon tomorrow. My room number is 819. If I don't hear from you, it'll be my turn. I've gathered enough proof to do more than spread a nasty rumor." Georgia patted her briefcase. "Thanks for the tea."

Before she left, Georgia turned back, pulled an envelope out of her briefcase, and waved it. "Too bad you didn't give me more time. I wanted to tell you what some of your vendors told me—about late payments, or no payment."

Driving back to her hotel, Georgia's hands kept trembling, even though she tightened her grip on the steering wheel.

On Sunday, fearing to leave her hotel room even for a moment, Georgia waited for Abigail's call. She waited until ten after twelve. No call. She had to leave to catch the last flight to Omaha.

CHAPTER 55

She told her father the whole story about Abigail during their ride home from the airport. "The facts we uncovered were good, but the bluff failed. Hoffman said the board meeting will be Friday, and the vote on my proposed vice presidency would be final. So that's that."

Her father patted her hand. "Regardless of negative odds there's always the chance of victory. Watch your thought process."

"Meaning what?"

"Say you're in a row boat headed for an opposite shore. Your plan is to go straight to that shore. You come upon an obstruction—heavy floating logs, as far as you can see. What do you do? Stop? Turn back?"

"Find a way around them."

"Good. It's a long way around but doable."

She smiled. "You told me that when I was ten years old."

"Glad you haven't forgotten."

"I know my trip to New York and this thing with Abigail dropped into the middle of things, but I want to hear about your evening with Matt. I saw him before I left for New York and the night before Emeralds board meeting. He seems . . . different since his meeting with you."

"Different?"

"Yes, Dad. tell me what was said. All of it."

Parker reflected. "Well, we talked about our work, our devotion to what we do. We revealed our backgrounds, some of the tough times, some of the good."

"Did you talk about what relates to Matt and me?"

"I told him about your mother, how she died. I told him how devastating the loss was for you."

He's dodging my question. Something's happened.

"What part of Matt's meeting with you might have affected him?"

"I . . . don't know."

"He just keeps telling me he'll always love me, in a way, as though, I don't know, like he's going away or something. Did he tell you he wants to marry me? I mean, did he ask you for my hand?"

Her father smiled. "He asked if I felt he was the kind of man who could make you happy."

"And you said?"

"I said he was the kind of man who could make any woman happy."

"What kind of an answer was that?"

"He's a great guy, Georgia. I really like him."

"But?"

"Nothing. Except . . . I only wish his chosen field wasn't so dangerous. Or required him being gone so often."

"Really? I don't remember you being around too much. You worked day and night, traveled, always something urgent made you an absentee husband and father."

He sighed. "Your mother was miserable. And so were you. I just wanted him to reflect on the challenge of a wife and family and the toll it takes on everyone when separation and, in his case, danger are involved."

"How could you? I love that man. Do you think I'd accept a loveless safe marriage for Matt? Never. Never. You call him. Please, and tell him my happiness depends on spending my life with the man I love and tell him you give us your blessings."

She opened the car door the moment they reached Regal Towers. "Dad, Matt could make any woman happy, like you said, but I want it to be me."

She got out of the car, but turned back to her father. "Matt's job isn't dangerous. We're not at war."

As she entered her building, she noticed her father had waited until she was well inside before he drove off.

Georgia picked up her mail—only three pieces of advertisements it appeared—and headed for the elevator. The house manager was holding the elevator door for her. "There's a nice surprise waiting for you in your apartment, Miss Parker. Welcome home."

After only a few seconds, she guessed what the awaiting surprise must be. Riding up in the elevator she speculated on the delivery and the doorman's wink. *Matt's here! It's so like him to do something cute like that. He's here waiting for me.* With anxious fingers she unlocked her door and ran in. "Matt?"

She hurried from room to room and finally reached the kitchen. There, near windows admitting a generous shaft of sunlight, was a huge vase holding two dozen red roses. The card read, "To the most wonderful woman in the world. My love will be with you always. Matt."

There it was again. That sound of . . . goodbye?

She took off her suit jacket, hung it up, replaced her gloves and briefcase to their original place and fell into a chair in her study, holding Matt's card. *What does he mean? Where can I reach him? The florist. Of course. The name's on the card.*

"Yes, I remember him. Nice fellow. He made me promise I would include only my best roses. He wrote his card, paid me in cash."

"No address?"

"No, ma'am."

But he was in Omaha. And why send me flowers and not come to see me?

All of the ideas she examined fell short of reality. Perhaps she should review her meeting with Mrs. Stone. What other steps could she take? Useless. The board meeting coming up so soon will end it all.

The mail. Why not look at that? Where did she leave it? Georgia looked in every place she had been since returning to her apartment.

Oh, well. It was only three or four envelopes, and all looked like bills or advertising. They'll show up. And if not, I know I'll receive duplicates.

Despite her logic about the mail, she couldn't envision a clarification about Matt's note and flowers. Matt had recently met with her father. All seemed to go well. Was the color issue over or was she assuming too much?

CHAPTER 56

Jean signaled Georgia for a phone call on "Line one."

"Miss Parker?"

"Yes."

"This is Abigail Stone."

Georgia hoped she wasn't hallucinating. "Mrs. Stone?"

"Yes. I will make this brief. I take great exception to the accusations you made in my office Saturday. I have nothing to apologize for. However, in the interest of avoiding further confrontations, I agree never to use your name again in association with the Bonnet's fire."

"Nor my father's name," Georgia added.

Abigail's annoyed sigh was very audible. "Nor your father's."

Georgia tapped a pen on her desk. "Not good enough."

"What?"

"I need all that in writing. Also, Mr. Scott told me that you and he hired a private investigator. I want whoever is responsible for the distorted information to rescind all the accusations against me and my father. Send one copy of the letter to Mr. Scott, one to Mr. Hoffman, and one to me. The letters must be here before Friday." Georgia said all this in one breath, not daring to pause.

"Absolutely not. And I'll not be ordered around by the likes of you," came Abigail's quick response.

"Then I'll have no choice but to pursue my plan."

"That's blackmail!" Abigail shouted, raising her voice for the first time, and hung up.

Damn. That bluff didn't work, either. Georgia had no time to reflect on what to do. Jean had stepped in.

"The Catalina show is ready to go. One o'clock on the second floor. But you have to meet with Mr. Ashe and Larry Lasondo in the executive dining room at eleven forty-five. Lunch and briefing. Go. Oh. One more thing. At three this afternoon you have to be at the TV station to tape three commercials."

The day flew, but the next three were agony. She hadn't heard one word from Matt after his flowers. Her calls to him hit a dead end.

Friday came and no mail from Abigail.

Jean walked into Georgia's office shortly after ten. "Sorry. Nothing from Abigail."

The phone rang at eleven. "Tell whoever it is I'm busy."

Jean answered the call, then popped back into Georgia's office. "It was Mr. Hoffman. I said you'd be right up." As Georgia headed out, Jean shouted, "Tell them you'll wear pantsuits and change your name to George."

Georgia attempted a chuckle but failed. Too defeated. Not just because of the vote, but mostly regarding Matt. Why all this mystery? If it's over between us, why doesn't he just say so?. *I'm in that damn row boat . . . got to get around the obstruction. But how?*

Hoffman welcomed Georgia into his office. "We just finished our meeting, Georgia." He walked over and put his hands on her shoulders. "You're in for a lot of work, young lady." With a warm smile, he held out his hand. "Congratulations, Miss Parker. You're Emeralds first female vice president."

"But . . . how? I mean . . . did Mr. Scott—?"

"Confirm you? Oh, yes. He got a letter from Abigail Stone—and I got a copy. Seems she had been misled by unreliable sources, and that you were not responsible for her fire. She had also been misinformed about your father."

This was unbelievable. What about Bladerton's boss? He had a vote. "Was every board member present?"

"Oh, yes. No, I take that back. Our vice president of Operations was absent. Had an emergency call with some problem in our Des Moines store. One has to be present to vote, you know."

I wonder who orchestrated that. "Thank you, Mr. Hoffman. I'll do everything I can to justify your faith in me."

He smiled. "I've always known that."

Georgia needed to be alone with her thoughts. The fire escape. She sat down on a step. Just moments ago she was aglow with victory. The victory was still there but not the glow. She longed for Matt more at this moment than she could have imagined. How glorious it would have been to share the good news of her victory with the man she loves, to tell him every detail of how The Satin Bonnet had impacted her life. She could see him smile when she told him about how she mentally battled obstacles from an imaginary row boat.

Matt declares he loves me, but his goodnight kiss Sunday and his words of endearment sounded as though he's . . . what? Been diagnosed with cancer? Going to die? Could the answer be with the discussion Matt had with her father? Her father being black hadn't disturbed Matt, but what if her father's reference to Matt's work-related absenteeism and danger was enough to push him away?

She stood up. *I don't need anymore what-ifs in my life. If I have to get out of the damn row boat and swim, I'll do it.*

CHAPTER 57

1980

The new decade meant only one thing to Georgia—she had reached it without Matt. Time heals everything? So far, time had done nothing but magnify the enormity of her loss.

Rudy, on the other hand, had found Utopia. Georgia glanced at the gossip tabloid Jean had left on her desk. Along with a picture of Rudy and Alfredo, was the provocative headline: "Who is Rudy Ascot? Seen everywhere with New York's hottest fashion designer Alfredo." Georgia read on: 'Has hot fashion designer Alfredo dumped famous model Maurice of *Gentleman's Quarterly* for unknown Rudy Ascot as his latest *assistant?*"

Later, Jean rang Georgia. "Guess who's calling from New York? Line two. "

"We're not hiring any skinny red-headed male models," Georgia said into the phone.

"That's no way to talk to a vice president."

Georgia's smile segued to a squeal. "Oh, Rudy! Vice president of Alfredo, Inc.?"

"How about that? The story of my appointment will be in *Women's Wear Daily* tomorrow. I'm happier than I've ever been in my life. When you coming to New York?"

"Not until the end of the month. Will you be there?"

"Probably. The launching of Alfredo's new perfume and fashion accessories, together with next season's fashion collection, drained him. We're leaving for a two-week vacation on the French Riviera."

"Great," she said. "I'll call before I come."

"I want to hear about you."

"Well, my office staff has been increased to a whopping five."

"At last," he said. "Emeralds has what—eighteen stores?"

"Yep. In six states."

"How are you covering all that?"

"Barely, I have coordinators in the bigger cities, but with increased responsibilities here, we're in about the same shape as before. Not complaining. This heavy schedule has been a blessing."

"Seeing anyone?"

"No."

"And Jesse? How's he behaving?"

"His work is excellent. To his credit, he's not giving me any trouble."

"I can't believe you waited until I left to tell me what he was doing to you."

"I had my reasons." After they said goodbye, Georgia recalled Jesse's long-ago threat. "The higher you climb the harder you'll fall." She shuddered. Would he reveal that incriminating picture of her and Stratley?

Three weeks later Georgia called Rudy. "How was the Riviera?"

"Rotten."

"What happened?"

"Alfredo's sick. Very sick."

"Has he seen a doctor?"

"Several. They're unsure. It may be cancer."

"Oh, God."

"We haven't told the press, but they're speculating something's wrong. Everyone in the fashion industry is deeply concerned."

Three days later Rudy called Georgia. "It's not cancer."

"Thank God."

Rudy's voice quivered. "It's far worse."

"What could be worse?"

"I don't understand it completely. They're just beginning to discover cases in Los Angeles and New York. They said it's a disease that attacks the immune system and little is known about how to treat it."

"Oh, Rudy, I'm so sorry."

Seven months later, Rudy reported that the glamorous Alfredo was nothing more than a shadow of himself. Then, early one morning, Rudy called her at home. He was sobbing. Alfredo was dead.

"Oh, God, I'll be there on the next plane."

"No. Don't come. There'll be no funeral. He'll be cremated. He died of pneumonia."

"I don't feel right not being with you. Please let me come."

"Thanks, love, but it wouldn't be fair to you. There's so much that has to be done. Shipments of the current collection have yet to go out and decisions about what to do about next season—"

"Can't you find another designer and use the Alfredo name?"

"Maybe. I don't know. Right now, I don't care."

Georgia learned two months later why Rudy didn't care.

"They didn't even have a name for what killed Alfredo, but they're calling it AIDS. I guess it's contagious, sexually transmitted." He dropped his voice almost to a whisper. "I'm sick. Don't come. All our friends have fled. No one came to see Alfredo, and no one is coming near me, either."

"Any chance your family has had a change of heart?"

"A family that had disowned me long ago? Do you think they'll rally around me now? Funny, for years I tried to hide my being gay, but no one has caused me greater pain than my own family. They probably believe I got what I deserved."

Georgia went weak with anger and grief. *Greatest pain from his own family? Why am I thinking of my father right now?*

265

CHAPTER 58

Just before Georgia was to leave for her New York business trip, Jean came into her office. "This just arrived. Marked confidential."

"Good heavens, Jean. You're a blonde again."

"Need to be. I haven't been having much fun lately."

When Jean left, Georgia opened the large manila envelope. "Damn. Damn it to hell!" It was an enlarged picture of her and Stratley from Jesse. It had a note attached. "Suitable for framing." Georgia groaned. *You aren't kidding, buster.*

She started to tear it, but felt that wouldn't be safe. Even if she tore it up, someone might piece it together. Nor was she going to carry it with her. What if she dropped it?

She had to leave for the airport. She rummaged through her desk and found matches left over from Jean's birthday party. She lit the corner of the picture and watched the flames devour the ugly sight, until the fire's tongue came too close to her fingers. She dropped it into her wastebasket. When she felt sure it was burned, she grabbed her coat, handbag and luggage and locked her office door.

The severity of Rudy's illness was apparent before Georgia was admitted to his hospital room. She saw it in the face of the aide who dispensed a disposable gown, mask and gloves. Georgia walked quietly into the dim room where her beloved, once-vibrant friend lay like a ghost. His beautiful hazel eyes, always so mischievous, were sunken and glassy. Several minutes passed before she could speak. "I'm here, Rudy."

"Don't expect me to take you dancing."

"Oh, heck."

He managed a weak smile. "We had fun as kids." He closed his eyes as though trying to recapture old memories.

Taking his gray hand, she tried to sound cheerful. "Remember our first Halloween? We were about the same size then. We traded costumes and fooled everybody. I intended to be Dorothy from *The Wizard of Oz.*

And you were to be—?"

"The Scarecrow."

"Right. With my wig you made a lovely Dorothy. You were prettier than I was back then."

"Still am."

Keeping him from hearing her cry was a struggle. *Oh, God, Rudy, who will make me laugh now? Matt could and he's gone. If you leave me . . .*

His dinner of chicken broth arrived, but he was asleep.

She looked with disbelief at this ravaged man. He opened his eyes. "As always, Rudy, you're late for dinner."

On her way to the hospital the following morning, she bought music tapes, a tape player, and books of poetry. At a florist, she ordered fresh flowers delivered to his room daily. For the next three days, she fed him, read poetry, and played soothing music.

His room was stark and foreboding—a private room in an isolated area. It was as though he had already been removed from life.

Each night, when she reached her hotel room, she prayed for sleep. It was always too late to return calls received from her office. Finally, on the third day, she called.

Jean answered. "At last. Did you get my messages?"

"Yes, but I've had my hands full with Rudy. What's going on?"

"We've had an . . . accident."

"What kind?" She heard Jean's deep sigh.

"A fire. It happened the night you left."

"Where?"

"It started in your waste basket. Your pretty office was scorched."

A spark must have caught onto something in the basket when she burned Jesse's infamous picture. "Did they get it under control?"

"Yes, but your office is a mess. There's lots of smoke and water damage to merchandise on the selling floor too. Mr. Scott is livid. When he was here inspecting the damage, I heard him tell the store's attorney that this isn't the first time you've been involved with a store fire."

A call to Mr. Scott's office told Georgia he wouldn't be back until Monday. His secretary was gone, so she left word with the store's operator.

Georgia's market week began five days after she arrived in New York. She attended meetings, covered resources with Emeralds buyers, and met with Larry Lasondo and private label developers.

"I'd like to see Rudy," Larry told Georgia, "but . . . maybe it's better to remember him as he was."

Every day, Georgia went directly to the hospital, got into her gown, mask and gloves, and stayed with Rudy as long as permitted. She called Rudy's parents, urging them to give him this last moment of peace. "If he could see you, even for a moment—" Click. They didn't come. No one came. If she left now he'd be totally alone.

She would not lose the chance to say goodbye to Rudy. *I didn't have that chance when Matt dropped out of my life. Nor to my mother. Why must the three dearest people in my life leave me?*

One day Rudy asked her, "Don't you have a job?"

"I'll get there when I get there." She tried to make small talk. "Can you believe I've worked at Emeralds for ten years?"

"How old are you?"

"Almost thirty-three. You want to hear a story?"

"Like stories." His voice was a whisper.

"Customer service used to be a top priority," she said, fluffing his pillows. "Service is disappearing. The perfect metaphor for that is in the mannequins we have now. Remember those beautiful life-like ones you bought when I shopped with you? Now we have headless, legless body forms."

He closed his eyes and Georgia almost dozed off in a chair when she heard him say "What else?"

"Well, we're doing fewer fashion shows. No more in school gyms and church basements. Only gala benefits and in-store events."

"What else?"

"Jesse and Steve are still working together."

She offered him a sip of water. He refused it.

"What else?"

"Display things are still disappearing. Remember?"

He nodded. "Stores here . . . things stolen." His eyes opened. "Check packing slips. Freight bills. Pink and blue. And weight." He closed his eyes again. "If I had known . . ."

Georgia listened to his laborious breathing.

He opened his eyes. "Let's . . . have lunch." His words were halted but somehow stronger. "BLT and Coke."

At first she thought he was hallucinating, but he turned his head towards her. "Our favorite lunch."

She went to the nurse's station and gave the order.

"He can't eat that," the nurse protested.

"I know. Just order it."

The nurse reached for the phone. "I'll have to get permission."

Georgia put her hand on top of the nurse's. "Please. Order it."

The sandwiches and Cokes arrived. Georgia slid Rudy's serving table across his lap and turned up the head of his bed. She spread out the food.

"Thanks, love." He looked at the BLT and Coke, smiled and closed his eyes.

It was over.

CHAPTER 59

Rudy's body was cremated. A total of three weeks in New York working and watching her best friend let go of life left Georgia with the greatest loneliness she had ever known. Soon after her plane landed in Omaha, she dragged her luggage, and weary self into the Fashion Office. No one was in sight.

A faint smell of smoke still hung over the area. She turned towards her personal office. The door was not only closed, but sealed with duct tape. A sickening flutter started inside her. She could almost hear Scott giving the order to shut her out. The vision of everything in her lovely office scorched was sad, but if the leather chair Rudy gave her was destroyed it would be unbearable.

"Georgia." It was Jean, with her arms full of mail. "Welcome home . . . such as it is."

"Is it really awful?"

"Not good, but if you don't mind a dull office for a while, I've moved out of mine. I've already moved the other girls in together."

Georgia nodded.

"I hate to bring it up," Jean said, "but Scott said he wants to see you as soon as you arrive."

"I expected as much. I'm on my way."

Jean put her arms around her. "I'm so sorry about Rudy."

On her way to the seventh floor, Georgia rehearsed—as she had on the plane—what she'd say to Scott. Actually, she felt she owed him and the store an apology for the fire started in her wastebasket. And, while she was at it, even though he had been so nasty about it, she'd thank him for the extra time off to be with Rudy. She knew he'd be hostile, but at least she'd do the right thing.

"Well, here at last," Scott said, in his best sardonic tone. "I'll make this short and to the point."

Georgia indicated she wanted to speak, but he stopped her by raising his omnipotent voice. "In view of the neglect of your responsibilities and irresponsible damage to company property, I should ask for your resignation."

The man who never smiled is smiling? He's enjoying this. He's found a way to get rid of me.

He paused long enough for Georgia to speak, but her words wouldn't come. Scott looked like Henry the Eighth—a mountain of fat in elegant attire. Off with your head, girl.

"I will delay taking final action until Mr. Hoffman returns from vacation. That's Friday, in time for our executive board meeting. We'll deal with you then."

Emeralds executive board met to discuss the first quarter. Trying to stay focused on business, Georgia struggled now, as she had all week with how she would defend herself when Scott put her on trial. Most of the board members were nice enough people, but they pandered to Scott. Except Larry Lasondo. He pandered to no one.

Georgia had called him after her confrontation with Scott to ask his advice. "Mr. Lasondo is home sick, Miss Parker," his secretary told her. "I don't expect him back until next week."

Her strongest ally absent. But Mr. Hoffman would be there. He certainly would see the truth in all this.

Everyone was carrying coffee and pastry to their seats when Georgia arrived at the meeting. As Faith handed her coffee, Georgia noticed Hoffman wasn't present. "His plane is late," Faith said. "If he can, he'll be here."

Georgia found an empty chair at the long conference table. Sitting directly across from her was Paul Stratley. Oh, God. Lasondo absent. Hoffman absent. What a wonderful opportunity for Stratley and Scott to devour her.

Scott began. "It appears that 1980 had a good start," Scott said. "And the new stores we added put us over the top. This year will be a challenge. Any bright ideas?"

The new Accessory and Cosmetics divisional, who replaced Harry Ralston, put up his hand. "Several celebrities have created or endorsed numerous accessories. I wonder if we could have more of those names in ready-to-wear."

Ralston's replacement was a much younger man. He knew about big names endorsing scarves, handbags, and hosiery. Signature accessories sold well, but he lacked knowledge of ready-to-wear. Larry Lasondo had shared his thoughts about this with Georgia. This may not be a good time to enter into a controversy, but with Lasondo absent, she felt she'd better speak up. She lifted her hand.

"Larry Lasondo mentioned often he was disenchanted with such offerings," she began. "He said John Travolta's line of casual wear sold for a short time, but had no staying power. Same with Johnny Carson Men's Apparel. And the flack the store faced with Jane Fonda's workout clothes angered some of our customers and made the papers. Lasondo found celebrity offerings not worthwhile."

Mr. Scott stiffened, then, with a demeaning grin, asked Georgia if she had anything better to suggest.

"I do have an idea, but there's something I need to share with you first." Out of the corner of her eye, she could see Stratley lean forward. She took a deep breath and turned to her boss.

"Mr. Scott, I want to thank you for permitting me to spend time with my dying friend, Rudy Ascot." She turned to the others. "You know what a remarkable contribution he made here. His artistic influence is seen in every store." They all nodded. She turned back to Scott. "I want to extend my deepest apology for my office fire."

"Enough of that," Scott barked. "Let's stick to the subject. We have a busy agenda to cover."

"I know, sir, but one more thing." Now she turned to the entire group. "The fire in my office was an accident. I tossed a burnt object into my waste basket. If any damage is not covered by insurance I feel obligated to pay for it."

A buzz of appreciation encircled Georgia. Paul looked at her with what she felt was amusement, at least he was smiling.

Scott turned a glaring shade of red. "One question, Miss Parker. Are you in the habit of burning papers in your office?"

"No."

"Could it be that you feared something incriminating would be uncovered?"

Georgia stirred under Scott's condemning glare. "It had nothing to do with company business."

Scott produced a half smile. "Well, then, to alleviate any doubt in our minds, perhaps you'd be kind enough to tell us what it was that required burning on store property before you left town?"

Oh, God. I've trapped myself. Without thinking, she looked at Paul. "I apologized and I—"

"Apology accepted." It was Hoffman. He had slipped in unnoticed. "Sorry I'm late." He took his seat at the table. "Did I miss anything important?"

"No," Scott said. "We were just trying to get some ideas from the group."

"Georgia was about to share an idea with us," Paul said.

What's he trying to do? Make points with me?

"Good," Hoffman said. "Let's hear it."

Not to appear to be gloating, she addressed her comment directly to Scott. "I agree with our accessory DMM, celebrities are a draw. I'd like to see us bring in someone who could make the cash register ring throughout the store."

"Like who?" Scott asked.

"Like Sheri Lewis and her puppet Lamb Chop for our children's area. That would pack the store with people. When children come, so do entire families. And if we had a storewide sale event at the same time it could be a real winner."

Scott said he'd pass that along to Special Events.

At this point Hoffman took the floor. "I have an announcement to make. That is, unless you have something you'd like to say first, Mort."

Scott threw down his pen. "No."

"Thank you, Mort. Well, I've been considering closing this huge store for some time. It's a monster to keep filled with merchandise and even harder to bring people downtown." Hoffman rubbed his eyes. "It's a sad time in Emeralds history. This was the first store, and for some time, the only store. With eighteen now. It's important to discard those that are unprofitable. Our bottom line is good." He smiled. "Seems the only time we really make money in this business is when we open a store or close one."

Hoffman announced that a press release would go out in June and the closeout sale would begin in July. "Everyone needs to get busy buying closeouts, over-runs, and promotional goods. We can mark these down drastically and they'll walk out. When the merchandise is gone, we'll sell fixtures. Any questions?"

"Yes," Georgia asked, "what will happen to that beautiful Emeralds symbol—the big clock?"

Hoffman shrugged. "I haven't gotten that far yet."

Preston McCarty, the V.P. in charge of Store Operations and Security expressed his concern about the problem of internal theft. "Missing property continues to plague the Display Department. I've talked to Jesse. He's very cooperative. As you might remember, things of value in that department began to disappear when Rudy Ascot was here. He left right after some major losses."

Georgia felt her face flush with anger. *Was he inferring that Rudy was responsible?* Scott had told Rudy not to worry about it.

Georgia had no doubt that McCarty was still smoldering from her demand that Bladerton apologize to two black boys wrongly accused of shoplifting. She also knew McCarty was incensed that his absence deprived him of a vote to keep her off the board.

As Georgia left the meeting, she saw Scott and McCarty off in a corner, talking in hushed tones. One way or another, she sensed, they'd find a way to eradicate her.

CHAPTER 60

Georgia returned from an exhausting ten days abroad. "The best part was the Hotel Crillon on the Place de la Concorde in Paris," she told her staff. "I had a beautiful suite, with fresh flowers and breakfast in my room. All the rest was grueling, including fighting rude crowds at every show."

"Did you see Gwen Val-Wray?"

"Yes. She was in tears. She said she loved modeling but the pay was too meager."

Jean asked, "Did she ask for a raise?"

"She did. And they said she was receiving the limit and she should get a lover like other models have done."

"Are you kidding?" the staff responded almost as one voice.

"No. I bought her a ticket and she flew to New York with me, where we both agreed she should try. So, what's new here?"

"Rudy's being blamed for display merchandise that disappeared before he left Emeralds," Jean reported. "Idiotic gossip."

"How dare they. Emeralds never had a more honest, devoted employee."

Scott called at four and Georgia worked very late reporting the details of her private label trip abroad. Scott was in his usual admonishing mood. Perhaps even worse since his failure to get her to resign or fired.

"You people better be sure of what you're doing. We've almost doubled the budget for this endeavor."

"Well, with a dress buyer and two sportswear buyers along, Lasondo and I had excellent input on what private label items they felt would sell."

Scott looked at his watch. "I had no idea it was so late. I was due to pick up Mrs. Scott ten minutes ago. Stay and finish the proposed plan. My secretary will let you out."

His secretary looked unhappy when Scott left. "I assume you'll be a while," she said, observing the papers spread on the conference table. "I need to pick up my mother. Just shut the door when you leave."

Georgia was alone. The file room. Maybe that's where she would find some answers to what was going on with the losses in Display.

"Check the packing slips," Rudy had told her, "pink and blue."

She had to grab this opportunity. She opened the outer office door to be sure no one was in the hall. As she gathered her papers together, she saw Scott's briefcase on the floor.

Georgia tried the file room door. It was unlocked. She ran her hand along the inside wall and found a light switch. Rows of steel gray files, all four-drawers high, lined both sides of the long room. Scott was well known as a pack rat.

A careful glance at several drawers indicated that everything was categorized by department, and the top drawer showed the latest date. She read on until she located Display. The top drawer was dated 1977-1980. Perfect.

Georgia opened the drawer. She thumbed through the file tabs to find 1977. Next, she found files labeled Orders, Invoices, Packing slips, Freight bills. That's it. Rudy had mentioned packing slips and freight bills. She pulled out two files—pink packing slips and blue freight bills. She took both and headed for the conference table.

All the slips were filed by month, but since she had no idea which month, she knew she'd have to check page by page. All of this would take time. She did remember, however, Rudy telling her about four display items that disappeared—the huge Raggedy Andy doll, two palm trees and, later, a baby elephant and a treasure chest.

She heard something. Footsteps. She froze. She heard a key in Mr. Scott's outside office door.

Move, damn it, move! She grabbed the folders and dashed into the file room, closed the door, praying it wouldn't squeak. Whoever was there had yet to open Scott's inner office door.

She crouched against the back wall, clutching the folders. Oh, no. She had forgotten to turn off lights.

Unable to move, she waited. She could hear some movement. Was fear playing tricks on her? No. The file room's door handle moved. The light under the door had been seen. *I've lost my chance to clear Rudy.* She covered her mouth to suppress even the sound of her breath. How could she explain why she was here? She was transfixed by the door moving.

I've buried myself this time. In disbelief, she watched the door open only wide enough for a man's arm to reach in, lift his hand to the wall switch and snap off the light. It was Scott. She recognized his huge gold ring. She heard another light switch, hopefully being turned off. It must have been, because she heard Scott's office door close. She remained crouched on the floor, unable to trust the silence.

Eventually, she turned on the file room light and replaced the files she had removed. *How stupid am I? What if he stayed behind as a trap?* Her hand trembled as she reached for the door handle, but waited. After a five-minute eternity she stepped out.

Scott had been here. His briefcase was gone. Maybe he knew that burning lights meant intruders and went to call the police.

Clutching her own folders, she dashed down the hall. In the dark she had to walk down the unmoving escalator to her office to get her coat, handbag, and car keys. Shaken and in a cold sweat, she made her way in eerie darkness to the exit door.

Coach was sitting and reading a magazine. "Georgia? Why in hell are you still here?"

"Just had so much work to do I forgot the time."

"I went by your office not more than twenty minutes ago and I didn't see any light. You work by candlelight?"

"Well, the truth is," she stammered, "I . . . I'm still experiencing jetlag from my trip abroad. I turned out the light and fell asleep on my couch."

He smiled and handed her the sign-out book. He went to a wall phone and called the alarm company.

"They'll think we're night owls here. This is the third time I've called tonight. Mr. Scott came back for his briefcase, now you. "

He said he had called *three* times. For her, Scott and who was the third? Maybe she could sneak a look in the sign-out book. She looked quickly at the book on Coach's chair.

"You look pretty beat," Coach said. "Better slow down, young lady. This business can be a killer."

CHAPTER 61

Michelle, Lasondo, and Georgia watched shoppers tossing fashion merchandise around on markdown tables, pulling things off round racks, and grabbing armfuls of bargains off shelves.

"Closing the downtown store is tougher to watch than I expected," Lasondo said.

Michelle looked grim. "After thirty years I'm watching my career being sold at sixty percent off."

Georgia sighed. The Designer Salon and Michelle's job were to be eliminated. Knowing that soon everything would be gone, her thoughts drifted back to Scott's file room. Would she have a chance to get back in before everything was moved out?

"This lovely old store," Lasondo said, "looks like a rundown warehouse." Some display fixtures had been ripped out, leaving walls raw, bare and useless. Lasondo stepped away from one aching wall.

"The customer who appreciated a fine store is gone," Michelle lamented. "She bought things as soon as they came in. And look at these shoppers—behaving like a pack of predators."

"I've had enough," Lasondo said. He started to leave, then turned back. "Stop in to see me, Michelle. Maybe we can work something out."

Georgia was wrapping autographed pictures of celebrities she had known or worked with at the store, plus awards she had received. These had once covered the only wall the fire hadn't reached.

"Here's another picture you'll want to frame," Jean exclaimed, rushing into Georgia's office with the current issue of *Vogue*. "Look who's on the cover!"

Georgia could feel her eyes widen. "Gwen? This is Gwen-Val Wray? Wow! She's as beautiful as the first black model who made a Vogue cover. Beverly Johnson."

Jean blinked. "How did you remember that?"

"I'll never forget that 1974 Vogue issue. It made me consider using black models here. Know what, Jean? They provide *Vogue* in the ladies lounge at Windsor Country Club. Oh, to be there when Mrs. Farnsworth looks at this issue."

Jean volunteered to frame Gwen's picture. "So glad you encouraged her to try New York, Georgia." She looked around. "It's a good thing they decided to close this store before you redecorated your office."

Yes and no, Georgia thought. It had been hell living for months with the reminder of how the fire started in her office.

Georgia was wrapping a picture of Polly Bergen when her father appeared. As always, he was dressed in a black suit, white shirt and black tie, exactly how he was dressed that rainy day he picked her up at school in Landing. No wonder everyone thought he was her driver. *What a terrible thing I did not telling my classmates the truth.*

"Well, this is a surprise," Georgia said. He had dropped in to see her less than a half dozen times in the ten years she had been with Emeralds, usually when he was Christmas shopping.

"I wanted to take one last look at the grand old store. Looks pretty grim." He glanced around. "So does your office."

"Can you stay a while? You have the choice of hard boxes or one dusty chair." When he moved towards the chair she grabbed a rag, dusted it off. "That's the chair Rudy gave me. It needs some refinishing, but escaped being destroyed by the fire. Guess angels were watching over me."

"Angels are always watching over you, Georgia."

"How do you figure?"

"The first female vice president here, and one with a black heritage? The work of angels."

Georgia shrugged. "Maybe."

"In coming years, parents will tell daughters they can be president."

Georgia laughed. "President of what? Their garden clubs?"

He was looking over her shoulder. With her back to the door, she guessed what he was seeing. Matt. He's here. That's why her father came today. Slowly, she turned around.

"Hi, Georgia. The door was open. May we come in?"

It was Larry Lasondo and Paul Stratley.

"We're touring the store and stopped by to see if you need any-thing," Lasondo asked, then looked towards her father, extended his hand. "I'm Larry Lasondo."

"Ben Parker," her father responded with a hand shake. "Georgia has mentioned how supportive you've been."

"She's the greatest. This is Paul Stratley, a new addition to our company."

Paul had plunged his hands into his pockets.

Georgia was chilled with fear. Her father had never met Stratley. At the sound of Strately's name Georgia saw him pull himself up, look-ing like a boiling volcano about to erupt. Instinctively, she grabbed her father's arm, fearing he would tear Paul to pieces as he had often threat-ened. Parker was taller and bigger than Stratley and could easily do just that. "Sorry you have to leave, Dad, I'll call you later."

Georgia noticed immediately that tension between the two men was not lost on Lasondo. When he saw no handshake, his eyes darted from one man to the other. Parker stood focused on Stratley, his eyes hard, his arms at his sides, with fists tight.

"Dad," Georgia's urgent tone was a breathy half-whisper. "I know you *have to leave*."

Lasondo stepped between the two men. "What a pleasure to finally meet you, Dr. Parker. I've heard great things about your work. I'd like to hear more. How about lunch tomorrow?"

"Sorry, I'm leaving town tomorrow."

Standing behind Lasondo during this encounter, Stratley slipped out.

Coward, Georgia thought, but she was relieved he was gone.

With eyes blazing and his mouth held firm, Parker flashed an accu-satory look at Georgia and left.

Soon after she reached home, her father called.

"When did you start lying to me, Georgia?"

"Let me explain?"

"If you can," he barked. "You assured me Stratley would stay at People's Savings and Loan. When did that change?"

"A . . . while ago."

"How long ago?"

"Dad, I didn't want you to worry. Rudy urged me not to give up what I had earned. We have so many stores now, Stratley's in charge of out-state properties, so he's away most of the time. I can handle this."

"Maybe you can, but I can't. When I get home we're going to bring a finish to this. One way or another I'm going to find a way to bury that bum."

The opportunity to get back into Scott's file room looked slim. *And what will I find on those freight and packing slips?*

Only one person could be trusted to help her. Larry Lasondo. He, like everyone else, was packing boxes to move.

"Larry, I need your advice."

"Regarding what?" He poured two cups of coffee.

She told him of Rudy's concern about internal losses, about Scott's telling him he'd take care of everything. "And have you heard the rumor that Rudy left because things disappeared only from his department?"

"Yes, but anyone with half a brain would know that's bunk."

She told him what Rudy had said in the hospital. "I understand the pink packing slips and the blue freight bills, but why did he say 'wait'? Wait for what?"

"How are you spelling that?"

"Wait? w-a-i-t."

He chuckled. "I'm sure he meant w-e-i-g-h-t. He meant the weight of what was shipped. We check freight bills on the basis of a shipment's weight."

"But what has weight got to do with losses?"

"If a shipment arrives much lighter than what is noted on the freight bill, something has been left out or taken out."

Georgia shook her head. "Where to begin?"

A knock on Larry's door preceded Stratley. "Am I interrupting anything?"

"Paul," Lasondo said. "I thought you were out at the distribution center today?"

"I was. It's looking great. Got anymore coffee?"

Lasondo obliged.

Before being invited, Stratley chose a chair next to Georgia. "I visited the new building and saw the office layout. Lasondo's office is on one side of yours, Georgia, and mine's on the other."

Lasondo's secretary stepped in to tell him he had a visitor. He excused himself.

Stratley closed the door. "Seeing your father the other day was a first. Handsome man. Sorry I couldn't stay, but had a lot of ground to cover."

Smart decision. My dad would have covered a lot of ground with you, coward. She didn't answer, just sipped her coffee.

"I called your office and they said you were here. There's a lot I need to explain."

She wanted to dash her hot coffee in his face. "How's Lyndy?"

"She's so busy with the boys and her social stuff she hardly knows I'm alive." He moved closer. "Georgia, I'm discovering it takes some time for a jerk to stop being a jerk. Maybe it's like trying to stop drinking. But, believe me, I'm trying. All I want from you is to hear that you forgive me."

Forgive him? Oh, what a speech she wanted to make, but not here. She only shot him a disdainful look. Lasondo returned.

"Thanks for your advice, Larry. I'll get right on it."

CHAPTER 62

The persistent buzzing of her apartment doorbell brought Georgia out of the shower in a rush. She tied a terry robe around her, and hurried to the door.

"Who is it?"

"Flowers, Miss Parker."

Cautiously, she opened the door. The man holding an armful of flowers in front of his face moved in quickly.

"Wait a minute," she said. Then she recognized Stratley. "Out!"

"Now, Georgia. Is that the way to treat a man bringing flowers?"

She leaned back from his whiskey breath. "Out," she repeated, and dashed to the phone.

He dropped the flowers and grabbed the phone. "If there's going to be any talking, it's going to be between you and me."

Georgia calculated her next move. She'd die rather than let him touch her. Better yet, *he'd* die. Slowly, she backed away towards the kitchen.

"Am I so frightening?" he chuckled, following her.

He walked straight. She estimated that he wasn't drunk, at least not enough to negate the brute strength in his arms.

She reached the kitchen and he had edged up closer. "Mmm." he breathed. "You smell good."

Georgia turned quickly, yanked a knife from her cutlery holder. "Out! And I'm not afraid to use this."

"I'm not going to hurt you. I just want to talk." He put his hands in front of him, palms facing her.

"My father's coming over. If he sees you here, he'll kill you."

"No, he's not. He's out of town. I heard him tell Lasondo in your office."

"I don't want to hear anything you have to say."

"Oh, I think you will, after you see this." He reached into his pocket and turned the item towards her.

Oh, my God, it can't be. He was holding the picture Jesse had taken of them at the wedding.

She was so distracted he was able to dart forward, twist her wrist, and dislodge the knife.

"You could hurt yourself with this."

She took a step back, clutching the neck of her robe. "Where did you get that?"

"It came by mail. You know anything about this? His smile made her shudder. He turned it over as if there might be a clue he had missed. He looked at the picture and smirked. "I'm surprised whoever took this hasn't tried to blackmail me." He wielded the knife playfully under her chin. "What about you? Anyone contact you about this picture?"

Did her face reveal that she had seen it? If Paul had the slightest suspicion, he'd demand to know when and who took it. Barely able to move, she shook her head.

Paul's eyes narrowed. He pulled her arms behind her with one hand, and slid the knife under the belt of her robe with the other.

She swallowed hard and uttered a weak, "I don't know."

"Sure?"

Fear found a hiding place in her stomach. She watched him scrutinizing her, but she shook her head again.

"Hmm," was all he said before slowly pulling the knife away. "Someone just took this picture for sport?" He ran one hand along the side of his dark brown hair. "If the mystery photographer isn't putting the screws to us, then maybe I can make use of it." He smiled again, that lecherous smile she had seen long ago, when he had sexually assaulted her.

"You're wasting your time, Stratley. Knife or no knife, if you touch me, I'll kill you."

His vituperative laugh robbed her of breath. "Don't worry, baby. What would be the fun of fucking you at knife point?"

"What happened to your resolution to stop being a jerk?"

He laughed.

Georgia's eyes sought out the poker at the fireplace.

"Nothing's going to happen tonight. This time, sweetheart, you're coming to me." His words were terrorizing and his voice fierce. "Friday night. My office. Be there at six. Come or I show this picture to Lyndy."

Georgia's hand went to her throat. "You would do that to her? Why?"

"I've covered my tracks. As soon as I received the picture, I dropped little remarks about how you've been coming on to me. In the picture, who can pick out the aggressor?"

Her legs went limp. "Why hurt Lyndy?"

"She won't be hurt. She'll believe me. Only you'll get hurt. And fired." He drew her savagely into his arms and kissed her hard. "Friday. At six. Be there."

"We're out of packing boxes. I'll go get some." Jean told Georgia. "Lyndy Stratley called. Here's her number."

He showed her the picture! This is my fault for not telling her about Paul. The moment Jean left, Georgia dialed the number.

Lyndy answered. "Georgia, I know you're terribly busy, but I'd like to see you."

Georgia was puzzled and fearful all at once. She hadn't heard from Lyndy in years. *Why now?*

"Could we have lunch later this week?" Lyndy's voice sounded shaky.

I'm not a good friend, Lyndy. I should have told you. "Yes, I think so."

"Good. Noon on Friday at my house."

Friday? Stratley had demanded that she be at his office Friday at six.

The words he had said to her the day he attacked her, when she was only fifteen, flashed in front of her like a blazing billboard. "If you don't want me to hurt you," he had said, "do exactly what I tell you." How in God's name was she going to avoid going to his office today at six and dodge his threat? Although he may not remember those words, a vicious punishment would still be forthcoming.

"Boy, did I walk in on a dramatic scene," Jean announced when she returned with the packing boxes.

Georgia was looking out her window, reflecting on Lyndy's invitation. "What?"

"I was on my way to the storeroom and, as you know, I have to pass Jesse's office. I heard Jesse shouting at the top of his voice. His door was partly open and I could see it was Steve he was shouting at."

"What were they fighting about?"

"Don't know, but Steve had some blue papers in his hand, and Jesse was trying to get them away from him. That's about it. What should I pack next?"

Blue papers? I'd like to see those.

Georgia had her own opportunity to overhear Jesse in a heated dispute three days later. She arrived for Scott's strategy meeting when she heard Jesse's strong protest floating out of Scott's office.

"I don't give a damn if he is Hoffman's son-in-law, he has no right to take our wooden soldiers for his kid's birthday party. They're eight feet tall, hand painted, and very expensive."

She stayed outside the door.

Jesse's voice was filled with anxiety. "They're central to our Christmas theme. Besides, they're not assembled."

"Calm down, Jesse," Scott said. "Paul has assured me he'd return them right after the party."

"You don't understand. Since we're moving I had them sent to the distribution center. To dig them out and assemble them is a day's work. When returned, we have to take them apart and repack. That's crazy."

"Just assemble them and don't take them apart," Scott said. "I don't want to hear another word. Tell your people the truck will pick them up tomorrow morning."

To allow the negative flack to clear out of Scott's office, Georgia darted down the hall into the Ladies Room. She rationalized why Lyndy had picked Friday for lunch; she was having a birthday party. Georgia had planned to bring gifts anyway.

When she returned to Scott's office for her appointment, she noticed blue freight bills, wrinkled and partly torn, on his desk. Jesse or Steve must have brought them here. But which one? Before she could get a closer look, Scott tucked them into his desk drawer.

I've got to get back into Scott's file room.

CHAPTER 63

For two long days and two sleepless nights Georgia wrestled with possibilities for thwarting Paul's plan. And during that time Paul was ubiquitous. Visions of his threatening form, face, and voice shadowed her every moment.

The more she thought of her lunch with Lyndy, the worse the scenario became. Imagine having lunch at their home, making girl talk, cooing over the children, then telling Lyndy her lecherous husband was blackmailing her into a sexual rendezvous. Who could advise her on how to handle this mess? Her father would be out to kill. No need for him to suffer too. Oh, how she needed Rudy. And Matt.

When Friday came, Georgia felt worse than the proverbial basket case.

"You sick?" Jean asked. "If you want to go home, I'll drive you."

"No, I'm okay." After a half hour she decided to cancel her lunch date with Lyndy. But how could she lose this last chance to tell her the truth?

As she gathered gifts out of her car and walked up to the magnificent house, Georgia heard sirens. A distraught, sobbing maid opened the door and motioned her in. Moments later, three police cars sped into the driveway. Georgia stood frozen, as police rushed in with guns drawn.

One officer approached Georgia. "What's in those packages?"

"Gifts for the Stratley children."

"Leave them here, please. And your name?"

"Georgia Parker. I was invited here by Mrs. Stratley."

"Yes, sir," the maid said, still sobbing. "She was to have lunch with Mrs. Stratley."

The officer turned to Georgia. "Don't touch anything, and don't leave."

The elegant two-story foyer was a shambles. Planks of wood, nails, and sand were spread everywhere. Georgia recognized the splintered bright red pieces as the wooden soldiers. Handsome heads, with tall hats and leather chin straps, were detached, like victims of a guillotine.

Several police scattered elsewhere in the house. Two stayed behind, one to talk to the maid, and the other stood at the front door. "What happened?" the officer asked the maid.

"Four men came into the house," she whimpered.

"What did they want?"

"The wooden soldiers." She doubled over with intense sobs, and the officer helped her to a chair, waited for her to regain composure.

"How were the men dressed?"

"In coveralls with Emeralds name on the back."

"Did you answer the door?"

"No, Mr. Stratley did. He told them . . . the soldiers were delivered only this morning and weren't to be picked up until late tomorrow." Her tearful words sounded like crackling static.

The officer pulled up a chair facing her. "Then what happened?"

"Mr. Stratley told them to leave. He walked over to the telephone . . . near the staircase, and . ." Sobs washed away her words.

"Take your time," the officer said. "When you're ready, tell us what happened."

"One man said the soldiers were too big to fit into their panel truck. Two went out and came back with sledge hammers." She wrung her hands. "That's when Mr. Stratley started to run and one man ran after him." Her sobs escalated. "Those soldiers looked so fine standing here. They were for the birthday party tomorrow. They smashed them. It was awful . . . awful."

"Did they say why they did that?"

"No. They smashed them one at a time. Pulled out big sandbags and slashed them open. Sand spilled everywhere."

"And then?"

"When they slashed the sandbags in the last two soldiers, they didn't find much sand."

"Those men were looking for something," the officer said. "Did they take anything with them?"

"Nothing but some bags of stuffing they pulled out of the last two soldiers."

The officers exchanged glances. "What kind of stuffing?"

"White bags . . . they cut open the sandbags and pulled them out."

"Where were you during all this?"

"At the top of the stairs, behind the banister. Over there . . . past the big pillars. You can see down here from up there."

She was sobbing hysterically now. "And I saw the man who ran after Mr. Stratley . . . and shot him."

Georgia looked towards the big pillars. Soon she was walking past them to the base of the staircase. A police officer stopped her. On the bottom steps, lying face-up, sprawled out like a drunk, was Paul. He was staring straight ahead, his eyes wide open.

Georgia was less shocked by what she saw than by her numb reaction. Suddenly, a wave of intense sadness washed over her. How awful for Lyndy and their children. Where was her relief that she would no longer have to deal with him? Where was her gratitude for not having to tell Lyndy anything?

About ten feet away, Lyndy was looking down at Paul.

"Lyndy," Georgia called out.

Lyndy didn't move. She just stared with a blankness that resembled a store mannequin.

"Lyndy? It's me. Georgia."

"He's dead." Her voice was flat.

The officer directed Georgia to move back. He also recommended that Lyndy leave when the coroner arrived, but she didn't move. All during the examination of the body, Lyndy remained tearless, wordless. She still hadn't looked at Georgia—only at Paul's body until it was rolled away on a gurney.

Georgia turned away. *Now my silence about Stratley leaves me with a lifetime of guilt.*

Lyndy was escorted to a small couch. Georgia sat down beside her.

Aaron and Karen Hoffman arrived, and Georgia had never witnessed such pain as she saw in their eyes.

"I'm fine," Lyndy assured them. "The children are at school, and their nanny will pick them up. I've told her to take them to your house. We need to get things cleaned up here."

Respecting their privacy, Georgia went back to the entryway. One of the officers identified the white dust on the floor. "Cocaine."

Georgia grabbed a chair for support. Drugs? Hidden in display items? Wouldn't they need someone to work with inside Emeralds?

A detective in plain clothes was talking to the maid. "How did these soldiers happen to be here?"

"Mr. Stratley borrowed them from the store."

"Thank you, ma'am. You've been a great help."

Georgia approached the officer and asked if she was free to go.

"Sorry we had to open your gifts. Are you related to the Stratleys?"

"No. Just a friend."

"A long time friend?"

"As long as I've worked for Emeralds. May I go now?"

His expression changed. "You work for Emeralds? Would you be kind enough to join me in the library? I need to talk to everyone."

The Hoffmans and Lyndy were there.

"The system of using stores' merchandise for contraband shipments has been showing up throughout the country," the detective told Mr. Hoffman. "Those soldiers, your property, contained contraband. I'm sure you understand that until a thorough investigation is made, the store will be under scrutiny."

"You'll have our complete cooperation," Hoffman said. "Emeralds has never had any negative publicity. I want our name cleared as soon as possible."

"One thing we do know," the detective said, "these thugs are working with someone inside your company. Can any of you throw any light on that?"

Georgia thought of the strong protest Jesse had voiced when Scott overrode him and loaned the soldiers to Stratley. Her thought translated into a nervous movement.

The detective noticed. "You'd like to tell us something, Miss Parker?"

She looked at Mr. Hoffman for guidance. He nodded.

Shaken and feeling like a traitor, she told them what she had overheard in Scott's office.

The Hoffmans looked at her with surprise. *I think my being honest is ill timed. Should I have discussed this with Mr. Hoffman first?*

"And who is Jesse?"

Hoffman answered. "Jesse Wiggins. He's our display director."

A clock chimed three thirty as the detective left.

"If there is anything at all that I can do," Georgia began, not knowing what else to say. The Hoffmans thanked her. Lyndy remained wordless.

Georgia moved towards Lyndy with the intention of hugging her, but Lyndy's glare stopped her. *Why is she looking at me like that? Is it because I revealed Jesse's protest? Maybe the gossip about things disappearing while Rudy was here—and our having been best friends—created suspicion . . . of me.*

CHAPTER 64

Georgia entered Scott's file room without turning on the light. This time she brought a flashlight. Scott always left early on Fridays. His secretary, who had to care for her mother on weekends, left promptly at five-thirty, and like clockwork, made a stop to the restroom at five fifteen. That's when Georgia entered the unlocked office and hid in the file room.

Once Georgia heard the outer door close and lock, she turned on her flashlight, found the Display drawer and pulled out the file labeled Freight. She looked for the wrinkled blue freight bills over which Jesse and Steve had fought. There they were right in front, stapled together and mended with Scotch tape. These were freight bills for four wooden soldiers. Each bill represented two soldiers.

What to look for? The soldiers shipped in two separate crates should weigh the same. One freight bill listed two custom-made nutcracker soldiers, eight-feet tall, red. The other freight bill listed two soldiers, eight-feet tall, red. The same. Check weight, Rudy had said. She found the column where weight was noted. The first freight bill showed 566 pounds. The second bill showed 484 pounds.

Paul's maid had said the men had smashed the soldiers, cut open sandbags, but found the white bags in only two soldiers. *That was it!* The two soldiers with the heavy sand bags were shipped separately from the two with cocaine. Somebody at the other end goofed. They should have made sure the weight of the two crates was identical. And who bought those soldiers for the store? Jesse.

And something else. If Scott had compared the two freight bills he'd know immediately something was wrong.

In order to clear Rudy's name, she needed the old freight bills on things that had disappeared earlier. Who had okayed those?

And Larry Lasondo. Earlier today, she had asked for his help. "This is dangerous, Georgia. Better leave it to the police." Georgia disagreed. If Scott was involved, delay would give him time to destroy the evidence.

Georgia was searching for that evidence when she heard something. She turned off her flashlight. When she looked toward the file room entrance, a strong light was shining in her face. Had Scott come back?

The glare was so powerful, she couldn't tell who it was. She shielded her eyes. Then she recognized him. "Oh, thank God," she sighed. "I'm so glad it's you. For a moment I thought I was in serious trouble."

It was Coach making his usual rounds. "Georgia? What in hell . . . ?"

"You've heard what happened to Paul Stratley today?"

"Of course."

"Well, in this file . . . stop shining that damn thing in my face and turn on a light."

"Sorry." He turned his flashlight off and the wall switch on.

"The proof is here that contraband has been coming into this store through props in the Display Department."

"My God."

"Someone has to check the freight bill against the orders, right? Then he or she signs the bill for approval."

"Right."

"The wooden soldiers, shipped in two crates, should have been identical in weight. Well, one had the heavy sand bags and the other crate, containing the contraband, was much lighter."

"Wow."

"The difference in weight of the two crates should have been immediately noticed by whoever approved the freight bill."

"Right."

"What I need to do now is find the freight bills of a couple of other shipments Rudy had found missing—a huge Raggedy Andy, some palm trees, an elephant, treasure chest. We find those, compare the signatures and—"

Coach lifted his walky-talky. "I need you. Now. Scott's office."

"What's that all about?"

Coach put his flashlight into its holder and drew out a gun. He pointed it at Georgia.

The warm, friendly gleam she had always seen in his eyes disappeared. His face had hardened and his eyes were iced.

"Georgia, you've always been one of my favorite people, but you've gotten in over your head. I've invested too much to have anyone screw it up."

"You? You've been running contraband through the store? You . . . alone?"

"Oh, no. I have a very good team. Harry Ralston had the New York contacts. And there's nothing a druggy won't do to support his habit and appetite for nice things."

"Steve."

"I hate to do this," he said with an ominous grin, "but business is business." He lifted his gun.

"If you shoot me they'll get you for murder."

"Oh, no, dear. I was only doing my job. I saw a burglar and shot in self defense."

"Self defense? I don't have a gun."

"Your flashlight. In the dark, how was I to know it wasn't a gun?" He smiled. "It's well known how much I liked you. I'll show such remorse everyone will rush to comfort me."

"Why did you do this?"

"Do you think I'd be a night watchman after having my own accounting firm? I stopped drinking, but I lost everything anyway." He lifted the gun.

"Wait. I just want to understand. What happened to you after you lost your company?"

"I went to prison on a trumped-up charge. But I learned some useful stuff there."

"How did you get this Emeralds job?"

"I asked for it. They offered me better jobs, but I insisted I didn't want any stress."

"Why be a night watchman?"

"It gave me the run of the place. Keys to everything, control of the alarm system. Steve gave me the names of vendors where Jesse placed orders. Ralston found or placed insiders at those vendors. Now that's enough talk."

"At least finish the story."

"Where the hell is that guy?" He lifted his walky-talky again. "Burdette. Get the hell down here. Scott's office."

"What happened when the merchandise arrived?"

"I advised the organization to make the pickups. A fun game and I'm a rich man."

"Who were those men who destroyed the soldiers?"

"I have nothing to do with them. They do the pickups and deliveries. I never touch the stuff."

"Why did they kill Stratley?"

"I guess they get uncomfortable when a big shipment like that ends up in a place, shall we say, unscheduled?"

"Was Stratley involved?"

"Naw, he just got unlucky."

"And Scott?"

Coach laughed. "He's a pain in the ass, but straight as an arrow. He was just making nice with the boss's son-in-law."

Other things were falling into place now for Georgia. "Remember that night I checked out after Scott came back for his briefcase?"

"Yeah. So?"

"When you called the alarm people, you said you had called three times that night. Yet only two names were noted in the sign-out book—Scott's and mine."

"So?"

"Something clicked, but it didn't seem important then. Now I know the third was for you. To open the dock for something to be taken out."

"Very good. But all this talk won't help you, sweet Georgia." He lifted his gun again.

Georgia saw it before Coach did—the muzzle of a gun pointed at Coach's head.

"All this talk won't help you either, mister. Drop the gun." It was the detective Georgia had seen at the Stratleys.

"Put it down carefully. Easy. That's it."

One police officer picked up Coach's gun and another swung Coach away from Georgia and handcuffed him.

Along with the detective were three uniformed police officers and Larry Lasondo.

She smiled at Larry. "So, you changed your mind to help me. Why?"

"I knew you wouldn't change *yours*. You okay?"

"I'm fine. Did you know Coach would show up here?"

"No. I just feared someone might."

"What made you think I'd be caught in here?"

"After what happened to Paul today I wasn't sure of anything, but I shared my concern with the police and they decided not to take a chance."

Georgia kissed his cheek.

Lasondo smiled. "And how did you have the guts to keep talking with a gun pointed at you?"

"On television, they didn't shoot until they cocked the gun."

"Coach wasn't carrying an automatic that you hear being cocked. He had a pistol. All he needed to do was release the safety and shoot." She opened a file drawer. "Now what are you doing?"

"I missed something."

"What's going on here?" It was Jesse.

A policeman approached him. "Who are you?"

"Jesse Wiggins. Display director."

Jesse stared at Coach as he was led away by two officers. The remaining police officer held Jesse's arm as the detective asked, "Are you aware that drugs were smuggled into this city through things you ordered?"

"Drugs? No. But I was trying to help the store find out why things were disappearing. I found some freight bills with weights that were highly irregular and okayed by Steve Burdette. When I showed them to him he said he hadn't noticed. Next thing I knew, he tried to destroy them."

The detective looked doubtful. "Maybe it was the other way around. Why are you down here?"

"I heard Coach beep Steve, but he was too stoned to respond, so I came to see what Coach wanted."

"Yeah? Well, if you do all the ordering for display, who else knows what's coming into the store?"

"Just the people I buy from. And Steve."

Out of the file drawer she reopened, Georgia retrieved the tattered blue freight bills. "These show the shipment of the four soldiers. See the signature? It's Steve Burdette. Steve was working for Coach."

The detective took the evidence from Georgia.

"And here are other freight bills. Notice these all came from the same supplier, all okayed by Steve, all things that disappeared."

The detective shook his head. "That doesn't prove Wiggins isn't involved."

"I think it does," Georgia said. *I can't believe I'm saying this.* "While Coach held a gun on me, it was Steve he called for, not Jesse."

Scott's reprimand of Georgia for invading his file room came the following morning.

"Sir, I apologize for opening your private files, but I couldn't think of another way to clear Rudy's name."

"I understand."

She was prepared with her next defensive statement, but not for this quiet, passive response. *Why isn't' he shouting at me?*

He pointed for her to sit. "You were very lucky not to have ended up like Paul Stratley." He lit a cigarette, and exhaled a stream of smoke that reached her face.

She coughed. "I wasn't thinking of danger."

A scathing verbal reaction would have been more welcome than his smirk that indicated—you weren't *thinking*, period.

"You were very clever to have put the pieces together and dig out the truth."

"I wasn't clever at all. Rudy gave me the clue."

"Indeed? Perhaps he did know what was going on."

Anger rushed to the roots of her hair. "He knew only what I told him at his bedside. He was trying to help."

Scott's mouth moved into what Georgia assumed was a smile. "I was very aware of the evidence I had in my files. As soon as I saw what happened at the Stratleys, I knew the answer was right here. Seems you got here first."

Where was he going with all this? She knew it wasn't good. "I know a simple apology for my unauthorized intrusion is inadequate, but at least the result was rewarding. We uncovered the culprits."

"We? Come now, Miss Parker. You accomplished all that by yourself."

I know a trap is hidden here somewhere.

Scott put out his cigarette. "Good results, good intentions do not erase the fact that you acted in an unethical manner."

Georgia almost had to agree with him.

"We cannot tolerate employees—and certainly not executive board members—playing detective and raiding company files without permission. You knew you were breaking rules."

Georgia could feel her lip twitch. "I'm guilty of all that."

"It seems you're not a team player. This time you've stepped over the line."

"I know." She couldn't tell him the reason for not asking permission—he was a suspect. "I was afraid if I asked you'd say no."

"Damn right." His voice remained low. "Maybe you've been reading too many mystery novels. Or, maybe, your devious dark gene has surfaced. I've put up with a lot from you. You're through here, girlie. Your resignation within two weeks or you're fired."

CHAPTER 65

"Georgia, Mr. Hoffman just called a special board meeting for eleven thirty," Jean announced.

Minutes later, Faith called, asking Georgia to come to Mr. Hoffman's office immediately. When Georgia arrived Faith wasn't there and his inner office door was open. "Mr. Hoffman?"

"He's not here."

Georgia identified the voice and stepped inside. "Lyndy. How are you? I sent food and flowers. Called several times."

Lyndy shrugged. "Thank you for the food and flowers."

"How are the boys?"

Lyndy avoided eye contact. "Fine."

"What's wrong, Lyndy?"

She shot Georgia a cold glare. "Don't pretend you don't know."

"I don't know. Can we go somewhere and talk?"

"Here's fine. If you want to talk, let's talk."

Lyndy shut her father's office door, and sat across from Georgia at the conference table. Lyndy looked pale, and her grey suit didn't help. Her hair was pulled back and knotted on her neck, making her look far older than thirty. "Paul had told me you had been coming on to him. He said that you were showing up at his office uninvited, calling him with one lame excuse after another."

Georgia was stunned. "You believed all that?"

Lyndy stiffened. "I was well aware of his escapades, but *you*, Georgia?"

No wonder Scott was so confident about getting rid of me. Lyndy had told her father, and Scott was given the go-ahead.

"Good God, Lyndy, how could you believe I would do that? Didn't our friendship tell you anything about me?"

"Don't try to con me, Georgia. When I told him I didn't believe that about you, and berated him for saying such things, he showed me proof. *Proof!*"

The picture. *Jesse will delight in seeing me executed. And Scott. And Bladerton.*

"Is that why, after years of silence, you invited me to lunch that Friday? To confront me?"

"No. Actually, I needed to talk to a *trusted* friend. Thursday night, when he was saying derogatory things about you, I was defending my *trusted friend* until he proved me wrong."

"Lyndy, I tried so many times to tell you about Paul, but you were glowing with happiness. I tried when we had lunch at Club 21, and when you showed me sketches of wedding dresses, even while I was dressing you for your wedding. I failed you as a friend with my silence. Couldn't face seeing your heart break."

Now Georgia was on her feet and pacing. "Oh, God, Lyndy, that man made a pass at me every time he saw me, even before he recognized me."

"What do you mean before he recognized you?"

Now Georgia was in tears. "He didn't recognize me because he hadn't seen me since I was fifteen."

"You knew him when you were fifteen?"

"Yes."

"Were you . . . lovers?"

Georgia's head snapped around to face her. "Hell, no. I hardly knew him." Georgia stopped again. *I can't tell her.*

"You hardly knew him? Then, what's this all about?"

"The bastard tried to rape me!"

Lyndy gasped. "When?"

Georgia turned to the windows. The thought of repeating the awful details produced hot stabs in her chest. *I must, to be done with this.* She wiped her eyes, sat across from Lyndy and related the story.

Georgia waited for a response. Shock. Outrage. Heartbreak. Sympathy. Something.

Lyndy had been motionless, listening with cold eyes throughout.

"You know what, Georgia? You should be on the stage. What a performance. I almost believed you."

"Why almost?"

"Because, Bette Davis, I've had a private detective following Paul. The night before Paul was killed, he was seen going into your apartment."

Still shaken from her confrontation with Lyndy, Georgia expected more trauma here at Mr. Hoffman's special meeting.

Scott hadn't arrived yet. Hoffman opened the meeting, his eyes focused on Paul's empty chair. "My daughter Lyndy will replace her husband on the board . . . when she's ready."

On any other day, that would have been happy news. Hoffman's eyes were ringed with fatigue. "Coach, Steve Burdette and Harry Ralston have been indicted. We need to double our awareness of any irregularities. We can't afford such negative publicity again."

Hoffman's voice revealed sadness. "We're on the threshold of change. Emeralds, like any forward-thinking organization needs to be updated. Change has to start at the top." Hoffman stopped and sipped some water.

At the top? Emeralds without Hoffman? Unthinkable. Georgia noticed everyone looked tense.

Hoffman cleared his throat. He looked around and his gaze stopped on Georgia.

He's never looked at me like that before. He's seen the infamous picture.

Hoffman turned to the group. "Mortimer Scott has been with this company for thirty years. He's brought us success with remarkable merchandising decisions."

Georgia watched people squirm. Were they all thinking what she was—Hoffman's retiring, Scott will be president.

The time has come, Georgia felt. Hoffman will avoid painful gossip about the infamous photo by using my invasion of company files—the perfect excuse to ask for my resignation. Damn Stratley. I always feared he'd ruin my career. *That bastard is raping me from the grave.*

"I owe a great deal to Scott." Hoffman stopped and leaned back. "Fashion retailing isn't the exciting business it once was. It's tougher, more demanding. Scott wants less pressure. So, he's chosen an early retirement. Scott's taken a position with Emily Gold Stores in California."

Mr. Hoffman stood. "I propose as replacement for Mr. Scott, a young man with vision and totally in tune with today's fashion customer, Larry Lasondo. May we have a vote?"

The vote was swift and unanimous. Faces that revealed apprehension now displayed relief.

Hoffman asked Lasondo to take the floor.

"Thanks to all of you, and I hasten to assure you that the merchandising team as it stands right now will stay intact." Lasondo looked at Georgia. "And I'm counting on you, Georgia, to help all of us make Emeralds an even stronger fashion leader."

With his first smile, Hoffman congratulated Lasondo, adjourned the meeting and left.

I'm not fired. No more Scott. The heavens are opening up. Imagine working on a team dedicated to propelling Emeralds to the lofty position it deserved.

Lasondo was surrounded with congratulations, and as soon as they dispersed, he walked out with Georgia.

"Larry, did you know Scott had asked for my resignation?"

"I did. His being sexist became a vital management concern."

"I never forget when Scott said, 'Women belong on their backs, not on boards', I was devastated."

"I know. He'll have an interesting experience with Emily Gold Stores." Lasondo smiled. "Their new president is a *woman*."

CHAPTER 66

"Good morning," Georgia greeted the Stratley maid, "Is Lyndy in?"

"Yes, Miss Parker. She's in the library. I'll call her."

"No. I'd like to surprise her, but thank you. I know the way."

The library door was open. Lyndy at a desk, writing.

Lyndy looked up. "Why are you here? Don't answer. Just leave."

"I'm not leaving. Not until you hear what I came to say. And, damn it, you're going to listen."

Being careful not to miss a beat, Georgia began. "Paul came to my apartment under the pretense of delivering flowers. I ordered him out. Not taking a chance of another sexual assault from him, I grabbed a knife from my kitchen. I told him if he tried to touch me, I'd kill him."

Lyndy started to stand, but Georgia quickly blocked her with a strong hand on her shoulder and in-her-face command. "You're going to hear it all, Lyndy. I'm not going away with this rot festering inside me anymore. Sit. Paul showed me the picture Jesse Wiggins had taken at your wedding and I almost fainted when he told me what he was going to do with it if I didn't submit to his demands. *He'd show it to you.*"

Lyndy's eyes glared. "He said you lured him out into the garden and had the picture taken to blackmail him."

"There was blackmail, alright. Jesse Wiggins snapped that picture and held me hostage with the threat of sending the picture to your father."

Lyndy dropped her head.

"This isn't easy for me, either, Lyndy. Paul Stratley has been a black cloud over my life longer than I care to remember."

"But the fact remains you and Paul were kissing on my wedding day. How can you explain that?"

"Easy. Paul said 'Can't we kiss and make up?' and even though I said *absolutely not*, he grabbed me. That's what Jesse caught on film."

"Nonsense. The picture doesn't lie."

Georgia opened her handbag. "Oh, yes it does. This is a blowup of the picture. Look closely."

Lyndy examined it. "I don't notice anything different."

"Look at my eyes. On the small print it isn't very noticeable. But see, my eyes are open. Ever see a woman lost in the ecstasy of a kiss with her eyes open? And notice my hands. Are they laid tenderly against his chest? Hell, no. My hands are fists, trying to push him away. Both Paul and Jesse assumed no one could tell who the aggressor was, but a woman can."

Lyndy checked the photo again, then dropped it on her desk. "What else happened at your apartment that night?"

"He grabbed the knife I held, and during the struggle, I scratched the top of his hand, either with the knife or my nails. So, then—"

Lyndy raised her hand. "How long did he stay?"

Georgia thought a moment. "About eight minutes. I remember my clock chimed shortly after he left."

Lyndy opened a desk drawer, pulled out a folder. "This is the private detective's report of that night. He says . . . here it is . . . 'Paul carried flowers in. He left nine minutes later." Lyndy reflected. "I never mentioned flowers when we talked in my father's office. And when Paul came home that night and showed me the picture, I noted that he had a deep scratch on his hand. He said he had tried to pet the neighbor's cat and she clawed him."

Georgia braced herself. "Lyndy, did you show the picture to your father?"

"No. I couldn't hurt him."

"I'm sorry, Lyndy. I was so wrong not to tell you about Paul long ago."

"It wouldn't have changed anything. I was warned by others. He was not only unfaithful, but abusive and a poor father. I never told anyone. That's why I avoided you. Too often I had bruises I couldn't hide."

"Oh, Lyndy."

"My mother had chided him about seldom doing anything with the children, so he decided to do something spectacular for our son's birthday party. He borrowed those wooden soldiers. That's what his grandiose gesture brought us." Lyndy walked away from the desk, dropped onto a couch. "I should have known it was just another one of his lies, but the picture was so convincing."

When Georgia left she was shaking. The memory of Paul's attempted rape rushed back. The vision of his slapping her, separating her legs, telling her she was nothing but a nigger, almost pushed her over the line. So long ago, and here she was suffering the residuals of that awful day.

She had only one wish—to find refuge in Matt's arms.

CHAPTER 67

On the celebrity wall of her new office, Georgia hung up a framed picture of Arthur Ashe, the tennis great. Next, she picked up one of baseball Hall of Famer, Bob Gibson.

"Did you know those guys?" It was Jesse Wiggins standing in her doorway.

"Yes. They're good friends."

"Lucky to have such friends."

She was surprised that he sounded so sincere. She hadn't seen him in over a month. "Why are you here?"

He took a couple of steps towards her, reached out his hand with an envelope.

"What's this?"

He nodded for her to open it. It was the negative of the picture of her and Stratley.

"Why did you send a copy of this to Stratley?"

"I hated the bastard. He treated me like dirt."

Georgia tilted her head in doubt. "Only that?"

"Well, when I witnessed how he came on to you at his wedding reception, I felt he was devious enough to use it to make trouble for you. That is . . . I hoped he would. I'm sorry. I screwed myself, didn't I? I got fired."

Georgia waited.

"Steve told the cops that Rudy knew nothing about the smuggling through the store."

She nodded.

"The damage done to your father's car? The scratch and obscene words? I did that. I called your father. I apologized and offered to pay for damages."

"What did he say?"

"He said my apology was worth more than the money."

Georgia wasn't surprised.

"And the late night calls? I did those too. I wanted to upset you." Jesse pulled out another envelope from his jacket pocket. He handed her a picture of him in the short red jacket with brass buttons and white gloves he had worn as a teenage ticket taker in Landing. "It looks kind of wimpy to me now."

"Back then, I thought you were kind of cute."

He looked downward. "You could have allowed me to be arrested that night in Scott's office."

Georgia shrugged. "I have strong feelings about injustice."

"I've got a job at Carson's in Chicago thanks to your good recommendation."

"I felt the quality of your work warranted that."

"A grudge-holder like me can't understand why you did that after all the garbage I dumped on you. Hell, I held that picture over you for years. Blackmail's a felony. How come you didn't press charges?"

She pulled herself up to her full height. "I knew you weren't a career criminal—but a stupid bigot, a man who drew his strength from feeling he was in control. Frankly, I knew a felony charge would leave an inescapable mark on you, and maybe ruin your chances of growing up. Besides, I wasn't about to bring myself down to your level." She looked at her grey leather chair. "You have talent. Rudy recognized it and he had faith in you. I think he would have liked to see that faith justified."

Georgia had looked straight into Jesse's face and was surprised to see a shimmer of sadness. "Now, if you'll excuse me."

At the door Jesse paused. "When I was living in Landing, I wasn't good at figuring out stuff. I took on my father's beliefs. Maybe now, I can find my own."

CHAPTER 68

After several calls to air bases, Georgia gained zero information about Captain Matt Fields.

"Oh, Rudy, what did you do when you didn't know what to do?" She pondered and paced. *I remember. Clean closets.*

She surveyed her walk-in closet, in disarray from weeks of neglect. Where to begin? Handbags. She replaced them by color in their individual slots, the taupe suede briefcase she had used when confronting Abigail Stone caught her attention. Better empty it. She removed all the so-called documentation of her case against Abigail—file folders, manila envelopes, white envelopes, all went into a waste basket. She moved to her shoe rack. Halted. "White envelopes? I don't remember having . . ." She retrieved the white envelopes. Two were bills, one was from . . . "Oh, my God, from Matt!" This is the mail she had received the day she found Matt's roses. She had slipped the mail into her briefcase, forgetting it when she read the card Matt sent with his flowers.

Her entire being trembled as she read it. The first paragraph was endearing, but when she read the rest aloud, the words became stabs of pain.

"After you've examined all your concerns and love me enough to endure my military commitment, write to me in care of Diana and Marty. It's the only address I can give you because I don't know where I'll be. If I don't hear from you by my birthday, I'll understand it's a no."

She read it again and the tears never stopped.

"Diana? This is Georgia Parker."

"Georgia. How great to hear from you. Would you believe I was planning on calling you? How are you?"

"Fine. And you?"

"Wonderful. I'm pregnant. We hadn't heard from Matt in a long, long time, but he called on our second anniversary. Marty told him if he wanted to be our child's godfather, he'd better come see us. Matt will be here Saturday. Could you join us for dinner?"

Georgia gripped the arm of her chair. "Does Matt know I'm invited?"

"Not yet."

"Could we . . . surprise him?"

"Good idea. Our house, say, seven? There'll just be the four of us, so dress casual."

Georgia thought she'd be elated when Saturday arrived. Instead, tension mounted like a gathering storm. She felt scattered in several directions, trying to find the right words to say to Matt.

Let the moment guide me. That's all I can do.

Georgia arrived at Diana and Marty's home fifteen minutes early. She stared at their shiny brass house numbers 2736—numbers she knew she'd never forget.

She handed her hosts a magnum of champagne and a baby gift. She was overwhelmed by the reception she received—hugs and lavish thanks for her gifts.

"You look so chic in your white sweater and slacks," Diana exclaimed as she led Georgia into the living room. "So smashing with your navy blazer. And, oh, that necklace."

"Matt gave it to me."

They sat. They smiled. No one spoke.

Georgia looked around. "Nice room. Very cozy."

"The style is early accumulation," Diana said, "from parents and grandparents."

Again. Silence and smiles.

Saved by the bell, Georgia thought, as Marty dashed to answer the door. Judging by the sound of energetic greetings, Matt and Marty were overjoyed to see each other.

"Here's the man of the hour," Marty announced.

Diana ran to Matt. "At last, you bum. And look what's been going on," she chuckled, pointing to her belly.

"Congratulations," Matt said, holding her at arms length.

And, Matt," Diana exclaimed, "look who's here."

Georgia stood up, and suppressed the urge to run to him.

The room became as quiet as a shadow.

Diana grabbed her husband's arm. "Come into the kitchen with me, Marty. I need help with the heavy lifting."

Matt looked thinner, Georgia thought. He was dressed in dark blue jeans, a white sweater and navy windbreaker.

An indescribable vibration reached her when his face turned from shock to smile. "You look wonderful, Georgia."

She managed a half smile and a nervous little laugh. "Well, what do you know? We're both dressed in navy and white." *Please walk over here, Matt, and take me in your arms.*

He slipped his hands into his pockets and surveyed himself. "We're a perfect match."

Oh, Matt. We are. We are.

Georgia pushed herself to speak. "Recall your letter asking for a reply by your birthday?"

"Of course."

"I had misplaced it and just found it the other day. I need for you to know . . . things would have been different if I had read it when—"

"You hadn't read it?"

"No. I'm so sorry. I would have written you, at this address as you instructed, and—"

"And? Said what?"

"I would have explained those signals you said I sent you—that I didn't want to make a lifetime commitment, and . . . " Her throat felt parched.

"And? What?"

And . . . why I was afraid to tell you I had a black father."

I'm talking too fast, but if I don't I'll lose my courage.

"In Mississippi, I was trashed when my high school friends saw my father. I was almost raped because I was just a nigger. I was harassed and blackmailed by a southern bigot who had had a dispute with my father over theatre seating. Abigail Stone –I told you about her—not only refused me service, but labeled me an arsonist."

I don't dare tell him here how I feel about having children.

"It was horrible, all of it, and it left an indelible scar on me. I need for you to know this. Matt. I love you."

He dropped his focus to the floor.

Her hand went to her throat. *Oh, God. He's involved with someone. Maybe married?* She felt she was one breath away from no breath. "I think . . . I'd better go."

He stopped her at the front door. "Where are you going?"

"Please, Matt. I don't want to know that you love someone else. I don't want to hear it." She opened the door and ran out. She had almost reached her car when he grabbed her and pressed her against a tree.

"I listened to you, now listen to me."

When she tried to break free, he planted his hands against the tree trunk, one on each side of her head.

"Put yourself in my place, Georgia. I told you I loved you, but needed you to be aware of the pitfalls of marriage in the military. When I hadn't heard from you by my birthday, I figured it was over. After that, I avoided my friends so I wouldn't be tempted to visit here. I knew if I did, I'd try to see you. I was miserable without you."

Georgia felt so much she almost broke in two. She held his face in her hands. "Oh, Matt. My misplacing that letter has caused us so much pain. Seems I continue to put our relationship in danger."

He put his hands on hers. "I'm accustomed to danger."

She slipped her arms around his neck at the same time he had drawn her to him. "There's no one in my life, Matt." She waited. "And . . . you?"

"Well, no one except Patsy."

His serious tone belied the gleam in his eyes.

He took her hand. "I think we've held up this tree long enough." He led her to the porch steps. "Patsy lives in the apartment next to mine. Doesn't have beautiful long legs like yours, but she really touched my heart."

"Oh."

"She's a dachshund." He kissed her tears before exploring her eager lips.

"Even through tears you can make me smile." But her smile was short lived.

He was looking at her without a smile. His kiss had been amorous and filled her with soaring longing. But when he drew away, he looked . . . stone cold.

Didn't he feel what I feel? Have time and distance diluted what we once had?

People change.

To have reached such a high, then a low in the space of seconds left her terrified.

At the front picture window, Georgia saw a curtain flutter and their hosts peaking out. Matt saw it too.

"Guess we'd better go in to dinner," he said, standing and extending his hand.

Throughout dinner, Georgia was bewildered by Matt's cryptic attitude, and even when he walked her to her car, he remained uptight.

I'm not going home with unanswered questions.

Matt spoke before she could. "Got a minute to talk?"

"Sure."

"I had no idea you'd be here. If I had, I wouldn't have scheduled a flight back tonight. But probably just as well. There's something I need to say."

Just say that you still love me.

He halted. "You seem to want to say something."

Ask him. "When you kissed me tonight on the porch, I felt . . . wonderful. Happy. And you?"

"Same."

"But you pulled away . . . became kind of distant."

To her surprise, he took her hand, lifted it to his lips, and held it there, seemingly contemplating what to say.

"Before we met, I was preparing for the work I always wanted to do—be a test pilot. I had the college degree I needed and was accumulating flight experience. Then, when you came into my life that changed."

"Then what?"

"It became an on-again-off-again thing. *Off* for the two years we dated. *On* after our Valentine's fight; *Off* when we made up."

"So, when you didn't hear from me on your birthday?"

"I applied. I had the required flight experience and was accepted."

Georgia pulled her hand away. "You're a test pilot?"

"Yes."

"Like it?"

"Love it."

"Does that affect . . . us?"

"Yes."

His work is his love. How can I compete with that?

"I'm at Edwards Air Force Base in California. While it's not unheard of, it's very unlikely that I will ever be back to Offutt in Omaha. You understand?"

She understood. *My job is here. His job is there.*

"In time, you'll know it's the right thing. . . to say goodbye."

They spotted Marty waiting by his car.

"Marty's taking me to the airport."

Please don't leave me like this.

He walked away, turned and saw her standing by hers. He quickly got into Marty's car.

This can't be happening.

They drove away.

CHAPTER 69

The evening Georgia arrived at her father's house with an overnight bag, her father greeted her in pajamas and robe and holding a bowl of cereal.

"Georgia?"

"It's only six, Dad. Are you ill?"

"No. It's cook's day off." He looked at her distraught face. "What's happened?"

They sat on a living room couch while she told her story. "Matt's gone, Dad. It's over."

"A noble gesture."

"What?"

"He's fearful of robbing you of your high achievement."

"How do you know?"

Parker paused. "That night he came here to talk, he doubted that he'd always be attached to Offutt Air Base, and wondered how you'd feel about leaving Emeralds."

Georgia felt anger surfacing. "Is that what you based your noble gesture theory?"

"Well, while your mother and I were dating, scathing public opinion hurt her. Once, we were sitting on a park bench with a picnic lunch. Some boys walked by and yelled, 'Hey, Gretchen, is it true black men are dynamite in bed?' The pain in her eyes tore at my soul. I thought I'd eliminate her pain by leaving her."

"How could you do such a thing?"

"Being noble."

"Matt's being noble? About my job? Why wouldn't he discuss that with me?"

"The same reason I didn't give your mother a voice before taking drastic action. Stupid male logic."

"What makes smart men so stupid?"

He shrugged. "Later, your mother said she didn't care what people thought."

Georgia felt lost. "I can't lose him. I love him."

Parker folded his arms. "Well, first, why not resolve your greater fear."

"Like what?"

His look held a challenge.

My fear of having a child that's not white. "Remember how badly we were treated in Landing? I don't want my children going through that."

"That was your childhood. It need not be your children's. Things are changing."

"Really? I witnessed an injustice at Emeralds—our security humiliated two innocent black kids falsely accused of stealing."

"Don't expect a perfect world, Georgia. Just a better one."

"Did you and mother discuss having children?"

Her father moved a couple of raisins around in his cereal. "Yes." He didn't look up. "We planned . . . not to have children."

So I was an accident.

"With you, our world overflowed with joy."

Because I was white? "When did you tell Mother about your heritage?"

"On our first date. I also told her both my biological parents were white."

Something frightening was emerging inside her.

"Do you still carry your birth certificate, like you did at that Landing theatre, proof that you're white?"

"No. I realized I married the woman I loved, have a beautiful daughter, doing work I'm proud of, and I did it all being the man that I am."

Georgia stood up. "When did that realization come to you? In Landing, wasn't it? In the home of one of Landing's most distinguished families. And me in the center of the room. You picked that moment to declare that you're my father? The daughter you raised to be white? You sent me to an exclusive, southern *white* school, and then threw me to the lions. Because you had a sudden surge of honesty and pride?"

He stared at her, not moving.

"Do you remember when I fell trying to leave, and got strawberry frosting smeared down the front of that beautiful white gown? I've had nightmares about that. I didn't see strawberries stains, Dad. I saw blood.

"There were times," she said, as she returned to sitting, "when I longed to be done with the pretense, but you said no, the time wasn't right. Other times, recalling the horror of that humiliation, I wanted to remain white. I've seen how my black sisters suffer. It's all crazy making. I didn't know who I was before. Don't know who I am now. What am I, Dad?"

She walked over to her mother's portrait. *Mom, I needed you so often—like when I started to menstruate, how to dress for my first prom, and, oh, how I needed your advice about falling in love.*

Georgia felt a tightening in her chest. Only men were available to advise her—Rudy, God bless him, or her father, who was ineffective or unavailable.

Georgia closed her eyes for a moment. Her head felt light. Her heart felt heavy. Never before had she lashed out at her father in such a manner. What was gained?

She looked at her father. *Is he crying?*

Georgia was torn. She had burdened this elegant, accomplished man with more guilt than he seemed able to bare. She knelt beside him, put her arms around him, laid her head on his.

In the morning, after a silent cup of a coffee, it was her father who insisted they talk. From breakfast until bedtime, they talked and learned more about each other than they had in their lifetime together.

"At college, when I first saw your mother, I didn't dare speak to her. But she extended her hand and congratulated me on being elected vice president of our senior class."

He told Georgia how they dared to overcome the odds against them. "Her parents were adamant. But when her father learned I graduated summa cum laude and had more money than he had, he became more accepting. Later, he gained a great deal of respect for my profession—you remember, he had diabetes."

"Georgia, you're another generation away from my black great-great-grandfather. But your fear of having a black child is something only you can face."

But my father is black. "Your history proves I can't be sure."

"Georgia, you'll find bullies even at all-white schools. The poor hating the rich. My God's better than your God. Which of us can totally avoid disapproval, rejection, hate?"

After they said goodnight, she sat wide awake on the edge of her bed. She was able to revisit positive memories—when her father's gleaming bronze skin seemed far more beautiful than her own, so pale and colorless. She recalled the affection between her parents, and she loved him more than she was able to express. All of this was hers until Mississippi, where the brutal consequences of his color overshadowed all that was good between them. Were those southern paper dolls worthy of her denouncing a loving parent?

A wide chasm still separated them. While she was growing up, he was often absent. On her birthdays, there were gifts but he wasn't there. Sometimes even on holidays—gifts but no hugs, no loving words. All that was true only part of the time. Strange what a child chose to remember.

The morning she was leaving, her father's sad, moist eyes touched Georgia, but not as profoundly as his words. "Thirty four years ago your mother and I eloped. We had little choice. Things have changed, but not entirely. If you can find a clergyman who would accommodate you, would you consider allowing me to walk you down the aisle?"

Her heart was sending her unfamiliar signals. Her voice shut down.

He kissed her forehead, hugged her as though he couldn't let her go. He hadn't done that since she was a very little girl.

Driving home, she realized there was more than her fear of having children. Could she endure the repeated agony of awaiting Matt's return after testing unproven planes?

CHAPTER 70

Even though Georgia hadn't heard from Matt since he left a month ago, she had hoped he would remember her birthday today. He did not. *When am I going to let go?*

Jean had arranged to take her boss to dinner. "I've picked a perfect restaurant."

"Oh no. Not here," Georgia protested, as Jean drove up to Mario's.

"It's changed since you've been here," Jean said, "New decor. New band. Besides, my new boyfriend Tony is a chef here."

Everything was different—from tables around a fountain, to deep red walls radiant with gold-framed Italian art. Little resemblance to the Mario's where Matt took her for their first and last date.

"Tony said tonight's check is on him, Jean said. "Isn't that sweet?"

The food presentation was superb. "Tony's an artist," Jean exclaimed. After the entrée, she stood up. "Look over the dessert menu. I'm going to the ladies room."

The waiter approached with a plate covered with a silver dome. "Your dessert, ma'am." He quickly left.

Oh, my God, déjà vu. "I didn't order dessert."

"I did," came a voice behind her. He walked around and sat in Jean's chair.

"Matt!"

"Happy Birthday."

"How did you know I was here?"

He pointed to Jean, who was standing a few feet away behind Georgia, smiling and dabbing her eyes.

He was in uniform, and looked deliciously handsome. Georgia fell into his smile. She loved the strong, wide spread of his shoulders. And what's that? "Your captain bars are gone. Is that a gold leaf?"

"After a year's test pilot training, I was made a major." He leaned forward. "Remember the night we had dinner at Marty's? All the way to the airport he lectured me on my stupidity."

"Stupidity?"

"I told him that if you gave up your position for me, you'd regret it. Marty said it was stupid to *assume,* not letting you speak for yourself."

"Bravo Marty."

"So, I got to thinking. Why does anyone have to give up anything? After two years as a test pilot, I'm burned out. It happens a lot, they tell me. I'm up for a strat com assignment—that means I'll serve on the ground, but not sure where. What do you think?"

Georgia's eyes gleamed. "I think . . . I like how you think."

Matt lifted the silver dome. On the plate was a small box.

Georgia opened it and gazed with amazement at a diamond solitaire ring. "It's beautiful, Matt. I hope you didn't—"

"I did. I sold some military equipment—a couple of jeeps, one plane, stuff like that."

"Really?"

"No," he chuckled. "Only robbed one bank."

This big, brave Air Force officer looked like a frightened little boy as he got down on his knee.

"Georgia. Please forgive me. I need you—the love of my life, for *all* of my life. I love you. And I'll do whatever it takes to make you happy. Will you—*please*—marry me?"

Tears gleamed on her cheeks. "Yes. Oh, yes."

The room exploded with applause as he slipped the ring on her finger. He noticed her necklace—the one he had given her—and took her into his arms. "Thank you for wearing it"

"It kept you close to me."

The moment they reached her apartment, Matt took her key and opened the door. "Too soon to carry you across the threshold?"

Georgia smiled. "Tradition says not until after the wedding."

"The hell with tradition. I'll do it now and on our wedding day I'll let you carry me." He swept her up and placed her gently on the white couch in her study. "God, you're beautiful," he said, looking down at her. "I don't know what I would have done if you hadn't asked me to marry you."

Georgia's laughter was full of gratitude for his humor and constant smile.

Suddenly, the mischief left his face. "To think I almost lost you."

"What made you come back?"

"When I realized I didn't want to live without you."

"Then what happened?"

He gulped. "Well, I called your father, asked if you were . . . seeing anyone. I told him I was on my way and coming with a ring. I said I wanted to surprise you, 'In that case,' he suggested 'you'd better call Jean.' He gave me his blessings and I called her."

"Oh, my. Knowing Jean, I bet she had plenty to say."

"Big time. She revealed in graphic detail what you had been through. I was overwhelmed. Scott, Coach, Paul, Jesse. My God. And the infamous picture. You've destroyed it?"

"Every copy, plus the negative."

He shook his head while holding a sad focus on Georgia. "I should have been here for you. Forgive me."

"When did you change your mind about us?"

"When I realized I didn't want to live without you."

She took his hand and pressed it to her lips. *How can I tell him now the one secret I've always kept from him?*

He didn't move for a long moment, savoring the joy of her loving gesture. When he took her hands and kissed her fingertips, he halted. "Your hands are as cold as ice. All this talk has been too much."

"No, no. It's something I need to tell you. I would have told you long ago, but you disappeared and—"

"Nothing you could tell me would change my mind."

If only I could believe that. I can't deceive him about this. Now. Tell him now.

Georgia touched his cheek and as he held her for a long silence. She could feel his tears mingle with hers.

Georgia smoothed his rich, dark brown hair, and moved back enough to face him. "Matt, . . . it's about . . . children."

He looked stricken. "You can't have children?"

"No. That's not it. I'm sure I can."

"I love children. I was an only child and so were you. Our kids should have brothers and sisters. What do you think?"

"I'm not sure, Matt. I can't seem to get rid of fear."

"What can I do to dispel that fear?"

Say you don't need children to be happy with me. "I don't know. I love children, but I can't see myself as the mother of a child who is . . ."

"Black," he provided.

"We're both white, Matt. There is a chance that we'd have a black child. That would be unfair to the child or us. Whispers. Snickers. I've seen it all. It's awful."

Matt had listened with his chin resting on folded hands. His intense gaze, which had remained focused on her, now shifted.

What's he thinking? My beloved has returned. A miracle. And I'm pushing him away. But I can't deceive him.

He returned to Georgia, removed her shoes, her earrings, released her upswept hair until it fell to her shoulders. "Comfortable?"

"Yes." *What's he doing?*

He took an authoritative stance, but his voice was gentle. "I want children. Color doesn't concern me. How a child is raised does. Unlike you, Georgia, our children would have two parents with loving understanding."

"I started out with two parents, but not you or anyone can predict if either or both will always be around."

"True. And every time I put my plane into a dive or pulled out of one, I didn't know how it would turn out. I didn't consider failure. I applied what I had learned—stayed focused. Did my best, one step at a time. I know of white couples who adopted black children. Why would they do that?"

Georgia stirred. "I don't know."

"Because that particular baby touched their heart."

"I agree, but what has that to do with us?"

Matt bent down in front of her. "When two people are as blessed as we are to find the mate we love above all else, to create life is a reward beyond description. If we were to discover we couldn't have children, we could adopt, but to deny the blessing of having our own would fly in the face of a gift many pray for."

Is the old fear so deeply imbedded that I can't relate to what he's saying?

"On the other hand," he continued, "maybe you're right. With your job, you travel a great deal—New York every month, Europe twice a year, trips to California. We'll barely have time to see each other."

He stood up, walked away, as though trying to regroup. He turned back. "Marriage is also a risk, Georgia, but less risky with real love. I want to marry you, with or without children, but I wonder if, in later years, *regret* of not having your own children wouldn't be more painful than the fear you hold today."

He held out his hand to her, and said no more.

The church for the Fields-Parker wedding was filled with Emeralds management and associates, Lyndy Hoffman (she had dropped the Stratley name), Mr. and Mrs. Jon Roberts—they had kept in touch since their chance meeting in Chicago's airport. Dr. Parker's cook, doctors and research associates, Matt's college and Air Force buddies. And, adding great excitement, when recognized, was super model Gwen Val-Wray. Georgia's closest models were bridesmaids. Marty was best man. And Jean, Georgia's maid of honor, dyed her hair pink to match her gown.

After the attendants took their places, the organist made a segue to the Wedding March. Guests turned to see the bride, and a collective gasp escaped. On the arm of her father, Georgia winked at smiling Dr. Parker.

On the first seat, first aisle on the bride's side was a large golden wreath, covered with Tootsie Rolls arranged like flowers. Across the wreath a blue satin ribbon bore the name, Rudy Ascot. Georgia paused, threw an air kiss and whispered, "This is a first, dear Rudy. You're on time."

At the altar, Matt handed Georgia a note. It had only four words. *Offutt Air Force Base.*

"A wedding gift from The United States Air Force," he whispered.

"Really?"

"No," he grinned. "Just lucky."

"May I begin?" the clergyman whispered.

When the time came for their personal vows, Georgia went first. *God help me say this right.*

"I hope all our sons grow up as smart, funny and loving as their father."

Matt's smile seemed as broad as his shoulders. "I love you, Georgia, and I will tell you so every day."

After the reception, Georgia told Matt, "You'll never guess what the Hoffmans gave us for a wedding gift. The magnificent jeweled clock that hung in Emeralds downtown store for generations. Now that the downtown store is closed, the Emeralds family felt it needed a home where it would be cherished. Rudy always said I had the perfect wall for it. I loved that clock. It was a gift of love—a reminder that *time* is precious."

Matt kissed her gently. "I wonder if a lifetime will be enough *time* to show you how much I love you."

On the first evening after their honeymoon in Hawaii, they had dinner with her father at the Nebraska Steak Barn. They sat at Parker's usual table, and his waiter, Charlie, greeted them.

"Haven't seen you in some time, Dr. Parker. Glad you're back. You too, Miss Georgia. And who's this young man?"

"My husband, Matt Fields."

Dr. Parker leaned towards Charlie. "I know he'll love the food here."

Georgia smiled. "My father loves this restaurant, Charlie."

"I don't believe I've had the pleasure of meeting your father."

Georgia reached across the table to touch her father's hand. "Yes, you have, Charlie. Dr. Parker is my father."